Well, look what snuck in while I was in the kitchen.

Zach should stay away—he really should—but knew he wouldn't. Casually making his way across the room, he stopped to check in at a few tables while keeping Sadie in view. Her laughter, her smile were beautiful things, though she wasn't overtly flirting. Still, a surprising surge of anger streaked through him. He found himself circling slowly, almost like a lion studying his prey from all angles.

Coming in from behind, he could no longer see her face, but he could finally hear her words.

"So did they know someone was sabotaging the mill before this?"

Every cell in his body went alert at the question. Why was she asking?

"Oh, yeah," one of the locals eagerly replied. "Of course, those of us that work there knew it way before any manager did."

She nodded, which caused the muted lighting to glint off her ruby curls.

Standing right behind her, Zach felt a moment of evil satisfaction that he stood so close, yet she seemed unaware. Every time he was around this woman, his hackles rose.

He wasn't sure whether to shake her or kiss her.

* * *

Expec
is part of the s
fi

EXPECTING HIS SECRET HEIR

BY
DANI WADE

MILLS BOON

First Published in Great Britain 2016
By Mills & Boon, an imprint of HarperCollins*Publishers*
1 London Bridge Street, London, SE1 9GF

© 2016 Katherine Worsham

ISBN: 978-0-263-91876-2

51-0916

Our policy is to use papers that are natural, renewable and recyclable products and made from wood grown in sustainable forests. The logging and manufacturing processes conform to the legal environmental regulations of the country of origin.

Printed and bound in Spain
by CPI, Barcelona

Dani Wade astonished her local librarians as a teenager when she carried home ten books every week—and actually read them all. Now she writes her own characters, who clamor for attention in the midst of the chaos that is her life. Residing in the Southern United States with a husband, two kids, two dogs and one grumpy cat, she stays busy until she can closet herself away with her characters once more.

To the Worshams, Tates, Nelsons, Schafers and Raymos, for teaching me all that family can mean during the highs and lows of life.

One

From her crouching vantage point, Sadie Adams sized up the composition before her with an artistic eye.

Wide, straight shoulders of a towering man, silhouetted against the smoking buildings and rubble. A small strip of dead cotton plants in the foreground. The sun lightening the top of his thick head of hair, leaving the rest of him in shadow. Standing in profile, hands on his hips, head hung as if in despair.

As the shutter clicked, she wondered about his story. Had he been an employee of the ruined mill behind him, or was he there to help? As several men approached, he raised his head, giving her a clearer view of his rough-cut features.

I should have known.

Those broad shoulders, clothes that fit a tight, strong body in all the right places—he was the most capable man she'd ever known. The most incredible lover she'd ever had. The one it had almost killed her to walk away from.

Zachary Gatlin was the reason she was back in Black Hills, South Carolina. But he could never know that.

She took a few more pictures, surreptitiously inching in the other direction, as he talked with the men surrounding him. Yet she kept Zachary Gatlin in her line of sight. Five years ago, he had blended in with the crowd. A worker bee. Now, he was clearly in charge, directing those around him with decisive gestures and a firm tone that reached her even though she couldn't make out the words.

Had he worked his way up into management at the mill? Would that change how he treated her? Would it change how he saw her?

Moving along the edge of the parking lot, she attempted to get closer to the ruined buildings. Her high-quality camera had some amazing close-up capabilities that she was eager to test. The piece of equipment was a luxury she couldn't afford—but her employer could, and he was pulling out all the stops to ensure she got the information he needed. She should feel dirty for accepting the camera, but it was the one thing—the only thing—she didn't regret in her current situation.

If Zachary knew the truth, he'd make sure she deeply regretted ever coming back here. He wouldn't rage or get physical. He wouldn't need to. That dark stare and hard features would be enough to make his point. At least, that was the Zachary she'd known—or thought she'd known.

Would he be the same now?

Turning to the smoking ruins, she focused on the things she knew. Angle, lighting, depth, perception. Her circumstances had prevented her from pursuing photography at a professional level, even though she'd had a few photographs published, thanks to a friend. But if her life had been different, with fewer obligations, maybe she could have followed her own dreams instead of lying awake at night wondering how her family would all survive.

Lost in her art, she'd almost blocked out her surroundings until a masculine voice spoke near her. "Ma'am?"

For just a moment, her heart jump-started. Had Zach finally spotted her? But she turned to find a generic security guard by her side. "Yes?"

"If you'll come with me, please?"

Though it was a question, his firm gesture in the direction he wanted her to go brooked no arguments.

After ten steps she had no doubt where he was leading her. Desperate to delay the inevitable, she paused. "Excuse me? Could you explain what happened here?"

Possibly fooled by her innocent expression, the man stopped, too, and cocked his head to the side. "You aren't from around here, are you?"

She shook her head. "No. I've visited before, and really wanted to come back. But I didn't think I would find the quiet place I remembered in such an uproar."

That was the truth. The single hotel in the area had been booked full. Sadie had managed to get the last room in the last B and B with an opening. From the types of people she saw coming and going, most of the influx consisted of firefighters and construction crews. From the looks of the half-full parking lot, quite a few of those guys were out here today.

"I kinda guessed, based on the accent," he said with a smile.

Yep. No matter how she tried to tame it, her Texas breeding colored her every word.

The guard went on, "Well, the admin building on this side of the plant had a bomb go off in it."

Sadie made herself look surprised, even though she'd picked up this tidbit of information around town already. "Really? Who would want to do that? This is the main source of employment for the town, if I remember right."

"It sure is," the man said, shaking his head. "They say they have a suspect in custody but haven't released any names yet." He stared up at the building for a moment, looking confused. "I have no idea why someone would want to ruin the mill, but after all the bad stuff that's happened around here in the last year—"

"Steve," Zach barked from over a dozen feet away.

"Oops. Better get movin'," the guard said.

Each step felt like a final walk down death row, but Sadie forced herself to move. After all, making contact with Zach was the reason she was here. She needed to spend as much time with him as possible—and she hoped their previous one-night stand might give her a bit of an in, even if the fact that she'd disappeared after it wouldn't make it a positive in.

Zach still had a group of workers around him who parted as she drew near. She expected them to skedaddle now that the boss had new business, but no. Not a single one moved away.

Her petite five-foot-five stature had been the bane of her existence ever since she'd realized she wouldn't be growing anymore, and being surrounded by a bunch of six-foot-tall men did not set her at ease. She felt like David approaching Goliath against his will.

Not that she had any sort of righteousness on her side.

There was only a moment to study Zach up close.

His thick jet hair was a little longer than it had been the last time she'd seen him. Remembering that night long ago, she couldn't help the itch to bury her fingers in those silky strands again. Or to run her fingertips over the weary lines of his chiseled features until the tension melted away.

Her sensual memories were dimmed by the current hard look on his face. There was no glimmer of recognition or softening as she stood before him, even though she could remember every detail of the body that now towered over her. No smile of welcome softened his sculpted lips as he asked, "What are you doing?"

"I'm just taking some pictures," she said quietly, lifting the camera still in her hand.

If anything, his dark eyes hardened more. "On private property."

She glanced around, uncomfortable under the stares of the other men. "This is…was a business, right? There aren't any signs posted about private property or trespassing."

"That's because they were all blown down by the bomb."

Really? She wanted to challenge him, push past that stony facade to find out if he was simply making that up. Was he trying to punish her for walking away? Or did he really not recognize her? Had she been that unmemorable? The thought made her slightly ill.

She settled for a simple, "Sorry, I didn't realize."

Zach stared her down. What would he do next? She had a feeling this wasn't going to end as a friendly little chat. Her cheeks started to burn. Inwardly cursing her fair skin, she tilted her chin up to counteract the feeling of inadequacy. So what if he didn't remember her…she'd still find a way to get what she needed.

But she couldn't force her gaze back up to his.

"As you can see, this is still an active fire zone, and we've got a great deal to investigate before we know how safe it is."

She smirked at the lame excuse. "I wasn't anywhere near the fire. I was in the parking lot with a bunch of other people."

The crowd around her shifted, as if uncomfortable with her spark of courage. But Zach didn't back down. "Do you have a press pass?"

"What?"

"A press pass," he said, enunciating each word with careful control. "Do you have permission to be taking photos of the scene?"

She seriously wanted to roll her eyes at his show of dominance but held herself in check. "No."

"Steve, please escort this lady back to her car."

Startled, she snapped her gaze up to meet his eyes once more. Surely he wasn't throwing her off the property?

He stepped closer, close enough for her to catch the scent she'd missed all too often, mixed with perspiration from his work despite the cool October air. His fingers— the same ones that had explored her body that long-ago night—caught her chin, tilting it up just a touch more until it was uncomfortable. Then she had no choice but to meet his gaze, despite their height difference. Her heart thumped hard, though she didn't know if it was from his nearness or fear.

"I suggest you stay away from where you don't belong."

As the guard escorted her back to her car, she had only one thought.

Guess he does remember me after all...

* * *

Zach Gatlin stood behind his desk, lost in thought as he stared at the large monitor. Where had she come from? Did he really want to know?

Unfortunately, he did.

As much as he wished he could forget the red-haired beauty he'd taken to bed five years ago, the memory of her eager passion had resurfaced all too often. As had the memory of her love of sunsets and people and nature—her artistic eye had taught him to see the gentler world he'd forgotten in the midst of war.

Then, with no warning, she was gone. He'd consoled himself with the thought that if she hadn't been willing to say goodbye, she wouldn't have stayed in the long run anyway. Probably for the better, since Zach's responsibilities were a heavy load.

Sometimes he wondered if that inner voice lied.

Shaking off the memories, Zach focused on the present. The question was: Did he look into her or not? Running a background check would be all too easy, especially now that he ran his very own security business. The tools were within close reach. Close enough to make his fingers twitch. He could know all he wanted within minutes, every small detail of her life within days.

But was it the right thing to do?

Maybe he should have asked himself that before he threw her off mill property yesterday. He'd had a gut reaction to seeing her there, so close but seemingly oblivious to him. He wished he had controlled himself, but what was done was done. He couldn't go back.

With his life, he knew that all too well.

Turning away from the computer, he decided to confront this problem head-on rather than hide behind snooping. Security might be his business, but it didn't have to be his life.

Thirty minutes later, he wondered if he should have taken the easy way out. Figuring out where Sadie was staying had been easy—this was, after all, a small town. Getting past the nosy owner of the B and B? Well, that was an altogether different problem.

"Gladys, I know she's here, I just need to know what room she's in."

"Is she expecting you?"

"Probably." At least that much was the truth. If Sadie remembered anything at all about him, it should be that he was a man of action.

Gladys leaned against the high desk in the foyer. "Now, why would Black Hills's newest hero want to see some strange woman who just came into town?"

Lord, this woman wanted a pound of flesh, didn't she? "I haven't always lived here, Gladys."

"So you met her somewhere else?" Was that a gleam of excitement in her eyes? How sad that his life had gone from daily drudgery to full-on gossip mill fodder.

He'd met Sadie right here in Black Hills, but it had seemed like another time and place. "The room number?"

Probably recognizing the obstinate look on his face and realizing she wasn't getting any gossip from him—outside of his very presence here—Gladys relented. "Room three."

Back straight, he refused to look over his shoulder to see her watching him as he climbed the stairs. He hesitated before knocking, but luckily there was no one to see it.

The door opened, revealing Sadie. She was just as he remembered her, with smooth, translucent skin, an abundance of fiery red hair and green eyes that appeared guileless. A trap he wasn't falling for this time.

"Zachary," she said.

He stalked through the doorway. The suite was more spacious than the tiny hotel room she'd occupied the last time she'd been here. This was open and airy, with a lightly feminine touch. His gaze bounced away from the bed in an alcove and came to rest on the laptop in a low sitting area in front of a fireplace. He made his way forward with measured steps.

"It's been a while, Sadie," he finally said.

"Five years," she murmured.

He paused, giving away the fact that he'd heard her when he would have preferred not to show any reaction at all. He was ashamed to admit, even to himself, that he'd often thought about what he would say if he ever saw her again. He'd pictured himself as calm, slightly condescending as he asked her why she'd left without a word, without any explanation.

Nothing in that scenario came close to the amped-up emotions he was experiencing at the moment.

Eager for a distraction, he paused in front of the open laptop. Several pictures shared space on the screen, showcasing the smoldering mill from different angles. He'd never had much time for art, but to his inexperienced eyes, these looked pretty good.

Which for some reason made him even angrier.

"You weren't authorized to take pictures there."

"Did you tell that to every bystander in that parking lot with their cell phones in their hands? Or just me?"

He glanced in her direction, mildly surprised by her return salvo. He hadn't known her to be very confrontational. Not that they'd spent much time arguing, but they had talked—a lot. He wouldn't have called her a doormat, exactly, but she'd shown a lot more spirit in the last twenty-four hours than he'd seen in the week he'd known her five years ago. A week that had ended in a night he couldn't forget.

She raised one fine brow. "There were no signs posted. No one said I couldn't be there…at first."

He studied the images a bit longer. Damn if she didn't have him stumped. What exactly had he wanted to accomplish by coming here? To go over the same territory as at the mill? To find out why she had returned? To get information without having to ask any direct questions?

To put himself out there to be hurt again?

Gesturing toward the screen, he asked, "So you came back just for pictures?"

It was as close as he'd let himself get to addressing the elephant in the room. He really wanted to know why she hadn't come back for him. She was the one woman he'd ever felt he could actually let into his life, have a real relationship with. And she'd walked away without looking back.

"I was in the area and heard about the explosion. I wanted to check it out."

She looked too calm, acted too casual. And she just happened to be in the area? He shook his head. When had he gotten so suspicious?

"What about you?" she surprised him by asking. "What were you doing there?"

That's when he realized she wasn't the only one who had changed in five years. "I'm head of security for the Blackstones—"

She smiled. "Wow. That's really great. Going from maintenance to head of security is a big jump."

He knew he shouldn't, but he said it anyway. "I'm not head of security for the mill. I handle security details for the entire family and all of their interests. I run my own security firm." Bragging did not come easily to him. Not that he'd ever had much to brag about. But somehow it felt good to rub his success in Sadie's face.

He wasn't the same man she'd met then—recently returned from combat in the Middle East, fighting the nightmares while maintaining a strong facade for the women in his family he'd spent a lifetime supporting.

Then one night he'd let her in, and he wished she'd never seen that side of him.

"Until we can get a good look inside and evaluate the damage, the mill is a huge security risk. So the Blackstones have asked me to oversee this initial part of the investigation."

"I heard it was a bomb."

He nodded. Yep. A bomb set off by a crazy man.

"Any suspects?"

It was a natural question. Simple curiosity. So why did his muscles tense when she asked?

"Yes, but that information is not being released to the public."

The words came out in a more formal tone than he would have normally used, but it was all for the best. Keeping their distance meant keeping himself sane. Instead of leaning in to see if her hair smelled the same as it did before.

He did not need to know that.

He eyed the bright waves dancing around her shoulders. He definitely didn't need to know.

"So it would be better to stay away from there right now." *And away from me, so all these emotions will respond to my control.* "Wait until we can guarantee it's safe."

"In the parking lot?"

"Right." He didn't care if she wasn't buying it. A man had to do…

Suddenly realizing he'd accomplished nothing but torturing himself during this visit, he stalked back to the door. Unfortunately, she followed, until she was within arm's reach. He was too far away from the door to escape.

It all flooded back—all the memories he'd struggled to hold at bay since that first moment he'd seen her again at the mill. The way his heart pounded when she laughed. The way her soft voice soothed his nerves as she told him a story. The way his body rose to meet the demands of hers.

So many things he couldn't force himself to forget.

But he could force himself to walk away this time. "I'll be seeing you, Sadie," he said, as casually as he could.

She pulled the door open and smiled. "Definitely."

Something about her tone, that confident edge, ruffled him, pushed him to throw her off balance. He couldn't stop himself. He stopped in front of her, bending in low to place his mouth near her ear. He sucked in a deep breath. "So…" he said, letting the word stretch, "aren't you gonna tell me why you really left?"

Her gasp left him satisfied…for now.

Two

Sadie's entire body instantly snapped to attention. She might not have moved, but every nerve ending was now awake and focused on the man before her.

She hadn't thought he'd directly address her leaving. Indeed, he'd seemed to do everything but ask the all-important question: Why? She'd thought she was prepared. Her flippant answer rattled around in her brain for a moment, but she couldn't force it out.

Instead she stared up into his brooding dark eyes and lost her breath. She'd known she would hurt him, leaving like that. He'd never tell her so, but she couldn't help but wonder if it were true from his somber gaze.

His body seemed to sway a little closer, and her mouth watered at the thought of his lips on hers once more. Then the trill of her phone broke the moment of silence.

Suddenly he was back to arm's length, leaving her

to wonder if she'd imagined that moment. Wished it into being.

His eyes grew wider, reminding her that her phone was still ringing. She ignored both him and the phone. Her mother called late in the evening, when her duties for the day were done. Only one person would be calling her at this time of day, and she wasn't about to speak to him in front of Zach.

Her heart pounded. She licked her lips, trying to think of something to say.

Instead of waiting for an answer, Zach gave a quick smirk and then walked out the door without another word. She waited until he was down the stairs and out of sight before pushing the door closed. Then she dissolved against it like melting sugar.

Tears welled, along with the wish that things didn't have to be this way. She quickly brushed both away. Her life had been one long lesson in dealing with reality, not dreaming of fairy tales.

At least he hadn't forgotten her.

Forcing herself to her feet, she crossed to the sitting area and picked her phone up off the low table. The very name she expected flashed across the screen. She sucked in a deep, bracing breath, then touched the screen to call him back.

"I'm listening."

She hated when he answered the phone like that. The part of her that rebelled against what she had to do forced her to hold her words just a minute longer than necessary, garnering some petty satisfaction from making him wait.

"What do you need, Victor?" she asked.

"Ah, Adams. Where were you?"

The impersonal use of her last name grated on her

nerves, but she was, after all, simply a servant. "Away from my phone."

"Don't get uppity with me, Adams. Just because you're hundreds of miles away from Texas doesn't mean you're off the leash."

Right. Remind her of the dog she was—that would make her work harder. But it was an apt description—she was a hunting dog. Sent to search for and fetch exactly what her owner wanted.

"I apologize," she said, hoping he couldn't tell her teeth were gritted. "But I didn't think you wanted me to answer the phone and give you an update in front of Zachary."

"Very good, Adams. I knew I could trust your judgment."

As if it had been all his idea. If Victor Beddingfield had an original idea ever in his life, she'd be shocked. Of course, this little expedition was his idea—and here she was. But the idea wasn't original to him. His father had tried it first.

"So you've already made contact? Good girl."

Yep, she was definitely a dog to him. "I have, but he's not happy about it."

"You simply have to make him like it. You know how to do that…don't you?"

She wished to goodness Victor had never found out the truth about her last visit to Black Hills. Not that he cared about her choice to deceive his father, telling him that Zachary couldn't possibly be the son he sought. The longer Zach had been out of his life, the more of their father's money Victor could spend. Still, the knowledge had given him a weapon to use against her—but not the biggest one.

"This might take some time." Although, even if she

had all the time in the world, Zach would probably never forgive her—then or now.

"Well, we don't have time, remember?" he said, his voice deepening in a way she perceived as a threat. "I need money. Now. And I'm sure you do, too—or rather, your sister does."

Not really. Amber didn't worry about that sort of thing. The hospital treated her cancer, that was all she knew. It was all Sadie wanted her sister to know. The practical aspect—bills, scheduling, medical decisions—all of that was handled by Sadie. Some days, it was enough to make her feel like she was drowning, but she did it anyway. It kept her sister alive, for now. It allowed her mother to be at her sister's side for however much longer they had her. That was all that mattered. Still, the reminder struck home.

But Victor wasn't done. "So get me the dirt I need to disinherit him, and we will all be in a much better position. Got it?"

How could she not? "I understand. I'll do my best."

"Good girl."

One of these days, Sadie's teeth were going to be worn to a nub, just from the irritation of listening to this guy. "He's not giving me much to work with," she said, consciously relaxing her jaw.

"Then get creative," Victor said. Without another word, he disconnected the call.

Get creative.

Sadie sighed. Easy for him to say. Victor had always had someone to do the dirty work for him. Her role in his father's household made her a convenient option. Her role in his father's investigation of his older son five years ago told Victor she wasn't just convenient, but experienced.

Now he wanted the investigation into Zach reopened so he could discredit the man who didn't know he was Victor's older brother.

Time for Sadie to earn her keep.

Plopping down onto the couch, she stared at her computer screen. Get creative. How? She couldn't think of any way to get around Zach's present uncooperative state. She needed to get close to him, learn everything she could about him. But he wanted her nowhere near him.

Glancing around to remind herself that she was alone, Sadie clicked on the computer folder she'd closed when Zachary had knocked. Instantly the screen filled with images of him. There were pictures from all different angles, taken while he wasn't looking. Not for Victor's benefit. Not because she had to. Because she wanted to.

Because the single photo she had of him from her last visit wasn't nearly enough to last her a lifetime.

She hadn't dared take home any more, certain that her employer, Victor and Zach's father, would discover them and realize she was lying about how much she'd found out about Zach.

She studied the haunting image she'd gotten of Zach silhouetted against the smoking building from yesterday. The contrast of his strength with the ruins of the mill reminded her of his conscientious care for his family, his quiet way of watching those around him until he saw a need that he could fill. If only he could fulfill her needs, free her from this mess of a life so she could be with him once more.

No, she couldn't think like that. This was her problem to solve, as always. If Zachary knew what she was involved in, he'd lead the mob running her out of town. The town didn't know her, either. They'd protect their own.

At least, that was the perception she had from watching him at the mill. But did she really know? What could the town tell her about Zach that he wouldn't tell her himself?

She studied the picture once more. She needed to find out, and she had an idea how she might make that happen.

I need more information.

And she wasn't going to get it moping in her room. Grabbing a light jacket against the autumn chill, Sadie threw a quick glance at the computer to make sure it was off, then headed out the door.

She shouldn't worry about her laptop. But Victor had taught her that people did all kinds of things that served their own ends—and invaded other's privacy. She never wanted to be caught off guard again.

Not that she had many secrets, but Victor had managed to find a doozy.

She paused on the stairs. Zach had said he owned a security firm now. Would he have checked her out?

Even now, had he figured out who she was? How long after that would he find out who her employer was, and what he meant to Zach?

Once that happened, her mission would be over before it even began. The ticking time bomb had been set.

Luckily, the overly friendly proprietress of the bed-and-breakfast was at the front desk when Sadie reached the office. The woman's husband was as reticent as she was open, so he wouldn't have been nearly as helpful. For now, luck was with Sadie.

The woman even started the conversation in the direction Sadie wanted it to go.

"Wow! New to town and already getting visits from the local hero."

Technically it was a statement, but Sadie could hear the question beneath the words. And Gladys wasn't finished. "Of course, not everyone feels that way…"

Interesting.

"Why is that?" Sadie didn't feel the need to beat around the bush. Subtlety wasn't Gladys's forte.

"Oh, there was a big to-do when he came home. He graduated to officer in the military, survived combat. Then came home to take care of his family after his mama's heart attack."

Sadie murmured a few encouraging words, even though Gladys didn't need them.

"But then all those plants got poisoned earlier this year—"

That made Sadie's ears perk up. "What plants?"

"Cotton fields." The older woman leaned toward Sadie over the high desk in what Sadie had learned was Gladys's favorite position. "One of the things Zach did to earn money was crop dust. Early this spring he dusted nigh on half the county in a day. By morning, the plants were dead. Boy, did that cause an uproar."

"I bet." Probably more like a riot. Killing the cash crop of choice for the area… "Did the police get involved?"

"You bet. Quite a spectacle it was, though I wasn't there. Handcuffs and all. But they released him the same day."

Gladys lowered her voice, though they were the only two around. "Them Blackstone brothers got involved. And they obviously believe in him, because he's the biggest news story around here…besides the bomb, of course."

"You mean his new job?"

The woman nodded, her tight gray curls bouncing.

"He don't have to work three jobs now, that's for sure. I hear his business is taking off like hot cakes."

See, he doesn't need the money.

Sadie pushed away the seductive thought. She wouldn't sugarcoat what she was doing. Regardless of his current circumstances, Zach deserved the inheritance her late boss had wanted to give him. The one she had denied him because she had lied and told Victor's father that Zach wasn't, in fact, the son he sought. She'd been afraid he would corrupt Zach the same way he had everything else around him.

Still believing his firstborn was out there somewhere, Beddingfield Senior had willed him his inheritance. The only way for Victor to get it was to ruin Zach. Because he knew the truth…the truth behind the lies she'd told.

Desperate times called for desperate measures.

Gladys had just given her a place to start looking for Zach's dirty laundry. And if Sadie succeeded in her mission, she'd steal away every last dime.

From Zach.

Three

"I heard there was an incident at the mill yesterday."

Of course she had. Zach glanced over at his sister. Despite her engagement to the richest man in town, KC had kept her bartending job, and she heard everything. "You mean besides the fire?"

"Well, this was a bit more interesting than a bomb, in my opinion. It was about you…and a woman."

Only KC would find that more interesting. But since there was never any gossip connecting him to any women in town, he could see her point of view.

Zachary hated that he paused before answering, practically admitting his guilt. "You heard about that?" His sister was too smart for him to bother pretending he didn't know what she was talking about.

Her sassy attitude was displayed in a raised brow and hand on her hip. "Seriously? This is a bar. In a small town. People in here have nothing to do but talk all day…" She studied him in a way that made him want to squirm. "Did you really throw her off the property?"

"You make it sound so much worse than it was."

KC's eyes widened. "Zach! Why would you do that?"

He wanted to use his lame security excuse again, but he seriously needed better lines. Instead, he focused on pulling a beer. "Let's talk about it later—we're kinda busy right now."

"That we are," KC said, filling her tray with drinks for a rowdy table of off-the-clock firefighters. The dinner hour was just approaching, and Lola's bar was already filled to capacity. "But you're not off the hook," she warned him.

He wanted to let his rare bad temper loose and tell her to mind her own business, but knew his sister's fiancé, Jacob Blackstone, wouldn't pull any punches putting him in his place if Zach made his own sister cry. Besides, it wasn't KC's fault.

It was Sadie's.

He hadn't been able to stop thinking about her, to the point that he wished his brain had an off switch. Even sleeping hadn't given him any relief. Ever since seeing her two days ago, he'd dreamed of the single night they'd been together, and the glorious sensuality of her body.

The images in his brain were not calming him right now. Any part of him…

He distracted himself by checking on his orders in the kitchen, along with the two new hires he'd put in place a month ago. One was a veteran chef from the military who'd put in ten years of duty before losing a leg in Afghanistan. The other was a hardworking kid who reminded Zach a lot of himself at his age, with a single mom and baby sister at home to support. Only Miguel's dad had been killed in a car accident. Zach's had simply walked away when supporting a wife and child got too boring for him to handle.

Despite the rush, he found everything moving along smoothly in the kitchen. There was no need for Zach to be working at Lola's. In fact, he refused to let his mother pay him anymore. The last thing he needed these days was money—a concept he couldn't quite absorb. But he couldn't stay away.

Taking care of his grandmother, mother and sister was a way of life for him. He'd only been away from them while he was in the military. No matter what his job was now, his day still wasn't complete until he'd touched base with them. And he wasn't the kind of man to sit around while the women worked. He wasn't like his father—uncaring enough to walk away from the people who needed him. Nor KC's father, who'd done the same when the going got tough. Zach had never let down the women in his life, and his new millionaire status wasn't an excuse to start now.

So here he was on a Friday night, carrying a tray of appetizers out to a table surrounded by several couples eager to eat before hitting the dance floor. Lola's was crowded tonight. Lots of people were in town needing to blow off steam, especially those who worked out at the mill. Too many probably thought about the disaster they would have faced if it hadn't been a mandatory shutdown weekend when the bomb had gone off.

Zach talked to the customers for a few minutes about the damage, then left them to their food. As head of security, he'd done his best to spread the most positive outlook. He hoped he was having some effect, because the last thing this town needed was for the people living here to give up. Regardless of the damage, the Blackstone brothers were not going to let the mill close and the town disappear. They'd all worked too hard to have that happen to the people they cared about.

Hearing some boisterous laughter, Zach glanced at the table of firefighters only to spot an unexpected red-headed beauty in their midst.

Well, look what snuck in while I was in the kitchen.

He should stay away—he really should—but knew he wouldn't. Casually making his way across the room, he stopped to check in at a few tables while keeping Sadie in view. Her laughter, her smile were beautiful things, though she wasn't overtly flirting. Still, a surprising surge of anger streaked through him. He found himself circling slowly, almost like a lion studying his prey from all angles.

Coming in from behind, he could no longer see her face, but he could finally hear her words.

"So, did they know someone was sabotaging the mill before this?"

Every cell in his body went alert at the question. Why was she asking?

"Oh, yeah," one of the locals eagerly replied. "Of course, those of us who work there knew it way before any manager did. But we needed proof, right?"

She nodded, which caused the muted lighting to glint off her ruby curls.

"They say they got someone in custody," the man continued. "Whoever it is, they're gonna get a sh—oops, not supposed to say that in front of a lady."

Was that a hint of a blush on the curve of her cheek he could actually see?

"But the whole town, they're already up in arms."

"That will just give them a target," she murmured, nodding her understanding.

Standing right behind her, Zach felt a moment of evil satisfaction that he stood so close, yet she seemed unaware. One by one the men at the table spotted him. Oddly enough, none gave away his presence to the lamb in their midst.

Every time he was around this woman, his hackles rose. He told himself it was because he'd found her at the mill, where she didn't belong, but he was afraid the reason was much, much deeper.

"Why would you want to know?" he finally asked.

Sadie jerked around to face him, causing her drink to slosh over the rim and drip from her fingers. "What are you doing there?" she asked before lifting her hand up and gently sucking the moisture away.

Zach ignored the tightening in his groin, ever aware of his surroundings and a half dozen pairs of eyes glued to their interactions…and that was just at this table. Zach gave a short nod in the direction of the men, then cupped Sadie's elbow with his palm. "Let's get you a fresh drink."

Without waiting for a response, he ushered her around a dozen tables to get to the less crowded, more utilitarian end of the bar. The whole time his heart pounded with intensity, though he wasn't sure why the conversation affected him that way. He forced himself to speak quietly. "Why are you asking all those questions?"

Sadie didn't jerk away, but she kept up a firm pressure with her arm until he let her free.

Zach ignored KC's curious glances from several feet away, grateful that there were enough customers to delay her interrogation. He turned back to his prey. "What was that all about?" he demanded again, letting anger seep through his self-control.

At first, he thought she would cave and spill her guts.

His stomach churned as he realized he wanted to know everything about why she was here, why she'd walked back into his life and turned his emotions on their head.

Then her thick lashes swept up, revealing those gorgeous green eyes, and somehow he knew he wasn't getting what he wanted tonight.

She wiggled her glass. "I thought I was here for a fresh drink?"

He wasn't sure whether to shake her or kiss her, but he felt relief as he moved behind the bar. Being that close to Sadie only encouraged his circuits to misfire.

So he tried a different tactic. He let his fingers slide slowly over hers as he lifted the glass from her hand. Her lowered lashes told him she had something to hide. At least that secret he could guess, if her reaction was anything like his.

"You know those guys?" he asked as he refilled her Coke. He wanted to grin at her drink of choice. As far as he'd been able to tell, she didn't drink, smoke or get into trouble. Her innocence simply hinted at an incredible sensuality that he'd never been able to forget.

She shrugged delicate shoulders. "A couple of the guys are staying at the B and B. The hotel ran out of room."

They'd been lucky with all the crews that had come in to help fight the fire and pull debris. Unfortunately, Black Hills wasn't very well equipped for visitors. Every last vacant room was in use at the moment. There were even a couple of fire chiefs bunking out at Blackstone Manor.

"I told them there was a great place for food and drinks out this way. They invited me to join them when I was free. I hope that was okay?"

The glance from under her lashes didn't seem to be seeking permission so much as a reaction.

It was his turn to shrug. "I've always been easy to find."

Her petite body stilled. She glanced around, as if making sure no one was close enough to listen. "Look," she said, "I'm very sorry about leaving. I just got... scared."

He stepped closer, bypassing the safety of the counter. "Why?"

She swallowed, hard. His instincts were to follow the movement with his mouth, taste what he could only see.

Reaching out, he forced her chin up with demanding fingers. "Why?"

"It was just too much for me," she whispered.

Without thought, he found himself murmuring, "Me, too."

Startled eyes met his. He could drown in all that fresh green color. Five years ago, her eyes had been just as vibrant. Just as alluring. He'd fallen for her seductive pull and received the rudest awakening in his life for it. But he still couldn't forget the night spent drowning in her green gaze.

Suddenly Sadie was bumped from behind, breaking the hold she had on Zach. Quickly he shuttered his expression.

He stepped back once, twice, until he found his breathing distance. "Now, what's with the questions?"

"Why? Do you see me as a threat?"

In more ways than one. But he wasn't giving her more ammo, so he bit his tongue. "Should I?"

Her gaze dropped at his question, causing his hackles to rise once more. Why was getting any information from her like pulling teeth?

"Just don't stir up trouble." He turned away, lifting a tray of dirty glasses off the counter and stepping through the opening behind the bar.

Only then did he hear her say, "And how's a busy guy like you gonna stop me?"

"Don't you know you don't have to do this anymore?" a male voice from right behind Sadie asked.

Zach turned back toward her, focusing over her shoulder with a grin that she wished was directed at her. But it was better than the glower she'd been sure to receive after her challenge.

"My mama doesn't care how much money I make," Zach said. "She simply points at a table and tells me to get busy."

When Zach came back out from behind the bar she was forced to step to the side, giving her a good look at the newcomer.

Or rather, newcomers. The trio looked like the epitome of wealth…and exhaustion. Zach shook hands with the blond man before turning to do the same with a man whose dark hair had a mind of its own. The woman between them received a light, social hug.

Based on her discussions with people in town, these must be the Blackstones.

If she remembered her gossip correctly, this would be Aiden Blackstone, his wife, Christina, and one of the younger brothers, Jacob. The utter weariness in their expressions spoke to the trials of the last week. Their brother Luke was currently in the hospital after being near the epicenter of the exploding bomb.

Suddenly another woman arrived through the break in the bar counter, pushing Sadie even farther back. The blonde beauty threw her arms around the one Sadie assumed was Jacob, holding nothing back. The surrounding people didn't seem surprised. The woman pressed light, quick kisses against his lips, then settled at his side. Her touch never wavered and never dropped. If Sadie remembered correctly from local gossip, Zach's sister, KC, was engaged to Jacob.

Zach studied them a moment, then asked, "How's Luke doing?"

"Much better," Jacob said. "They say he can come home tomorrow."

"No further damage to his legs?" KC asked.

Jacob shook his head. "None."

"Good," Zach added. "We don't need any more damn tragedies around here."

Everyone murmured their agreement.

"Anyway." Aiden stepped closer. "My wife is in firm need of sustenance that isn't hospital food, and I promised her some of your mama's fried chicken."

Zach grinned in a way that took Sadie's breath. "With a baby on the way, that woman should have anything she wants to have. She's doin' all the work, after all."

"Amen," Christina said, leaving the whole group laughing.

Sadie smiled, even though she knew it was a little sad around the edges. The group reminded her of her family. There were only three of them, but she, her mama and her sister had taken care of each other through a lifetime of heartache. They could often make each other laugh during the hardest times. And they never gave up hope that they would be together.

Zach stepped back to the kitchen to put in the order without so much as looking in her direction, intensifying Sadie's feeling of solitude in the midst of the crowd. She eyed the distance back to the table she'd come from, but the Blackstones simply took up too much space for her to squeak by without notice.

Then the silence around her registered and she glanced back to realize she'd become the center of attention. Four sets of eyes studied her. Her familiar technique of disappearing into the shadows where she wouldn't be noticed wasn't an option here, as she was boxed in by the wall on one side and the bar counter behind her.

Finally the woman she recognized as Zach's sister stepped closer. "Hi, there. I'm KC, Zach's sister. And you are?"

Sadie wasn't used to people offering her their hands, but she shook anyway. "Sadie Adams."

"Let me guess," KC said with a slight smile. "You must be Zach's new nemesis."

How had she known? "Um…"

"Oh, is this the woman from the mill?" Christina asked, interest lighting her eyes.

Suddenly Sadie felt as though someone had dialed up the spotlight.

"I believe she is," KC replied.

"How did you know?" Sadie asked.

"Honey, it's a small town." KC's smile was friendly, not condescending as Sadie had expected. "Trust me, everybody knows."

"I don't know," Aiden said with a frown.

Christina patted his chest. "I'll fill you in later, dear."

That didn't stop him from studying Sadie in a way that made her more reluctant than ever to stay. But KC picked up her now watered-down drink from the counter and dumped it before starting a fresh one. "Come on over and tell us about yourself," she invited.

Sadie hung on to that friendly smile, even though she knew more than anyone how deceiving it might be from a stranger. But she needed these people for her mission, so she forced her feet forward.

"What do you do, Sadie?" Christina asked.

"I'm a photographer." It wasn't the entire truth. She did take photographs. She just didn't do it for a living, as she'd led them all to believe.

"Oh, where's your camera?"

"Outside." She'd been afraid Zach would make a scene if she brought it in.

Christina didn't seem fazed. "Have you had anything published?"

"Yes, actually. A few pieces through Barnhill Press." The art press wasn't anything to sneeze at, so at least Sadie didn't feel like such a fraud.

Until another voice chimed in. "So you no longer describe yourself as domestic help?"

The people around her froze, unsure how to take Zach's comment. Sadie had no problem with being seen as domestic help. After all, she'd fallen into that category all of her life.

She'd tried to stick as close to the truth as possible. She'd only ever held two things back from Zach the first time around: her employer's true identity and her sister's situation.

Sadie raised her chin and spoke confidently. "Actually, my longtime employer recently passed away. I'm taking a bit of a break before looking for a new position."

"Good luck," Aiden said.

"Thank you." She took a deep breath for courage. "I have an idea I think might interest you."

Suddenly the trio on this side of the bar with her adopted that slightly uncomfortable look that rich people got when they know they were about to be asked for money. She'd seen it often enough back home. But that wasn't what she wanted…

"I wondered if I could have your permission to shoot a series of photographs about the rebuilding of the mill? I visited the town several years ago and became quite attached to it." If they only knew… "From what the people here have been telling me about your family and what you are doing to keep the town alive, well, it's incredible."

She smiled brightly at Christina, since the woman's calm features were easier to focus on. "If nothing else, I think it would make a wonderful memento for the people of the town."

Christina glanced back up at her husband. "Aiden, that sounds wonderful."

"I could talk to the publisher at Barnhill. I've worked with him on several projects…though this would be my first solo proposal," she added, feeling the need to be honest.

On the other side of the bar, she could feel a sense of frustrated resistance coming from Zach. He stared at her, though she refused to meet his gaze. Luckily, she'd already gotten a positive response or she had a feeling he would have blasted her before his employer, simply to keep her from getting close.

Though he still didn't know how close she planned to be…

KC must have sensed it, too, because she kept glancing sideways at her brother. But she didn't speak. Finally Aiden said, "That does sound good. I am a bit worried about safety issues—"

Before he or Zach could go further, she cut him off. "Not a problem. I've already seen the destruction at the mill, and I would definitely need someone to steer me in the safest direction. Someone local, with a lot of experience with the area who could introduce me to people who know the history, the ins and outs of the area. The people and places that make Black Hills so special…"

"That's a great idea," Christina enthused.

Jake and Aiden were nodding along with her. "Definitely," Aiden said. "Zach fits both those criteria and as head of security could keep us informed about your project, too. Would that be a problem?"

"Not for me," she assured him.

Only after speaking did she glance at her former lover, whose hard-won mask barely covered the resentment pushing to get out. Sadie wondered if anyone else could see it. Probably not, because they went on talking as if this were a done deal.

Only Zach kept quiet. Good thing he didn't know the whole story. Otherwise, she might have to worry about her safety.

But at least he would learn. She would get what she wanted…no matter what.

Four

"Just what the hell did you think you were doing?"

Sadie quickly suppressed her smile before turning to face Zach's rage. She and she alone knew the depths of despair she'd experienced since the last time she'd walked away from him. But she couldn't have realized she'd be thrilled to see him under any circumstances…including when he looked like he would choke her if he could.

"Who, me?"

Her innocent question only served to incense him even more. The show was quite spectacular, in fact. Zach's skin took on a ruddy color underneath, showcasing the extent of his anger. But a lifetime as help to people who only wanted things to go their way had taught Sadie to take her kicks where she could get them, even if she could only feel her amusement on the inside.

"You knew I didn't want to spend time with you. So why would you set this whole thing up?" he growled.

Ouch. That hurt, but she had known the way he felt before he even said it. "Look," she said, not afraid to push back. "You started this with your high and mighty attitude, not me."

"So this is all a game to you?" He waved a hand at the damaged building behind him. "This is not a game to these people. This place was their life."

"Yes, and I think it will mean a lot to them to have someone document its resurrection, don't you?"

She wasn't wrong in this. Knowing how much people got attached to places—like she had to Sheldon Hall, even though it would never be hers—gave her a glimpse of exactly how these townspeople felt. "Building positive memories will help shore up the community and keep people here. Isn't that what you want?"

She could see on his face that there wasn't a right answer. He did want that, but it meant spending time with her. Though the reality made her chest ache, she had a job to do just as much as he did. With just as much at stake.

Through clenched teeth Zach brushed her off. "I don't have time to mess with you right now. The fire marshal is here. Just go back to the B and B."

As he stalked across the parking lot, she couldn't help needling him a little more. "I can get some exteriors, though, right?" she called.

He might as well have flipped her the bird, considering the glare on his face. But he held his temper in a gentlemanly way, at least in the midst of the crowd of people he now walked through.

Sadie chuckled, simply because crying in front of everyone wasn't an option, either. She'd suspected that coming back here would be tough, but she could never have imagined the roller coaster of dealing with her own emotions while matching wits with Zach.

Ever comforted by her camera, Sadie set off around the perimeter, once more trying to capture the compound from angles that showcased both the tragedy but also the potential for rebuilding, because that was exactly what people needed to see.

Just a few minutes in, a bell sounded. Glancing around, Sadie saw numerous soot-covered men exit the site and make their way across the parking lot to a couple of huge tents that had been erected along the far edge near the fencing. Must be lunchtime.

After taking a few shots of the men, she edged away from the crowd. Her focus here was pictures, not food.

"Hey, there," a voice said from behind her a few minutes later.

Sadie sighed but finished up her shot before easing her camera down from her face. Had Zach sent another security guard to escort her away today? If so, he was going to have a hell of a fight on his hands.

Turning without any rush, she eyed the man behind her. There was no badge attached to his clothing, and he didn't look dirty like most of the men here. A buttoned-down shirt and Dockers weren't really appropriate attire for a disaster site. But at least he looked friendly.

"Hi," she said, her unease calming down a notch.

"Is that a Canon Mark III body?"

Warmth spread through her. A fellow photographer, maybe? "Yes, with a custom lens. You know it?"

"Ah, I admire from afar and spend my budget on paper and ink instead." The man grinned, looking young despite his thinning hair, and held out his hand. "I'm Lance Parker, editor of the local paper."

She met his hand for a firm shake. "Nice to meet you, Lance. I'm Sadie."

"You must be getting some good pictures, then."

Pulling the camera from around her neck, she clicked on the picture preview and turned the screen so they both could see.

Fifteen minutes of talking cameras and photo composition and lighting fed Sadie's artistic soul. None of her family were interested in photography. She had few friends because of all her responsibilities, but she had managed to join an artists' group near home that she tried to go to once a month. Sometimes it worked out, sometimes not. But she tried to get her fix in when she could.

"Would it be possible for me to use a couple of these in the newspaper?" he asked. "We'd compensate you, of course. These are wonderful and my two photographers are busy with the cleanup, which keeps them from snapping away right now."

Sadie barely had a chance to think before another voice cut in. "Hey, Lance. How's it going?"

She looked over the newspaper editor's shoulder to see Zach's sister, KC, approaching them. Lance smiled as she arrived.

"As good as can be expected, I think." He gestured to Sadie. "Just trying to convince Sadie here to share a few of her pictures with the community. They would be a great accompaniment to the recovery stories."

KC studied Sadie for a split second, but then her lashes swept down, shielding the expression in eyes so like Zach's. "That would be cool. So, Sadie, what do you think?"

That I don't like being put on the spot... "Yeah, I'll come by and we can look over them again. Tomorrow?"

"Great," KC said, as if she'd decided the subject was closed. "Now y'all want some lunch?"

Lance agreed enthusiastically, but Sadie shook her head. "I'm still full from the breakfast spread my landlady puts out, but I'd be happy to volunteer, if you'd like?"

KC's raised brow and hesitant "Sure" didn't make Sadie feel better. She knew it didn't really matter what KC thought of her, whether she approved. Sadie wouldn't be sticking around Black Hills long enough to make real friends…or sisters-in-law. Somehow that didn't stop her from wishing differently.

Although KC might be hesitant for completely different reasons. Had Zach told her about Sadie? How much did she really know?

Zach made his way back across the parking lot to the food tents KC and Christina had installed. He tried to keep an eye out for Sadie along the way, though he desperately wanted to curse himself for caring where she was in the first place. He could tell himself all he wanted to that it was about suppressing her plans, but deep down he was afraid there were far deeper reasons than that lame excuse.

He didn't see her until he was closer to the tents, and that fiery red hair came into view as she scurried behind the serving line. It wasn't entirely clear from this distance, but it looked almost as if she were in charge.

"Kind of amazing, isn't it?"

Zach glanced to the side to see his little sister approach, her arms filled with a box. He automatically reached for her burden, taking it on himself as he nodded his head in Sadie's direction. "What's going on here?"

KC didn't look at the other woman but continued to

watch her brother...making him very uneasy. "She volunteered to help after saying she wasn't hungry. I could tell she wasn't thrilled with the setup when she joined us, but she didn't say a word."

One side of KC's mouth lifted in a slight smile. "I wondered if she would, but she never did until I started asking for help. It took a few minutes to get her to open up. As soon as she realized she wouldn't offend me by making suggestions, she took the lead. We were whipped into shape in ten minutes and served hundreds in less than half an hour." KC shook her head. "She's good."

Very good. But Zach didn't want to think of that in front of his sister.

"She told me before that she made a living as domestic help, but never went into specifics," he mused as he watched Sadie navigate the chaos with the calm demeanor of a woman who had many pots on the fire but wasn't worried about losing one. He glanced at his sister, only to find her still studying him.

He was in trouble now.

"So you knew her before, as in before this trip to Black Hills?"

Why hadn't he just kept his mouth shut? "Hmm..."

But KC wasn't buying the noncomment. "Did you meet her while you were in the military?"

No, but those days right after he came home had been a blur of nightmares and worry over his mother, his family. He hadn't known how to tell them he was falling in love. After she disappeared without a trace, he'd been glad he kept Sadie to himself and not made her a thing—that thing he had to explain to friends and family, pretend not to miss, or realize hadn't been as real as he'd thought. He had happily done most of that without public scrutiny.

Now, though, he could talk about Sadie without having to get into all the ugliness of regret and pain. He'd never been a liar, but he kept it brief, strictly answering the question that was asked. "No, she's been to town before."

KC slapped her hands to her hips, making him wish he hadn't been gentlemanly enough to take the box. "She was here before, long enough for you to talk to her about her job, and you never mentioned her. Was she a customer? Or—"

"What's for lunch, my lovely?" Jacob's voice interrupted his fiancée's, much to Zach's eternal gratitude.

"Barbecue and fixin's," KC said, giving Jacob a big smile.

"What?" her fiancé's voice boomed over the lot. "Barbecued meat, a pretty lady and a cold beer? All I need is our son and it'll be heaven."

"Christina's got him at the manor," KC said, giving Jacob a quick kiss on the cheek. "Your mom started running a fever this morning, so she stayed home and offered to keep him, too."

Zach saw the flash of concern that crossed Jacob's expression, and knew that even the slightest bug could be very harmful for the Blackstones' mother, who had been in a coma for many years. But KC gave him a reassuring smile.

Jacob pulled her into his arms. "Well, how long is that gonna last? Forget the barbecue. Let's go home."

"Nope, sorry," she said, laughing as she swatted his chest.

Jacob buried his face in KC's neck. "Doomed" was all Zach heard before mumbling and giggling took over. He glanced away, grinning at the two lovebirds' antics. In the sea of chaos under the tent, Sadie stood oddly still. The look on her face, even from this distance, had a hint of sadness and longing before she blinked and it was gone. Actually, all emotion was gone, as if she were afraid for Zach to see too closely inside.

Funny, he felt the same way.

Finally Jacob and KC separated, walking to the food tent hand in hand. Zach fell in step beside them. They talked about the next step in their plan as they joined the dwindling line for food. Sadie certainly had stepped up the efficiency of the process, and now the parking lot was filled with hungry workers eating their fill.

"I'm so glad we could do this," KC said, surveying the scene.

Jacob kissed the top of her head. "Me, too. Whatever it takes to keep Black Hills alive, that's what we're gonna do."

They reached the steam table set up under the tent and chose their meal. Zach deposited the box in the serving area before taking his food tray. Sadie was at the other end in a cute apron with a pig on it, pouring drinks.

"Wow," KC said as she reached Sadie's table. "This was incredible. Thank you so much."

Sadie shrugged away the thanks. "It was no problem."

"No problem? I didn't think so." KC laughed. "Of course, I'm used to a well-ordered kitchen. Being outdoors and not knowing where everything is throws me off."

"Organization is key," Sadie said with a wink.

Jacob reached out to shake Sadie's hand. "Well, we are extremely grateful for your organizational skills."

Sadie shifted as if their praise made her uncomfortable. "I'm glad I could help," she said, handing him a large iced tea.

"Would you be free tomorrow to help some more?" Jacob asked.

Sadie blinked. "I'm sure I can," she said. "I'll be out here tomorrow to take more pictures anyway."

"Did you get any good shots today?" KC asked.

"Sure did."

Jacob looked over at Zach in a way that made him distinctly uneasy. He kept looking. Zach could see the wheels turning.

"Tomorrow," Jacob finally said, "we have a truck coming in with lots of supplies for the workers. Decent boots, heavy overalls, protective gloves and such."

Oh, no. *Jacob, please don't do this to me.*

Jacob didn't even glance in his direction. But his jaw twitched as if he were aware of Zach's dread…and amused by it.

"We need some help getting everything organized and out to the employees. I don't want them working cleanup without good-quality gear."

Zach looked at Sadie in enough time to see her eyes widen. "Isn't that costing a lot for a company that's not bringing in any money at the moment?"

Jacob nodded. "But we want them safe. Those that opted to stay on through the temporary closing and re-building are being paid wages to help with cleanup and reconstruction.

"We wanted to keep the work local, as much as possible," Jacob said, his tone firm. "We've got some donations, but everything else is at Blackstone expense. Ultimately, this is about the good of the town. The people who live here deserve to be able to stay."

KC chimed in. "Not be run from their homes by a crazy person."

"That's commendable," Sadie said.

"Not really," Jacob responded, giving her a puzzled look.

"Trust me." She met his look without wavering. "I've known some businessmen who couldn't care less about anything but their bottom line. They'd bring in the cheapest labor and not care who lost their livelihoods. Y'all are doing good here."

Zach could see Sadie mulling all this over, her brain working in overdrive even though she didn't ask any more questions. She simply picked at the puzzle, trying to unravel the complicated strands.

The fact that he could discern this made him uneasy. He didn't want to read Sadie's mind. Didn't want to feel her curiosity, her disbelief that the Blackstones were good people who cared about their workers. What had happened in her life to lead her to question that?

No, he didn't want to know.

"Sadie, if your organizing skills make this as easy as serving lunch, we'll be in business in no time. Zach will be here when the truck arrives in the morning around nine. He can make sure whatever you need is carried out."

Sure I will. Don't ask me what I want.

Then Zach wondered if his thoughts were showing on his face, because his sister was watching him—very closely.

Sadie, on the other hand, looked pretty pleased with herself. Considering how he'd treated her since she came back to town, he had to wonder why.

As his sister and Jacob moved on, Sadie smiled over at him. "Looks like it's you and me together—again."

Was that a statement...or a threat?

Five

"It's the truth, I tell ya."

Sadie couldn't help but grin at the man before her. Wearing the traditional farmer uniform of overalls, plaid shirt, ball cap and messy white hair, he was a perfect candidate for sitting on a bench in the town square. So were the other two grandfatherly types with him. But he was the talker.

"I think you're pulling my leg," Sadie insisted, knowing it would spur him on.

"No, I would never," he said with a sincere shake of his head. "But I betcha they're all in on it. The other cotton industries are pressuring the state to shut us down, because they want the business we've always had here. That's why all of this is happening."

She knew old men were prime candidates to become conspiracy theorists. They had too much time to sit around and think and talk and spin events into the way they wanted to see them. So she asked, "But Blackstone Mills has been here since the town started, hasn't it?"

"And still putting out quality product," one of the other men, Earl, said. "That's why they have to put us out of business."

Well, as much as she'd like to brush them off, the fact that a bomb had exploded here couldn't be denied. That was deliberate malice, so someone definitely had it in for Blackstone Mills. And the police weren't talking yet.

"I still don't understand why anyone would want to put you out of business," she said, hoping to get more gossip. "Wouldn't someone local have to be in on this? Have access to the plant?"

"Oh, they were," Mr. Farmer breathed.

"The other textile companies found someone local to do their dirty work, we're pretty sure," Earl said.

Farmer interrupted, "We heard about all kinds of things. Can't keep stuff like that secret. Equipment failure and missing shipments. But it was the cotton that was the kicker."

Now they were getting somewhere. Sadie forgot about the lines of men behind her, getting loaded up by fellow workers with their safety gear after she'd streamlined the process for them. Zach had introduced her to the lead volunteer then disappeared, which she was grateful for now, because she was pretty sure these old-timers wouldn't be speaking to her with him around.

Especially about the damaged cotton crop her landlady had mentioned.

"What about the cotton?" she asked, pretending ignorance.

"Oh, that Zachary Gatlin boy did it," Earl said, "though the police said he was innocent."

"We aren't so sure," Farmer said. "He's in thick with

those Blackstones, so…" He shrugged. "Why they'd want to damage their own business would be a mystery, but then again, there's a lot about all this that is."

Sadie nodded.

"But he sprayed the cotton, that's all we know. Either somebody loaded the poison in or he did it himself."

"Now he's heading up recovery efforts, so who knows."

"But poison the cotton, it did. Took a while, but they managed to get cotton in from elsewhere. Thank goodness, or the mill would have gone under by Christmas, for sure."

It was the same story she'd heard from her landlady. Something didn't add up, though. "Maybe somebody was trying to frame him?" she mused.

"Frame who?"

The voice from behind her had her stiffening. There was nothing like being caught red-handed talking about someone by the person in question. The men's wide eyes clued her in to their awareness of Zach's presence. Too bad she hadn't been watching them while she was overthinking.

Quickly, she twisted around. "Zach, there you are. I was wondering what happened to you."

Under his breath, so only she could hear, he said, "Didn't sound like it."

Her cheeks flushed hot, but she didn't tuck her chin down the way she wanted to. *Don't show weakness.* Always her first line of defense against the world.

"Gentlemen," he said, glancing over her shoulder. "Glad to see you here. Thanks for supporting us." Then he clasped her elbow. "If you'll excuse us."

He pulled her away, quickly enough that she had to double her short steps to keep up. Looking back, she noticed the men talking and laughing. Goodness only knew what they thought he wanted with her, but whatever their assumption, they thought it was amusing.

Not breaking stride, Zach marched her around the side of the parking area to a more isolated spot before turning to face her. "What was that about?"

"What do you mean?" She had a feeling her innocent look wasn't going to work here.

She was right.

"What right do you have to talk about me, about my life, with the people of this town?"

"Well, technically the conversation didn't start out that way—"

"I don't care how it started." His voice rose enough to sting her ears. "Just that it stops. Now."

Unbidden, Sadie could feel her backbone stiffening and her expression becoming a blank mask. A lifetime in service had taught her how to deal with difficult people, usually men, and their expressions of displeasure. She instinctively took steps to protect herself, even if walking away from the situation wasn't an option. Which it usually wasn't.

Her voice was awfully formal when she spoke. "I'm sorry you feel that way, but I was simply asking about the mill and they offered information. I didn't dig into anything."

"I heard you asking questions."

She narrowed her eyes at him. If he thought she would just take this, he was mistaken. He didn't know her as well as he thought. "A question. You heard me ask a question about you, and that's after Earl brought you up." She cocked her head to the side. "But I do have another question."

"I'm not telling you anything about myself." His snarl said she didn't deserve it.

Which she didn't. "And thus my question. Why do you care if I ask?"

Zachary Gatlin hated being caught off guard. He'd spent his military career planning for the unexpected, but that didn't mean he liked it.

Luckily, Sadie didn't wait for an answer.

"Look," she said, "I have to ask questions. How else am I gonna know what to take pictures of? Who to take pictures of? Talking to people is part of that."

She cocked her jeans-clad hip, the hand she propped there drawing his eye more than he liked. "If that's a problem, I can do it on my own. After all, you are only supposed to escort me through the mill."

"No," he said through clenched teeth. Not just from his anger, either. Being only a foot away from her seemed to be causing his entire body to go haywire. "That's not what Jacob meant, and you know it."

"I know nothing of the sort." Her brows rose. He didn't remember her being so sassy before. This time she was pushing all his buttons. "I only know that the mill is dangerous right now and they want you with me when I go inside. That's the only sure thing."

"It's my job to make sure *everything* you go over is safe." They both knew what his emphasis meant, even if she wanted to pretend otherwise.

"Then I guess you'd better stick a little closer, don't you think?"

For a split second, that sassy pink mouth and raised brow made Zach drop his protective barriers. Without thought, he stepped in. Her back hit the wall behind her. His hand planted right above her shoulder. There was barely a hand's breadth between their chests. Their lips were even closer.

Zach's heart moved into double time. *Remain impassive.* But he couldn't when his entire body was straining to press in close and make contact in the most primitive way he knew how. *Touch.*

Their breath mingled. He allowed one point of contact. Only one, when he wanted so many more. He reached out with his other hand and curled it around her waist, soaking in the warmth of her body beneath the T-shirt she wore.

"Oh, I'm gonna stick pretty damn close, sweetheart," he said, relishing her eyes going wide with something akin to nerves. "I'll be keeping an eye on every move you make. Every word you speak. Every picture you take." No matter how creepy that might be.

He could be dedicated to his job, couldn't he? "No more snooping behind my back."

"Roger that," she whispered.

It was the barest brush of her lip against his that broke the hold she had over his body. That accidental contact shook him to his core—which was the last thing he wanted her to know. So he stepped back. Removed his hand. Controlled his breathing.

And met her gaze. He could have sworn she'd just gotten exactly what she wanted.

Which filled his mind with images of other times she'd gotten what she wanted, only they were much more intimate things, things he didn't want to remember when he was standing this close to her.

Then she threw him off guard again. "I'm sorry," she whispered.

Zach blinked, not switching gears fast enough. "What?"

"I'm sorry that you're angry with me."

He met her eyes, studying their green depths, not sure if he wanted to go back to the time when he'd known her before. But his body spoke before his mind could catch up. "But you're not sorry you left?"

Her expression flattened, her pale skin going almost white. The spare sprinkle of freckles on her cheeks stood out in contrast. "I didn't have a choice," she finally said.

"Zach?" someone called before he could push for more. He forced himself to pull back, to let his arm fall to his side, to clench his teeth together so he wouldn't ask why. Then he deliberately turned his head to the side, blocking her out.

Because he didn't need to know why. Knowing that she had walked away was more than enough.

Six

"Zach, are you ready?"

Sadie tore her gaze from Zach to look at Jacob Blackstone, who stood about five feet from them. To her embarrassment, she had to blink a moment before her gaze would focus on him. Instead she wanted nothing more than to turn back to Zach and press her lips to his. No matter who was looking.

So close.

But Zach wouldn't be there waiting. He strode toward his future brother-in-law, not looking back. "Yeah, I'm ready."

"Ready for what?" she asked.

"They've cleared us to take a preliminary tour inside before the workers go into the parts of the building that were damaged to start cleanup."

She glanced at Zach's retreating back. For someone who said he wasn't letting her out of his sight, he sure was moving away at a fast clip.

"Are you coming?" Jacob asked. Sadie found herself on the receiving end of his inquisitive look.

"Yes, if I may," she said. Apparently, Zach wasn't so far away he hadn't heard that, because his shoulders had straightened, hard.

Jacob led her back to the trailer and got some boots and coveralls in her size. Once she was dressed and had collected her camera, she approached the men again where they stood with two soot-covered figures with clipboards. She steeled herself as Zach turned toward her, but he held out a bright yellow hard hat. "This, too," he said simply.

Jacob introduced her to the fire inspectors, then they headed for the building entrance. To her surprise, a large group of workmen formed a crowded semicircle near the door. Jacob paused to shake a few hands and speak, but the still, respectful patience of the hundred or so people brought out an emotional response in Sadie.

She wasn't used to this. She had more experience with the spoiled variety of the human species. But the simple look on their faces told her this place meant something to them. When Jacob gave the word that it was time, they'd put their backs into rebuilding it—paycheck or no.

Stepping back, she got some wide-angle shots of the crowd, then the entrance. As she took her turn stepping through, her chest tightened. To be the first to see the destruction of this place felt significant. And this wasn't even the worst part of the damage. Her hold on her camera got a little tighter. Hopefully she'd be able to do her subject some justice.

The smell of smoke lingered in the air outside the building, but it hadn't prepared her for the thickness of it inside. It seemed to immediately dry out her throat and threaten to choke her. She found herself panting, trying to limit the air's access to her lungs.

The outer rooms were relatively intact except for their blackened walls, but as they traveled deeper, more damage began to appear. Bubbled paint, peeled portions of Sheetrock, black marks following trails that she assumed were electrical wires in the walls.

"Wow," said a masculine voice near her.

Sadie turned her head to see a big bear of a man staring down the hallway. The hard movement of his Adam's apple told her just how much seeing this affected him.

The rest of the group that had come in were just ahead, leaving Sadie and the man behind a bit. "What did you do here?" she asked.

There was no doubt he had worked here. Someone didn't view a building, especially an industrial building, with such emotion if there wasn't a personal tie.

He turned to her as if he hadn't realized she was there. He blinked rapidly. She knew the feeling well. Working in Sheldon Hall for the Beddingfield family, she'd learned early on all the tricks to hiding those telltale signs of emotion. Instead of pushing, she waited to see if he was interested in talking to her or wanted to be left alone.

Once under control, he offered a halfhearted smile. "Oh, I'm Bateman, the day shift foreman."

She snapped a few pictures of the group ahead of them, getting a long-range perspective, so the foreman wouldn't feel as if she was too focused on him. "So you must have worked here a long time to reach that position," she surmised.

"Since I was a young'un," he said, and this time his smile was more genuine. She smiled back, her heart softening even more.

He went on. "I was hired by the old Mr. Blackstone himself. I tell you, I about wet my pants that day."

"Intimidating?"

"Oh, yes," he said, moving forward once more. "He was a fierce one. I just happened to get lucky—or unlucky, as it were. The hiring manager was sick the day of my interview. But I must have passed muster, because he hired me on the spot. I was seventeen."

They picked their way down halls, pausing beside rooms with water and smoke damage. Sadie managed some more artistic photos of the damage, along with pictures of Bateman while he surveyed the areas. The deeper they journeyed into the building, the harder it became for Sadie to breathe, though she tried not to let it show. Her body felt hot, as if it could still feel the flames, even though she knew that was impossible.

The effects of the explosion became more evident as they proceeded. Sadie could tell they were coming closer to the heart of the plant. Closer to the connection to the admin building where the bomb had been placed. Here pieces of the ceiling were missing; what parts of the walls were left were completely charred and the smoke lay like a blanket over them.

Bateman paused just inside the entrance to a long, cavernous room. As Sadie paused next to him, she noticed the remnants of two-by-fours that had once formed wall dividers, the twisted metal remnants of filing cabinets against the far walls. This room had once been either offices or cubicles. At the far end of the room, the group of men ahead of them also paused. Sadie tried not to watch but couldn't miss Zach's proud bearing and confident interactions with those around him.

Her heart ached, even if she didn't want to acknowledge it. So she turned back to Bateman.

"Since seventeen? That is a long time."

Bateman's smile was tinged with something sad. "Yes, I've been here a long time. My sons work here. And last year my grandson came to work here, too."

"Your family is very important to you."

"Always." Again she saw that sheen of tears, though he tried to hide it by turning his face in the other direction. "If this place closes, what will happen to us? We've always been close. But they're already looking for jobs elsewhere."

Sadie rarely found herself in this position in her day job, but she'd spent more than her fair share of time in hospitals. Her natural compassion asserted itself. She couldn't help patting his arm, though she pretended not to see his tears. Grown men almost always preferred it that way.

"I don't think that will be necessary," she said, hoping her words would soothe him. "From the sounds of it, the Blackstones are gonna do everything they can to keep that from happening."

In her peripheral vision, she saw Bateman blink several times and nod. To give him more privacy, she glanced back at the other men—and found Zach's dark stare trained on her.

This time, she couldn't look away. She felt almost paralyzed by the intensity, as if by sheer will he could see deep inside her.

And for once, she wished she could show him.

Suddenly the connection broke as Zach glanced up and his eyes widened. "Watch out," he yelled.

Sadie quickly followed his example and looked at the ceiling. Her mind barely registered some kind of debris falling before she flung her hands out to push Bateman away.

It happened fast. She pushed. Bateman pulled. Pain slashed across her cheek. The camera shattered. They both went down, then Sadie saw stars across her field of vision before everything went blank.

"Really, I'm fine."

Zach watched as Sadie went a few rounds with the nurse in the temporary first aid center they had set up.

"No, you're not. That cut needs stitches," the nurse, Marty, said.

If anything, Sadie paled even more. "Just butterfly it."

"And mar that gorgeous face forever?" The young guy was aghast. And no, that slinky dark emotion wheedling into Zach was not jealousy—or any form of territorial assertion. "No, ma'am."

As others crowded the opening behind him, Zach turned to KC and Jacob, who both wore concerned expressions. "How is she?" KC whispered.

Zach answered at the same volume, for some reason not wanting Sadie to know they were talking about her. "Very unhappy in the face of treatment." An unusually strong panic had graced her features every time any mention was made of going to the hospital. She seemed to only want to go back to the B and B and pretend she was fine. Zach did not care for the curiosity leaking into his thoughts. "And she'll be even more unhappy when she realizes what happened to her camera."

There was a general chorus of winces before the nurse joined their little group. "She'll need some stitches for that cut on her face. The hard hat did its job. Still, I'd feel better if she wasn't gonna be alone tonight. Especially once she's got some pain meds in her."

There were a lot of logical solutions to this problem. Sadie could stay at Blackstone Manor with Aiden and

Christina. After all, Christina was a nurse. But she was pregnant and Ms. Blackstone, the brothers' mother, had been fighting some kind of infection lately.

KC—or hell, even Zach's mother—could take care of Sadie overnight.

So why did he hear himself saying, "I'll do it."

He ignored the myriad glances that swung his way. "She'll be more comfortable at the B and B with her own stuff," he said, offering a fairly reasonable excuse. "And I'm the only single person with no kids in this bunch."

Marty gave him a nod, as if this were the given option. "I'll get some instructions put together, but I imagine you know what warning signs to look for?"

He sure did. Zach's military background had trained him for this and a whole lot more. Unfortunately, he'd had to put that knowledge into practice a time or two. Times he'd prefer to not just forget but to completely obliterate from his memory.

Marty went back to his patient and the others talked quietly together in that intimate way couples had. Zach watched as Bateman lumbered in across the small space. He knelt by Sadie's chair, the movement oddly humble in a man his size.

Sadie smiled at the older man, then immediately winced. As they talked, Zach thought back to earlier, to Sadie's comforting hand on Bateman's arm, to her push to get him out of the direct path of the falling debris… All those things matched the Sadie he remembered from before she'd pulled her disappearing act.

The new Sadie had been more of a challenge, demanding, secretive almost—instead of just sweet. He didn't want to be intrigued, yet he was.

What had brought on those changes? Obviously there

was some of that sugary-sweet woman in there some-where—so where had the new spice come from?

Zach suddenly realized Sadie was staring at him, her big moss-green eyes uncertain and almost fearful. The nurse must have told her about tonight's sleeping ar-rangements. He didn't care if it was the coward's way out; he made a quick exit.

There was still work to do—and if it helped him avoid any questions, all the better.

But he couldn't avoid Sadie a couple of hours later as he drove her slightly dopey self back to the B and B. He'd gotten her key before they'd left the mill.

When they went inside, there was no nosy landlady in the lobby to ask too many questions. Sadie leaned into him on the stairs. He told himself it would be rude to make her climb them on her own in her current shaky state. If only he could just ignore the softness of her body as it pressed against his—in such an achingly fa-miliar fit. The light caramel scent of her hair stirred an all-too-base hunger. He felt the echo of anticipation from another time when he had been leading her to bed.

No matter how many times he told himself it couldn't happen between them again, his urges were steadily drowning out the voice of reason.

"You don't have to do this," Sadie said in the same sexy drawl that featured in his memories of that one emotion-charged night five years ago.

"I take my job very seriously," he said as he unlocked her room and led her inside.

"I see that," she said, swaying slightly where she stood. Apparently Sadie couldn't handle pain meds very well. "You've always gone above and beyond."

Zach didn't deny it. That was a part of his nature he couldn't get rid of. Whether he was writing a grocery list, doing a job or taking care of his family, he was usually in whole hog.

A cute frown scrunched up Sadie's usually open features. "But I can take care of myself," she said. She shuffled toward the dresser. "After all, I've been doing it all my life."

He refrained from pointing out that she would have been driving impaired if he had let her go home alone, and watched her pull out pajamas. She shuffled to what he assumed was the bathroom and shut herself inside.

Right, he'd conveniently forgotten about the stubborn streak.

Dropping the overnight bag he kept stowed in his SUV, Zach strolled over and sank onto the couch to wait, banging his knee against the little coffee table in the process. The laptop before him sprang to life.

Four pictures filled the screen, all of him. These weren't the classic survey pictures he was used to seeing. Each one was artistically composed with strategic lighting and showed him absorbed in some task. Except for the one in the bottom right corner, in which he stared straight ahead with a sad look on his face.

The pictures had an indefinable quality portraying not just his emotion but the photographer's as well. Almost a wistful, yearning feel.

Looking at them, it hit him—Sadie had missed him after all.

The bathroom door opened. Somehow, Zach knew Sadie would not want him to see these pictures. With a flick of his wrist, he closed the laptop.

He looked away so he could avoid seeing the sway of her breasts beneath the short, fitted nightie she wore. Unlike the oversize T-shirts his sister had preferred as a teenager, Sadie was all girl when it came to pajamas and underwear.

Nope. Don't go there.

She plopped onto the bed then dropped back onto a mound of pillows. The minute her head made contact, she winced.

But her sleepy eyes met his defiantly. "See. I'm good."

Yes, you are. He smothered a smile. "Sure you are."

She ignored him, rolling onto her side. He could have been offended at her presenting her back, except he knew from experience that was the side she slept on.

He stood for a long time in the middle of the room, almost able to pinpoint to the second when she sank into sleep. His gaze traced the familiar S curve of her body he was desperate to curl around once more. He looked out the window at the darkening sky, then at the alarm screen on his phone that told him when he would need to wake her next.

And finally, the laptop.

He didn't have to open it to know what was inside. Those pictures were imprinted on his brain. Mixed with the yearning he'd seen on her face when they'd stood in the alley this morning, he knew deep inside that Sadie still wanted him, too.

Then he stripped down to his boxer briefs and climbed into bed beside Sadie. At some point, his body made up his mind for him. He might be a selfish bastard, but if this was his chance to have one more taste of the only woman who had tempted his heart, he wasn't going to turn it down.

Seven

Waking to the feel of strong arms and Zach's scent wasn't unusual for Sadie. He remained in her dreams no matter how many days they were apart. She let herself hover there between wakefulness and sleep, wishing the feel of him would never disappear.

Ever so slowly, the mist started to recede. "Zach," she whispered, her mind still not comprehending. "Zach, is that you?"

"Yes," he murmured. "I'm here."

"Please don't leave me."

"I didn't leave you. You left me."

"But I never really wanted to."

Only the sudden stiffening of the body beside hers awakened her enough to realize that he was real rather than a figment of her imagination. So warm and alive she could have wept in gratitude.

The confusion dissipated in a rush of fever as desire swept through her. She'd denied her need for too long.

His groan filled the air. The rough scratch of hair and smooth heat of skin graced her palms, telling her she had reached out to touch. To test whether the apparition of her dreams was indeed real.

And that's when reality returned in an unwelcome rush.

She shouldn't. She knew she shouldn't, that deep down it made what she was doing that much more despicable. Her betrayal then, and her betrayal now.

Her fingers curled, digging into the warm flesh as if to keep him with her just a moment longer. His quick catch of breath signaled a change in the air, a breach of a barrier that shouldn't be forgotten.

But it was too late.

Her mind cried out with joy as his body rolled against hers, sweeping over her to take control. He was the same Zach she remembered. His familiar scent and bulk enveloped her. Her need exploded deep inside. For this moment she would let go of the past, not worry about the future and do the one thing Sadie never did: enjoy the present.

For the first time in five years, she felt his lips against hers. Not the barely there brush from the mill, but a full meeting of lips that conveyed passion and want. Sadie's palms found the bare skin of his shoulders, tracing muscles bulked by years of true labor. For long moments his lips distracted her. It wasn't the tentative touch of new lovers, but the eager reunion, the rediscovery of each other.

Just as her hands traced sinewy muscle over his ribs, he dipped down. The heat radiating from him blanketed her, left her aching for more. She wanted freedom—freedom from her clothes, from her fear, from the secrets that stood between them.

The tips of his hair, much longer than the last time they were together, brushed her cheeks. It tickled, lightening her mood a little. She smiled against his lips. Her hands automatically burrowed into the silky strands, and she savored the thickness, the new weight that signaled his complete return to civilian life.

Her hands in his hair ramped up something for him, because his movements took on a frantic edge. A powerful purpose that plunged her into heaven.

He stripped her of her nightgown, then panties. His thighs settled between hers as he assumed possession. Then he traced her ribs with his palms, reminding her of the first time his hands had explored her body.

Time coalesced in a surreal effect, mixing this moment with a night five years ago when Zach had introduced her to an ecstasy she'd only ever dreamed of before. Now, as then, he touched every part of her as if committing her body to memory. Fingers kneading her muscles. Nails stimulating her skin. Palms controlling her hips.

From somewhere deep inside her a whimper erupted. His hands tightened at the sound, keeping her from lifting against him. The inability to move only ramped up her need. Her core melted in liquefied heat.

Suddenly his warmth receded as he crouched between her thighs. It took a moment of disoriented disappointment to realize he hadn't left her. Then he pressed his open mouth to her thigh. She tensed. Each sucking kiss brought him closer to the apex of her need, but never close enough. Her gasps filled the silence.

Just when she'd thought he would end her suffering, his mouth moved to her belly button, then out along her ribs. This time her breath caught, then she giggled at his touch. He growled, his approval obvious as he rediscovered every spot that made her laugh, sigh and moan.

Finally he stretched out over her once more. He buried his hands in her hair. The long strands wound around his fingers, and he took full advantage, tugging until her chin lifted. Sadie wanted to weep as control and guilt swept away from her. All she could do was enjoy.

His kiss against her neck was firm, demanding. This time there was no stopping her hips from lifting, her hands from clutching him to her. His mouth worked its magic while his other hand guided his hardness to her. The stretch right to the edge of fullness made her wince. It had been so long.

Too long.

But her nails dug into the cheeks of his ass, pulling him into her with devastating effect. Her entire body exploded into tingles as he moved within her. It was exactly as she remembered, and so much more.

His body demanded her response. She gave him her all. Hips clashing. Skin rubbing. Breath mingling. Until the night erupted into a million points of light and emotion.

Cementing her to him…forever.

Zach's eyes opened when he heard the click of the bathroom door the next morning…then the unmistakable turn of the lock.

In the military he'd trained himself to be instantly alert upon awakening, but the habit wasn't always beneficial in civilian life. For instance, at the moment, his clear mind began to play last night over and over and over again. Which wasn't what he wanted.

The feelings and memories urged him to get his naked ass out of bed and into the shower with her. If only he hadn't heard the telltale sound of the lock shutting him out.

So instead he covered his naked ass with a clean pair of jeans and headed downstairs for some coffee. At least he didn't run into the proprietress first thing—which was good for her. He wasn't in the mood to deal with Gladys before getting in a good shot of caffeine. The breakfast room was empty, though there were pans of fresh rolls and biscuits on the sideboard, and the dark smell of his favorite breakfast brew permeated the room.

The hot black coffee distracted him from what he would say to Sadie when she appeared, what he would do from this point onward.

Her agreement with the Blackstones meant he couldn't ignore her, couldn't get away. She hadn't been the clingy type—now or in the past. But he could honestly say this wasn't a situation he was used to being in with women.

His relationships since he'd been home from the air force had been few and far between. They weren't really relationships, per se. Life had been too full of obligations and change to indulge in something that required that level of commitment—and he'd never felt the urge for more than a good time.

Except with Sadie.

A flicker of movement in his peripheral vision had him looking to the doorway. Sadie straightened her gray sweater, smoothing it down over jeans-clad hips in the barest flicker of nerves. Then she continued into the room and joined him at his table. Her smile was artificial, but it highlighted the bow curve of her upper lip—the same lip that had felt so soft and hungry beneath his own the night before.

"Are you hungry?" Sadie asked quietly, tentatively

testing the waters. "Gladys's husband makes some incredible cinnamon rolls."

"I'm definitely not a man to turn down good food. My mama will testify to that," he said.

She waved him back as he started to rise, so he watched as she filled two plates with rolls and some fruit. Then she lifted a large metal lid and the smell of meat filled the air. She added a couple of slices of bacon to his plate. She'd remembered. He was an avid bacon lover.

Had she learned that so well in the week they'd danced around each other before giving in to their passion?

She laid the plate before him in silence, then fixed her own cup of coffee, doctored with sugar and a liberal dose of cream. This was a natural rhythm that he'd noticed from her before. Just like at the mill, where efficiency in a large-scale task seemed routine for her, so he'd also found her to take charge of these little, everyday domestic tasks, too. Not in an overbearing way, but with a calm efficiency that matched her approach to life in general—at least, as far as Zach could tell.

And probably a way to make herself more comfortable around here.

After she was seated, she drew a long sip from the blue-glazed pottery mug. He munched on bacon, but theirs wasn't a comfortable silence. He sensed Sadie wanted to say something, and wondered idly if he was facing the Dear John conversation he hadn't been subjected to the last time. Odd how the thought bothered him.

He would have preferred not to care one way or another.

"I didn't plan on that, you know," she said, her usual quiet, even tone belying the anxiety with which she stared at her food.

"I know." He noticed the slight puffiness along her upper cheekbone and the fresh bandage on her cheek.

She took another sip, her gaze still trained on her plate.

The least he could give her was honesty. "Neither did I. That wasn't why I brought you home."

Suddenly her gaze snapped up, and he found himself entranced by her brilliant green eyes. How could such a clear color hide so many secrets from him?

They both started as something heavy landed on the table. Zach had been so lost in their stilted conversation that he hadn't noticed the approach of Gladys. He glanced up, sure his expression portrayed just how much he appreciated her intrusion.

"Why, Sadie, you didn't mention you would have a visitor for...breakfast."

The overly long pause told Zach that Gladys was fishing. She must not have noticed him making his way downstairs earlier—surprising for a woman who seemed to know everything.

"Sorry, Gladys," Sadie said.

"Well, how lucky for me that it's Zachary Gatlin."

Zachary couldn't imagine a time when Gladys had ever been that happy to see him, except when she hoped to get a juicy bit of gossip. He looked up with an arched brow. This might be more interesting than he'd thought. "And why would that be?" Zach didn't believe in beating around the bush.

"Why, I get to be the first to congratulate you."

"On what, exactly?" There hadn't been a lot happening worthy of celebration lately.

"On being officially cleared for the cotton poisoning, of course."

She tapped the newspaper she'd dropped on the table with a well-manicured finger. The top headline read,

Founding Family Son Charged in Mill Bombing. Zach was still trying to put the pieces together when Sadie picked up the top section of the paper. Zach didn't need to read it. He already knew who was to blame. Which was a perk of being part of the inner Blackstone circle.

Sadie seemed to be devouring the text. Zach watched her for a moment, then glanced up at Gladys as she continued to stand next to the table.

"Isn't it great, Zach?" she asked with a gleam in her eye that said she couldn't wait to be on the phone the minute she had something to pass along. If he didn't give her something, she'd just make up something interesting. Of course, the fact that Zach was here, and had probably come down from Sadie's room, would be the first thing she'd offer.

"Yes, Gladys. It's very nice."

Even though I shouldn't need the validation of being proven innocent. His sister, his mother, Jacob and his new employers all believed in him, even when the evidence had been totally damning. Those were the people that mattered.

So he kept it simple.

As Gladys headed back to the kitchen with a disappointed look on her face, Zach turned to find Sadie's eyes on his. "Why blow her off like that?"

"Because she's looking for a scoop, something to share with the grapevine."

Sadie nodded. Her guarded expression held a hint of sadness, as if she understood his need to protect himself. But what he really wanted to know was what she hid behind the mask…and whether he would regret last night if he found out her true secrets.

Eight

"I'll finish getting ready."

At least, that's what Sadie told Zach to get a few minutes alone in her room. She needed to make a phone call before Zach took her anywhere this morning. Since her car was still at the mill, she didn't have any choice but to get a few things in order and hitch a ride into town.

Luckily, Zach hadn't pushed anything after their conversation at breakfast. She'd had the distinct impression he'd just as soon step out in the parking lot and get out of ready reach of Gladys. Not that she could blame him.

She was well acquainted with people who blamed first and asked questions later.

Sadie also loved the people who pretended she didn't exist, because it was easier than having to be polite.

Not that she was in a position to judge. As she picked up her phone, she was all too aware of that fact.

"I need a new camera," she said without preamble when Victor picked up.

He wasn't thrilled—not that she'd thought he would be. "What the heck does that have to do with me?" he asked.

Sadie explained how the camera had been shattered when she'd dropped it, then the falling debris had finished the job.

"My question stands."

"A photographer has a camera. A nice camera."

"Then I guess you should have held on to yours."

Why did she bother explaining anything to this guy? "According to our contract, you are responsible for all business expenses, including a camera. I could have considered it a regular expense, but it's not, so I'm actually giving you the courtesy of informing you that you need to pay for it." Sadie had covered every loophole she could think of in the deal with Victor. It was all completely spelled out in black and white. And he'd needed her, so he'd signed.

"So sue me."

"If you don't pay, I'll just have to wait for the insurance claim. They'll take care of it…eventually. But it will mean a delay—"

"Fine. What am I getting for my generosity?"

Nothing he was going to like…but Sadie kept that thought to herself. Better not to antagonize him any more than normal.

"Unfortunately, nothing at the moment. My biggest lead was blown away this morning." She explained how the newspaper article had laid out bombing suspect Mark Zabinski's connection to the local airfield and how his presence there would not have been questioned. This gave the police reason to look into his possible sabotage of the containers on Zach's plane. That meant Zach was innocent, and the crop poisoning couldn't be used to disinherit him. She'd have to find something else. Victor's curses rang in her ear even before she'd finished.

His voice rose in volume and ugliness with every word. "Then find something else. We're running out of time."

The sound of him slamming the phone down made her wince, but to her relief he disconnected the call. Letting her eyelids drift closed, she took a few moments to breathe. Her body and her emotions had been through a lot in the past few days. She was exhausted. Her head hurt. And she had to face the fact that she'd had sex with Zach, knowing good and well she would betray him before her time here was over.

Having to deal with Victor on top of all that was more than she could handle, as evidenced by the tremble in her fingers as she opened her laptop and accessed the internet. By the time she went downstairs to meet Zach outside, she knew exactly where she needed to go next.

"Would you mind if we went out to Callahan's before heading all the way out to the mill?"

Zach threw a glance her way but quickly returned his eyes to the road. "Sure. What do you need there?"

"Mr. Callahan can order a replacement for my camera. I'd prefer to get it done as soon as possible." Who knew what she might get involved in once she got to the mill? Plus, it was a long way from town. By the time she got there and got her car, it could be late afternoon.

If there was one thing Sadie wanted almost as much as Zach, it was her camera. Her fingers ached to curl around it once more. Only another shutterbug would understand the feeling, but it was there nonetheless.

"I was surprised when you dropped it," Zach said, his tone more than conversational somehow. "I knew before that your camera was your baby. This one was really nice."

She wasn't going to pretend she hadn't felt a twinge as it left her hands, because Zach already knew the truth in that. Still, she shrugged. "In the end, it's just a thing." And she knew all too well how little things meant in the long run. "Compared to a person...at least the camera can be replaced."

"Won't that be expensive?"

Goodness, yes. "That's what credit cards are for, I guess. The insurance will eventually pay me back."

Until then, Victor better have it covered.

"Why are we even having this conversation?" she asked, not backing down when Zach shot a glance her way. "Do you really view me as that heartless of a human being that I wouldn't value Mr. Bateman's safety over my camera?"

"No, but—"

"Wouldn't you drop whatever you were holding to push your sister out of the way?"

"Yes, but Bateman is a stranger."

"Who still has a family he cares about and who would miss him if something bad happened to him. You may not approve of all of my actions, Zach, but I still think I'm basically a decent human being."

"One who's grown a pretty decent backbone."

"I told you I was sorry. But I'm not gonna dissolve into sackcloth and ashes or let you whip me with the past. That isn't good for either of us."

She sucked in a breath, suddenly realizing the extent of her tirade. But she couldn't finish without saying, "It won't change it, either, much as I wish it could." Because in the end, honesty was important to her, so she would honor that where and when she could without harming her own family...

Zach didn't respond this time. Sadie's nerves tightened with every turn of the steering wheel, but she wasn't backing down on this.

It wasn't until they reached the little camera shop on one side of the town square that he finally spoke.

"You're right, Sadie. My apologies."

She'd have been happier if his tone hadn't been so formal, but in the end, it was for the best, wasn't it?

The store had a checkered awning that matched numerous others around the old-fashioned square, easily visible now that the leaves were mostly missing from the Bradford pear trees lining the streets. Sadie wondered what cute little Christmas traditions the town observed and whether those bare branches would be wrapped in holiday lights. She wished she could be here to see it, to walk along the sidewalks with Zach and soak in the atmosphere.

But her life was elsewhere. So were the people who were counting on her. She tried not to think about how quickly she might have to leave as she stepped through the door into a camera lover's paradise.

"Hello, my dear Sadie," Mr. Callahan said. "What an unexpected pleasure."

"For me, as well," she said with a smile, allowing the dapper Southern gentleman to press a gentle kiss to her cheek.

She caught a glimpse of Zach's surprised look as she pulled back. Why was he shocked? She'd made more friends than just him when she'd been here before.

"That is quite a large bandage you have there," Mr. Callahan remarked. "Did you, by chance, receive that yesterday?"

"Why, yes," Sadie said. "A cut, but it will heal. What I'm really worried about is my camera."

He nodded sagely, reminding her of a benevolent, skinny Santa. "Yes, I heard about that, too."

Well, this was a small town… "I see." After all, what should she say?

Zach wasn't having any difficulty coming up with words. "She was very brave, pushing Bateman out of the way of that falling debris."

For a moment, Sadie wondered why he was so open with Mr. Callahan when he'd practically refused to talk to Gladys at the B and B. But she knew it probably had to do with Mr. Callahan's integrity. He didn't need gossip as a source of entertainment.

"I'm glad you came to see me," he said. "Though there is no hope of repair?"

"Since the camera is sitting under a pile of loose plaster and two-by-fours, I doubt it," Zach answered.

Sadie winced as she remembered her last glimpse of the camera. "I was able to get almost all of my pictures off, since I download them to my laptop every night. But I'll bring in the digital card and see if you can get the ones from that day for me."

The gleam in the older man's eyes said he looked forward to the challenge. "It will be my pleasure."

"Until then, I need to order a new one."

Mr. Callahan moved over to a computer on the counter. "What kind?"

When she told him, he whistled. "You've stepped up in the world," he said.

"And now I'm in deep mourning." It was either brush it off or cry.

"Let's see if we can resurrect it," he said with a wink.

"The Blackstones would appreciate it," Zach said,

surprising Sadie. "She's using the camera to create a visual history of the mill's resurrection."

That had the older man's eyes widening. "Are you now? I can't wait to get a sneak peek at the digital card."

"I can bring my laptop down here later this week so you can see what I have so far. The building and people down there make fascinating subjects." Especially certain people. She'd have to make sure those photos were in a completely different folder.

"I imagine so," Mr. Callahan said, even as his fingers continued clicking on the keyboard. "I've always been interested in the juxtaposition of all that steel and metal with endless fields of cotton. From what I saw yesterday when I drove out there, the damage is quite picturesque."

He paused, staring into space for a moment. "Kind of interesting that James Blackstone's empire suffers ruin just over a year after his death."

"Was he the original owner?" Sadie asked.

"The original dictator," Zach scoffed.

Mr. Callahan agreed with a knowing look. "The original business was built several generations ago, and added to through the years, but it was James Blackstone who catapulted it into luxury quality linens."

"So he was a good businessman?" Sadie asked.

Zach was quick to answer. "Yes. And a miserable human being."

She studied his suddenly shuttered face. "That sounds like it comes from personal experience."

He simply shrugged and walked away, leaving her to wonder as he strolled around the length of the old-fashioned, quirky shop.

She glanced over at Mr. Callahan. He gave her a half smile. "I'm not big on telling other people's stories," he said, "but James was most definitely difficult. He ruled

Black Hills with an iron fist and had definite views on how things should be done." He, too, glanced over at Zach. "And he wasn't above using devious tactics to get what he wanted, either."

He finished putting Sadie's package together on the computer, checked it twice, then rang up a payment on her card that made her slightly nauseous. If Victor didn't come through with that money in her bank account by tomorrow, she was going to ruin him for sure.

He was used to throwing around that type of money, but Sadie definitely was not.

They headed back out to the car, Mr. Callahan's promise that the camera would be delivered in forty-eight hours drifting behind them.

Hopefully it wouldn't be a moment longer.

There weren't too many things that made Sadie impatient, but waiting on a camera was like a kid anticipating the bike they just knew they would find under the tree Christmas morning.

The silence in the car on the way to the mill wasn't helping her nerves. "So the Blackstone men I've met," she asked, "they're James Blackstone's grandsons?"

Zach nodded.

"You seem to know them well."

"Not really…at least, not until recently. Different circles and all that." The words were accompanied by a smirk, but at least he'd started talking.

"KC actually got involved with Jacob Blackstone first, months before I knew the family. Before that, I just knew *of* them. None of the grandsons lived here then. She met Jacob when he came home on a visit to his mother, and then she ended up pregnant with Carter."

The scowl darkening his features turned fierce. "That was my first up close and personal encounter with the patriarch of the family. He threatened my sister, scared her so badly she left town. I'll never forgive him for that."

Sadie recognized something in Zach's expression all too well. "Or yourself?"

He shot a quick glance her way before resolutely returning his eyes to the road. "She knew I wouldn't have held back. I've spent my life protecting my family. And I would have jeopardized my livelihood and my mother's bar to teach that son of a bitch a lesson." His knuckles whitened from his tight grip. "So she made a decision and left alone. She didn't come back until James was dead."

Zach took a deep breath, almost as if cleansing himself of the memories. "Jacob and KC were lucky. Their story ended in a happily-ever-after—but it never would have if James had had any say about it."

Zach's stiff shoulders and furrowed brow suggested that he was still angry. But it was obvious from seeing Jacob and KC together that they were very much in love. From the sounds of it, they'd overcome a lot to get there.

Sadie knew how Zach felt, though. It was his job to protect his little sister. He hadn't said it outright, but he must feel as though he'd let her down.

The question was, would he understand someone else needing to do the same for their family?

Almost a week later, Sadie stepped into Bella Italia with more trepidation than she'd ever experienced over a formal event. Mostly because she was usually at these things as the help, serving, blending in with the decor rather than standing out like a peacock in a brand-new dress.

She'd known exactly what she wanted to wear when KC had invited her to the Blackstones' party celebrating a new chapter for the mill. The bright blue dress had called to her from the moment she'd walked past the window on the square on the way to Callahan's. Sadie was used to admiring clothes she wasn't able to buy.

Not this time.

For once, she didn't blink at the price. She didn't even use the company card Victor had given her for regular expenses. Somehow that would taint the gift of being invited in the first place. This time she wanted to experience something on her own terms—even if it ended up being a fairy tale.

The sleeveless dress had a fitted bodice that hugged her generous curves and provided ample support. Her second favorite element, besides the color, was a mesh triangle cutout between her breasts, giving a shadowy glimpse of cleavage beneath. The flowy skirt was dressed in sparkles along the calf-length hemline, adding to her festive mood.

She'd indulged in a pair of sexy silver heels without once wondering how many other outfits they would match. Practicality had no place tonight. She wore a single piece of jewelry. The necklace had been a gift from her mother on her twenty-first birthday, the length perfect to nestle a teardrop opal encircled in silver wire in the indention at the base of her throat. A silver shawl completed her dream outfit.

She wasn't sure what had gotten into her, but tonight she would simply go with the flow. Especially since it meant more time with Zachary. A quick look over her shoulder let her watch her prince as he stepped in the door to the restaurant behind her. She'd seen him plenty at the mill in the past few days, but never alone. And there had been no repeat of the night at the B and B.

She wished he had come to get her because he wanted

to, not because Christina had asked him to, but the flutters in her stomach were the same, regardless. And the way his dark eyes widened when he saw her in this dress for the first time was very much appreciated.

Zach was a sight to behold himself. The fitted black suit and burgundy tie complemented his dark good looks, making her fingers itch for her camera to record tonight for posterity. She had a small one in her clutch— she was never without one—but wouldn't intrude on a personal gathering by breaking it out.

As Zach took her arm to lead her in, the look on his face was proud—at least, she liked to think so. Even though it didn't dim the wariness that would forever linger in his eyes when he looked at her, still, it made her happy.

This, at least, she could have.

"Well, somebody cleans up good," KC said, giving her brother the once-over before a quick hug.

Zach's gaze flicked to Sadie when she murmured, "I agree."

He wiggled his tie a little to adjust it. "You know I hate these things."

KC shook her head as if she were disappointed in his response. "What's not to enjoy? Great food, friends— even Mom's here." She looked between them, giving Sadie the distinct impression that she was sizing them up together. "Go introduce Sadie, why don't you?"

That definitely started the butterflies in Sadie's stomach. When she'd been here five years ago, she hadn't met any of Zachary's family, though she'd heard a lot about them.

Luckily she had time to compose herself before doing the family thing. She and Zach couldn't get more than a few feet across the floor without someone stopping them to chat. The Blackstones had spared no expense in renting out the entire restaurant for this impressive soiree, and they'd invited all of the upper management from the mill and their families, as well as Zach and KC's family, the mayor and some city officials.

To her surprise, she was almost as much in demand as Zach. The people at the mill and in town had been beyond friendly, and it was no different with tonight's crowd. Sadie felt more at home here than she ever had in Dallas, where she'd lived her entire life. Mostly because the people of Black Hills actually saw her. The real her...or as close to the real her as she could risk showing them.

Suddenly a man with an authoritative bearing appeared at Zach's side, reaching to shake his hand. "I told you this would eventually be cleared up," he said.

"You didn't say it would take this long," Zach answered with a knowing look.

"This is true," the man said with a laugh.

"Sadie," Zach said, pulling her into reach of the conversation, "this is Officer Stephens, my arresting officer."

"What?"

To her consternation, both men chuckled. "Sorry, ma'am," Officer Stephens said. "A little joke. I didn't actually arrest him... I just brought him in for questioning." His wink set her at ease.

"And question me he did," Zach said.

"Just doing my job. But you did good, buddy. Real good."

Zach shook his head. "In the end, it wasn't even me who caught him. It was Luke."

"But you kept pushing," he said, patting Zach's back in that casual way comrades have. "The truth always comes out, my friend."

Sadie forced herself not to shift in her three-inch heels as she heard the words.

"How is Luke?" the officer asked.

"Good." Zach nodded. "He's home, but he opted to stay with Ms. Blackstone tonight. He's had enough of the spotlight for a while."

The officer laughed, shaking his head. "I bet he has."

The men chatted for a minute more before Officer Stephens moved along. Then Sadie turned to Zach. "Luke is the brother who was there when the mill exploded, right?" She'd heard the name all over town, but never met the man himself.

"Yes, Jacob's twin."

As they approached the table where Jacob was solicitously getting KC settled, Sadie studied him. "After seeing the damage, I can't imagine how scary that must have been."

Zach nodded. "They were able to dig him out, along with Mark Zabinski, who set the bomb. They were both injured, though Mark ended up in worse shape than Luke. A wall came down, pinning his legs to the floor."

Sadie winced. "Ouch."

"Ouch, indeed," Zach said as they reached the table.

Not long after everyone was seated and introduced, Aiden and Christina Blackstone also made their way to the table.

"How's Mom?" Sadie heard Jacob ask after giving Christina a quick hug.

"About the same," she replied.

For a moment, Sadie was struck by the silent communication between the Blackstones. Each gaze was tinged with sadness, with a knowledge no one wanted to admit about their beloved mother. But the words weren't spoken aloud. Her own shared glances with her mother were the same. Sadie's heart ached for what the Blackstones were going through; she was going through it with her sister's illness.

From her understanding, Lily Blackstone had been comatose for many years, but in good health...until recently. A series of infections had raised concern for the matriarch. And for Christina, Sadie realized as Aiden pulled his wife close for a moment, resting his palm against her pregnant belly. Sadie was sure the added worry of being Lily's primary nurse did not help in any way.

"What? No camera?" KC asked, distracting Sadie from her sad thoughts.

Sadie lifted her clutch. "In here. I'm rarely without one. Mr. Callahan let me borrow one of his smaller digital cameras, but I didn't want to intrude on a personal gathering. Sometimes people have a hard time enjoying themselves when a camera is in the room."

"What a lovely consideration," Zach's mom said.

"Yes," KC added, "we appreciate the thought, but please feel free. We don't want people to see Black Hills as simply a pile of burning metal and soot." She waved her hand around the room. "Life is a mixture of good and bad, not just the bad. Parties have their place, too."

Sadie signaled her agreement with a smile, but she couldn't help but wonder why everything good in her own life had always led to heartache.

The rich, decadent Italian food only served to make the atmosphere even merrier. Laughter and the scent of tomato sauce mingled in the air. After eating, Sadie excused herself to take a few photographs but seemed to keep Zach in her peripheral vision no matter where she ended up.

He stayed close to his mother, making sure she had

everything she needed, though she was far from frail. The family talked easily and continuously, leaving the impression of a perfectly formed group of people that life had brought together. Sadie knew, probably more than most, that it wasn't perfect, though. Zach's father had been a selfish man, leaving Zach's mother with a legacy of heartache and a child to raise alone. The fact that KC's father did the same years later made it that much sadder. And she knew about the Blackstone brothers' sadness over their mother and the danger they had personally faced during the mill's destruction.

But it looked postcard perfect. As did the darkly handsome man in their midst. The man who so easily cared for his family—and possessed the strength and the means to do it.

Unlike Sadie.

Suddenly feeling as if someone had dropped a bag of bricks on her chest, Sadie hurried outside. For long moments she couldn't breathe, couldn't think beyond the need for the cool, fresh air. Ever so slowly, her lungs loosened, letting the air inside, until she no longer felt that her body had seized up. Without thought she drew her phone from her pocket. A quick swipe and she was calling her own mother, almost desperate for the reassurance that she still had some semblance of a family to go home to.

Only no one answered.

There could be a lot of reasons for that. Her mother was in the other room, or tending to Amber. Still, tears welled beneath Sadie's eyelids. She missed her mother so much. And her sister, who was often too weak to talk for more than a few minutes on the phone.

Careful steps took her to the window. She looked in at the party, which was still in full swing. Raising the camera, Sadie took a few shots of the people inside, framed by the decorative greenery on the window casing. She hoped to capture the essence of revelry, especially the family who had so generously offered this opportunity.

But she was on the outside looking in.

And just as Sadie started to feel sorry for herself, Zach turned to face her. His gaze unerringly found her, holding her immobilized with a simple look. A look that laid his soul open, telling her he could be trusted. That a man so beloved by those around him didn't have any dark secrets to hide.

No. The secrets were all hers.

Nine

The minute he'd seen her through the window, he'd known he had to go to her.

Zach wanted to hold her, touch her as he had too few times. But now that he was here, he found himself hesitating. Her beauty in the half darkness, illuminated by the twinkling lights surrounding the window, took his breath away.

She didn't look at him, remaining in profile. "Your family is beautiful," she said.

So are you.

But the yearning in her voice kept him quiet. Somehow he knew, though he could easily seduce her, that this wasn't the time.

"You've built a good life here," she went on. "Are you happy?"

"For the most part," he conceded. Though even surrounded by family and friends he was often lonely, aching. His nature made him a protector, yet he yearned for someone to share the burden with him. "Are you?" he asked, curious.

Sadie had talked very little about her life away from him. Oh, they'd discussed books, music, photography and many other things. But looking back, he realized how little of herself she'd actually given him. As if she were afraid to do so.

"Not often."

In the dim glow he could see her eyes widen; she was surprised by her own response. Why? It was certainly honest. Was she surprised because she'd told him the truth?

And that would be the crux of his wariness when it came to Sadie's return. The more he was with her, the more he was convinced she was holding back, keeping things from him. That wasn't what he wanted. That was why he hadn't gone back to the bed-and-breakfast with her again, even though he wanted more than just one night with her.

So he asked, "What about your family?"

Her hesitation sparked impatience deep inside. "You do have a family, don't you, Sadie?" He took a step closer. "Or are you alone in the world?"

The thought brought sadness for her, tempered by the knowledge that he could have kept her from being alone…if she had let him.

"Tell me, Sadie." *Something. Anything.*

Then she turned to face him, and his impatience melted away. Tears stood in her eyes like small puddles left from a wintry rain. "I miss my mom," she whispered.

Those gorgeous green eyes slid closed, cutting him off from the aching vulnerability. When they opened again, her gaze was still glassy, but more controlled.

"Where is she?" he asked.

"Dallas." A small smile graced her lips. "I'm not a complete vagabond."

She went quiet once more, a long silence that made him wonder if she would speak again. Just when he gave up hope, she said, "Your mom reminds me of her—hard-working, concerned over her children, never giving up hope." Her deep breath cracked his heart. "I wish I could take care of my mom the way you take care of yours."

"I'm sure she knows that, Sadie." He glanced through the window, seeing people in various groups having a good time. Then he looked at Sadie once more, here on the outside. She wasn't a loner, by any means. He'd seen the way she got along with people, could draw out their stories and make them feel comfortable with her. But yes, she did still keep a part of herself distant.

Just as she did with him.

"If she needs you, why are you here?"

For a moment, he thought she wouldn't answer. Finally she shook her head. "It's the only way I know to help her now."

She didn't elaborate on the cryptic words, so Zach asked, "Your father?"

Sadie shook her head once more. "I don't remember him. He left when I was little. We're a lot alike in that, you and I."

Zach stiffened, bracing himself with one hand against the wall. "How did you know that?" He never talked about his father, preferring not to give attention to someone so utterly lacking in human decency. "You've been snooping around again?"

Her eyes widened, appearing almost scared in the twinkling light. "I wasn't snooping about that. I promise." Her brows drew together. "I can't help it if people like to talk."

"About me?"

"Well, I like talking about you, so why not?" Her lashes lowered over her expressive eyes, as if she knew she'd revealed too much. Suddenly she shivered, drawing the sparkly shawl closer around her shoulders. "Goodness, I didn't realize how cold it had gotten. We should go back inside."

Not yet. As she tried to pass him, Zach reached out. His arms encircled her, his body warming hers in the only way he could in public. Then he leaned down and kissed away the chill.

When he finally pulled back, he felt rather than saw her grin. "Zachary Gatlin, are you coming on to me?" she asked.

That's what they needed—a little light, a return to the celebration inside. "I don't know—are you willing to risk another interrogation by Miss Gladys?"

He felt her breath catch beneath his palms on her back. "Oh," she whispered. "I think it might be worth it."

As they walked back inside, Zach let his arm remain around her shoulders. Anticipation built, bubbling beneath his skin, only to fizzle out as they rejoined their table. The Blackstone brothers were quietly gathering coats, readying everyone to leave.

"Luke called," Aiden said, turning dark eyes Zach's way. "Mother's temperature has spiked again, but something else is going on. He's concerned. We need to skip out, but I don't want to ruin everyone's evening. Can you take over from here?"

Luckily the mingling of the crowd and the dancing in the back room distracted most everyone from the family's departure. As Zach started making final arrangements, he noticed Sadie falling into organization mode—directing the restaurant staff, taking care of last-minute requests from guests, coordinating cab rides for those who needed them.

Then Zach was left with a final conundrum: the Blackstones' butler and chauffeur, Nolen, had taken them all to Blackstone Manor, where KC and Jacob had a suite with all the baby stuff they needed. That left Zach's mother without a ride home—and her house was in the opposite direction of Sadie's B and B…by quite a distance. While he pondered, Sadie appeared at the table. "It was a pleasure to meet you, Ms. Gatlin," she said, her voice smooth and in control.

Which simply reminded him of just what drove her out of control…

"And you as well, young lady," his mother said. "You handled this party like someone in the know."

"Cleanup is an art form," Sadie said with a slight smile and dismissive wave of her hand. "Just not one normally appreciated by others."

Her words left him to wonder just who she was always cleaning up after.

"Let me just get Mother home, then I'll come by—"

"Nonsense," Sadie said, her eyes overly bright. "The last thing I want to be is trouble. I booked a cab for myself." She patted his arm. He tried not to notice how her touch lingered for a few seconds longer than normal, because it reminded him of an opportunity missed.

"Y'all have a nice night," she said.

Uncomfortable would be more like it.

Sadie told herself she'd come to Lola's because four days was way too long to go without seeing the object of her investigation. Also, a woman had to eat, right?

The impulse had nothing to do with her body's

mourning over the lost opportunity or lack of a Zach fix. Not at all. Even though she knew it would have been wrong to accept, she couldn't help but think of his invitation the night of the party with longing. She wished she hadn't given him—and her—the least complicated way out, when her heart had wanted nothing more than to take him home.

The last week had been a busy one for him. The Blackstone brothers had been less hands-on at the mill, splitting their time between there and home with their dying mother. At least that's what gossip around town said: Lily Blackstone's precarious health was finally failing.

The woman's tragic story—of being comatose for many years after a car accident followed by a stroke—left Sadie weepy. She tried not to think about it. Her own sister's terminal illness made the story hit too close to home.

The situation had left Zach with a lot of administrative work on his hands, along with directing his own business. She'd watched at a distance, waiting for the moment when he'd invite her back into the inner circle... but he never did. She told herself he was tired, overworked, but a panic had started deep inside. Yes, she needed to get close to him. She seemed to have found all the superficial evidence about Zach's character she was going to get from the town. Family history, rumors and accusations—none of it would disqualify him from his inheritance. She needed to dig into the parts of his life that no one else could see. In order to find something truly damning, she'd have to find it out from Zach himself.

But the truth was, as wrong as she knew it to be, she wanted that time with him. His attention. His intensity focused on her…for just the few minutes she had left with him.

She'd guessed that he'd be here tonight. He couldn't be spending a lot of time with his family during the day, and family meant a lot to him. That much she'd learned about Zachary Gatlin. So even though he didn't have to work at Lola's, she figured he would be here in some capacity to check on his mother and sister.

The restaurant was full, but not as packed as the last time she'd been here. The scents of grilled meat and some kind of spicy barbecue sauce had her mouth watering in anticipation. She waved to a few friends she'd made as she crossed the floor to nab a small two-top along the wall near the bar, hoping the position would help her see and be seen by one very specific person.

Her disappointment mounted as a waitress took her order and served her food. She'd shared a smile with Ms. Gatlin, Zach's mother, as she busied herself behind the bar. But as dinner wore on, there was no sign of Zach, or even his sister, KC.

As Sadie finished up, the arrival of three women distracted her. They claimed the table directly in Sadie's line of sight near the dance floor. As she looked closer, she noticed that only two of the girls were young, probably early twenties. The other was significantly older. They settled in the chairs and ordered from the waitress.

As soon as she headed back to the kitchen, the older woman smiled at the other two. "You girls head onto the dance floor. It will be a while before the food is here."

They each kissed one of the woman's cheeks, then walked toward the dance floor with eager steps. She smiled after them but didn't look sad to be left behind in the least.

Without warning, her gaze swept over the room before coming to rest on Sadie. They shared a smile.

"Hello, my dear," she said, their tables close enough together that she didn't have to yell, though her voice had certainly not been weakened by age. "Are you dining alone tonight?"

Sadie nodded. "Yes. Just finishing up, actually." She wiped her lips with her napkin, hoping she'd removed any stray barbecue sauce. "Lola's has some of the best food I've found in town."

The woman patted the empty chair next to her. "Indeed they do, which is the excuse I give my granddaughters for bringing me here," she said with a knowing smile. "Join me for a moment. Are you visiting Black Hills?"

"Yes," she confirmed, sliding into the chair. "Thank you, Ms...."

"Saben, dear."

"Ms. Saben. I'm a photographer, working on documenting the rebuilding of the mill."

"Ah, yes. I heard about that. Very exciting."

It certainly had been, but probably not in the way Ms. Saben meant.

"The town—and the Blackstones in particular— have had a very exciting year," she went on. "What with young Aiden coming home and marrying Miss Lily's nurse. Christina is such a lovely young lady."

Ms. Saben smiled at the waitress as she served the drinks. Sadie asked for a refill on her tea and got one. "You doing okay, Miss Saben?" the waitress asked.

"Sure am. Glad to be back in for a bit."

As the waitress went on about her way, Ms. Saben explained, "I've been coming up here for a long time. Ms. Gatlin and I are old friends. But we each have very busy lives." She took a sip of what Sadie had overheard to be a rum and Coke. Ms. Saben tipped the drink in salute. "My granddaughters say it's bad for me to drink, so I've gotta sneak in a little tipple when I can. Otherwise I'd be left watching them down margaritas while I'm drinking water."

Her sass had Sadie laughing out loud.

"Especially now," Ms. Saben went on with a small smile. "I'm just fully recovered from pneumonia. Off all my medicines and pronounced one hundred percent by my doctor. If I had to stay in that house one more second, I'd have gone stir-crazy. So I offered to come out here with the girls.

"They get a fun night out from watching me," she went on. "And I'm not afraid to get out on the dance floor myself in a bit."

"I'll bet you know a thing or two about dancing," Sadie said, inspired by the older woman's daring.

"Honey, you've gotta dance while you still can. Besides, I'd rather break a hip that way than push a walker at the old folks' home."

"Amen," Sadie said with a salute of her tea.

The same muscular server who had delivered Sadie's food earlier came bearing Ms. Saben's potato skin appetizer. Sadie suppressed a grin when the older woman said, "It's a vegetable, right?"

"You got that right, Ms. Saben," the man said before ambling back to the kitchen area.

"I'm so glad Zach was able to hire some decent men to work around here, now that he and KC have so much going on in their lives," Ms. Saben said. "But life does go on, especially new babies." She eyed Sadie. "You have any babies at home?"

"Not yet," Sadie said. Babies were far in her future,

if ever. Right now, she had her mom and sister to take care of.

"Well, that little Carter is a joy, and KC deserves her happiness."

"I heard James Blackstone tried to keep KC and Jacob apart…" Sadie prompted, sensing the woman enjoyed telling her stories.

"Indeed he did. And KC had every intention of telling Jacob about the baby, but she was fearful—for herself and her family. James threatened their livelihood, you know."

"No, I didn't."

"Oh, yes. He owned the land Lola's is built on. Luckily, Jacob and Aiden have deeded it over to KC's mother. You know, so she could feel secure."

Sadie murmured her approval.

"Jacob Blackstone is a good guy. Not like his grandfather. None of the boys are, but there's a lot of men who are none too happy about having the responsibility of a child sprung on them. A lot who would walk away. Ignore it. Not Jacob. And soon there will be a wedding to celebrate, once the, well, sadness is done."

For Lily. They would definitely need some celebration after losing a woman so important to all of them.

As if she were a hunting dog, Sadie suddenly caught the deep timbre of a man's voice and knew immediately that Zach had arrived. Her eyes searched restlessly until she spotted him coming out from the kitchen area, where she knew there was a back entrance.

Apparently Ms. Saben didn't miss her interest. "So that's the way it lies, huh?"

Sadie swung guilty eyes in the older woman's direction. "What?"

"Oh, honey, don't be embarrassed."

Too late. The dreaded heat had bathed Sadie's cheeks already.

"There's not a woman your age who hasn't pined over that one…and a few not your age, too." Ms. Saben giggled like a schoolgirl. "Talk about another good man. One who's had a hard life, but powered through. Nothing like his daddy, either."

And just like that, the seed was planted. There was a theme in both their families' lives—unwanted children. Did Zach have any kids out there he'd neglected? The heart that had yearned for him for five years said he was too responsible for that, too protective. But people were crazy sometimes. Did he have an ex hovering on the fringes, waiting to pounce or holding a child as leverage?

One glance at Ms. Saben told Sadie she had an inkling of the direction of her thoughts, so she might as well be honest. "Does he date a lot?"

Admiration shone in the older woman's gaze. "Honest answer? No. I haven't seen or heard of him dating more than three or four women—why, since he got home from the air force, I guess." She studied Zach as he greeted his mother behind the bar.

So did Sadie. The strong, protective stance drew her, as did the hug he gave his much smaller mother. Her heart instantly melted.

"Maybe that's why…" Ms. Saben mused.

Sadie turned her way. "What?"

Ms. Saben's gaze met hers. "He loves his mama."

Sadie nodded. "And his sister."

Approval lightened the older woman's gaze. "Men who know how to take care of women don't normally play around, because they know how it affects the woman being played with."

Like a ton of bricks, the knowledge hit Sadie. Zach

hadn't been playing with her—he wasn't that type of man and didn't have that kind of reputation. And she'd ruined it by walking away…even if she'd done it to protect him.

She couldn't face him with that knowledge so fresh in her heart. Not tonight. Maybe not ever.

Ten

Sadie had been to several impressive mansions throughout her lifetime. Her boss's home was essentially a villa at the end of a lane full of overblown palatial residences that offered every amenity imaginable, including an entire apartment for her in the refurbished barn whose rent came out of Sadie's salary.

But Blackstone Manor gave the impression of a family home despite its grandeur, starting with the red-rimmed eyes of a very fragile-looking butler. "Good afternoon, madam," he said solemnly, prompting an urge to hug him close and comfort him with hot tea.

Neither of which Sadie did, because this wasn't her home or her rodeo. But her natural sympathy, coupled with the fact that she genuinely liked the Blackstones, made it hard to remain objective.

Lily Blackstone had lingered into January. The family had been able to celebrate Christmas at home, and the announcement of another brother's engagement, without the black cloud of death intruding. That had come with the frigid winds and gray skies of deep winter.

Sadie had been around Black Hills long enough now to give her a tempting feeling of belonging. Some days she wished she could live forever in this sleepy friendly town, with its good, its bad and its quirks.

And except for a brief flight home one weekend to visit her mom, she had.

She and Zach continued to participate in a dance of sorts, a waltz that separated them and brought them close again, but not nearly close enough. Sadie began to recognize that she was procrastinating. She didn't want to have to make a decision, didn't want to figure out what she'd do back home if she didn't get the money to bail her sister out.

At least she was being paid for her current job, even if it meant phone calls from a yelling, screaming Victor almost every night.

Today, she wouldn't think about that. She wouldn't give him the satisfaction of knowing how much he upset her, and she would hold on to the knowledge that his private investigator hadn't had any more luck digging up dirt on Zach than she had.

She greeted Mr. Callahan, Ms. Saben and the Batemans as she made her way across the front parlor. Finally she was beginning to feel welcome. How would she ever live without this when she returned to Texas?

Christina and KC remained at the back of the parlor near the fireplace while many townspeople mingled throughout the room.

"Hello, Sadie," KC said, pulling Sadie into a hug. "We were hoping to get to see you."

"I'm so sorry," Sadie said, feeling the inadequacy of having no true way to comfort them.

"Thank you," Christina replied, ever gracious. "I'm glad you could come by."

Sadie glanced around. "This place is incredible."

KC grinned. "I felt the same way when I first stepped inside. I bet your photographer's senses are at full attention."

"Definitely."

The sound of a large group of people in the foyer had them all turning their heads in that direction. Several couples who had all arrived at the same time made their way to the Blackstone brothers first.

"Looks like we're about to have our hands full," Christina said, patting Sadie's arm. "We'll see you more in a little while, but please feel free to explore."

"And Zach is around here somewhere, too," KC added, her smile looking a little sly to Sadie.

KC hadn't made any secret of her approval as the two women had gotten to know each other more, and had hinted a time or two that she didn't understand why Sadie and Zach didn't at least go on one date. Obviously Zach had not filled his sister in on their history. Sadie wasn't going to do it for him.

It was simply another dark mark on the friendships she was creating here. She told herself she need never see these people again after she betrayed one of their own, which only reinforced the notion that she didn't want to cut them out of her life.

Dangerous thinking.

Sadie wandered around the room, studying the architecture and antiques while she conversed with more of the townspeople. Several of the men she'd gotten to know at the mill introduced her to their families. The

Batemans led her across the breezeway into a glorious dining room that had a full spread of food laid out.

They met up with another couple and were distracted talking, so Sadie wandered to the front of the room to look out the window. A man in a dark suit stood to one side of the front windows. He reminded her of other men she'd just passed in the breezeway and front parlor. They were so still they almost faded into the woodwork.

Security.

Then Sadie saw another man approach. She took in the dark tanned skin and close-cropped hair for the first time since she'd returned. He wore a dark suit and tie, along with dark sunglasses to protect his eyes from the winter glare. He paused beside the first man, the angle of his pose allowing her to see the wire for a communication device running up to his ear.

The entire time Sadie had been back in Black Hills, the impact of Zach's new position hadn't really become a reality to her. He'd been directing cleanup and safety crews at the mill. There were other days when she didn't see him at all, and she knew he had taken over an old, established house not far from the town square as his new business headquarters, but she'd never really asked what actually running a security firm entailed.

It made sense that a family who had been targeted for over a year and a half would want this time of grief to be peaceful and safe. They knew the most prominent people in the county, not to mention in the region, and all of the brothers had contacts elsewhere. A lot of people were going to be in and out of this house over the next week.

As he glanced up at the window, it hit home that it was Zach's job to ensure all ran smoothly and safely. Ever the protector. Ever the hero—without all the glory.

Looking at him only brought home just how opposite

they were in this situation. He was here to protect those around him. She was here to betray the one they trusted.

Turning, Sadie took her shame with her as she walked away. Surveying the people mingling and eating in the room, she noticed a small woman at one end of the sideboard picking up a half-empty tray and moving toward a door at the end of the room. Sadie hurried her steps to reach the door just as the woman did.

With a smile Sadie held it open so the woman could slip through unhindered. Sadie herself had performed the maneuver many times, but a helping hand had always been appreciated...and rarely offered.

"Thank you so much, sweetheart," the woman said.

Sadie followed her into a large kitchen filled with the scents of baking. "No problem," she replied, feeling her body relax almost instantly into an environment that held some familiarity for her. Being behind the scenes was much more her forte. "Is there anything I can do to help?"

Stacks of prepared foods in boxes lined several feet of counters. Coolers ran the length of the wall beneath the windows. A glimpse into an open pantry showed shelves lined with dishes and glasses. "Are you doing all of this yourself?" Sadie asked.

"Bless your heart for asking," the woman said, wiping her now empty hands on her apron before extending one toward Sadie. "I'm Marie, the Blackstones' cook and housekeeper." She glanced around at the organized chaos. "And while they know I can work miracles, no, they didn't leave me to do this alone. But the girls who are helping me have taken a quick break."

She shrugged her tiny shoulders, making her Kiss the Cook apron dance. "I thought we would have a bit of a lull, but I was obviously wrong. Normally Nolen would help, but he's got his hands full, too. But those girls have been on their feet all day—they deserve to at least eat lunch sitting down."

"And you don't?" Sadie asked, but she knew exactly how this went. When an event was in full swing, you simply performed the most urgent task, then the next, and the next, until everyone was satisfied. But this event would go on for a few days, which could get grueling.

Reaching for an apron hanging nearby, Sadie draped it over her dark gray dress. "Just point me in the right direction."

They chatted seamlessly for a good twenty minutes as they prepared and replaced platters. Sadie brushed aside Marie's protests as she loaded the dishwasher. It needed doing, so she did it.

Until a six-foot-two hunk of dark charisma walked through the doorway. Sadie couldn't help it—her every motion stopped, including her breath. Not too long, but long enough for Marie to notice.

Long enough to earn her a knowing grin from the older woman.

"So you're still here," Zach said.

If she hadn't been glancing in his direction, Sadie wouldn't have known he was speaking to her. She straightened. "Where else would I be?"

"When you disappeared, I assumed you went home without at least saying hi."

Her heartbeat resumed, a little faster this time. For a moment, she'd thought he meant here as in Black Hills, not here as in Blackstone Manor. "No, I'm just trying to lend a hand."

His dark gaze slid over to Marie. "She's good at that, isn't she?"

"Most definitely."

He approached the older woman and folded her carefully into his arms, as if she were too fragile to be in charge of an army's worth of food. "I'm sorry, Marie."

Tears prickled behind Sadie's eyes as the older woman seemed to melt into him. She'd given Sadie, and probably everyone else, the impression that she was coping just fine, thank you very much. But one hug and the facade shattered. She didn't cry, but the pain showed on her aging face nonetheless.

"I'd been with her since she was a baby," Marie said.

"I know," Zach murmured, so tender Sadie had to look away.

"The car accident was hard," Marie went on. "But she was still here, still with us. Then the stroke…she's really been gone since then, but it wasn't real, you know."

The words struck Sadie's heart unexpectedly. There were times when her sister got so sick that she disappeared into unconsciousness for days. One time the doctors had to put her in a medically induced coma. But she always came back…there was always hope. Lily Blackstone had had none.

A rustle of fabric drew Sadie's gaze once more. Marie had straightened and was smoothing down her apron. "I wish she could have been here to see all the boys come home." She smiled at Zach, though it was a little shaky around the edges. "Your sister. Carter. This new young'un on the way. She would have loved all of it."

Life. It had been all around Lily, but she'd been unaware. Amber was the same, in certain ways. Her life was a series of doctor visits, debilitating treatments, recuperating and quiet nights at home with her mom and sister.

How much longer before she had no life at all? The

weight of the thought sat on Sadie's chest, constricting her breath.

"Yes, she would have," Zach said. "She created a beautiful family."

"A legacy," Marie agreed.

And Amber would have none.

Suddenly the walls wavered. Sadie knew if she didn't get out of there, she was going to embarrass herself by either weeping copiously or passing out. Neither option made her very happy.

Her throat was too constricted to speak, to excuse herself. She lurched for the back door, stumbled through a closed-in porch, then burst into the weak sunshine. Not sure why, she kept moving forward, as if the motion would somehow jump-start her body into behaving again. But suddenly she was halted by a set of heavy hands on her shoulders.

Her body was pulled upright, then back against a solid, muscular chest. The warmth soothed her, making her aware that she was out in the cool January air with no coat over her dress. Just an apron. The thought made her want to laugh, but her lungs were strained.

Zach leaned in close, burying his face against her neck. His heat surrounded her. "Just breathe, baby," he murmured against her ear.

Zach felt Sadie's body unlock as if he'd turned the key. Breathing deep, she rose up on her toes. Then she collapsed back against him.

Leaving him feeling like he'd won the lottery.

He sensed her beginning to relax. The feel of her ribs expanding beneath his palms. The loosening of her muscles against his chest. The sigh that finally graced his ears.

He waited for her to sag as the tension drained from her, but Sadie was too strong for that. Instead her knees locked. She didn't pull away, but she wasn't relying solely on him for her stability, either.

That was the essence of the woman he'd come to know.

And she was kind, compassionate, hardworking. Today, he was determined to learn something new.

Stepping back was a hardship, but he substituted holding her hand for the embrace. A poor substitute, his body said. He led her to a bench near this end of the sloping back lawn. During the summer, irises bloomed plentifully here, but the now-barren leaves didn't detract from the richness of the view.

He took a quick inventory of her. Breath steady. Eyes closed. Pulse slowing beneath his palm. He waited a few minutes more before pushing.

"Tell me what that was about."

"A panic attack," she said simply. "I've had a few over the years, but they're so rare that I never feel quite prepared for them."

Her deep breath drew his gaze down to the fullness of her chest, even though he knew that's not where his focus should be right now.

"Marie's words…they just brought up some bad memories for me."

"Did you lose someone you love?"

She shook her head, but it wasn't really an answer— more the movement of someone trying to deny reality. "Not yet…but I will."

He waited, trying to wrap his mind around her words. Was it her mother? That was the only relative she'd ever mentioned.

"I have a sister…a baby sister."

Zach felt his world tilt slightly, then right itself.

"She was diagnosed when she was a teenager. The cancer is terminal at this point." A sad smile tilted the corners of her lips. "She's a trouper—it's been six years since her diagnosis. They said she would only live two."

Zach could read between the lines. "But she won't be able to fight it forever?"

Sadie shook her head, her lips pressed tight for control. Fortunately, he could read all her emotions in those expressive eyes.

"No," she finally conceded. "She's fought long and hard, but her resolve is weakening. As is ours—mine and my mother's. We take the best care of her we can, but there's only so much we can do."

"And that's heartbreaking."

"My poor mother—she's handled the majority of Amber's care, but it's too much. We had to place her in a type of halfway house. Not hospice…yet." Sadie looked away, but Zach could still see her neck working as she swallowed.

As he'd done with Marie, he reached out to comfort her. Only this wasn't Marie. He reacted in a completely different manner that shook him deep inside. But he didn't let go.

"I was still young myself, but about a year into her treatment I took over my mother's position as housekeeper for our former employer so she could stay home with Amber full-time. This trip is the longest I've been away from them, ever."

In her voice, Zach heard an echo of his own struggles with responsibility. The burden of doing whatever you had to in order to care for someone you love, regardless of where you wanted your own life to go. It was a heavy weight, one he hated to think of on Sadie's slim shoulders. But it came with its own rewards.

He was sure she knew that by now also.

"Why did you leave now, Sadie?"

She went still beneath his touch, and for a moment he worried that his question had seemed judgmental. But Zach was the last one to judge. He'd left his entire family behind for the military because that's what he'd needed to do to provide a better life for them.

"The trip—it was a legacy, of sorts, from our former employer," she said. "The chance to travel outside our little world. My mom wouldn't hear of me giving it up—neither of them would."

He knew he shouldn't ask, but he couldn't stop himself. "So you could go anywhere, and you chose to come here."

She quickly glanced at him out of the corner of her eye, which told him she realized the significance of the question. "Zach, this is the only place I wanted to be." She wiped shaky fingers over her cheeks. "I'm sorry. This is just a little too close," she whispered.

For a moment, he thought she meant him. But now she clutched his arms, her body leaning into his. Then he understood. Marie had been talking about life, the life Lily should have had.

The life Amber should have had.

"I know it is," he said. "And that's okay."

With a jerk her gaze swung up to meet his. He could read the conflict in her eyes. The woman she'd shown him was strong, independent, but soft with others. Now she needed to take care of herself.

"It's okay, Sadie. Feeling that way doesn't make you weak. It makes you human."

That's when the tears appeared, just like the night

she'd told him she missed her mother. They pooled like shiny puddles in her eyes, reflecting that incredible green color. He knew then, no matter what he really wanted, he would never be able to get over Sadie.

Whether she stayed or not.

Eleven

When her phone rang, Sadie was surprised to see Zach's name lighting up the small screen. But her hesitation lasted only a second before she answered.

"Pack a weekend bag and meet me downstairs."

She opened her mouth to reply, but the line went dead. Was he already downstairs? Should she go question him? Why was she even thinking about this?

Letting go of her worrisome thoughts, she packed her travel toiletries and enough clothes for two days into an oversize purse in record time. The sound of her feet on the stairs as she descended ramped up her heartbeat.

It had only been a day and a half since she'd seen him, but it seemed like forever. She'd chosen not to attend Lily Blackstone's funeral today, figuring she'd simply be lost in the throng of people who would be there. But Zach had surely braved the crowds for the family who had done so much for him.

When he'd last said goodbye at Blackstone Manor, he'd told her he would be in touch, but not when. That made sense, considering his position as head of security for the family. She definitely hadn't expected to speak with him tonight after what had undoubtedly been a long day.

Shouldn't he be home relaxing? Sleeping?

Yet there he stood in the foyer of the B and B, looking a little tired around the edges, but fresh in a pair of jeans and a T-shirt. She wished she could run her fingers through his hair or savor the sexiness of his gaze as he did a little inspecting of his own.

But he didn't linger. He quickly took her bag and led her out to a low, dark sports car. Still without an explanation, he seated her in the front, then stowed her bag in the trunk. Her first clue as to his intentions was his quick lean across the seat after he climbed behind the steering wheel. His lips on hers were hot and hard, telling her without words of the need he barely held in check.

Her anticipation exploded into full-blown excitement.

Good thing he wasn't dangerous, because she had no recollection of where they drove. Her entire focus was on the smallest of things: his hands on the steering wheel, the barest hint of music on the radio—too low for her to tell what it was—the shaking in her core that had nothing to do with fear and everything to do with Zach.

It wasn't until he pulled the car into an almost empty lot and parked that reality hit. She realized she needed to know. "Zach," she stalled, before he could open his door.

"Yes?"

His low voice only sent further shivers up her spine. "I'm guessing we're not going out to dinner?" She tried to keep her tone light, but Zach plunged straight into the deep end.

He leaned closer, invading her comfort zone. "We both know what's happening, Sadie. I think it's time to stop beating around the bush, don't you?"

"Um…"

"Don't pretend this isn't what you want." If his words didn't convince her, the way his lips traced her jaw definitely did.

But for once, she needed honesty between them. "I won't." Heaven knew she couldn't. "But how can it be what you want?" She swallowed hard but forced herself to finish. "After I left?"

"You were trying to do the right thing, weren't you?"

He would never know it, but she had. Her attempt to protect him from the callous, self-centered man who had been his father might not be the right thing in his mind, but it had been in hers. "Yes."

"That's the most important thing to me, Sadie."

She instantly cooled as he got out of the car and walked around to her side. If she hadn't known she would ultimately lose Zach, those words had spelled it out loud and clear. But she didn't have time to contemplate. Zach opened her door. His hand folded over hers, and he eased her out onto her feet. "I want you," he said, no longer holding back. "You have responsibilities away from here. I totally understand that."

He lifted her chin with his other hand, positioning her lips exactly right for his kiss. "If I only have you for this weekend, so be it."

Her defenses and resistance fell with his words, and she had a feeling she'd never be able to rebuild either again. Instead she took a deep breath and nodded. "Okay." Her voice wasn't too shaky, at least.

As he locked up the car, she glanced around. Parts of Black Hills had become fairly familiar to her by now, but she had absolutely no idea where she was at the moment. Zach grabbed their bags, then her hand and led her across the asphalt to a large metal building.

They were spending the weekend in a manufacturing plant? It certainly didn't have the romantic feel she would expect, but then, Zach was a guy. The dark night kept her from reading the sign farther down the wall. It wasn't until they passed through the double doors that Sadie got a clue.

They'd arrived at the small municipal airport. The too bright, fluorescent-lit space wasn't big enough for commercial traffic—mostly crop dusters and shuttle planes. Which also explained why it was mostly deserted at this time of the evening.

Zach dumped their bags near a grouping of chairs and waved her into a seat. "I'll just get everything set up."

Sure he would. She remembered him talking about loving every minute of learning to fly in the military, and he'd done some crop dusting in town until the notorious cotton killings last year.

"Zach, would you mind telling me what we're doing?"

He paused a few feet away, his expression filled with an almost childlike excitement. "Do you like surprises?"

A frown started between her brows. "I haven't had any good ones in my life."

"Well, let's try this one and see."

Zach felt like he'd spent the entire two-hour flight grinning—and he wasn't a grin type of guy. He preferred a smirk or a glare. But the reaction to Sadie's every gasp and sigh was unstoppable.

Despite her initial shock, it was clear she'd enjoyed the view, no matter their altitude. Zach's new private plane, no matter that it was small, made the trip pure pleasure. It was the first thing he'd bought for himself since he'd hit the big time. Add on the anticipation of being with Sadie, and yeah, he grinned.

He was giving himself a gift, and hopefully giving her one, too. He'd told her the truth: the past was the past. He didn't need a crystal ball to guess the future was uncertain. But for this weekend, they would have all they wanted of each other.

No more interruptions.

He took the plane down and handled the technicalities at the airport with ease but not nearly enough speed for his liking. It took way too long to get everything loaded into the Jeep he kept at the airport and get started on the road.

"We'll be at our destination in about twenty minutes," he said.

At least, he hoped so. He hadn't checked the weather forecast the way he normally did before his trips, and a light snow had started to fall as they ascended the mountain.

"Where are we going?" she asked.

"My favorite place in the world."

She didn't question him further but grinned herself. Then she turned her gaze back out the window to the darkened landscape. "Well, I already know it's beautiful," she said in a hushed voice.

As did he. The real estate agent was the most trusted in Black Hills, a woman Zach had known most of his adult life. He'd laid out his specifications, and in a week she had an even dozen options from a trusted network of agents all over the South. This one had stood out from the rest at first glance. He'd made the purchase without hesitation—and without familial consent. Heck, his family didn't even know the specifics about this place. And they'd never actually been here.

He came to the cabin regularly. Always alone. It was the one place he could let down his guard, let go of the ever-present responsibility and truly relax. He'd never wanted anyone else's personality to imprint on the place...until now.

Maybe he should have planned this a little more, but Zach knew all about trusting his instincts. The impulse was true. At least when Sadie was gone, he'd be able to come here and remember her.

Even he had to admit that the cabin looked charming as they arrived. The light, fluffy snow had started to accumulate on the nooks and crannies of the log house and roof. He parked out in front instead of pulling in close. The cabin wasn't large, though it did have two bedrooms and two baths. The second story held only the master bedroom, bath and sitting area.

Not big, but it had all the amenities he'd wanted. A wide wraparound porch perfect for relaxing. A balcony with a hot tub, accessible from the master suite. An environmentally friendly exterior finish. And the whole thing was surrounded on three sides by a forest dense with cedar and pine.

"Wow, Zach. This is gorgeous."

He helped Sadie out of the Jeep and grabbed both of their bags before leading her up the stairs to the porch. Her red hair glinted with snowflakes, tempting him to keep her outside to admire her beauty. But his body protested any further delay.

The security system and locks were a minute's work for him. Then they were stepping through the door into the slightly cool interior. Dropping the bags, he made a beeline for the opposite wall and adjusted the thermostat.

"I keep it cooler in here when I'm away—just high enough to keep everything from freezing—but it will warm up soon."

She nodded, her eyes twinkling with excitement as she surveyed the interior. "I'm serious, Zach. This has to be your best-kept secret. I love it."

Arms tucked around her to combat the chill, she wandered through the downstairs area. But her words held him still. Because the cabin was a secret of sorts. He never talked about it with anyone; he'd never even described it or shown his family any pictures, even though they knew of its existence.

Because deep down, he felt guilty for taking this time, this space for himself.

The admission stunned him. Guilt was a weakness he couldn't afford and didn't have the time to wallow in.

Suddenly Sadie stood before him, her appearance shaking him from his daze. "You're right," he told her, "it is my secret. You're the only person I've ever brought here."

Her green eyes widened. He could almost see the impact as his confession hit her. Then she narrowed her gaze on him. "Why, Zach?" she asked, soft-spoken but demanding in her own way. "Why wouldn't you want people to know about this part of your life?"

"They wouldn't understand why I want to be here… need to be here." The explanation burned in his throat.

Sadie reached out to him, offering comfort instead of the passion he'd planned on when he'd first walked through the door. "I understand. Sometimes life is overwhelming, and you need to recharge—somewhere away from all the things you feel like you have to take care of."

She stepped in close, the arm around his waist making him wish there was nothing between his skin and hers. "You've worked incredibly hard, Zach. You deserve this sanctuary for yourself."

"Sometimes it doesn't feel like it."

"Why?"

He shook his head. "If it wasn't for the Blackstone brothers, I'd probably be rotting in jail from that crop dusting incident. To have everyone patting my back… it just feels false."

Sadie wasn't buying it. "You've worked at the mill a long time, right? Long before you were head of security for the Blackstones."

Zach nodded.

"You've known most of those people all of your life, right?"

"Yes."

"I saw you with them, Zach," she said, squeezing him a little tighter. "I've watched you interact with them since that first trip out there. They respect you. Your direction and judgment."

Her gaze remained clear and direct, pulling him in.

"That doesn't come from Blackstone backing. You have to earn that. Which you did with your integrity and hard work. They know you because you've proven yourself time and again. And that's why they won't judge you for indulging in some of what we girls call me time every so often."

Her assessment left him speechless and in desperate need of a few minutes to himself. As if she completely understood, she graced him with a sweet smile and continued on her exploration.

Leaving him and his emotions behind.

Twelve

Eager for something to do, Zach carried the bags up the stairs to the master suite. Simply furnished in beige suede with accents reminiscent of the nearby woods, the atmosphere was soothing without being feminine. He dropped the bags, wondering where he would put Sadie's stuff.

With a self-deprecating shake of his head, he conceded that he hadn't thought through his plans for this visit very well. He could put her bag downstairs, but he wasn't about to give even a ghost of an impression that he wanted her that far away. Upstairs, he had a few drawers built into the closet, filled with his own clothes.

Maybe they'd stay busy enough that clothes wouldn't be necessary.

They definitely weren't necessary for what he had in mind. He glanced from the bed to the French doors leading to the balcony and hot tub. For the first time, Zach planned to explore every fantasy he could with a woman. Until now, he'd always held back. The intensity of his nature kept him cautious.

But tonight he was cutting the caution tape and diving in headfirst.

As he heard her footsteps on the stairs, a tremble started in his hands. Not hard enough to be seen, just subtle enough to be felt. He clenched his fists, unwilling to give in to the need to pounce the minute she strolled through the doorway.

But when she came in, she didn't look around, didn't inspect her surroundings with the curiosity she had downstairs. Instead her gaze rested solely on him.

Just as she had downstairs, she reached for him. Only this time, her touch wasn't intended for comfort. She moved in close. The faint scent of sugar drifted over him as her hands traveled across his chest to grasp the edges of his open flannel shirt. Slowly she pulled down, just hard enough for him to feel the weight. Then she let go and slipped her hands inside. The same feeling of need came over him, multiplied by a hundred.

But he refused to take the reins...just yet.

The light scrape of her nails against his ribs through the undershirt tested his resolve. His eyelids slid closed. A few deep breaths might help...

She pressed her mouth against the underside of his jaw.

...maybe not.

His heart raced as she nibbled and licked her way to his neck, then down along the sensitive skin of his throat. He growled a warning.

And heard her giggle.

With a quick move, he lifted her by her arms and tossed her lightly onto the bed behind them. A high-pitched squeal signaled her surprise. He stood his ground at the mattress's edge, staring down at her with the knowledge that the game was now his. He was in control. He would make the next move.

For both their pleasure.

"Strip."

The command sounded loud in the room, firm in its intent. Her eyes widened, and he didn't miss the catch in her breath. Slowly, as if to tease him, she crawled to her knees, then straightened. Her fingers traced up her sweater to the trio of buttons right below her breasts. He could almost feel the seconds tick out as she released each one with agonizing delays.

If she only knew just where that teasing would lead.

Next came the long-sleeved T-shirt beneath. How could a woman make pulling a shirt over her head so incredibly sensual? As she reached for the button of her jeans, the tremble in his hands became a reality.

The zipper traveled down ever so slowly. Just when he wondered how she would complete the move, she rolled confidently down onto her back. Holding his gaze with her own, she braced her knees and lifted her hips into his line of sight. She worked the heavy material down over her hips, then paused with her palms flat against her thighs.

Now it was his turn.

His patience at an end, he grasped the material and pulled. The jeans came off in one easy move. Sadie lost her balance as her feet were swept off the bed and fell back with a little bounce. The lamp on the bedside table left no shadows to hide her body. Zach was free to savor every inch with his gaze as much as his touch.

He took advantage as he systematically stripped his own clothes away. As he crawled onto the bed, a new feeling took hold of him. He didn't recognize it at first.

When he did, he probably should have been ashamed. After all, this was the age when women weren't owned by men. But deep inside, the urge to brand her as his was undeniable. To cover her body with his own and take her until no other man would dare touch what was Zach's alone.

Primitive. Forceful. Necessary.

He could concede that this relationship wasn't forever as long as he wanted to…but his body would never believe it.

Straddling her stomach and arms, he bent low over her upper body. Just as she had earlier, he pressed kisses along her lower jaw. Only his were openmouthed and hard, drawing moans from deep within her throat. He moved lower, sucking at the base of her neck where the delicate indentation between her collarbones begged for his attention.

She squirmed, but he wasn't giving her the chance to distract him with her touch. As he traveled out to the delicate structure of her shoulder, he swept the strap of her bra aside. Then he stripped the bra itself down to reveal pale, trembling mounds of succulent flesh. Pressing them together with his palms, Zach admired their strawberries-and-cream color before lowering his head to drive her wild.

Because he remembered everything that made Sadie moan, sigh and cry out. And he used that knowledge to his full advantage.

As much as he wanted to hold out, to extend their loving to the brink of insanity, the throbbing pulse between his thighs insisted otherwise. He made quick work of her undergarments, then took immense satisfaction in lifting her legs and wrapping them around his waist.

She needed no prompting but immediately pulled him

in tight. He barely had enough reach to snag a condom from the bedside table and cover himself. Then he slid home.

This time, there was no controlling his rhythm, no holding back. Their bodies strained in time with each other. Her cries filled the air. The feel of her fingernails on his back sent a sharp zing down his spine.

Almost over. Not yet. *Not yet.*

He buried his face at her throat, absorbing the vibration of her hoarse cries with his mouth. Her body tightened around him, a long, slow squeeze that pulled him in and sucked him dry.

It was many moments before Zach could open his eyes to the glare of the lamp beside them, even more before he could ease away from the tangle of their limbs. He made them both comfortable, then plunged the room into darkness.

A dim glow from outside permeated the French doors. Not the light of the moon, but maybe its shadowy reflection off the ever deepening snow on the deck. He lay on his side watching it, Sadie pulled close and secure against his chest. As he listened to the deepening of her breath, he had the same feeling he'd had on the nights before a few missions gone wrong. The sense that he'd made a mistake, missed something that was going to come back to bite him in the ass.

But he was too happy to care. If Sadie was a mistake, she was by far the best mistake he'd ever made.

"But I didn't bring a swimsuit."

The amused, calculating look in Zach's eyes told her he didn't care. Not in the least. "Well, I have one, but I promise not to use it."

Oh, she was in trouble. But she tried to protest anyway. "It's cold out there." The idea of the hot tub in the snow sounded romantic, but she'd have to actually go outside naked to accomplish it.

"So…"

As Zach tracked her around the bedroom, Sadie tried to think of another motive for staying inside. Normally, dawn was something she only saw for photo shoots. But this seemed to be her punishment for trying to ease out of bed and find a robe to cover her naked body. Now she attempted to both avoid Zach and keep the robe, which proved useless as he pounced.

Her squeal echoed in the room when he swept her into his arms and stalked for the French doors. The first blast of cold air on her bare bottom made her gasp.

Yep, exactly what she had wanted to avoid.

The Neanderthal carrying her didn't appear fazed. "Zach," she said. "I'm naked."

"And all the more beautiful for it."

Thankfully Zach had prepared the tub while she'd been in the bathroom. The cover was already off and steam rose in smoky tendrils from the water. After a few steps, he tilted her until her toes met the blessed warmth. Inch by inch he eased her in until the water covered her like a blanket. Then he slid his sleekly muscled limbs in behind her.

The water bubbled against her skin, reawakening the sensual needs that simmered below the surface whenever Zach was anywhere close. Zach's strong hands kneaded her shoulders, further weakening her resistance.

"See," he murmured. "This is worth the walk, right? Or rather, the ride?"

"Totally," she mumbled back. "And I'll believe that until the minute I have to get out and walk back into the house."

Zach laughed, the sound echoing around them. "Then I better make the interim worthwhile, huh?"

You always do.

But she didn't let herself say the words out loud. She let her body speak them instead.

It wasn't long before Zach's hands moved from working their heavenly magic on her shoulders back up into the wildly tangled locks of her hair. He alternated hands, squeezing and pulling one at a time, just enough to release the tension from her scalp.

Sadie thought she might melt into eternal bliss.

Every touch, every word spoken became a treasure to hide in her heart. The only gift she might ever be able to give herself, because once she had to leave him, nothing else would ever compare to these memories.

Suddenly his hand in her hair was guiding her. A nearby seat hidden in the bubbles became a shelf for her to brace against. The vista before her swirled with dancing snow swept up from the forest floor, and the saturated pinks and blues of sunrise reflected off sparkling icicles.

She felt Zach's warm skin against her back, forming a shield between her and the cool air. Not that she noticed. Her mind was too focused on the moment when he made them one, bringing their bodies together in a connection as glorious as the beauty around them.

He moved inside her, all around her. The water splashed and bubbled in an accompaniment to their harsh breath. His fingers continued their ballet of tightening and letting go, building her anticipation.

"You're so beautiful, Sadie," he murmured with his mouth against her shoulder, only adding to the myriad sensations.

How could she ever let go of such perfection?

In response to the thought, her body clamped down, desperate to hold him within her for as long as she could. She arched her back, trying to take him deeper. To make him as much a part of her as she could.

He moved in and out, every drag and pull intensifying her response. The low rumble of his voice added to the tingles, coaxing her into submission, commanding her response. Finally, just as the sun peeked over the horizon, her orgasm rolled through her, forcing Zach to catch his breath. He held still, buried in her inch by glorious inch.

Her mind exploded along with her body, screaming the knowledge of her love for this man. So loud, she had to bite down on her tongue to hold the words inside. Instead tears fell, mingling with the steam surrounding them.

Zach groaned, thrusting a few last times before he slowed down with a sigh. He pressed firm kisses along her shoulder as his arms surrounding her trembled ever so slightly. He murmured tender, soothing words against her skin.

Something inside Sadie died at the thought that she couldn't have him forever. But as her eyes drifted closed, she did her best to imprint every second to memory.

Then again, how could she ever forget any of these incredible moments? She only hoped she never did.

There was a lot to be learned about another person when you spent several days in a row alone together, just as Sadie did during their time snowed in at the cabin. Sharing the same bed brought a whole wealth of knowledge.

And not just about sex.

For instance, Zach was a side sleeper. He cuddled in

close every night, but her position didn't seem to matter. She could face out spoon style, or snuggle her cheek against his chest. Either way, he almost never moved more than the barest shift. He wasn't a tosser and turner, which made sleeping with him a bit like having access to her own human pillow that supported her body and didn't self-adjust after she'd made herself comfortable.

It might have sounded uptight, but Sadie had learned after many interrupted nights' sleep with her sister that she could only be awakened so many times before her brain started to short-circuit. Sleep was, quite frankly, important to her.

Tonight, their third here, started the same as both the other nights. Sadie drifted off to sleep wondering how many more nights she would have like this. Would they be going home tomorrow? Were the roads safe up here? She hadn't had more than the briefest of glimpses out at the road and wasn't sure that she wanted one.

Frankly, she didn't want their time together to end.

An adulthood spent in a sickroom had given her the unfortunate ability to instantly wake up at the slightest noise or movement. Only Zach's movements weren't slight.

First he flopped onto his back so that his side bumped against her back. She rolled over to face him then snuggled up to a pillow instead. He was probably trying to get comfortable. Then he jerked again, mumbling something under his breath.

A little odd for the man who usually slept like a rock for six hours a night. Reaching out, she laid her palm against his bare chest. His skin was hot, with a light sheen of sweat.

A few seconds later, he jolted again. Then again, and again. It took her a few minutes to realize that the man she thought couldn't be shaken was having a nightmare. Seconds later he rolled over, this time throwing out an arm that caught her unawares as it struck against her side.

Her gasp sounded loud in the room. Suddenly, Zach sat straight up, his body at attention. Sadie froze, too, not sure whether or not it was safe to reach out again. Who knew what Zach was reacting to—and she had a feeling he wasn't entirely awake.

So she held still, counting the spaces between his breaths, waiting for him to gain consciousness. As he did, the feel of the room changed. His muscles loosened one by one. Then the sound of a ragged breath met her ears, interrupted by a hard swallow.

When he turned to her, she couldn't see his expression in the gloom, but she could hear the emotion in his voice. "Sadie? Sadie, are you okay?"

Now she sat up, automatically reaching out a hand to rest against his biceps. "I'm okay, Zach."

She barely made out the shadow of him shaking his head. "I think—I think I hit you." His ragged breathing continued. "I'm damn sorry, Sadie."

"I'm perfectly fine," she assured him. "It was more like a bump. I was just in the way, Zach. No harm done."

"I still shouldn't have…"

That's when she realized there was a slight tremble beneath her palm. Not a full-blown reaction. Something she suspected he was using all his might to control. But it was there, all the same.

"That must have been a doozy of a nightmare," she said.

Even Sadie, who kept a lot to herself, would have wanted to talk something like that out. If for no other reason than to rid herself of the haunting images that could linger after a very intense nightmare.

Apparently Zach didn't, because he was silent. Which was fine. It wasn't for her to decide what Zach wanted to share. But that didn't stop her protective instincts from surging to the front.

Being protected, being taken care of, was as foreign to Zach as it was to Sadie. She wasn't going to let that hold her back.

Curling her fingers around his elbow, she pulled him in her direction. He resisted at first, but she wasn't giving up. As he twisted toward her, she reached for his other arm, then used them to guide him down against her. She lay back against her pillow, positioning him along her side.

"It's okay, Zach," she repeated softly.

Her heart leaped as he buried his face against her neck, but she held still. It took time. Soon his skin was flush against hers, his breath puffing gently along her collarbone and his arm heavy across her waist. There were no more signs of the shakes, but she sensed a struggle for balance. One she couldn't influence, but she could provide a safe haven until he found it.

She embraced his shoulders, securing him to her. Then she closed her eyes and measured her breaths. Soon his breathing matched hers, his rhythm evening out. Only then could she truly relax deep down inside, no longer worried that the nightmare would win.

He might not sleep well, but at least his body could rest.

But sleeping didn't seem to be what he had in mind. Just as she began drifting toward slumber, his leg shifted over hers, sliding between her thighs. Languidly his hand explored what flesh it could find.

And she was more than happy to welcome his touch.

She kept waiting for him to speed up, to channel

the adrenaline from his dream into a headlong rush for oblivion. Instead, he seemed to lose himself in pleasuring her, drawing out every caress to gift her with the ultimate in sensation.

Sadie found herself drowning in the unexpected sensuality that lasted longer than she could have dreamed possible, until every inch of her body was imprinted with the memory of Zach on a cellular level that meant he would be with her forever.

She still wasn't sure if a forever without him was something she could survive.

Thirteen

Zach let Sadie sleep.

It was the least he could do after waking her up last night. The thought that he could have hurt her during his dream hung like a chain around his neck.

Something he wasn't proud of.

But he'd survive. He'd learned long ago that he could do this. He would do this. Healing just took time.

As did other things.

He remembered staring down at Sadie's back as he made love to her in the hot tub. The flex and pull of her muscles fascinated him, because they represented the strength and character of a woman who worked hard and provided for others when she could. A woman he loved.

If he'd had any doubts before now, they'd been obliterated last night. But emotions were much easier to face and acknowledge in the dark of night. Now he was about to face her across the breakfast table, and he had some explaining to do...

Which always went down better with food. His mama had taught him that.

He was in the middle of cooking up waffles, scrambled eggs and bacon from the supplies his caretaker had brought in when Sadie made her way into the kitchen. The sexy tumble of her hair made him think of all the things he'd done to her during the night. His body's elation muted the slight panic over his plan for this morning.

Her gaze followed him as he moved, but she didn't ask any questions. He could go with it and not bring up the nightmare he'd suffered for the first time in a year or more, keeping his secrets to himself. He hadn't even fully shared the experience that caused the nightmares with his family.

But he saw that as the dipwad way of handling this. He wasn't going to take the easy way out—that wasn't the kind of man he was.

"Are you trying to butter me up?" she asked, peering over his shoulder. "Because waffles are definitely the way to go."

He'd noticed her love of both waffles and pancakes whenever Gladys served them at the B and B. So he might have been working with a little insider knowledge.

"Do I need to?" he asked, glancing at her over his shoulder as he plated the food.

Sadie didn't look away or back down. Her gaze held his. "Absolutely not."

Good to know. He hadn't hurt her when he was thrashing around last night. She'd told the truth—she was fine. Now he would do the same.

He let her dig in first, lifting forkfuls of buttery,

syrupy goodness to her lips before he got down to the dirty details.

"A lot happens in the years you serve your country," he started. "Some of it is good—very good. Like the men and women you serve with. They become like a second family."

He chewed thoughtfully on a piece of bacon. Sadie had slowed her own bites, as if her initial hunger had been eased somewhat.

"Some of it is bad—very bad."

"I'm sure." Her soothing voice coated his nerves like a balm. It was the very thing that had drawn him to her five years ago, that voice.

"One particular day was beyond bad." He blinked, questioning for a moment whether he could actually do this. With a deep breath, he forced himself to continue. "I thought we were all gonna die. My platoon. My brothers." Without warning his throat tightened, closing off his voice, his breath. The memory of that day could still tear him up even now. "But a friend, my best friend, actually, saved us all by throwing himself over an IED."

Unable to handle whatever sympathy he might see in her face, he stared down at his plate. "He died instantly."

Abstractly, he noticed the tight grip his fingers now had on his fork and forced them to loosen one by one. This mere exercise in concentration helped get him back on track.

"The nightmare is always the same," he said. "I go back through the entire day, but I'm only observing it. I can't stop anything from happening. I see all of the things I missed, everything I could have done to stop it."

He clenched and unclenched his fists. "I yell at myself until I'm hoarse, but it does no good. I watch helplessly, unable to prevent his death like I should."

Her gentle voice intervened. "Why should you?"

"It's my job," he said, handing over the rote answer, the least complicated one.

"You're right," she answered. "You are responsible."

That had him looking up, misery snaking through his heart. But she reached out to cover his hand with her own. "Because you've made yourself responsible. But your friend would not want you to spend your life beating yourself up.

"Just like my sister doesn't want me to stay home—" she pulled back from him "—to stop living, just for her. Their wishes don't ease the sense of obligation or guilt, but ultimately, they want us to live, even though they can't."

Sadie dropped her fork onto her plate. He thought about her sister and how hard it must have been for her to encourage Sadie to leave her. He thought about his own mother and the many times she'd told him to go out and have fun.

Yet the only way he could do that was at an isolated cabin in the woods, because everywhere else he went there were things to do and people to take care of.

"Is that why you left the military?" Sadie asked.

Zach sat for long moments, unable to answer. The turmoil and confusion of that time complicated his thoughts. He finally said, "No. I really did want to come home to take care of my family. I hadn't planned to re-up for another tour. After the inquiry, I didn't have the heart for another go-round anyway."

He glanced over at Sadie, surprised to find her eyes had widened as she stared at him. But her expression quickly melted into a compassion he hadn't even known he was hoping for.

"Your family needs you," she said, then waved her

hand through the air. "You need this. There's nothing wrong with it."

Taking the few short steps around the table, Zach knelt next to Sadie's chair and buried his face in her lap. His eyes were squeezed tight. He stayed there for a few minutes, taking comfort from her wisdom and willingness to share.

His grip tightened for a moment, unwilling to let go, and for the first time in over five years, he started to believe.

Sadie knew what she had to do the minute she got back to Black Hills, but still put it off for a few days. Every phone call from her mom increased her procrastination instead of spurring her to finish this farce. Every angry email, text and phone call from Victor increased her guilt.

The excuses were growing slim.

It hadn't helped that she'd been completely out of contact for four days. Rather than risk a call while she was with Zach, she'd simply shut her phone down, turning it on only to call her mother each night. She'd sent her pictures of the gorgeous scenery covered in snow, including some she took when they went hiking in the dense woods.

Those four days seemed like a space and time outside harsh reality. Now she had glorious memories of Zach to hold on to for years to come—years that were sure to be even lonelier and colder than the last five.

But she had to check one more thing about Zach. This was the last avenue open to her. If nothing came of it, she'd already determined that she wasn't going to lie just for the money. No matter how scared that left her.

She would call the lawyer, bypassing Victor completely, and tell him she would give an affidavit testifying to what Victor had hired her to do, all the avenues she'd explored and that Zach was squeaky-clean and eligible for his father's inheritance.

Then she'd walk away once more. At least if she disappeared she wouldn't have to see Zach's face when he realized who she really was, why she was really here.

It was the coward's way out—but her reserves of strength were leaking out with the speed of an hourglass. So she was looking into the only option left: Zach's military service.

The chance that she might have to use something so personal—his very intimate confession—against him…

Well, the thought made her sick to her stomach.

She'd done a preliminary search on her laptop, just to see if there was anything out there. Gaining access to military records wasn't an option, but if the incident was big enough, it might have been reported by local media outlets in the US, especially in the deceased's hometown.

Quite a few hits had shown up, but she didn't dare read them when Zachary could walk in at any moment. Lately he spent more time with her at the B and B than he did at home—though he never offered to take her to his place.

They spent so much time together, the landlady had casually mentioned charging her for a second person. Sadie had adopted a deadpan expression and said, "Sure"—which had left Gladys a little startled.

Now Sadie glanced around the local library, wondering exactly how to use the computer system. She figured doing this anonymously on a public computer was the safest way to go. If she signed in as a guest, no one would be able to trace it back to her.

Finding the bank of computers near the back of the

building, she was grateful to see they were mostly un-occupied. She signed in at the desk, using her sister's name on the form. Then she chose the last computer on the end of the row, figuring there would be less chance of people reading over her shoulder.

Logging on, she retraced her internet search on this computer in a safe browser. Odds were, it was a useless precaution. After all, who would think to look at her browser history here? But just in case…

The first link happened to be to the website for the local Black Hills paper. Following it brought her to the electronic archives for the paper, but it needed a log-in for access. Deciding to come back to that, she tried a few more links.

The local paper for a small town in Pennsylvania wasn't password protected. Sadie was able to learn the name of Zach's friend who died, read the basics of his death and see pictures of him, his fellow soldiers and his grief-stricken family.

Sad. Very sad.

As if that wasn't heartbreaking enough, there were excerpts from Zach's speech at his friend's memorial service, held after the soldiers made their final trip home. But it was a random sentence, late in the article, that told her she had to search further. As commanding officer, Zach had faced an inquiry into his friend's death. No results were mentioned there, or in any other articles she read.

Frustrated, Sadie dropped back against her chair with a short sigh. What should she do now?

"Are you finding everything you need, ma'am?"

No. Sadie looked up into the face of a young woman who had a library volunteer tag on her shirt. No one had bothered her here in the corner, and Sadie had been grateful for the privacy. But maybe this young woman would know…

"Does the library have access to the local newspaper's archives?"

The woman smiled. "We have the oldest editions on microfiche, but we have a subscription to the modern edition that's available online."

Well, wasn't that handy. Sadie might have been happy if this wasn't such an awful thing to be doing.

The young lady got her logged in and showed her how to search the archives.

"So I can just put in a date range, like this?" Sadie asked, typing in the dates for the two months after the incident.

"Yes," the volunteer answered. "When you do that, it comes up in this neat preview version." The screen filled with rows of little preview boxes, each with a thumbnail picture inside and a date directly below it.

"Cool," Sadie said, scanning the pictures.

"You're the photographer lady, right?"

Startled, Sadie looked up at the girl. Cautiously, she nodded, but the other woman didn't seem to notice her sudden reticence. What if she started blabbing about Sadie's search?

"I thought so," the young woman went on. "I saw you at the mill one day when I was there to take my dad some medicine while he was working on the cleanup. I heard some of the workmen talking about you." She reached across to take control of the mouse so she could choose one selection pretty close to the middle. "You might find this interesting, since I heard you were spending a lot of time with Zach Gatlin."

Sure enough, the preview had a photo of half of Zach's face on one side, something that Sadie hadn't had time to scan down to see yet. When the woman clicked, the front page of the paper loaded, including a story with the headline Hometown Hero Returns After Tragic Ending to Tour.

Sadie sat frozen, unwilling to believe the woman had picked out the very story she needed to read.

"It was the talk of the town, even before he came home," she went on. "He was lucky to even be alive. I just happened to be in Lola's when KC brought him home from the airport. I'll never forget his mama's face."

Having met Zach's mom and seen how much she loved her son, Sadie could very much imagine.

The young lady looked up as another employee appeared on the other side of the computer terminals and said, "Sweetie, Miss Jane needs a bit of a hand with story time, if you don't mind."

"Sure," the volunteer said with an eager smile, then turned to Sadie. "Hope that helps. If you need anything else, just flag one of us down." Sadie was grateful for her eagerness to help, but she needed to be alone…now.

"Will do." But Sadie sincerely hoped this was her last avenue of investigation.

It wasn't until the women walked away that Sadie read through the story. It looked as though Zach's involvement had indeed been questioned. But right below the picture of him and his sister embracing at the airport, it stated that he'd been found not guilty of any wrongdoing.

Sadie searched through nearly a month's worth of articles until she finally found the most in-depth account she could have gotten. It was obvious from the cautious tone of the article that the author didn't yet know the outcome of the inquiry.

According to the author's source, there were accusations of inadequate planning and reconnaissance, which could have meant anything, since the military was unlikely to release every detail that was being questioned. Zach was being held responsible in his friend's death, since he was the highest-ranking member of the team and had given the orders during the mission.

After reading all the way through, then one more time for good measure, Sadie cleared her browser history and closed the window. She leaned back, then looked up at the ceiling, as if the answer to her question could be found there. Even without her bias toward Zach, Sadie could tell this was just an instance of wrong place, wrong time. Zach had gotten off without even a reprimand, as far as she could tell.

But that didn't stop him from searching for what he could have done differently to save his friend. The nightmares were his mind's way of playing out his questions and his guilt. They were lessening with time, but would probably never go away.

That was punishment enough.

Now Sadie knew the truth. Her own search was over—her own guilt just beginning.

Fourteen

Sadie was once more wearing her fancy blue dress from the Blackstones' party, hoping those who had seen it before would understand she was from out of town and hadn't traveled with a steamer trunk full of formal gowns.

Her heart pounded as she waited for Zach, nausea welling up inside her. He'd paused to talk with the country club valet, whom he knew from working at the mill. If she could just stand here and watch him forever, she'd be so happy.

But deep down, she knew she had to end this tonight. Somehow she would find the courage to tell him the truth. He deserved to know how to claim his inheritance, and she'd decided he should hear it from her.

But first, just one more night together. One last memory.

Finally he headed her way, his dark good looks set off by the black suit and tie. She savored the way his gaze traced her body. No other man would make her feel as wanted as Zach did. She knew that beyond a doubt.

They joined the Blackstones at their table. Sadie realized she must be getting used to attending these events with Zach, because that feeling of unreality she usually experienced had disappeared. Too bad this wouldn't last. As soon as she returned to Dallas, she'd be extra busy looking for a new position. Hopefully in the same social circles her former boss had enjoyed, so she could continue to keep their heads above water as best she could.

Victor had continued to pay her regular salary, in addition to all of her travel expenses, as if she were on a regular business trip, instead of seeking to ruin a man's reputation. But when she came back empty-handed, all of that income would end.

She had some contacts within those social circles, so that might help. But her foremost concern was that her sister needed to remain close to the hospital and doctors who currently treated her. Sadie would hate to be separated from her family, but without the bonus from Victor, for finding dirt to disqualify Zach from his inheritance, finding work would be essential.

Wherever she could find it.

Christina sat opposite Sadie. The tired cast to her face prompted Sadie's concern. The poor thing must be exhausted after handling her mother-in-law's death, plus her own grief and her pregnancy, too. "How are you, Christina?" Sadie asked quietly, not wanting to draw undue attention.

The other woman's smile seemed bittersweet. "I'm managing. Just trying to focus on what's right in front of us, you know?"

Sadie didn't, but she could imagine, so she nodded.

Before she could respond further, Aiden rose from

his chair to look over the table. Everyone's attention turned to him. He appeared comfortable in his role as head of the family. His normally tough gaze as he took in those around him seemed to soften and glow. "Thank you for being here tonight. We wanted our family and closest friends here to celebrate the joy that is coming to our family—our newest baby, who will be joining us soon, along with the return of our brother Luke and his engagement to one of Black Hills's own treasures, Avery Prescott."

Quiet applause and smiles erupted. Sadie glanced down the length of the table, noting the people she recognized. Luke Blackstone and his fiancée were new to her, along with an older couple someone had mentioned were a doctor and his wife, friends of both the Blackstones and Prescotts, and mentors of Avery Prescott. Zach and Bateman and his family were there from the mill. She was impressed to see both Nolen and Marie present, along with a younger woman Marie had introduced to Sadie as her niece, Nicole. There was a mix of ages, stations in life and connections, but Sadie had found that the Blackstones embraced others based on their presence in their lives, not what they were capable of doing for them.

The viewpoint was refreshing for Sadie. She only hoped she could find future employers who were as real as the people she'd come to know here.

As they were served their meals, Sadie felt Zach's hand circle around her own. She turned to find him watching her with the fire and need she so desperately wanted to see in his eyes.

"You look beautiful tonight, Sadie," he said. "I love you in this dress."

Her throat closed for a moment. Hearing those first

three words on his lips meant the world to her, even if he didn't mean them the way she wished. "I love you in that suit," she finally whispered. "Very dashing."

"Dashing, huh? Debonair, too?"

Oh, that grin was dangerous. "Most definitely."

"Well, I promise to be a gentleman." He leaned forward to brush a kiss high on her cheekbone, right in front of her ear. Then he whispered, "For now."

The shiver that worked its way down her spine caused her to squeeze the hand still holding hers. How much longer could she hold him to her?

They were interrupted by the arrival of their food. Sadie leaned back as her soup was placed before her, followed by a plate of oysters for their end of the table to share. As she glanced over the half shells coated in some kind of breading and cheese mixture, her stomach turned over again.

She sucked in a breath through pursed lips, then slowly released it. *Nope, not helping.* "Excuse me a moment," she murmured to Zach.

Luckily she'd seen where the restroom was on their way inside. Her stomach had calmed again before she reached the door, but she went inside anyway. Running cool water over her wrists helped also. Lord, she needed to get her nerves under control. Life was never easy, but why ruin her last night with Zach by anticipating the earthquake that she knew was coming?

Did she even believe what she was telling herself right now?

The door opened behind her. Christina and KC stepped inside. Both women flocked to her with concern in their expressions.

"Are you okay?" Christina asked, patting her back gently.

She nodded as KC asked the same. "Yes, I've just been feeling a little off somehow."

"Zach was worried when you left so quickly. I told him we would check, though you were probably fine."

"Sorry. Didn't mean to scare anyone."

"Well, I only have to make about fifty trips a night to the bathroom right now," Christina said with a laugh as she headed for a stall. "So I'd be here soon enough anyway. If it had been any earlier in my pregnancy, those oysters would have turned me green. I wouldn't have even made it back here." She flashed a grossed-out face over her shoulder before shutting the door.

"Oh, me, too," KC said from beside Sadie as she patted over her hair. "Of course, any kind of seafood got to me. It wasn't so much the look of it as the smell. Yuck." She grinned. "I was so glad when that stage went away, because I love me some shrimp."

Sadie felt her stomach twist again as her mind conjured up the image of shrimp scampi, usually one of her favorites. She breathed carefully, glancing at the mirror to make sure her queasiness didn't show on her face. No need to cause more concern.

KC opened her little clutch purse and proceeded to touch up her already perfect makeup. Christina returned and washed her hands. "It's not completely gone for me," she was saying. "The nausea isn't nearly as bad as it was in the first trimester, of course, but some things will still set it off sometimes. And the exhaustion. Oh, boy."

"I know what you mean," KC agreed. "You have more than just the pregnancy to make you tired, but I sure remember trying to wait tables with swollen feet and that bone-tired feeling weighing me down. That was rough."

As the women talked around her, Sadie stared into the mirror. She could actually see the blood drain from her already pale skin. Her light dusting of freckles stood out in stark contrast, as did the glossy pink of her lips. Nausea. She'd put it down to nerves. Exhaustion. She'd simply pushed it aside as too many late nights with Zach.

Her gaze dropped to her chest, as she suddenly remembered the recent tenderness of her breasts. She'd chalked it up to hormones, but this would be about the third week they'd been unusually sensitive.

That wasn't normal.

"Are you coming, Sadie?"

She glanced up, realizing the others were readying to leave. "Oh, I'll just, you know." She nodded toward the stalls. "Then I'll be right out."

They smiled, sure they'd done their duty, then headed back out to their dinner. Sadie couldn't have felt less like eating.

As the sound of their chatter faded, she closed herself in a stall, leaning heavily against the inside of the door. Her mind raced, frantically counting out the days she'd been in Black Hills, the number of days since she'd first seen Zach again. Finally, the number of days since they'd made love that first time.

Please. Could she please just stop thinking? Stop remembering? But it was no use. She didn't have experience with pregnancy herself and had never been around anyone who was having a baby. Her time with Christina was as close as she'd gotten.

Which wasn't much. But based on how off she'd felt the last few weeks—something she'd chalked up to guilt, nerves and grief—Sadie was afraid she'd added one very large complication to her already tangled situation.

Heaven help her.

* * *

Zach lengthened his stride, hoping to make it through the foyer before Gladys heard the door close behind him. He didn't have long before he had to be at the office. KC was helping him get their newest team member settled in town. They were signing the paperwork on his new apartment before she brought him by the office for the first time.

Zach needed to be there.

But he was worried about Sadie. She'd gone home early from the dinner the night before, afraid she'd come down with a stomach bug. She'd even insisted on taking a cab home, expressing concern about interrupting the event and also about infecting him.

He'd let her go, only after she'd promised to text when she got back to the B and B. There were still things they didn't know about each other—for all he knew, she was the type who wanted to be left alone when she was sick. Like him.

She'd texted him when she got back and had even mentioned that she'd stopped at the pharmacy for some meds to help calm her stomach. He hadn't heard from her since.

A quick peek to assure himself that she was okay would be enough for now.

But later, they needed to have a talk. Zach was perfectly happy to let her be, as long as she touched base every so often to let him know she was okay. Preferably from the other end of the room, rather than the other end of town.

Otherwise, those dang protective instincts kicked in, and he worried something had happened—

Zach paused outside Sadie's door, hand raised to knock. The contrast between what he wanted with Sadie and what he had with her hit him hard. He'd proceeded on tiptoes, not demanding too much too soon, not asking for what he truly needed, afraid that if he pushed too hard, she would leave again.

Maybe he'd been overcautious. They were practically living together, and yet he'd let her go home sick without him the night before. He stood outside her door right now, waiting to knock, because he didn't want to intrude. How ridiculously careful all of this was.

With a frown, Zach tried the doorknob. It clicked, then opened. He walked inside. It was that easy.

Glancing around, he was alarmed to see the bed empty, blankets half hanging off the side, as if they had trailed after the person trying to leave them behind. No Sadie in sight. He heard the shower running.

Okay. She was steady enough to want to shower. Good deal. He'd just wait until she got out. After making sure she didn't need anything, he'd head over to the office for a while, then come back. He crossed to the bed to straighten up the covers. A tissue box and mound of crumpled, used tissues covered the nightstand.

Odd, she'd said her stomach hurt, not that she had a cold.

Once more he looked around, this time hunting for the small trash can he knew to be around here somewhere. He finally located it under the low table in the sitting area. It was already filled with tissues. That explained one thing, at least. As he stood there wondering if he should risk calling Gladys for a new trash bag, Sadie's phone lit up.

An incoming text message.

He didn't recognize the name Victor Beddingfield, but the preview of the message on the screen below the name made Zach do a double take.

Hell no, I don't care what happens to Zach Gatlin, as long as he doesn't show up here wanting…

Wanting what? And why was this stranger texting about him?

The mere use of his name gave Zach the right to pick up that phone, in his opinion. And right now, his was the only opinion that mattered. He swiped his thumb over the screen. Zach only wished he could honestly say he didn't know Sadie's combination to unlock the screen. Unfortunately, it was a connect-the-dots picture that he'd watched her swipe in many times. The order of the combination played out in his mind's eye with ease.

He didn't even hesitate.

As a soldier, Zach knew that doing ugly things was sometimes necessary to get the job done. Right now, breaking into Sadie's phone was one of those necessary things. Regardless of how other people would see it.

A violation of her privacy? Sure. Overstepping his boundaries? Definitely. A decision he'd regret in time? Absolutely not.

Zach would rather know the truth than live in a fantasy world. The phone blinked its notice that Sadie had a text message at the bottom. He clicked on it and saw the truth in full color.

At the top of the screen, there was a text from Sadie in a white bubble: I will call soon.

Then a blue bubble from Beddingfield: If you don't call me within the hour, this is gonna get really ugly. I want this over. Do you hear me?

Followed by Sadie's response: Don't you care at all what happens to Zach? I'm trying very hard to do the right thing.

Hell no, I don't care what happens to Zach Gatlin, as long as he doesn't show up here wanting our father's money. You said you would dig up the dirt and I want it now. If you have to lie to disqualify him, that's what you'll do. I make the rules here. You simply obey me.

Deep in Zach's chest, coldness bloomed, then spread. Questions whirled in his brain. First and foremost: Who was this person? And what did he mean by "our father"? Was Victor Sadie's brother, talking about the two of them when he said "our"? But they had different last names.

Or was he Zach's brother?

Zach didn't know his father, so half or stepbrothers were definitely a possibility. Though the fact that his father would want to have other children when he couldn't be bothered to care for the one he already had was hard to take.

The second line of thought was the more painful one. He didn't even want to think about it. Didn't want to form the words that would rip apart the foundation he'd thought he was standing on for the last two months. But as the water shut off in the bathroom, he knew the detonation was coming.

The phone was still in his hand. He didn't bother to put it down, didn't bother to move. By the time Sadie came through the door, he'd even stopped breathing. That cold, cold part of him wanted to thaw, wanted to go to her.

Her long auburn hair was piled in a messy bun atop her head. She looked tired, her features slightly drawn. Her naked body was wrapped in one of the fluffy towels he'd often used to dry her. When she saw him, her eyes widened, but then she produced a small smile.

"Zach, you startled me," she said. "I didn't know you were coming."

Before he could speak, the phone in his hand rang. Her gaze flicked down to it, alarm invading her expression when she saw it in his hand. It played through an entire ringtone, then went silent. Zach's fingers tightened. Almost immediately the ringing started again.

Zach reached out, offering the phone to her. "Beddingfield wants an answer to his question," he said. "Don't you think you should take his call?"

Fifteen

The fact that she could take the phone from Zach's hand and switch it to mute actually amazed Sadie. Her body shook so hard she wouldn't have thought the move was even possible.

But she did it. Because she had to—because she deserved whatever Zach was about to dish out.

But she'd rather not do it in just a towel.

Turning away, she dropped the phone on the bed and reached for her robe. She hadn't even gotten it over her shoulders before Zach's questions started. She was actually surprised he'd waited at all.

"Who is Victor Beddingfield? Your brother? Your lover? Your what? Employer?"

Sadie's stomach turned, this time from more than just the pregnancy she'd confirmed after a stop at the drugstore last night. She couldn't think of that now. Luckily, she hadn't eaten, so there wasn't anything to come up.

"Tell me now, Sadie."

She absorbed the blow of the staccato words as she tied the robe's belt around her waist. Then she faced Zach, attempting to keep her expression blank.

"Victor is my current—temporary—employer."

As if her calm answer infuriated him, Zach spoke next through gritted teeth. "And what the hell does he have to do with me?"

She slowly drew in a breath before answering. "He's your half brother."

Should she say more? This was one reason why she'd put off this moment—there were no guidelines telling her how much or how little information she should give to the man that she'd lied to for two months...no, five years.

"That doesn't tell me what he wants with me." Zach's harsh expression didn't give her any clues or guidance as to how to proceed.

Okay, here goes... "Your father recently passed away." She paused to give him a moment to absorb that, but his expression only grew harder. "There is a rather, um, large inheritance."

"Then this Beddingfield should take it and leave me alone. My father never wanted anything to do with me. Why would I want his money now?"

That wasn't technically true, but Sadie wasn't going to explain that his father had sent her before. At least, not now.

"It isn't that easy," she said instead. "Victor can't inherit your father's estate because it has been willed to you."

Zach frowned, but didn't say anything.

"On one condition."

Then his gaze flipped to her phone on the bed before returning to her face. "The dirt?"

Reluctantly, she nodded. "You've been selected to receive the bulk of your father's estate, provided you haven't been immoral or corrupt in any way. There can be no arrests, convictions, scandals or incidents showing distinct lack of character in your—" she had to swallow "—history. Your father wanted to reward you for being a better man than he was."

"That's ridiculous."

Sadie shrugged. "Mr. Beddingfield played by his own set of rules."

"So you're, what, here to spy on me?"

Leave it to Zach to get to the heart of the matter.

"Wait. Were you here to spy on me before, too?"

Straight to the heart. "Yes." Why prevaricate? He was going to hate her anyway. She might as well cut the ties cleanly, even if the frost encasing her heart was starting to bite. "Your father sent me the first time." She could go into details later, if necessary. "Victor sent me this time—"

"To find out the truth? Or to make up some plausible lies?"

"Victor doesn't really care either way."

"He made that clear."

"But I can assure you, I'll be telling your father's lawyer the truth."

She couldn't stop herself from flinching as Zach stalked to her. He seemed to grow larger and more menacing as rage lit his features. "You know nothing about the truth. You've lied to me from the beginning, haven't you?"

"Not about the things that matter."

Rage mutated into disgust. "I doubt you have any idea what matters to me. None at all."

Oh, but she did. He valued family, loyalty, honesty, compassion, helping hands and going the extra mile. He was everything Victor wasn't. With each thing she'd learned about Zach, Sadie had known she fought a losing battle for his heart.

Because the core of her mission was the opposite of everything he held dear.

Only she couldn't turn away from these few weeks of pure bliss. That had been selfish on her part—indecisive, too. But she couldn't change it—not her choices, nor what had pushed her into those choices.

But she wasn't making excuses or asking forgiveness. She didn't deserve it.

"I'm sorry, Zach." It was as far as she could let herself go. Anything more and she'd fall to her knees right here, begging for the one thing he would never give her now: his love.

She expected him to let loose that rage on her. To rant or throw things or scream. His father would have. His half brother certainly would have.

Zach did none of that.

Instead he turned and stalked to the door. He was probably done with her. But despite her resolutions, she found she couldn't keep one thing inside. The one thing he deserved to know.

"But I do have one last thing to say, Zach. And I mean it with everything in me. That you are a good man."

He paused before the door but didn't turn around, didn't grant her one last glimpse of a face carved in stone. Instead he said, "Pardon me if that offers very little consolation."

She was sure it didn't.

* * *

Somehow, some way, Zach managed to get through what he absolutely had to that afternoon without exploding, and then he ditched the rest of his appointments. His car ate up the miles to the airport. His only thought was of running, fast and far, but where—he didn't know.

The cabin wasn't an option right now. The memories were too fresh, would be too painful. Only now did he regret taking Sadie there, because even a complete makeover would never erase her presence in what had once been his sanctuary.

Anger had him pressing on the gas that much harder. He was anxious for speed even though it wouldn't really help anything. That's when his phone dinged to signal an incoming text.

Sadie. He knew it before he even looked. His instinct was to hurl the phone out the window, but that would be giving in too easily, so he forced himself to pull over and read the text instead.

I've gone home. The room at the B&B is paid thru end of week. Left some of ur things on table and some important papers for you. I'm so sorry. S

Zach let his eyes slide closed. He didn't want to see the screen, didn't want to read about how sorry she was. If she'd been sorry, she never would have lied to him. Hell, she never would have come here. Why would she do something so incredibly dishonest?

No, he didn't want to know. Motive didn't matter, because he refused to feel sorry for someone who would go to so much trouble to integrate herself into his life, his bed, just to find out if he was a bad person.

And who was his dad to judge? That man had never

done anything good in his entire life. He'd abandoned Zach's mother when he was little, simply vanished, never paying a lick of child support or sending so much as a single birthday present or Christmas gift. They'd been okay. They'd made it without the old SOB. But that seemed to make the terms of his will even more ironic.

There had to be more to the story than what Sadie had told him.

Some important papers for you.

Dammit. He spun the car into a U-turn and headed back into town. No matter what he told himself, he really did want to know what was going on.

He flashed a strained smile at Gladys when she glanced out at him from the dining area as he made his way through, but didn't speak. Neither did she. Did she realize Sadie was gone? Or had Sadie simply left without saying anything so Zach would have a chance to come by and collect his stuff without Gladys's interference? He didn't know what to think anymore.

He let himself into the room, noticing Sadie's absence at once. The low table no longer held her laptop, just a pile of odds and ends. Her robe wasn't thrown over the high back of the winged chair near the dresser. Her extra fluffy blanket no longer graced her side of the queen-size bed.

But her vanilla-caramel scent still lingered in the air. Tantalizing, but also a reminder of how deceptive that sweetness truly was.

Zach dropped onto the couch in front of his stuff. A T-shirt he'd left here. A toiletry bag with an extra toothbrush and deodorant and things for his overnight stays. His black leather belt. He wished now that there hadn't been so many nights, that she hadn't made it so easy.

Next to the pile was a manila envelope. Zach stared

for a long time before he made himself reach out and open it. The quality of the fax wasn't the best, but it was still readable. The time stamp along the top showed she'd had this sent not long after their talk this afternoon.

The letterhead was from a lawyer's office in Dallas. The text below explained that this lawyer was in the process of executing Zach's father's last will and testament. Based on his father's unusual requests, adequate time had been given to search every avenue necessary. If Zach had any questions, he was welcome to call them for explanations.

Should he wish to refuse his inheritance, there were instructions on how to do that and what that would mean for him in terms of future claims. The exact sum wasn't mentioned, but Zach was guessing it was significant for a lawyer to have been hired to set up something this elaborate.

The lawyer seemed like a man who knew what he was doing. Zach planned to reserve judgment until he had experience with the guy himself.

The envelope also contained what looked like legal papers that Zach would look over in more depth later. There was a photograph of a man Zach assumed to be his father. It was blurred with age. But Zach wasn't that interested in the picture; he'd put his father out of his mind long ago. After all, his father hadn't been willing to think about Zach or his mother when he'd left them. Zach had been four at the time.

There was a professional bio. From what Zach read, his father had hit oil when he'd traveled to Texas a couple of years after abandoning them. Of course, he hadn't looked back to the family he'd left behind. Zach's mother had worked her fingers to the bone to provide for him, and later KC. She'd deserved better than that.

As if she'd known he would be curious, Sadie had printed an article about his father's stroke and how it had affected his company. Apparently he was well-known in the Dallas area. Zach scanned it and moved on to the next piece. It was another photo, this one of a younger man with distinct features matching his father's. This one was labeled Victor Beddingfield.

Zach couldn't help it—he studied the picture for any resemblance to his half brother. There were a few. Zach certainly hoped he didn't share the petulant expression and self-indulgent softness that didn't sit well on an adult male.

All in all, the envelope contained straightforward information that Zach could take or leave. It all depended on his plans. He put the papers back. He could find out pretty much everything he needed to know about the players in this game at his office, now that he knew where to start.

This time, he wasn't about to hesitate to dig hard and deep.

Standing, he loaded his arms with everything that belonged to him. He had no intention of leaving anything of himself in this place. As he moved toward the door, he remembered another time, the first time, when he'd faced the same choice. He'd had the chance to exit and never look back, but the lure of Sadie had been too strong.

He glanced toward the bed. The same one that had tempted him that first night here. Memories of nights wrapped around Sadie under those covers made him ache with a mixture of desire, sadness and anger. He wasn't sure if he'd ever get over that. Maybe one day he would. Maybe one day he wouldn't think of her at all, and he could live the rest of his life without thinking her name or remembering her face.

Maybe one day.

As he turned toward the door, a glimpse of something that didn't belong flashed in his periphery. Something neglected on the floor between the antique nightstand and the bed. Zach should leave it. After all, the odds of it being his were slim.

Still, his feet carried him forward, and he cursed himself the entire way for caring that she might have left something of herself behind.

He shifted his load into one arm then bent low and patted around for whatever it was. Finally his fingers brushed against something hard. Long and rounded, it fit easily in his hand as he picked it up.

Zach glanced down as he stood, then totally wished he hadn't.

His mind flashed back to another day. One when he found his sister crying all alone at the bar, late at night after everyone had left. In her hand was an identical white plastic stick with a plastic cap on the end. There were two solid pink lines in the little window in the middle. He dropped onto the bed, and wondered if this day could get any worse.

Sixteen

Sadie quietly let herself into her apartment early the next morning, her body beyond tired. Sitting at the airport on standby was hellish on a good day. Yesterday had been almost unbearable.

She set down her luggage and made her way down the hall into the living area. Maybe she could catch a few winks before her mother woke up to get ready to go to the treatment center to see her sister. How in the world Sadie would explain to either of them what had happened was beyond her at the moment.

Zach hadn't been the only person she'd lied to. Despite their desperate need, Sadie had known her mother and sister would have never condoned her cooperation with Victor's diabolical plan to disqualify Zach from his inheritance. So she'd told them the same story: that their former employer had gifted her with the trip of her dreams to explore her photography.

Now she had to find a way to tell them the truth.

As she came into the spacious room, she saw her mother sleeping on the overstuffed couch. Sadie frowned, worried for a moment that something had happened. Or maybe her mother had fallen asleep waiting for her to arrive. But a soft sound drew her gaze in the other direction, where she found her sister propped in the recliner Sadie kept angled toward the line of windows along the front of the room.

But her sister wasn't watching the early-morning sun as it lit up the rolling lawns of the Beddingfield estate. Instead her gaze met Sadie's. Tears stung Sadie's nose and eyes as her sister gifted her with a weak smile of welcome.

Quickly crossing the room, she bent over and carefully pulled Amber close. She still had an IV attached to keep her from dehydrating. But otherwise she was awake, and the staff must have thought her well enough to come home for a while.

Bending down, she met her sister's eyes, green like her own, and whispered, "When did you get here?"

Amber grinned, though she didn't lift her head from where it rested on the chair. "Just yesterday. We were gonna Skype you last night, but when you called to say you were coming home we decided to surprise you."

"Well, I definitely am."

Her sister's thin hair had been cropped close, leaving a pale auburn halo of curls that highlighted the too-prominent cheekbones in her pale face. Sadie brushed her fingers over the softness. "How are you, kiddo?"

"My white blood count is closer to normal, for now. Electrolytes are good. And I tolerated this latest round of treatments better than they expected, so I got to come home a few days early."

"That's great."

"She's getting stronger," their mother said. Sadie glanced over at her; she hadn't moved but had opened her eyes to watch her daughters. "The doctors are quite pleased."

"I bet."

Any improvement in Amber's condition was considered wonderful at this stage. Their goal now was to halt the deterioration from the disease and keep her as pain-free as possible, without the disorientation and fatigue that could come from the wrong drug combinations.

"I'm so glad you're home," Amber said, reaching out to squeeze Sadie's hand.

The chill from her sister's skin always startled Sadie. She reached up with her other hand, creating a little sandwich pocket in an effort to warm the cold fingers with her own. It never seemed to help, but Amber told her it felt good, so Sadie had formed the habit over time.

"And just why are you home?" her mother asked.

Her tone said she knew something was up. Not that Sadie was very good at hiding things. Or maybe she was too good, since she'd been able to deceive Zach for so long. "It was time," she said simply.

It was more than time to cut the ties. Maybe Zach seeing that text was for the best, even though her breaking heart didn't think so. If it had been up to her, she inevitably would have delayed. And then where would she be?

She pressed her sister's hand a little more tightly. "You rest a bit. I'll fix you some tea," she said.

"That would be good." But Amber didn't close her eyes. Instead she turned back to gaze out the window. She'd often told Sadie that she slept enough at the treatment center, pumped up on pain meds and other drugs.

When she was home, she wanted to experience life, even if it was only through the window of their apartment.

Trying hard not to let a new wave of tears overwhelm her, Sadie retraced her steps down the hall to the kitchen. As expected, Sadie's mother joined her.

"For someone who has just been on the trip of their dreams, you do not look like you had a very restful time," her mother said quietly.

Sadie appreciated her mother's attempt to keep Amber from hearing her.

"That's because I lied," she said, figuring the straightforward approach was probably best.

There was no shock from her mother, only an understanding nod. "I see."

Why did life have to be so hard? "I did a very bad thing, Mom."

"I'm sure you did."

Sadie glanced over in surprise, spilling a bit of water over the edge of the electric kettle. "What? Why would you think that?"

"Sadie," she said with a sad shake of her head, "when was Mr. Beddingfield ever involved in anything good? Yes, he might have changed his perspective somewhat on his deathbed, but that man never did something only from goodness. There was always an ulterior motive."

Ulterior motive indeed. "Mr. Beddingfield didn't send me on this trip. Victor did."

Her mother's eyes widened. "Yes, I can see why you didn't share that with me. There is nothing benevolent in that man. I was surprised to even come home to find our stuff still here yesterday. I couldn't figure out why he hasn't made us leave the estate yet."

"It was part of our agreement," Sadie confessed.

Then she went on to tell her mother the how and why

of her trip back to Black Hills, South Carolina. About halfway through she looked away, unable to bear what was sure to be her mother's disappointment in her. She managed to keep the tears at bay until she mentioned the baby she was now sure she carried.

The silence of several minutes was only broken by the release of steam from the kettle. Sadie couldn't bring herself to steep her sister's tea. Instead she remained with her arms braced against the counter, praying that the pain in her heart would ease enough to let her breathe again.

"So this man, Zach, will we be seeing him again?" her mother asked.

Sadie nodded. "I'll have to tell him about the baby, but it was so new, I just…couldn't." A deep breath braced her for her latest decision. "I will contact him soon enough, but I want to be established in a new job, a new place to live. I just couldn't bear to give him the impression that I told him about the baby to get some of his money."

"But Sadie, how will we afford—"

"I don't know. We just will. Somehow." But she knew beyond a doubt she couldn't face asking Zach for money. She wasn't even sure she would be able to take it if he offered. So much of this whole situation had been motivated by her struggles to simply keep their heads above water.

But other people would only see it as greed.

"We will figure something out," she assured her mother with a false smile. "I'll start looking for another job today. One thing—the only good thing—Mr. Beddingfield did was to safeguard me against any attempt Victor made to discredit me. I have a certified reference from him, with his lawyer's signature as witness. That will at least give me a place to start."

Some of the strain on her mother's face eased. "Yes, it will help. I could look for something—"

"Absolutely not." They'd had this discussion time and again. "Amber needs you with her. We both know that. I'll fix this, somehow."

Even if the solution was a complete and total mystery to her right now.

Zach took a seat in the substantial waiting area at the offices of Beddingfield's lawyer, Timberlake. Apparently, Beddingfield Senior had been a big man in town, and he'd paid for the best in everything. Including lawyers.

Zach couldn't bring himself to think of the man as his father. He'd contributed DNA, but that was about it.

Except now, after his death, he was about to gift Zach with a fortune that still boggled his mind, according to his phone conversations with the lawyer. Beddingfield hadn't just hit it big in the oil business after coming to Texas, he'd then diversified, which had protected his assets from market fluctuations and downturns. Zach would be in a tax bracket far removed from the one he'd moved into after opening his own business. The thought was so far outside reality that he'd stopped trying to comprehend it.

But in terms of the man who'd sired him—it was a case of too little, too late.

Zach had chosen to make an impromptu trip to Dallas before telling his family all that had transpired. He preferred to have all the facts at hand first.

Besides, his sister had become increasingly curious about Sadie, not buying Zach's excuse that she'd returned home for a family emergency. Of course, after his investigation into her history, that excuse might not have been as far from reality as he'd thought when he made it up.

Sadie had told the truth about some things. This time around, Zach hadn't held back, using all the resources at his disposal when it came to investigating her. She'd used her real name. According to her tax records, she'd indeed been an employee of Beddingfield Senior for several years. And her mother had held the same position for the same employer until the year Sadie took over. Her mother had no employment records since then.

The few things Zach had been able to find out about Sadie's younger sister's illness had confirmed what he knew: she'd been ill a very long time and her prognosis was terminal.

The most eye-opening portion of his investigation had been his inquiries into Sadie's finances. That's when he'd started to feel dirty. She didn't have the usual expenses of a woman her age. No apartment or housing loan. No car loan, either. Two maxed-out credit cards that hadn't had any activity recorded in two years, other than payments. And astronomical debts to several medical institutions in the Dallas area.

Sadie was apparently financially responsible for all of her sister's medical bills.

As much as Zach didn't condone lying and dishonesty, factoring Beddingfield's huge fortune into Sadie's crippling financial situation didn't add up to a woman spying on him on a whim. He wanted more information before he confronted her about the little bombshell he'd discovered at the B and B after she left.

Feeling restless, as thoughts about Sadie often made him, Zach stood up. He prowled around the empty area for several minutes before coming to a stop in front of a long bank of windows overlooking busy traffic on the streets below. Coming to the office at the end of the day, he'd known he would wait for an extended period of time. Probably until after Timberlake's last client left.

But he'd see Zach—the man about to take the place of his, and his firm's, biggest client.

Zach heard a rumble down the hallway, the sound of a raised voice behind a closed door. He glanced over at the receptionist, who looked uneasily toward the glass wall behind her. When she noticed him watching, she flashed a strained smile and pretended to get back to work.

The rumble increased, and Zach realized other voices had joined the fray. One of the lawyers must have a very unhappy client. Just as a door in the back hallway opened, the receptionist's phone rang. She answered with a clipped, "Yes, sir." Then she immediately hung up and redialed. "We need assistance on floor four near the conference room, please," she said in a slightly raised voice.

The commotion in the hallway got louder. Zach wasn't sure what was happening but decided to offer his assistance regardless until security could arrive. Just as he reached the receptionist's desk, a man's voice rang out.

"I will get you for this. You will never work in this city again, you hear me! Not only will you not see a dime from me, but I'll see to it that you'll never find a way to support that dying brat, either."

The sound of men's voices protesting and the shuffling of dress shoes carried through to the reception area. One was louder than the rest. "Mr. Beddingfield, stop right now. There's nothing to be gained by this behavior."

"There's nothing to be gained by me being a Goody Two-shoes, either. This bitch just cut me off from my inheritance. She's gonna pay."

The elevator dinged as the doors opened, heralding

the arrival of two security guards. But the raucous group in the hallway now appeared around the corner, plainly visible through the glass wall behind the receptionist.

Zach saw Sadie jump backward just as a male hand grabbed for her. A sharp cry rang out. The men around her dropped their polite facades. Yelling commenced as they tried to force Victor Beddingfield back. The security guards waded into the fray, quickly subduing the man Zach now knew was his half brother. He watched as they cuffed the tall man, whose blond good looks made him Zach's polar opposite.

As did his spoiled attitude.

A stocky, gray-haired man guided Sadie back with an arm around her shoulders. For the first time in a month he glimpsed her wealth of auburn hair and full features through the wavy glass. He couldn't make out her expression with precision, except to tell that her lips were pulled into a frown. By the time he looked back at Victor, the security guards were leading him back down the hallway.

A few low words were exchanged with the other two gentlemen, then one broke away and followed the guards. After a few minutes, the gray-haired man led Sadie around the opposite side of the glass wall and over to the elevator bank.

They never even glanced in Zach's direction.

"Thank you again, Ms. Adams, for coming in to give your deposition. I'm very, very sorry for the commotion. I have no idea how Mr. Beddingfield found out you would be here today."

Sadie shook her head, but Zach could see that her hand remained clasped over the front of her throat. Her arms were pressed close against her torso. "No, it's not your fault. I just hope I've done what I can to make sure y'all know the truth about Zachary Gatlin."

An electric pulse set Zach on edge as he heard his name on her lips. He knew it shouldn't affect him—or rather, he shouldn't let it affect him. But he was a man who'd been in love, after all.

He stood quietly as the two finished their conversation. The lawyer, whom Zach now knew to be Timberlake, delivered her carefully into the elevator, as if worried about any lasting effects from the confrontation. Only as she faced the reception area once more did she glance beyond where the lawyer stood.

Her eyes widened in surprise just as the doors slid closed.

Seventeen

"Will she?"

"Pardon me?" The lawyer's confused look confirmed Zach had spoken out loud, even though he hadn't intended to.

"Will Sadie be able to support her sister? Or will Beddingfield be able to keep her from getting work?"

The confusion cleared. "Oh, no. He won't be able to poison future employers against her—I drafted your father's reference letter for Ms. Adams myself. Plus, she has a good reputation with the people who have visited his home over the years. She'll be fine, professionally."

Zach sensed something more. "But?"

"I'm afraid I don't know of a job in her field that will pay enough to take care of the medical bills."

Zach knew about that all too well.

Timberlake leaned forward, his expression earnest. After their conversations over the phone, Zach had found him to be someone he felt pretty comfortable with. The man's motives seemed straightforward.

"I wouldn't normally say this," he started, "but I know you've met Sadie personally. The deposition she gave is proof of that."

"Was it now?"

"The contents will be made public in court, but yes, she was very clear about your values, your family and the respect you have from your business associates. She explained in detail her efforts and inability to find any complaints against you or any criminal activity."

Zach hadn't realized that she would be so thorough in her report.

The lawyer went on. "I wonder if you know what a gift that is?"

Zach raised his brows in question.

"She didn't have to do that. She could easily have lied. If she had, she'd have been set for life."

What? "I don't understand."

"She confided to me, when she first came in, that Victor Beddingfield had offered her a quarter of the inheritance if she could find anything that would disqualify you. That money would have more than paid for her sister's treatments. Sadie would never have had to work again."

That was the truth. From everything he'd seen, a quarter of the inheritance, even after exorbitant estate taxes, would still be a fortune. A fortune Sadie desperately needed.

"But she never spoke against me?"

Timberlake shook his head. "Not a word." His gaze met Zach's directly. "Look, I'm not telling you this because I expect anything. I'm going to connect Sadie with some organizations that might be able to help her with her sister's treatments from here on out. But once you have that debt, it often can't be wiped away…at least not in any way that Sadie would accept."

The lawyer smiled sadly. "I could tell from the way she spoke that Sadie is not neutral in your case." He raised his hands. "I don't know what happened, and I don't care. But I think she should at least get credit for trying to do the right thing—in the end."

Could he do the same? Zach wasn't sure. He wanted to, and Lord knew he and Sadie had one more major hurdle to cross before their future was decided. He would never be able to leave the mother of his child behind completely. And he wasn't enough of an asshole to cut her out of their lives, even if that had been his first instinct.

Everyone made bad decisions when they were angry.

"There's something else," the lawyer said. The curiosity in his eyes making Zach just a little nervous.

"Yes?"

"Sadie has asked me to contact a family named Blackstone, and see that the pictures she took in Black Hills were copyrighted to them to do with as they wish."

Holy hell.

"She also provided the name of a publisher who was interested in the story."

Why? Zach thought back to that pregnancy test and tried to imagine how she must have felt when she took it. She could have been elated…could have imagined all of her problems were fixed with the luck of the draw. After all, one DNA test and he would be legally liable for at least child support. With the inheritance he had coming, she could probably have jockeyed for a lot more than that. But if that were so, why would she have subjected herself to Beddingfield and having to give her deposition alone? Given up the rights to pictures that he knew meant more to her than the money?

One phone call to Zach could have put her on top of the world instead of the bottom rung. One call she'd refused to make to save herself from a lot of worry and fears.

But was this proof enough that he could trust her?

A quick change into clean clothes had helped Sadie feel more in control after her ugly experience with Victor at the lawyer's office. But she also felt an increased need to get them packed and out of the apartment over Mr. Beddingfield's renovated horse barn.

A need that rose exponentially after realizing Zach was now in town.

She could have gone back into the office, could have asked what he'd seen and heard and tried to defend herself against any ugly things Victor might tell him about her. But what was the point?

Zach already had enough ammunition to blast her out of his life. Anything more would just be overkill.

Still, she needed to get her family moved. The probate of the will would be moving forward, and hopefully one of the interviews she'd had over the last week would pan out for a new job. She'd found a medical halfway house that would let her mother and sister stay temporarily while Sadie arranged for a new place. All the apartments on the cheap end had been scary, but with her credit, something small in a bad neighborhood was the best she could do.

If her luck turned around, her new position would also offer living accommodations, or at least a supplement toward her rent. Fingers crossed on that one.

She moved down the hall to her sister's bedroom,

stepping into the circle of cardboard boxes and packing tape and scissors she'd left there earlier. She'd splurged by hiring a mover, simply because her mother was completely unable to lift anything. Moving furniture alone wasn't an option, but Sadie wanted to pack all of the keepsakes and items with sentimental value herself.

The sun had completely disappeared by the time a knock sounded on the apartment door. She must have lost track of time, moving from her sister's bedroom to her own. The five full boxes now standing in the hallway attested to her progress.

The knock sounded again as she crossed the kitchen into the hallway. "I'm coming," she hollered, wondering if it was one of the staff from the big house.

Even though she wasn't technically employed anymore, they still showed up to ask her questions about various things. With that in mind, she flung the door open without thinking…and came face-to-face with Zachary Gatlin.

Panicked, she turned on her heel and strode back to the kitchen. Her quick steps took her all the way to the other side of the kitchen island. Only when she was facing the door with something solid between them did she feel a little more secure.

And slightly stupid for her reaction.

As he came through the door, words started to tumble out of her mouth. "Zach, I want to assure you we are in the process of moving. I've gotten everything arranged and we will be out—"

"Shush."

Sadie felt her eyes bug out a little at his harsh tone, though she wasn't sure why. It was nothing more than what she'd expected. "I just didn't want you to think—" she spotted his glare, but couldn't seem to stop "—we were…taking…advantage…now that you own the estate."

"Well, it's a little early in the process, but I will be looking into the estate and how it is run pretty soon." Zach spoke a little more mildly this time. "Still, I don't believe I said anything about you leaving."

"I just assumed…"

His raised brow told her exactly what he thought of that.

Maybe he was right. She should just shush. Everything she said right now was coming out wrong.

"Do you know why I'm here, Sadie?"

"Apparently it's not to throw me out of what is now your apartment."

He simply stared. "Sarcasm isn't pretty."

No, but it was her go-to option in this bizarre situation that she was completely unprepared for. Unless she chose honesty—and that was a scary thought. "No, Zach. I really don't know why you would want to see me."

He took a step closer to the island. "No reason at all?"

Sure—if he knew about the baby. But he didn't, and she wasn't ready to tell him yet. She would later, after everything was settled. "After what I did to you, Zach? No."

"The lawyer told me about your deposition."

Shock shot through her. That was the last thing on her mind. "Oh. I thought it would be kept private until the hearing."

Zach shrugged. "Does it really matter when I learn what's in it?"

"I guess not," she murmured, though she wished he hadn't learned about it while she was here. She could have done without a face-to-face discussion.

"And about the photos. Why, Sadie?"

Then his tone caught her attention.

She simply couldn't meet his gaze. "It's not right for me to keep them, not after…"

"You lied to me, Sadie."

"Yes, yes, I did," she said, dropping her gaze to the countertop. "I'm sorry, but I did lie to you." What more could she say?

"Why?"

This was exactly what she didn't want. She shook her head. "Zach, excuses won't change it."

"Try me."

She straightened her shoulders but still couldn't force herself to look at him. "The first time, I didn't know you."

"But then you did."

Why torture herself by admitting the truth? Why torture him? But with him standing so close, yet so far out of her reach, her need prodded her. He deserved the truth—the whole thing. "I did know you," she said, though her voice was so weak as to be almost nonexistent. "And it scared me so badly, all I knew to do was run."

"Five years, Sadie." The pure anguish in his voice twisted her heart. One look confirmed the same emotion in his expression. "Why didn't you come back to me?"

His cry echoed inside her, forcing her reality into words. "Why would a man like you want a woman with all my problems?" She grasped the edge of the counter until her knuckles turned white and her fingers went numb. "I'm sure the lawyer must have told you—the real me is nothing like that Sadie."

"She's not?" His voice softened. "Are you sure?"

"Yes." *Most definitely.*

He moved closer until he was flush with the other

side of the counter. They were as close as they could be in this space. "I'm not sure, Sadie. Because the woman I knew was compassionate and interested in people. Organized and hardworking. Artistic and able to see the beauty in the world, even in the midst of destruction."

Tears welled up, forcing her to squeeze her eyes closed.

"Isn't that the same as what you do here? Take on a hard job at a young age so your mother can stay home with your sister? Care about the people you meet in your job every day? Worry about your mother being tired, even though you're the one on your feet for twelve hours? Teach your sister to appreciate the world around her, even though she's dying? Sounds like the same Sadie to me."

She couldn't stop the tears. They dribbled down her cheeks without her permission.

"But she's also prideful."

Her lashes automatically lifted, her gaze connecting with his. "What?"

"Sadie only wants to be the caregiver, not the receiver."

So? "Doesn't everyone?"

"No." Zach's dark eyes offered compassion, but he didn't back down. "Lots of people want their dirty jobs done for them. They ignore the hard parts of life. You power through them."

"That's a problem?" she asked.

"Only when it makes you blind to other people's desire to help care for you." He leaned forward over the island between them. "It took me five long years to become vulnerable to you, Sadie. Don't you think I deserved the same?"

She took a step back, needing space, needing to

breathe. "But me being vulnerable, opening up to you would have placed an obligation on you. A demand, even if it was unspoken, for you to take care of me and my problems."

"It's never an obligation when you love someone."

That took her breath away. "I've never had someone love me that way," she murmured.

"Haven't you?"

That dark gaze wouldn't let her look away, wouldn't let her pretend to not see the truth. "Yes."

Silence stood between them for long minutes, almost as if the world held its breath, waiting to see what came next. Sadie wasn't sure what it was.

Finally Zach spoke. "I want you to do something for me, okay?"

She nodded, not trusting herself to speak.

"When you're ready, truly ready, for me to love you that way…you let me know. Okay?"

A tremble started deep inside. What he asked seemed like almost too much.

"Okay?"

She could barely get the word out. "Yes."

"Goodbye, Sadie."

Her whole body screamed in protest, but she kept her lips sealed as he walked away. She could hear his footsteps down the hallway, then the click as he opened the door.

"Wait. Zach," she called, then forced her timid feet to follow him. She paused a few feet away from where he waited by the front door. "I—I know I disappointed you." She swallowed at the lump trying to form in her throat. "But there's something you need to know. You can't leave without knowing…two things, actually."

He nodded, but didn't encourage her by word or any further gesture.

"One is... I love you. I'll always be glad that I experienced loving you, even though I screwed it up so badly."

His expression didn't change, and she died a little inside. But this had to be done.

"And two?" he asked.

She almost couldn't say it, almost told him to leave, but that was as selfish as every choice she'd made up until now. "Two is—I'm pregnant."

"I know."

"I don't want you to feel obligated—wait, what?"

Now she detected a touch of amusement in his voice. "I already know."

And from his softening expression, she knew he accepted it. "How?" she breathed.

Very gently, he closed the door. "You dropped the test. I found it when I went to get my things."

Sadie groaned, collapsing with her back to the wall. "Oh, goodness. I was putting it back in the box to bring home with me. I knew if I threw it away there—"

"Miss Gladys would have found it and the whole town would know, not just me?"

"Right." She opened her eyes to find him right in front of her. "I was trying to figure out how to tell you without making you feel..."

"Obligated?"

She nodded. "And I knew I couldn't do that with you looking at me, touching me. So I thought it was better to wait." She offered a halfhearted smile. "After what happened between KC and Jake, I couldn't keep your child from you. I wouldn't do that, Zach."

"I know that now."

"You do? How?"

"You just showed me. Thank you for trusting me with the truth, Sadie."

"So you aren't angry?"

He shook his head, stepping in until they stood body to body. "I'm not angry. We have a lot of things to work out, and I think we will both have to learn to let someone else take care of us, instead of always being the strong one." He brushed his lips gently over hers, leaving her weepy and boneless.

"We can make all of this work," he said, "but I think it's gonna take the two of us."

"You don't mind?"

"Never have."

That's when she started to weep in earnest. And Zach stood right there with her, supporting her through the storm.

"I love you, Sadie," he said when she finally quieted.

"Oh, Zach, I love you, too."

For long minutes neither of them spoke. They simply held each other and let their bodies confirm what they had known all along.

"Just promise me one thing," Sadie finally murmured.

"What's that?"

"That you will never do anything for me or my family that you don't feel completely comfortable doing," she insisted.

"The same here," he said.

After she nodded, he added, "And never walk away without letting me know where you're going."

"It's a deal."

* * * * *

Lucinda knew that she needed to do something.

Say something, maybe even shut the door.

But Josh had just short-circuited her brain.

"I have Thai," he said, leaning back but not stepping clear. "A bottle of California chardonnay, and some ice cream from this new place I've heard of—Calhoun Creamery?" He winked at her. "I hope it's good. I got you mint chocolate chip."

He kissed her. He remembered what her favorite kind of ice cream was.

And, more than any of that, he was here.

Josh was still standing over her, smiling down as if he was enjoying her complete and total befuddlement. "I'll just put this in the kitchen, shall I?"

"Oh. Yes." She gestured in the general direction of her kitchen and managed to get her door shut. She was suddenly very aware of why, exactly, having Josh at her place made her so twitchy.

It was because they were alone.

* * *

Claimed by the Cowboy
is part of the
Dynasties: The Newports series—
Passion and chaos consume a
Chicago real estate empire.

CLAIMED BY
THE COWBOY

BY
SARAH M. ANDERSON

MILLS
BOON

First Published in Great Britain 2016
By Mills & Boon, an imprint of HarperCollins*Publishers*
1 London Bridge Street, London, SE1 9GF

© 2016 Harlequin Books S.A.

Special thanks and acknowledgement are given to Sarah M. Anderson for her contribution to the Dynasties: The Newports series.

ISBN: 978-0-263-91876-2

51-0916

Our policy is to use papers that are natural, renewable and recyclable products and made from wood grown in sustainable forests. The logging and manufacturing processes conform to the legal environmental regulations of the country of origin.

Printed and bound in Spain
by CPI, Barcelona

Sarah M. Anderson may live east of the Mississippi River, but her heart lies out West on the Great Plains. Sarah's book *A Man of Privilege* won an RT Reviewers' Choice Best Book Award in 2012.

Sarah spends her days having conversations with imaginary cowboys and American Indians. Find out more about Sarah's love of cowboys and Indians at www.sarahmanderson.com and sign up for the new-release newsletter at www.eepurl.com/nv39b.

To Charles Griemsman, who occasionally
lets me run completely wild with a story.
Thank you for trusting me with your stories!

One

"May I help you?"

Josh Calhoun whipped off his Hollister-Whitney trucker hat and beamed a grin at the receptionist. "I sure hope so," he said, unconsciously letting his country accent bleed through a little more. He couldn't help it. This was the first time he'd been back in Chicago in five years and so much had changed.

Once, he'd tried to hide his accent. He'd tried to blend in with the big city.

Not anymore.

"I'm looking for the Newport boys," he went on, leaning his head toward the receptionist. Her eyes widened and he thought he saw a little bit of color come to her cheeks. He wasn't flirting—not intentionally—but Sydney, God rest her soul, had said that this was just his way. His down-home charm was what had attracted her to him in the first place.

Damn it. He hadn't been in Chicago proper for more than thirty minutes and he was already thinking about Sydney again.

He hated this town.

"I'm Josh Calhoun," he went on. "They asked me to stop by."

Which was the only reason he had bothered to come back to Chicago. Brooks, Graham and Carson Newport were old college friends, and all three men had called him recently—apparently, without the others knowing that they were making the same call. Brooks Newport had asked for Josh's help in dealing with a rather stunning set of revelations about Sutton Winchester—Josh was still having trouble putting it all in order.

Apparently, Sutton Winchester was Carson's father and for a couple of months, Brooks and Graham had suspected that maybe the old real estate baron was their father, as well. But the paternity results had been conclusive—Brooks and Graham didn't share a father with Carson.

Ever since Sutton's involvement with their mother, Cynthia, had come to light, the Newport boys had been locked in a fierce battle with Sutton's daughters—Eve, Grace and Nora Winchester. As best Josh could gather from scrolling through the news stories on his phone, Sutton was on his deathbed.

The Winchester girls—particularly Eve—were not that happy to have a newly discovered brother who had strong opinions about staking his newfound inheritance claims. The rumors on the internet were flying fast and furious, and Josh had had trouble figuring out what was real and what were strategic PR leaks.

Brooks wanted Josh's legal advice on how to make Sutton pay for getting his mother pregnant with Carson and leaving her high and dry. His twin brother, Graham, wanted Josh's help in finding out who their father was, since it wasn't actually Sutton. And Carson, the baby of the family, desperately wanted Josh to come help calm Brooks down.

Josh wasn't sure he could actually do any of that. He was a former corporate lawyer and a dairy farmer. He negotiated with representatives and senators on legislation governing the dairy industry. He ran a multi-million-dollar dairy company. Sure, he had a reputation for being ruthless behind his good-time smile, but he wasn't a miracle worker.

Not for a single second did he think that anyone named Winchester would so much as give him the time of day. What did Chicago real-estate moguls care what a guy who made ice cream for a living thought? But he had to try. He owed the Newport boys.

The receptionist turned her attention to her computer screen. "Ah, yes. I see. Sadly, none of them are available." She looked up at Josh and he noticed that she had some dimples. "Brooks is in a private meeting and asked not to be disturbed. Graham is off-site, as is Carson."

"Off-site?" Chicago wasn't exactly a two-horse town. *Off-site* could mean anywhere. "Can you tell me where Graham and Carson are? They are expecting me." Irritation snaked up the back of his neck. At their request, he'd sucked it up and braved coming back to Chicago for the first time since the funeral, and they weren't even there to meet him?

The receptionist looked contrite. "I'm not at liberty to say where Graham is. However, Carson is on-site at the new children's hospital that the Newports are funding and constructing. I'd be happy to give you directions to the work site or..." She batted her eyelashes at him as her dimples deepened. "You're more than welcome to wait here."

Just as he had over the course of the last five years whenever a pretty lady made eyes at him, Josh did a gut check and waited to see if he'd have a reaction. Any reaction.

But there was nothing. Nothing other than the simple observation that this was a pretty girl who was flirting with him. He felt no attraction, no desire. There was absolutely no interest.

He ignored the black loneliness that existed in place of temptation and slapped on one of his best smiles. "I do need to speak with Carson," he said in his most apologetic tone. It wasn't the receptionist's fault that Josh was incapable of feeling anything.

The disappointment that crossed over her face was fleeting. "Let me get you those directions," she said in a much more professional tone.

"Thank you kindly," Josh said.

He was vastly out of his league and he knew it. He had vowed never to come back to Chicago, but there he was. The Newport boys were the only people on this earth who could've gotten him back inside city limits. They had been there for him at the hospital and at the funeral. In all likelihood, they'd probably saved his life. Not that Josh would ever tell anyone that, but when the people he cared for kept dying on him, it made it hard to put on a brave face and keep moving forward.

He was Josh Calhoun, heir to the Calhoun Creamery fortune and its current CEO. To the rest of the world, the fact that he had buried his parents and then his wife didn't matter as much as being one of the most powerful dairy owners in the country.

Well, it mattered to him. Sydney mattered to him.

And when she'd been taken away from him, the Newport boys had been there.

Brooks, Graham and Carson mattered to him. It was the only reason he was in this godforsaken city, because if something happened to any of them, well, it just might be the end of the world. His world.

"Here you go," the receptionist said. It was a pity that Josh couldn't work up any attraction for her, but he just couldn't. "Shall I let Carson know that you're on your way?"

"Much obliged," Josh said, settling his hat on his head. "It's been a while since I drove in the city—how long do you think it'll take me to get there?"

The receptionist turned her attention back to her computer. After a few keystrokes, she said, "At this time of day, it shouldn't take you more than forty minutes."

Josh didn't try to hide his groan. Back home in Cedar Point, Iowa, forty minutes would put him three towns over. Here, forty minutes on a good traffic day would take him all of three miles.

The dimples were back on the receptionist. "It could be worse—it's only two in the afternoon."

"I know." He touched the brim of his hat and headed back out to his truck. It stuck out like a sore thumb there, parked among the sleek Jaguars and shiny sports cars of all sorts. But he'd had his truck since high school. It'd outlasted college, marriage and his wife's death. He wasn't about to get a new vehicle to meet someone else's preconceived notions of what a multimillionaire business owner should drive.

Because, most days, Josh didn't feel like a multimillionaire business owner. Most days he was up by four checking on the cattle in the milking operations of the Calhoun Creamery farm. He got crap on his boots and broke a sweat nearly every day. The only break he got was times like now. He'd been on his way home from Washington, DC, after meeting with a lobbyist for the National Dairy Council about what regulations they wanted to see included in the FDA's new organic standards.

As the owner of one of the largest dairies in the country and the CEO of the Calhoun Creamery, Josh's word carried some weight in those discussions. It was the only time he left the dairy farm.

Sighing heavily, Josh fired up the old truck and merged back into the hell that was Chicago traffic. He hoped the Newport boys appreciated the sacrifices he was making. And he was thankful that the traffic was just bad enough that he had to really pay attention. People in Iowa did not run lights like they did in Chicago. There, when the light turned red, people stopped. Here, when the light turned red, people sped up. He almost got rear-ended three separate times because he couldn't make himself run the red.

Finally, the new children's hospital work site came into view. It didn't look much like a children's hospital at this point—half of the exterior didn't even have walls. Josh studied his directions and saw that the receptionist had made a note that he was to pull down a side street and park in the back. She was a good receptionist. He almost wished that he'd been able to feel something for her. If he was going to be stuck in Chicago, a little distraction could go a long way.

He parked in the construction zone and there, at least, his truck blended in a little better. Josh made himself a promise. He would only stay in Chicago as long as it took to help the Newport boys get some of their issues sorted out. The moment he stopped being useful, he was out of there.

He'd worked too damned hard for a sense of equilibrium after Sydney's death. He knew better than to tempt fate again, and he simply did not have the mental energy to let himself fall into another deep depression.

If it were anyone but the Newports, he wouldn't be there.

But he was already there. So he better get this over with.

"But you understand that he's not dead yet," Dr. Lucinda Wilde said, trying her very best to keep a grip on her temper. She rarely got mad at patients—it was a waste of time and emotional energy. "I can only prolong his life if he stays in the hospital, under constant care. You do see that?"

Carson Newport stood to the doctor's left, his hands on his hips and a determined set to his eyes. On the doctor's right, Eve Winchester was glaring at Lucinda, her arms crossed and her brow furrowed with anger. All around them, the sounds of construction filled the air—as did dust. So much dust. She was going to have to shower before she went on her rounds again.

Lucinda had to hope that the construction materials being used here at the new children's hospital weren't carcinogenic. She vastly preferred her own hospital, where everything was already hospital-sterile. And she was not happy about having to leave her patients to trek halfway across town to mediate yet another dispute between the Newports and the Winchesters about her patient, Sutton Winchester.

Lucinda sighed and pushed her glasses back up her nose. She would have a better chance convincing a pack of wild dogs than Sutton Winchester's children that the scion of the Winchester fortune needed to stay in the hospital.

Never in her nine years as a practicing oncologist had she run into such a stubborn set of relatives. She adored her job and Chicago, but days like these had her muttering "city folk" to herself and longing for the wide-open spaces of Cedar Point, Iowa. Even cows were more reasonable than this.

"I understand that you're not interested in doing your job," Eve Winchester said in a tight voice.

"There's no need to be rude," Carson Newport snapped. "The good doctor *is* doing her job. No one lives forever—especially not bitter old men."

Eve wheeled on Carson and most likely would have demolished him in a verbal barrage of slings and arrows, but a voice interrupted them. "What seems to be the trouble?"

Lucinda froze. Absolutely, completely *froze* as a voice out of her past floated up from out of nowhere and made her blood run hot and cold at the same time.

It couldn't be. It simply wasn't possible that she'd heard *him*. Not after all this time. Not right now, when she was barely keeping herself together in the face of one of her most challenging cases yet.

But then Carson turned and said, "Josh!"

And a little bit of Lucinda died because she wasn't imagining this. She couldn't be. Josh Calhoun himself had walked out of her nightmares and into her line of sight.

Oh, God. Her breath caught in her throat as Josh approached. He looked exactly the same as he had the last time she'd seen him. He was wearing jeans and a red plaid shirt. His longish brown hair stuck out around the base of his ratty-looking ball cap that looked exactly like the one he'd worn every single day back in school.

No, no, *no*. This wasn't happening. It couldn't be.

Josh Calhoun—a ghost from her past that she never wanted to face again—smiled widely at their small group.

Until his gaze landed on her.

Lucinda wasn't surprised when that good-time grin of his died on the vine. After all, they hadn't exactly parted on the best of terms when Lucinda had made an absolute fool of herself on the worst day of her life and Josh had turned her down flat.

They stared at each other and Lucinda was at least a little relieved that he was just as surprised to see her as she was to see him.

And then everything got worse. Because Josh Calhoun, the boy who'd shattered her already broken heart, lifted one corner of his mouth in what she knew all too well was his real smile.

Oh. Oh, my. Something about him had changed. He was a little taller and a heck of a lot more broad in the shoulders. His chin was sharper now and his eyes…

Josh Calhoun had grown up.

Lucinda did not allow herself to feel a rush of instant attraction. Lust had no place in her life. It was an inconvenient emotion at best, and she only had so much emotional energy to spare after spending her days as the head of the oncology department at Midwest Regional Medical Center. She couldn't waste a bit of it, certainly not on the likes of Josh Calhoun, the last person she had allowed herself to lust over.

But watching Josh's lips curve into that real smile instead of the big one he used when he was befriending every single person in the room? Lust hit her low and hard, and she wasn't ready for it. She wasn't ready for him. Not now, not ever.

But she refused to let any of that show. She didn't suck in air, even though her lungs were burning. She didn't allow her skin and circulatory system to betray her in any way. She didn't even bat a single eyelash at him.

He was nothing to her. She didn't need him; she didn't want him, and she'd be damned if she let him know how much he'd hurt her back in high school.

Carson's scowl broke into a wide smile as he said, "You made it!" Then he and Josh wrapped their arms around each other and performed a few manly thumps on each other's back.

Lucinda couldn't help but glance at Eve during this display of masculine affection. Eve was rolling her eyes.

"Man, I'm glad to see you," Carson said to Josh. "Josh, this is Eve Winchester—it turns out that she's my sister."

"Stop telling people that," Eve snapped.

Lucinda sighed heavily. She'd heard variations on this particular theme over and over again whenever it came time to make a decision about Sutton Winchester's care. The Winchester daughters—Nora, Eve and Grace—refused to acknowledge that Carson was their half brother and did everything within their power to make sure that he did not have any say in family decisions.

But Carson Newport wasn't exactly taking this decision lying down.

Just as he did every time Eve threw this insult in his face, Carson opened his mouth to retort that she didn't have any choice in the situation. Lucinda knew the script by heart.

Josh didn't. Instead, he cut Carson off with a warm smile and an extended hand. "Ms. Winchester, it's a pleasure to make your acquaintance. I'm sorry that we can't meet under better circumstances, but Carson has told me how impressed he is with how you've been handling all the new developments."

Lucinda had no idea if this was a true statement or not. Maybe it didn't matter. Josh's words went off like a little bomb in the conversation, completely resetting the discourse.

She shouldn't be surprised. Josh Calhoun had always been the peacemaker of their high school. He had a way of finding the common ground and making everyone happy.

Everyone except her.

"He…what?" Eve stared down at Josh's outstretched hand. "Who *are* you?"

If Josh was insulted by this lack of manners, he didn't show it. "Beg your pardon—I'm Josh Calhoun, of the Calhoun Creamery. I went to college with the Newport boys and I count them as some of my oldest friends. I understand that things have been challenging recently and I wanted to stop by and see if I could do anything to help." As he said this last bit, his gaze shifted back to Lucinda.

Oh, come on—was he seriously including *her* in that statement? If that's what he thought, he had another think coming.

But he was the Newports' oldest friend? Figured. As if the Winchester/Newport feud wasn't enough of a tangled web to be caught in, Josh Calhoun had to go and add another thread. A big, fat, *complicated* thread.

Carson jumped in, taking advantage of Eve's stunned silence. "Josh, this is Dr. Lucinda Wilde. She's the oncologist who's overseeing Sutton's care. If there's one thing that Eve and I can agree on…" At this, Eve snorted. "It's that Dr. Wilde has managed to stabilize our father. Without her, he would probably already be dead."

"Dr. Lucinda Wilde," Josh said, rolling each of the words off his tongue as if he was trying to figure out which part was the strangest. He leaned forward, his hand out. "Lucinda? And you're an oncologist now? I should have guessed."

She did not want to touch him. So she nodded her head and stuck her hands behind her back. "Josh. Sorry," she added in a not-sorry voice. "Germs, you know."

Eve and Carson shared a look. "Do you two know each other?" Carson asked.

She didn't answer. She didn't want to cop to knowing Josh. She didn't want anyone in Chicago to know about their tangled past, and she absolutely didn't want to be thinking about Josh Calhoun, past or present.

Sadly, it seemed as though she didn't have much of a choice. "Yeah," Josh said, letting his hand hang out there for a second before he lowered it back to his side. "Well, I knew Lucy Wilde."

She shuddered at the sound of her name. She'd left Lucy Wilde behind when she'd left Iowa, and there was no going back. "We went to the same high school," she explained to Carson and Eve. "But only for two years." She shot a warning glare at Josh because if he took it upon himself to add to that simple truth, she might have to kick him somewhere very important.

He notched an eyebrow at her and something in his eyes changed, and she knew—*knew*—that he remembered exactly how things had gone down between them. Or not gone down, as the case may be. But, thankfully, all he said was "Yup."

"I'm very happy for the high school reunion, but none of this brings us any closer to getting my father out of the hospital," Eve Winchester snapped.

Josh—without looking away from her—asked, "Is that a possibility?"

Right. Lucinda had a purpose here that had nothing to do with Josh Calhoun or Lucy Wilde. She had ventured out to this dusty, half-finished work site to try to talk some sense into Carson and Eve because they were the most invested players in this family drama.

Not that that was saying a lot.

"It would be best for the patient if he remained in the oncology ward at Midwest," Lucinda said as all three looked at her. "I want to keep him under my direct supervision, and there are several experimental treatments I would like to try—with his consent—that have the potential to increase his life expectancy. There are promising developments with low-dose naltrexone…"

"I don't understand why these experimental treatments have to be done in the hospital," Eve snapped, cutting Lucinda off. "Every day that he's in a public space—and no, you can't promise me that his privacy will be respected in that hospital—it becomes that much more likely that *someone* will access his records, take pictures of him while he's incapacitated or bribe a nurse for information they can use against him in the court of public opinion." She paused and shot daggers at Carson. "I want him home where I know that he'll be protected and safe."

Ah, so they were back on the script again. Josh looked to Lucinda for a reply, but she was unable to provide any other details of her patient's medical condition to him. She was not about to break her Hippocratic oath for him.

Instead, it was Carson who answered. "We've been over this, Eve. He's sick. He belongs in a hospital." He turned to Josh. "He's got inoperable lung cancer—years of smoking and hard living, I guess. It's spread to his lymph nodes. Stage three."

Josh had the decency to wince.

"But," Eve said as she jumped back in, "he's not going to die tomorrow."

"You can't just cut the cancer out?" Josh asked Lucinda.

She glared at him even harder. "I cannot share anything about my patient's condition with a nonfamily member."

Carson rolled his eyes at her. "As Dr. Wilde has explained to us, due to the original tumor's location, she can't perform surgery and traditional chemo, and radiation won't be powerful enough to eradicate the malignant cells that have spread to the lymph system."

Josh turned to Eve. "I'm so sorry to hear this," he said in a gentle voice. "This must be hard for you and your sisters."

Eve appeared stunned by this olive branch—and Lucinda appreciated someone short-circuiting the bickering.

Josh Calhoun was the same as he'd always been, that much was clear. This was what he did. She'd seen him talk down two guys in the middle of a fight so that, within minutes, they were all sharing a soda and laughing about good times or whatever it was men laughed about while one was wiping the other's blood off his knuckles.

Once, she'd admired him for that. Okay, honestly—she'd more than admired him. She'd been fascinated by him. She'd never been much to look at, but Josh had never treated her like the know-it-all nerd everyone else did.

Well, almost everyone else. Josh's best friend in high school, Gary, had asked her out after she'd verbally smacked down some bullies who were mocking Gary for being unable to lift his own backpack after a chemo treatment. And since no one else had ever even remotely looked at Lucy Wilde as someone they might like to go see a movie with—much less kiss—she'd said yes.

Lucinda shook her head out of the past. How long had it been since she'd allowed herself to think of Gary—or Josh? Years. It hadn't been that hard. She'd been busy with her medical career and dealing with the likes of the Winchesters and Newports. And the Winchesters and Newports took all of her attention.

She had, of course, expressed her concerns to Sutton's family—that was part and parcel of her job. She cared not only for her patients but their loved ones, as well. She'd had decades of helping people live and die—long before she'd become a doctor.

Long before she'd humiliated herself in front of Josh Calhoun.

But now that she thought of it, she couldn't remember witnessing anyone else expressing their sympathies to any of the Winchester daughters. Certainly not Brooks Newport or his brothers. Carson's grim acceptance of the situation had, until this moment, been as good as it got.

"Thank you," Eve replied quietly. Then she turned her attention to Carson. "I'm not giving up on him. I just want what's best for him and I don't think being in the hospital is it."

"What are the options?" Josh asked.

Why did he have to be here? Why did he have to be forging a peace between Eve and Carson?

Why did he have to be reminding her of things she'd tried so desperately to forget?

It was Carson who answered for her. "Eve and her sisters—*our* sisters—think it would be best to take him home. I'm not comfortable pulling him out of the hospital." He stared at Eve. "*We* have questions and I want him to live long enough to get some answers out of him."

It was blisteringly clear who the "we" was—Carson and his brothers.

Lucinda wanted to massage her throbbing temples.

Eve glared at him. "What you think doesn't matter. He's not really your father. You don't know him and you don't love him like I do—like *my sisters* do." Her gaze swung back to Lucinda and she looked more determined than ever, which was saying something. "Money is no object. I can have a private medical facility that meets your specifications set up at his estate in a matter of days. I want him out of the hospital and safely at home. And if you won't help move him," she threatened, "I will find a doctor who can."

"Beg your pardon," Josh interrupted in that gentle tone that Lucinda didn't really appreciate. "Does he *want* to stay in the hospital?"

It was a deceptively simple question and Lucinda knew it. What Sutton Winchester wanted was to go home and pretend he was not on death's door. He never wanted to see her face or the inside of a hospital ever again. But that was not what was best for him.

"Of course, he doesn't," Eve stated flatly.

"Because if he's got the means to be treated at home, maybe that would be best for everyone," Josh said as if this were the obvious conclusion instead of a solution that entailed an unnecessary health risk.

Well, that went sideways on her. Lucinda gave him a dull look and Carson was none too pleased at this announcement.

Undaunted by their open hostility, Josh went on, "Carson, you've got to realize that if he's more comfortable, he'll likely be willing to answer some of those questions, don't you think?"

She wanted to strangle him. It was bad enough that he

was here and worse that she was having to talk to him. But for him to come down on the wrong side?

That, however, wasn't the worst of it. No, what was the worst was that she could see Carson start to waver. Damn it. She knew there were many unanswered questions and she also knew that, currently, Sutton was in no mood to unburden his soul.

Carson Newport had been her ally in keeping Sutton Winchester in the hospital. But, before her eyes, she could see him switch sides. "Well…"

Josh didn't wait for Carson to talk himself out of it. "If it won't compromise his care, that is." He turned his attention to Lucinda and turned on his all-American charm. "If Eve can get the room set up to your specifications, would you be willing to release Mr. Winchester? I know that no one wants to risk his health. That has to come first. I think we can all agree that your word is final, can't we?" He glanced around their small circle, gathering approval to him like a cloak.

Lucinda blinked at him. Was that the bone he was going to throw her—that she had the final word? Very neatly, Josh Calhoun had sidestepped, diffused or completely undercut weeks of bitter arguments—and boxed her into a corner.

What she wanted to say was that he was out of his ever-loving mind and he could go crawl back into whatever hole he'd crawled out of.

But she didn't. She had a professional reputation to maintain, and she would be damned if she let Josh Calhoun take that away from her, too. "In no way would moving him at this stage of his treatment be a good idea," she said firmly.

This fell on deaf ears. "Okay," Carson announced. "If

we can get a room set up in his home, we can move him. But our brothers aren't going to like this."

"Graham and Brooks are absolutely *not* my brothers," Eve said just as her phone buzzed. She glanced at it and Lucinda saw a small smile break through her icy demeanor. "Dr. Wilde, if you could get a list of equipment we'll need, I'll have everything else taken care of."

"You do understand that this will be very expensive, don't you?" Lucinda tried a last-ditch attempt. "You'll need twenty-four-hour care to monitor him, as well—and not some random home-health nurse. He needs oncology specialists around him at all time."

Eve and Carson shared a look. "That's fine," Eve said with a smile that made Lucinda's blood run cold. "There's plenty of room at the house. I'll have the guest quarters prepared for your stay. Hire whomever you need."

"Ms. Winchester!" Lucinda gaped at her in shock. When had she lost complete and total control?

Josh cleared his throat. *Oh, yeah.* The moment he'd walked back into her life.

But she didn't get any further than that. Carson stepped forward and said, "That sounds like a good idea to me. Would you be able to do that, Dr. Wilde?"

This simply could not get worse. She had already been dragged into more than enough Winchester/Newport drama. Personally supervising Sutton Winchester's care at home would only double and then triple that.

She had opened her mouth to find the words to politely yet firmly refuse when Josh spoke up. "At the very least," he said, shooting her one of his big smiles that did absolutely nothing to her, "would you be able to see him settled?"

"I'm the head of the oncology department at Midwest," she told him with an edge to her voice. "I cannot simply disappear to a private home for days or what could even turn out to be weeks at a time."

Carson gave her a smile that bordered on predatory. "I'm sure, for an appropriate donation to that new cancer pavilion expansion they've been planning, they'll be more than happy to help you find a way to make this work into your schedule."

In other words, her medical services were going to the highest bidder—and there were no bidders higher in the greater Chicago region than the Winchesters and the Newports. The Newports were already funding this new children's hospital. In the grand scheme of things, the cost of an expanded cancer pavilion meant nothing to them or the Winchesters.

Lucinda *absolutely* did not want to be a pawn in this tug-of-war between the two families, but that pavilion would do a lot of good for a lot of people. Damn it all to hell. "I suppose I could move a few appointments around and take a couple of days. But I won't compromise anyone else's care. And if I don't believe your father will receive excellent care at home, I won't allow him to be discharged."

Eve sniffed, and there was determination in her voice as she said, "Fine. Do whatever you have to do. I'll have the guest quarters set up." Abruptly, she turned away and began texting rapidly.

Lucinda sighed. She turned to Carson—and Josh. "I just want what's best for my patient," she reminded the men.

"It sounds like *you're* what's best for the patient," Josh said as if he were seriously complimenting her.

Lucinda had never physically assaulted anyone in her entire life, but she was damned close to taking a swing at Josh. That did it. He needed to get his nose out of this medical situation—and her business—before she lost what was left of her temper. "Can I talk to you for a second?" she demanded, not bothering to smooth her tone over with a smile.

Carson's eyebrows jumped up, but Josh showed no sign that he understood the danger. "Sure."

Good. Great. She was going to tell Josh Calhoun off the way she should have done seventeen years ago, and then she was going to get on with her life.

Without him.

Two

Josh stood there for a moment in a state of total shock. His mind had to be playing tricks on him. *Chicago* had to be playing tricks on him. Because there was just no reasonable explanation for why he was here with Lucy Wilde. He stared after her as she stalked away.

"I take it you two aren't the best of friends," Carson commented drily as he watched Josh watch Lucy.

"Probably safe to say that," Josh admitted. But once, they had been. Lucy and Gary and Josh. Three peas in a pod, his grandpa had always said. Until it'd just been the two of them. And then Josh had done what had been the hardest thing he'd done in his life—say no to Lucy Wilde.

Carson pondered Josh's statement. "Old girlfriend?"

"No, nothing like that." Which was not entirely the truth, but Josh got the feeling that Lucy might personally tear him limb from limb if he gave anyone any indication of how close they'd been once. "Can you give me a few minutes?"

A grin twisted Carson's lips. "Given how she was trying to kill you with looks alone, you might need more than a few minutes."

"I didn't come here for her," Josh said in as good-natured a tone as he could manage. "Let me get this settled, and then we can go somewhere and get a beer and you can fill me in on what the hell has been happening around here." As if he could just "settle" the matter of Lucy when she was clearly out for blood.

Carson looked defeated. "That's going to take a lot more than one beer," he said. "Go on. Another five minutes isn't going to change anything."

"Thanks." Josh took a deep breath and began to follow Lucy Wilde.

Except she wasn't Lucy, not anymore. Lucy had been a wide-eyed, freckled girl who had been wildly in love with his best friend, Gary Everly. Josh had actually liked her—he'd liked her quite a bit. She'd had a dry sense of humor and a sharp wit that she only used when people had her backed into a corner, which they did at their own risk. She'd been smart—smarter than either of the boys.

And she'd loved Gary. It hadn't mattered that he'd been sick. More times than he could count, Josh had caught Lucy gazing at Gary with unabashed adoration. It had never bothered him. Really. Lucy had been one of the best things to happen to Gary, and Josh had not begrudged his childhood friend the little bit of happiness Lucy was able to bring him in a dark time.

Josh had tried to make Gary happy, too. Minigolf, cow tipping, the movies—together, they'd made a hell of a group, tearing up Cedar Point, Iowa. He'd had the car and the Calhoun cash; Gary had had his bucket list;

and Lucy had kept them from doing anything truly stupid. In fact, if Josh was remembering things correctly, it'd been Lucy who'd passed judgment on whomever Josh had dated. A lot of the time, they'd been a foursome.

But a lot of the time…it'd just been the three of them. Him, her and Gary.

Until Gary had died. Four days before his eighteenth birthday. Of leukemia. Because his folks hadn't been able to afford to bring him to Chicago or anyplace that had a really good oncology department.

Not that it would have mattered. After all, Sydney had had access to the best medical care in the country and it hadn't been enough to save her.

Josh was already clinging to his sanity by his fingernails just being back in Chicago, but to suddenly find himself confronted with Lucy Wilde and Gary's memory was almost too much. He wanted to bail and go back to his cows and stay far away from the people he loved because that was the best way of keeping them safe.

He did not want Lucy Wilde to remind him of yet another person he'd lost.

Not that he had a lot of choice in the matter. He walked toward her slowly so that he could try to put his thoughts in order. This was not the same girl he remembered. Oh, sure, she still had on a massive pair of eyeglasses that gave her an owlish appearance. And the only thing that seemed to have changed about her stick-straight blond hair was that she had pulled it up into a bun. But half of her hair had worked itself free and fell around her face and shoulders, making her look ethereal.

Josh almost smiled. Lucy had never had a head for fashion or style and, given that she was wearing a shapeless doctor's coat over equally shapeless black trousers and a mannish blue button-up blouse, that hadn't changed, either.

But the fire in her eyes? That was something new. Something that had made him come to a screeching halt and stare at her in openmouthed wonder.

The way he had the last time he'd seen her.

She reached her destination and spun, glaring at him. Her toe began to tap and he wouldn't have been surprised if she'd pulled out a phone and checked the time.

"It's good to see you again, Lucy," he began.

He didn't get any further than that. "What are you doing here?" At least she kept her voice to a fierce whisper.

"Like I said, I'm friends with the Newport boys. They called me and asked for help sorting out this mess."

"Don't give me that," she snapped. "Because rolling up here and turning on all of your charm to convince my patient's family that he would be best served outside the hospital is not exactly how I wanted to see you again, Joshua Calhoun."

Ouch. She was busting out the *Joshua* already. So much for warm, fuzzy reunions. But he couldn't help himself. Teasing Lucy had been so much fun because she always gave so much better than she got. He heard himself slipping right back into it. "So, how did you want to see me again?"

If looks could kill, he would probably need emergency medical help right now. "I didn't."

There wasn't a single thing about this situation that should make him smile, but he did. "I'm just going to go out on a limb here, but you seem upset with me."

Her eyes widened at the challenge. "Oh? Do you think? No. You obviously don't. Because if you did think, you would remember..." Abruptly, her voice trailed off into a new emotional place, replacing the anger that flamed out all over her face.

It almost looked painful.

He didn't like that pained look. Because he did remember. He remembered quite clearly. What had happened between them—it wasn't the sort of thing a man forgot. He may not think about it every single day of his life. But, no, he hadn't forgotten about going to Gary's funeral and Lucy clinging to his hand the whole time and then pulling him out back at the wake and telling him that she needed him, needed him so badly because she hurt so much and she just wanted to not hurt and would he…

"Oh, my God," Lucy gasped, recoiling in horror. "Stop. Stop right there."

Josh shook himself. He was pretty sure he hadn't said anything out loud. "What?"

"Don't." Somehow her eyes got even wider and, behind her thick glasses, even more owlish. Her back straightened and he realized that, despite the fact that she was wearing an almost sexless doctor's uniform, she wasn't the same girl he remembered. She was taller and, with her shoulders squared, he could see that a woman's curves filled out her body.

If she'd had those curves back then…

"Don't what?" he asked, although he knew that was a lame dodge. She'd always been so incredibly perceptive, and as for him—well, he'd always been an open book. He'd only ever been able to hide one thing from her— exactly how much he'd liked her.

The only other woman he'd never been able to hide anything from was Sydney.

Which meant Lucy had realized exactly what he'd been thinking.

"Just don't, Josh," she finished weakly. Then, she blushed. Hard. So hard that she went scarlet from the tips of her ears to the base of her neck. Lucy was so tomato red that he didn't even need to look at her hands to know they'd turned bright red, too.

"Lucy…"

But whatever vulnerability he'd glimpsed was gone in an instant. "Don't you dare 'Lucy' me," she interrupted. Everything about her body tightened as if she were fighting off some urge. He had no idea whether she was going to punch him or what. "I am Dr. Lucinda Wilde now, and so help me, Josh Calhoun, if you roll up in here and in any way, shape or form compromise the care of my patients, I will personally make sure the rest of your life is a living hell."

She spun on her heel and he knew she was done with him, but, damn it, he wasn't willing to let it go. He reached out and grabbed her hand. "Lucy, it doesn't have to be like this."

She froze. Her gaze dropped down to where he had her by the hand. Her skin was warm and soft against his, softer than he'd expected it to be. He closed his fingers around hers and, without really thinking about it, pulled her closer to him.

A feeling so unfamiliar, so foreign that he couldn't name it right away, hit him low in the gut. Lucy. This was Lucy, and against all odds he'd missed her. He took another step into her, closing the distance between them.

Dear God in heaven, what he was feeling right now? Desire. Want.

Need.

Josh Calhoun did a gut check and, for the first time in five years, his gut told him to go for it.

For Lucy Wilde, of all people.

His heart began to pound and his skin began to prickle. He inhaled deeply. She smelled of hospitals and antiseptics and, underneath that, a hint of something sweet, and all he wanted to do was lean his head down and taste her to find out what that sweetness was.

Then she looked up at him, her light blue eyes impossibly wide. "Yes, it does."

He wasn't going to accept that. "Have dinner with me."

That made her laugh—and pull her hand away from his grip. "Seriously? Am I not making myself clear? I thought you were smarter than this, Josh. I don't want to see you. We're not friends anymore."

"We are." Her eyeballs bugged out of her head at this declaration. "Well, we can be again."

"No," she said softly, turning away from him. This time he didn't try to stop her. "After what happened? No, we can't."

He watched her go, her words echoing louder in his head the farther away she got.

She hated him. Well, he supposed he deserved nothing less than her contempt. She'd needed him to comfort her after her high school sweetheart had died and he'd...

He'd forced himself to turn her down. He'd embarrassed her then and he'd embarrassed her again, that much was obvious. She only ever got that red when she lost her temper.

But she didn't realize how hard it'd been to say no to her. How much it'd hurt to know that he'd added to her pain. To have twice watched Lucy Wilde walk away from him and know that he'd screwed it up.

Damn it all to hell and back.

He watched a construction worker scurry out of Lucy's way right before she disappeared around a corner. He should let it go. She'd made her position more than clear. Just as she had seventeen years ago when he'd rejected her.

But it'd been different then. He'd been a kid in mourning for his best friend and due to leave Cedar Point in just a few weeks for college in Chicago. He'd rationalized that a clean break was best for all of them.

Now?

Now his gut was telling him that maybe it was okay to look at another woman and feel something. Something good. Something right.

He hadn't felt anything in so long...

No. He wasn't going to let Lucy Wilde walk away from him a second time with so much unsaid between them. He wasn't the same confused kid he'd been. He was a man now and he knew what he wanted.

He made his way back over to where Carson had been waiting for him, texting on his phone the whole time. With any luck, Carson hadn't been paying attention to his and Lucy's conversation.

"That seemed to go well," he said without looking up.

Josh sighed. One thing was abundantly clear.

His luck had run out.

Lucinda did her very best to ban all thoughts of Josh Calhoun from her mind as she moved through her afternoon. She'd spent more time at the children's hospital site than she'd meant to and was behind schedule. She hated being behind schedule. Things happened on time or there were dire consequences in her world. When it came to the health of her patients, waiting could be fatal.

This was what she kept telling herself as she moved around Midwest's oncology ward, her hair still damp from the quick shower she'd taken to wash the construction dust off. Like any other day, some people were making progress and some people were losing the battle. Mrs. Adamczak was sitting up in bed and smiling for the first time in weeks. Mr. Gadhavi, however, had not responded to treatment and, as hard as it would be, Lucinda was going to recommend that he be sent home for hospice.

This was where her focus needed to be—on the people she could still help. That did not include Gary Everly and it did not include Josh Calhoun.

It did, however, include Sutton Winchester.

It was madness that she was even going to consider allowing him to continue his treatment away from this hospital. If it were any other person in the entire city of Chicago, it wouldn't be an option. It wouldn't even be a figment of someone's imagination.

But Sutton Winchester wasn't any other person. And his children weren't going to let her forget it.

But before she could even get to his room, she was stopped by the vice president of Midwest, John Jackson, outside the nurses station on the oncology ward. "Dr. Wilde," Jackson said with an unnaturally bright look to his eyes. "Just the doctor I was looking for!"

Lucinda didn't have time for ego stroking right now. She knew that if Jackson worked up a proper head of steam, he could go on for hours. "How much money did they offer you?"

Jackson pulled up short and blinked at her. "How did you…"

"Because I'm not stupid, Mr. Jackson. I was there when Eve Winchester decided that this was going to be a reality whether I thought it was a good idea or not. You should merely count yourself lucky that you're going to get the money for the cancer pavilion expansion out of it, shouldn't you?"

Jackson didn't know her very well and it was clear that

he didn't know how he was supposed to take this attitude. But he hadn't made it to being a vice president of a hospital without understanding how to cover his tracks. "Just think of all the people that we'll be able to help," he said, putting all available lipstick on this pig of a situation.

"Yes, yes—I know. I hope you at least negotiated for the entire cost of construction?"

"The Newports and the Winchesters have agreed to $250 million!" The man actually did a little dance. "I've never seen anything like it. Whatever you did, Dr. Wilde, do you think you could do it again? We could use a new cardiac cath lab, too."

She glared at him hard enough that he took a step backward. God, this whole situation had left her with a bad taste in her mouth. What else could go wrong today?

At that exact moment, the ward doors opened and a cart laden with floral arrangements was wheeled in. This was normally a happy time of her day as she got to see the flowers bring a bit of hope to people's eyes.

"As I said to Mr. Winchester's children, I will only allow him to be treated in his home if they can get a room set up to my specifications and if it won't compromise the treatment of my other patients," she told Jackson as she kept an eye on the beautiful arrangements being off-loaded. She shouldn't like the flowers. She never got any, and the last time anyone had actually given her flowers had been at her senior prom with Gary.

He'd only been able to stand for the photos and for one dance. He'd gotten her a corsage, though. And then he made Josh Calhoun dance with her several other times throughout the night.

The last bouquet on the cart was a small arrangement of sunflowers and daisies—bright and sunny and full of the promise of tomorrow. The delivery guy set the bouquet on the nurses station counter and Lucinda saw one of her favorite nurses, Elena, glance at the card. Elena's eyes got very wide very fast, and then she looked up at Lucinda and smiled.

Elena must have a new boyfriend. That was sweet of him to send flowers to work.

Lucinda turned her attention back to Mr. Jackson. "...find a way to make this work," he was saying in his best salesman tone.

Elena held the card out to another nurse, who read the name on it and started giggling. "Fine," she told Jackson. Because who was she? Just Sutton Winchester's doctor, that's all. Just the one person who wanted him to get the best treatment in the best place from the best people.

Apparently, that made her the bad guy there.

Well, she knew when it was time to cut her losses. You couldn't hold back the tides and you couldn't hold back Eve Winchester when she made up her mind about something.

Jackson was still making noises about pavilions, patients and money when Elena carried the sunny bouquet over to Lucinda. "It's for you," she said.

Lucinda wasn't offended by the nurse's awestruck tone. She didn't believe it, either. "Seriously?" She grabbed the card out of Elena's hand. Yes, that was her name on the envelope. Typed, not handwritten: "Dr. Lucinda Wilde."

"When will you have a list of things Mr. Winchester needs to get ready?" Jackson asked in a tone of voice that was one small step removed from a flat-out demand. "I don't want to keep Ms. Winchester or Mr. Newport waiting."

"Give me an hour," Lucinda all but growled at him. Elena was watching her with naked interest, Jackson wasn't leaving her alone about the Newports and the Winchesters, and she was holding in her hands a card from Josh Calhoun, because who else would send her flowers?

No one, that's who. She'd always been something of an introvert. She had a few good friends and it was more than enough for her.

Never in her entire life had she wanted to go hide more than she did right now.

"Great! I'll check back in an hour, okay?" For the love of everything holy, Jackson looked so much like an over-eager golden retriever at this moment that Lucinda was tempted to dig a treat out of her pocket and throw it just to get him to go away.

"Yeah." She should probably work a little harder on sucking up to the hospital administrators, but she just didn't have it in her today.

Once Jackson was out of sight, Elena whispered, "Well?" and crowded closer to read the card over her shoulder.

Lucinda slipped the card into her pocket and grabbed the floral arrangement. There was no way in hell she was going to read it right now, with half of the nurses on duty pretending not to listen in. If she was going to turn beet red again, she wanted to do so in the privacy of her own closet. "It looks like I'm going to be picking up some extra shifts at a private residence. I'm going to need a few trusted nurses who can keep their mouths shut." The irony of the situation didn't escape her. She wasn't going to read Josh's note in front of them because she didn't trust a single one of them, but she was asking them to come to Winchester's estate and help her discreetly manage him there. "Are you interested?"

The difference was, of course, that patient privacy was the law and that law was drilled into them over and over again. Her personal life, however, was fair game and everyone knew it.

"Of course!" Elena's gaze darted over to Sutton's room. Yeah, everyone knew who they were talking about. "Any word on what it'll pay?"

"I'll make sure it's worth your while. Now, if you'll excuse me…" Lucinda juggled the flowers and her tablet and, randomly tapping on the screen to make it look as if she was doing something important instead of fleeing like a trapped rat, turned on her heel and started down the hallway.

She couldn't flee fast enough. "Is he cute?" Elena called after her. "Or she—it's fine with us either way."

As if Lucinda hadn't been put on the spot enough already. She had always avoided the *Grey's Anatomy*–style hospital romances that seemed to permeate Midwest. And, yeah, on some level, she probably knew that people assumed she didn't date men because she was a lesbian or asexual.

But was it really such a common assumption that Elena would announce it in the middle of the hallway like that?

"Don't you need to check on Mrs. Adamczak?" Lucinda shot back over her shoulder as she walked through the wide swinging doors. Without giving Elena a chance to catch up, she hurried to her office and blissfully shut the door. It wasn't much of an office. Part of the plans for the expanded cancer pavilion was redesigning the doctors' offices to make patients feel more comfortable when they sat down for life-and-death discussions. Right now, Lucinda barely had enough room for a desk and two chairs. But she had a door and a lock, and that was all she needed right now.

She pulled the envelope out of her pocket and realized

with horror that her hands were shaking. *No. No.* She was absolutely not going to let Josh Calhoun get to her again.

She slipped a small card out. "L—I will always be your friend. Let me take you out to dinner. J"

Below that was an Iowa phone number.

She had to stop thinking it couldn't get worse. Because at this point, fate was merely toying with her.

Three

"I might be stuck here for a couple of days," Josh told his grandfather, Peter Calhoun, who'd called just as Josh was getting into his truck after leaving Carson's place.

He wasn't sure what he hoped that his grandfather would say. Peter Calhoun was still the chairman of the Calhoun Creamery, although he was well into his eighties and little more than a figurehead at this point. For all intents and purposes, Josh ran the creamery as CEO. And he hated being away from it.

He almost wanted his grandfather to tell him to come home right now. To heck with the Newports and the Winchesters and the whole city. Chicago was not his town. And the longer he was there, the more everything would hurt.

But if he turned tail and ran—and there was no mistaking the fact that that was exactly what it would be— then what would they think of him? Brooks and Graham and Carson and, yes, Lucy?

He'd given up Lucy's friendship once without a fight. He could not willingly forfeit the Newports' friendship, too.

"No big rush," his grandfather said, his voice crackling with age. "You work too hard, son. Take all the time you need."

That was not exactly what Josh wanted to hear. "It'll only be a few more days," he said as if his grandfather had asked him to come home. "I think the Newport boys need me to be here long enough to see Sutton Winchester settled a little bit. I won't be here a moment longer."

There was a pause on the other end of the phone before his grandfather said, "Josh, I know it must be hard for you to be back in Chicago, but I'm serious. Your brothers and sisters are doing a great job holding down the fort. Take the time you need to take. The cows aren't going anywhere. Paige has the situation well in hand and Trevor is helping cover for you. You know, I think it's been good for him to have a little more responsibility."

Josh scowled, not that his grandfather could see it. He did his best to take care of his siblings.

"Unless there's something else bothering you?" Peter Calhoun asked tentatively.

"DC was fine," Josh quickly said. "I think we'll see some good things for the creamery in the new regulations. We should be able to capitalize on the push for hormone-free products and grow our market share." That wasn't what his grandfather had asked, but switching back into corporate-lawyer mode was almost automatic for him.

And they both knew it. "But…" the older man said in his gentle way.

Josh sighed. "You're not going to believe this," he said,

pinching the bridge of his nose between his fingers. "But Lucy Wilde is Sutton Winchester's oncologist."

"Is that so?" At first Josh thought his grandfather didn't remember who Lucy was, but then he added, "Have you seen her since graduation?"

"No." Josh left it at that. He didn't need to tell his grandfather that Lucy had looked at him with absolute venom in her eyes, and he also didn't need to mention that he had sent her flowers already.

"An oncologist? Well, good for her. You know…" His grandfather trailed off and Josh could infer what the old man was not saying.

You know, we always wondered what happened between you two. You know, she was such a nice girl. You know, you know, you know.

Shortly after Lucy and Josh had gone to their respective colleges far, far away from each other, Lucy's folks had moved out of Cedar Point. The Wilde family had no more connections with Iowa that he knew of. Lucy had not come back.

But Josh had.

And he would again.

Josh knew he shouldn't be sending flowers to anyone. What he had was his job and his family. And that was all he needed. He didn't need the feeling of desire that hit him low in the gut. He'd lived a good five years without it, after all.

And he especially didn't need to feel that desire for someone he had a messy history with. The less complicated his life, the happier he was.

And one thing was blindingly obvious—Lucy Wilde was complicated. With a capital *C*.

"If you see her again, you tell her I said hi," his grandfather went on as if Josh were actively participating in this conversation. "You know, she was such a nice girl. I'm glad to hear she is doing well. And Josh?"

"Yeah?"

"There's no rush. If you need to take a couple of weeks in Chicago, that's fine. Your brother and sisters and I have everything under control."

If Josh didn't know any better, he'd think his grandfather was actively telling him *not* to come home. "Yeah, okay. I'll let you know." And with that he hung up.

He stared at his phone. Why did his grandfather's insistence that he take some time off bother him so much? Josh didn't need to take time off. He was fine. He'd been fine for a long time.

His mind called up the images of the three women he'd had conversations with today—the Newports' receptionist, Eve Winchester and Lucy Wilde. He hadn't responded to Eve at all, but that feeling had been mutual. Nothing unusual there.

But that receptionist…she'd been actively flirting with Josh. He'd felt nothing other than noting she was a pretty girl. No reaction, no interest. As usual.

Then he'd come around that corner and seen Lucy. That had inspired a reaction in him, which was putting it mildly. Was it just the shock of seeing her again after all these years? Or was it something else?

Before he could fire up the truck, his phone buzzed and lit up with a text message. Josh jolted and almost dropped his phone, but he managed to keep a grip on it and prevent it from sliding down between his thigh and the seat.

For Pete's sake. His heart thumping along at a good clip, he looked at the screen. It was a Chicago area code. The text message read, I don't know if dinner is such a good idea.

Oh, thank God. Lucy had gotten the flowers. And she had not promptly told him to go to hell. On the whole, that was an improvement from their earlier conversation and, for some reason, made him feel...hopeful?

Why? Don't you eat dinner?

The little bubble popped up on the screen that meant she was typing something back. What do you really want?

The hell of it was, he didn't actually know. Why wasn't he letting this drop? Was it simply because he was in Chicago and it was easier to think about Lucy than it was to think about Sydney? Or was it because he wasn't sure what he was supposed to do to help out the Newport boys and this problem seemed less challenging?

Or...was it something else?

His fingers curved and he could almost feel her hand in his again, see the way her eyes had widened when he'd pulled her in.

It didn't seem possible that he wanted her. Not after five years without a single damned spark of attraction to any woman.

So he sidestepped the unfamiliar emotions and focused on what he could handle. To catch up with an old friend, he texted back.

The little bubble popped up, went away and then popped up again before he got a reply. You shouldn't send me flowers at work.

I didn't have your home address. It's just dinner, Lucy. He almost added, I've missed you, but at the last second, he changed his mind and backspaced over the words. Except he hit the wrong button and accidentally sent a partial text that read, I've mp.

Crap.

Sorry, he quickly texted. Hit the wrong button.

She didn't answer for the longest time—so long, in fact, that Josh was pretty sure she had decided to call it a day.

Then her reply popped up. One dinner. That's it.

Tonight? The moment he hit Send, he felt stupid. He hadn't come to Chicago for Lucy. He'd told Carson as much. He was here for the Newport boys and nothing more. Tonight was about settling in with a couple of six-packs and doing his level best to keep Brooks from going off the deep end.

But suddenly he realized he wanted her to come to dinner with him. And not just because they were old friends. Okay, because they were old friends—the very best of old friends.

Hell. He didn't know why he needed her to say yes. Only that he did.

Can't. Dealing with the Winchesters.

Disappointment unfurled in his chest, but then another text popped up. Tomorrow night. Meet me at Lou Malnati's on N. State. 7 o'clock.

Chicago pizza? I'm there, he texted.

All this was, he told himself, was two old friends getting together for dinner at a classic Chicago restaurant. And Josh would be lying if he said he didn't miss Chicago food. Cedar Point, Iowa, was a great small town and a wonderful place to grow up, but folks there considered Applebee's to be fancy and the ethnic food section of the grocery store consisted of refried beans and tortilla chips. Chicago dining was one of the very few things that he missed about the city.

His stomach rumbled.

So that was why he was suddenly excited. Not the fact that Lucy had said yes, but that he was going to get a good Chicago pizza for the first time in a long time.

Nothing more.

This was a mistake. Lucinda had spent the last twenty-four hours doing her regular job and dealing with the Winchester sisters. She understood that they loved their father, and she also understood that they only wanted what was best for him.

But they were going to drive her past madness in record time.

And what she wanted right now more than anything was to be curled up on her couch with a pint of ice cream—yes, Calhoun Creamery ice cream—and watching a Sandra Bullock movie.

She did not want to be walking into a pizzeria at 6:58 on a Thursday night. And she most especially did not want to be meeting Josh Calhoun.

Somehow, though, that hadn't stopped her from rushing home after work to change. Even worse, it hadn't stopped her from putting on one of her few dresses, a sleeveless navy blue wrap dress that she had worn to weddings and funerals alike. The evening was cool, and she'd put on a cream-colored cardigan so she didn't feel naked.

She knew that if the people from work saw her—especially someone like Elena—they would lose their collective minds, because Lucinda never dressed up, never put on mascara and lipstick, and she never, ever wore her hair down. All the things she was doing right now.

There was only one explanation. She had lost what was left of her mind.

This is not a date, she told herself as she forced her feet to carry her through the door and into the restaurant.

This was two old friends catching up—nothing more, nothing less.

Which did nothing to explain the way her stomach fluttered when Josh caught sight of her and stood up. Now that she was braced for seeing him again, it was easier to see how he had changed compared with what she remembered. He was taller and broader—a fact that was only emphasized by the heather-gray blazer he wore over a white dress shirt. He didn't have on his trademark hat, either. His hair was neatly combed and he was clean-shaven.

Two thoughts hit Lucinda at the exact same time.

God, he was the most handsome man she'd ever seen. So much more than the cute boy she'd been friends with.

And oh, *hell*. This was a date.

Those two things were quickly followed by a third, even more terrifying thought—it was too late to back out now.

"Lucy!" Josh came around the table and made a move as though he was going to hug her, but then he pulled up short and instead just put his hands on her shoulders. "You look great," he said.

It was the kind of thing that he could've just tossed off as a social nicety. But his gaze traveled over her body—which made her want to curl up self-consciously into a small ball and hide. This was painful. Excruciatingly so. She knew she was a failure when it came to sensuality. Heck, wasn't that why she'd put on the cardigan? Because it hid her shapeless body—and it was as close to her lab coat as she could get away with outside the hospital?

Then he added, "Wow. You've really grown up," in a tone that was uncomfortably close to reverential.

Was that a compliment? It had to be. There was no

mocking eye roll, no barely contained snicker behind his words. And, truthfully, she was pretty sure she'd be able to tell. She'd always been able to read Josh better than his own mother.

No, he was being sincere. And that somehow made everything worse. Lucinda forced herself to smile. "So have you. I'm surprised to see that hat isn't chemically bonded to your head."

"Hey!" Josh yelped in mock embarrassment. "At least I stopped sleeping with it on."

Against her will, Lucinda laughed. "Maturity in action, huh?"

Josh tried to look sheepish and didn't quite manage it. "Here," he said, stepping to the side and pulling out her chair for her. "Let me get this for you."

Yeah, this was a date. Back when they'd been friends in high school, Josh had treated her exactly the way he'd treated Gary—no special favors, no coddling. And certainly no holding chairs for either of them.

Her heart began to pound wildly as she sat. What was she doing? She didn't date. She didn't go out. She worked and she slept, and that was it. If this really was a date— and all signs seemed to be pointing to it—she had no idea what she was supposed to do or when she was supposed to do it without making a total fool of herself.

All she knew was that she was not going to make a fool out of herself. Not again.

Josh crossed to the other side of the table and sat down. "I don't know about you," he said in a light tone, "but I spent all day dealing with the Newport boys. I need a beer."

Okay, she could do this. As long as she didn't throw herself at him again, this would be fine. "And I was handling the Winchester girls," she admitted. That information didn't violate the HIPAA privacy laws, especially not when Josh already knew what was going on.

And a beer was exactly what she needed right now to get through this evening, too.

"What can I get you folks tonight?" a perky young waitress asked.

"I've missed Chicago deep-dish pizza like you wouldn't believe," Josh said, looking at her. "Is it okay if we get one to share?"

"That's fine." Lucinda also ordered a salad and Goose Island pale ale, while Josh ordered a Percheron Draft Stout ale.

Once the waitress left, Lucinda decided to go on the offensive. "Okay, so explain to me how you know the Newport boys, as you call them, and why you miss Chicago deep-dish pizza." Because if she could get Josh talking about himself, he wouldn't ask questions about her, and he especially wouldn't do something horrific like apologize for what happened all those years ago.

Josh gave her a look and she got the feeling that he knew exactly what she was about. But just as she began to squirm, he said, "I went to college with them. I lived in Chicago until about five years ago." As he said it, he dropped his gaze to the top of the table and Lucinda guessed that there were specific reasons he'd left Chicago. And whatever those reasons were, they weren't good things. She'd dealt with enough grief in her life to recognize sorrow when she saw it.

Her heart hurt for him. But she wasn't getting wrapped up in his problems, because doing that would mean that she still cared about him and she didn't. Not like that, anyway.

So she focused on keeping things light. "Wow—I had no idea you were here." Not that she would have done anything about it if she had. "What were you doing in Chicago? I mean, I knew you were going to go to college here, but I'd always assumed you'd gone right back to Cedar Point after you graduated and worked at the creamery."

He shrugged in that way he had. "College, at first. And then law school—"

"Wait, wait—law school?" She sat back in her chair and looked at him with new eyes. "You went to *law school*?"

"You don't have to be quite so shocked by it," he said with an easy smile.

Her cheeks heated. "No, I didn't mean—I mean, well, you were always really smart, you just..."

"Never did my homework?" His eyes crinkled as his smile deepened. "Yeah, I know. That maturity thing, it did a number on me. I grew up. I had to."

He said the last bit with that hint of sorrow again. And Lucinda knew what he was talking about.

They'd all had to grow up very fast after Gary had died.

She cleared her throat and caught sight of their waitress approaching with their drinks. "So, you're a lawyer. That's great! What's your specialty?"

Josh took a long pull on his stout. "I don't practice. My grandfather thought it would be a good idea if I knew corporate law—and I have to admit he was right—but I'm the CEO of Calhoun Creamery. So you weren't really that far off. I went home and started in the family business. Grandpa says hi, by the way."

"Really? He remembers me?"

Josh gave her a long look that made her stomach flutter—and her pulse flutter. And her eyelashes—they fluttered, too. Suddenly, she was one giant fluttering mass, like a butterfly having a seizure or something.

"Lucy," he said, and there was no missing the fact that his voice was deeper. It set off another round of quivering and she couldn't do anything but sit there and listen to what he had to say. "You're kind of unforgettable, you know that?"

Four

"Oh," Lucy gasped, which did some very interesting things to her chest.

Not that Josh was noticing her chest at the moment. He was also not noticing the way her cheeks colored prettily—nothing like the tomato red that she'd turned yesterday. No, this was a delicate pinking of her cheeks, and something inside Josh responded on a physical level that he hadn't anticipated and sure as hell couldn't control.

He hadn't been aiming for flattery. He knew Lucy too well to think that flattery would get him anywhere. He thought he was just being honest. She *was* unforgettable. The other day he'd recognized her the second he came around the corner and clapped eyes on her.

But seeing her physical reaction?

That feeling hit him again deep in his gut—*want*. Okay, so maybe it wasn't as unexpected as it had been yesterday, when it had caught him off guard. But it was still so new and unfamiliar that he honestly didn't know what to do with it. Should he compliment her again? Tell her how much he'd missed her? Should he tell her how lonely he'd been for the last five years?

All right, so the answer was clearly *no* on that one. No. He was in no mood to come off as pitiful and needy, a widower who was lost without the touch of a woman to soothe his wounded soul, blah, blah, *blah*.

He didn't want to tell her about Sydney. And he didn't want to talk about Gary, either. Or even his parents, for that matter. He didn't want to talk about people he'd lost, because that was in the past and there was no changing it. He just wanted to keep moving forward.

Plus, he'd made a promise to Lucy. This was just dinner between two old friends. He was out of practice when it came to flirting and seduction and, given the rough ending to their friendship back in high school, he didn't really think testing the waters with her was a smart idea.

Which meant he didn't know what he was supposed to do next.

Lucy came to his rescue, though. "Do you know," she said, and he didn't miss the way her voice was slightly softer than it had been just a moment ago, "you're the only person who's called me Lucy in years? I mean, besides my mom."

"And your father?"

She sighed wearily but waved away the comment. "He passed from a heart attack about six years ago."

So much for getting away from the subject of people they'd lost. "I'm sorry to hear that. I didn't know."

"Thank you," she said, but she didn't sound like she was on the verge of an emotional collapse. "My mom went through a brief period where every time she saw me, she would say, 'If only you'd been a cardiologist,

Lucy,' but she got over it. It's fine. She misses him—I miss him—but no one lives forever. It was his time."

Josh gaped at her. He remembered Gary's funeral. It had almost destroyed her—and then he couldn't help but feel he'd finished the job. "I guess as an oncologist, you deal with death every day?"

She nodded and took another drink. "It does go with the territory. I won't say it's gotten easier over the years, but I've come to accept that I can't save everyone." Incredibly, she even managed a small smile. "Although I do try."

Josh drained half of his bottle of beer in one swig. He hated this town. Everyone and everything in it represented an ongoing, never-ending struggle between life and death, but it seemed to him that death won a hell of a lot more than life did.

Desperately, he changed subjects. "Seems to me that you've been pretty successful at that. You're the youngest-ever head of the oncology department at Midwest—and the first woman. I could be wrong, but I'm guessing that they don't give those titles to just anyone."

Her eyes got wide again and he was struck by their light blue color, with a touch of gray around the edges. Something rare and wonderful and completely Lucy. "Did you look me up?"

"Of course," he said, figuring a little internet stalking was no big deal between friends. "I even read some of your published papers."

Her eyes narrowed and an old feeling of being busted floated up out of the past. Then she grinned at him. "You always were a terrible liar."

Josh laughed. This was better. Lucy might be unforgettable, but he had sort of forgotten how much fun it was to talk to her. She had always held his feet to the fire and expected more out of him. "Okay, okay—you got me. But I did read the titles of some of your papers, and some of them had a very helpful opening paragraph that summarized things in words I almost understood." She giggled, a sweet sound, and he heard himself say, "You're really quite brilliant, you know." Which even he knew was straight-up flirting.

There was that blush again. It made her look soft and, in a way, almost vulnerable.

Josh's arms began to itch with an unfamiliar urge to pull her against him, to settle his hands around her waist, to pull those massive glasses off her face and tilt her head back and...

What the hell was wrong with him? Seriously, aside from his sisters hugging him, he hadn't touched anyone in the last five years. But now he'd spent no more than thirty-five minutes, tops, with Lucy Wilde and suddenly he could barely control himself?

Thankfully, the waitress came back with Lucy's salad and Josh ordered another beer. He didn't normally drink quite as much as he had in the last thirty-six hours, but this was Chicago. He needed all the liquid courage he could handle.

"So tell me about you," he went on. He wasn't trying to make her blush, but the fact that it kept happening was... Well, it was something.

She gave him a look as she poured her dressing over her lettuce. "There's not much to tell. I went to college, I went to med school, I did my residencies, I do my job. It's a good job and I like doing it. We're making a lot of progress on alternative therapies and targeting the DNA structures of malignant cells and..." She wrinkled her nose in a way that Josh might have called adorable if the gesture hadn't been paired with one of Lucy's cut-the-crap looks. "I'm going to eat this salad and you're going to tell me about you because I, unlike *some* people at this table, have not Googled anyone recently." And then she shoved a huge forkful of salad into her mouth.

Josh couldn't help but grin at her. There was something comforting about the fact that, after all these years, Lucy was still just as snarky as she had ever been. "I'm sure there's more to tell than that." Her eyes narrowed at this. She chewed vigorously and held up her fork as if she were going to stab him in the hand with it. "Okay, I get the hint." Now it was his turn to feel uncomfortable because—

Because of Sydney.

"So you went to college with the Newports?" Lucy said in between bites.

"Yup. I met Graham first and then I became friends with all three of them. I was a little lost my first year." Which was kind of an understatement. He'd spent his freshman year in a daze. He'd been homesick and, because he'd lost Gary and, in a different way, Lucy, he felt very alone. "We all got along pretty well. They didn't seem to mind that I was a country bumpkin."

Lucy rolled her eyes at him. "I hate it when you do that," she said. "You were always underselling yourself back in high school. Used to drive me nuts."

He'd never really thought of it in those terms. "I wasn't underselling myself," he said defensively. "I was just immature as all hell."

She smirked at him. "No argument here."

He gave her a dull look. "If I was so immature, how come you put up with me?"

The question hung in the air and Lucy was the one to look away first. In that moment, Josh had to wonder if they would've been friends if it hadn't been for Gary.

Maybe she had been right yesterday when she'd said that they couldn't be friends anymore.

"Because you're a good person," Lucy said in a quiet voice. "I mean, you were the heir to the Calhoun Creamery fortune. You could've easily been a selfish, egotistical bully of a boy. Who would've stopped you? You were cute and charming and you could have run that entire town into the ground. And you didn't."

Josh didn't know what to say to that. Yes, he'd always been destined for the creamery. But his parents—God rest their souls—and his grandparents had never handed him a single thing on a silver platter.

"I always admired you for that," Lucy added. "You were an honorable man then and, even though you might have made me a *little* mad yesterday, it's clear that's still who you are. You came to Chicago to help some friends out and brokered a peace between two groups of people who've been driving me crazy for weeks. Of course," she went on in an unnaturally perky voice, "if you barge into a medical decision like that again, I'll take back what I said about you."

"That would be terrible," he agreed just as their pizza was delivered to the table. "You have no idea how good this smells. Iowa doesn't have a clue how to make pizza."

They both scooped slices onto their plates and began to eat. The silence stretched between them, but it wasn't uncomfortable. Josh was still trying to break down what Lucy had said and reconcile it with everything that had happened in the last twenty-four hours. There was almost too much information to process.

"So," Lucy finally said in between bites of pizza, "how long did you live in Chicago?"

"Almost twelve years. I used to work for the Newports." She was gaping at him. "What?"

She shrugged. "Just having trouble reconciling the guy who used to take me cow tipping with a corporate lawyer who worked for the Newports."

Josh couldn't help but laugh at that. "It's been a long time since I tipped a cow. Don't tell my grandpa," he hurried to add.

"You really have grown up," she said. And before Josh could think of anything to say to that, her phone buzzed. "Sorry," she said, digging into her purse. "It's probably the Winchesters. Just a moment."

"No worries. Take your time." He finished his first slice of pizza and dove into a second while Lucy stared at her phone, texting and grimacing. With a heavy sigh, she dropped her phone back in her purse. "Sorry," she said again. "I'm basically always on call. Especially when it comes to certain, shall we say, *difficult* patients."

"Everything okay?"

"That was Grace—have you met her?" Josh shook his head no. He would've answered out loud, but a proper Chicago pizza had a lot of cheese and he was still chewing. "She was telling me that they've got everything set up for her father at home and she wanted to know when I can come by and check it out."

Josh finally got past the cheese and took another drink of beer. "I owe you an apology, you know."

Everything about Lucy went stiff. It almost looked as if she was expecting a brawl to break out. "Oh?"

"For yesterday. It was never my intention to undermine you or make you look bad in front of your patients. I know how dedicated you are, but—"

"But you were just doing what you always do, Josh. Keeping the peace."

That didn't exactly clarify whether or not she was in a forgiving mood. But, then again, she had come to dinner with him and she hadn't stabbed him with her fork, so that had to count for something, right? "What are you going to do? That is, if you can tell me."

"I think I can. I've got surgery in the morning and the rest of my day is packed, so it looks like I'll be going over after dinner tomorrow night to check out the room." Her shoulders slumped and he could tell that she was not happy with this development. "They're basically buying the hospital's cancer pavilion expansion, and for that I had to agree to spend nights at the Winchester estate for as long as it takes."

This was his fault. And, more than that, he felt responsible for making it better. That wouldn't be easy, balancing what Carson and his brothers wanted against what the Winchester girls wanted, all while making sure he didn't undermine Lucy's authority.

"Tell me how I can help," he said earnestly. Because there had to be a way to make this work.

Lucy gave him a measured look. "I suppose convincing everyone that Sutton's better off in the hospital is out of the question?"

He had a feeling it was, but he said, "I can give it a try."

She shook her head, but she was smiling when she did it. "I appreciate that, but we both know that ship has sailed." She wiped her mouth on her napkin and tossed it onto her plate. She'd only had one piece of pizza and her salad. Somehow, Josh had eaten most of the rest by himself.

She had promised him one dinner. But that didn't seem like it would be enough, not now. "You know," he said in a casual tone, "the thing I miss most about Chicago is the food. The pizza, the Korean barbecue, the Indian naan—we have a Chinese restaurant back in Cedar Point now, and it's not bad. But it's not like what you can get here." He steeled himself for the rejection he was pretty sure was coming, but he asked anyway. "Let me take you out to dinner tomorrow night before you go over to the Winchesters. I don't know about you, but I would kill for some Thai food."

He wasn't necessarily asking her out on a date, right? No more than he'd asked her out on a date tonight. They were old friends, so why not catch up over dinner?

But he wasn't being honest with himself. Because the difference between having dinner with Lucy and having dinner with Carson or Graham or Brooks was so huge as to be laughable. The Newport boys were his best friends, but when he looked at them he didn't get the feeling in his gut that previously he'd thought was out of his reach forever.

He and Lucy were friends. And he *had* always liked her.

She wasn't looking at him. She had placed her fingers on top of the tablecloth and was staring down at them, and he got the feeling that she was about to deliver bad news. Hell.

Then she said, "I don't think I'll have time," which was not the same thing as *no, I won't*. "I have a busy day tomorrow and then I'll have to go home and pack up so that I can move out to the Winchester estate for who knows how long. I'm sorry."

"You know," Josh said, trying to keep from laughing at her, "they have this thing now—maybe you've heard of it? It's called 'takeout.' Modern technology at its finest. You order the food and then—it's the latest thing— you take it home and eat it there."

And just like that, they were back in high school. He was teasing her and she was glaring at him, and then she picked up her napkin and threw it at his head. He dodged and they both started laughing.

It felt good to laugh again. It wasn't that he hadn't laughed in the last five years. So maybe it just felt good to laugh with Lucy again.

When they finally quieted down—after several judgmental looks from other diners—Josh tried again. "I got you into this mess, sort of. The least I can do is bring you food and carry your luggage."

"You're right," she said with a smirk that meant that he had it coming and he had no choice but to sit there and let her cut him to shreds. "It is the least you can do. You're on. I like pad see ew—medium hot plus." She dug around in her purse until she came up with the stub of a pencil and a scrap of paper. She wrote down her address and slid it over the table to him. "I should get home by six thirty and, I told Grace Winchester that I would try to be out to the estate by eight thirty. That doesn't give us a lot of time."

That made Josh's eyebrows jump up. *Time for what?* He had meant it when he said this was just dinner—but was something else on the menu?

"To eat and get packed," Lucy hurried to add, her eyes getting wide again.

He couldn't fight the grin that took hold of his lips. Sure, this was still just friends having dinner. But there was no mistaking it—she had thought the same thing he had.

"I'm looking forward to it."

Whatever *it* wound up being, he was looking very forward to it.

Five

Despite the fact that Lucinda had told Josh that she would get home about six thirty, she managed to get home at six. True, she had to bend the truth to get out of the meeting with John Jackson by saying, "I've got to run—the Winchesters, you know."

It wasn't entirely a lie. She was heading over to the Winchester estate that very evening to set up camp.

But first she found herself doing some last-minute cleaning while simultaneously trying to apply mascara without putting out her own eye.

Needless to say, it was not going well. She'd gone— what? Six months without wearing mascara? Yes, the last time she'd caked it on had been to go to that gala fundraiser for the hospital. Coincidentally, that was also the last time she'd worn her dress.

Yet here she was wearing mascara for the second time in two days. And why?

Josh Calhoun. A man she'd convinced herself she never wanted to see ever again.

Six thirty came and went. Then six thirty-one. Six thirty-two.

Oh, God, she was going to drive herself insane. She forced herself to stand in front of her meager closet. What exactly did one wear when sleeping over at the billionaire's estate to make sure that he got his cancer treatments on time? Somehow, her fleecy pajama bottoms featuring frolicking penguins didn't seem quite right.

In general, frolicking penguins did not exactly scream professionalism and medical authority.

Maybe she would just sleep in a pair of her dress slacks. She'd be rumpled, but at least she wouldn't be humiliated.

Her buzzer sounded, making her jump. Six thirty-six. That could still be reasonably construed as being on time.

She hurried to the intercom. "Yes?"

"I have pad thai," Josh promised over the staticky intercom.

She pushed the button that would let him in. "Come on up." Although she didn't know how she was going to eat at this moment.

Her stomach was a hot mess, and as much as she tried to tell herself it was simply because she was about to put herself at the mercy of the Winchesters and the Newports for an indeterminate amount of time, that wasn't it. That wasn't it by a long shot.

No, the reason she was nervous was knocking on her door. "Lucy?"

She took a deep breath and opened the door. She hadn't thought of herself as Lucy in so long that the name still sounded weird. But she couldn't imagine Josh calling her anything else.

He was leaning against her door frame, his arms full

of grocery bags. "Good Lord!" she gasped as she stared at the bags.

"Dinner is served," he said in what could only be described as a gallant voice. He stepped into her apartment and then, before she could process what he was doing, he leaned down and kissed her on the forehead. "I have Thai," he said, leaning back but not stepping clear. "A bottle of California Chardonnay and some ice cream from this new place I've heard of—Calhoun Creamery?" He winked at her. "I hope it's good. I got you mint chocolate chip."

Lucinda knew that she needed to do something or say something. Maybe even shut the door. But he had just short-circuited her brain.

He'd kissed her. He'd remembered what her favorite kind of ice cream was.

And more than any of that, he was *here*.

Josh was still standing over her, smiling down as if he was enjoying her complete and total befuddlement. "I'll just put this in the kitchen, shall I?"

"Oh. Yes." She gestured in the general direction of her kitchen and managed to get her door shut. She was suddenly very aware of why, exactly, having Josh at her place made her so twitchy.

It was because they were alone. Dinner at the pizzeria last night had been out in public. But right now?

It was him and her. And some Thai food.

She realized that she had never had a man over to her apartment before. Which sounded pathetic, but it was the truth. At almost the exact same instant, she remembered the last time she'd been alone with Josh—that awful night she'd embarrassed herself so completely in front of him.

Right. He may have kissed her, but a friendly little peck on the forehead wasn't any kind of seduction. Therefore, it wouldn't do for her to act like this was anything more than a continuation of their conversation last night. They were friends. And there was no way she was going to risk humiliation a second time.

Josh Calhoun was off-limits.

She surveyed what seemed like enough food for a dinner party for ten. "Josh, how much food did you buy?"

"This?" Josh looked at the chaos he had unleashed on her kitchen island. "It's just some pad see ew, pad thai, crab rangoon, egg rolls, rice—it's not that much."

"You know it's just the two of us, right?"

He paused in the process of putting the ice cream in the freezer. "Actually, I wasn't one hundred percent sure. It's possible you have a roommate or…someone." He shut the freezer with more force than was necessary. Then he turned and gave her that easy grin. "We didn't discuss that at dinner the other night."

She blinked at him. "I'm not seeing anyone." Which was the truth. However, it also neatly sidestepped the fact that she had never really seen anyone except for Gary. But she was doing her best to avoid sounding pathetic on what was still probably not a real date, so she left that part out. "You?"

"No." Considering that he was the one who had brought up significant others, his clipped tone seemed out of character. "Let me get the wine open. Can you get some glasses?"

Oh. Right. She stepped around him—her kitchen was small—and got two matching glasses out of the cabinet. They weren't wineglasses, but at least they were clean. She gave them to Josh and then got out the plates and the silverware.

"Nice place," Josh said as he poured them each a glass of wine. "Have you lived here long?"

"About four years—since I joined Midwest."

"You have a hell of a view," he said, looking out toward the living room with its floor-to-ceiling windows.

She'd arranged the couch so that it faced the windows instead of the flat-screen television she only used to watch movies. She didn't have drapes or anything on those windows. She hadn't wanted anything between her and the sky and the water.

She glanced at him out of the corner of her eye. "To be honest, most of the time I eat on the couch so that I can watch the colors at sunset."

"Then by all means," Josh said, grabbing a plate and loading it up.

They carried their plates and wine over to the couch and settled in. The sun was just beginning to set behind the building, and the sky over Lake Michigan was going from blue to pink and orange. They ate for few moments before Lucinda worked up the nerve to ask him about that clipped *no*. "I'm surprised."

"About what?" Josh asked around a mouthful of crab rangoon.

"That you're not seeing anyone. I always assumed you'd settle down, have some kids." She knew immediately that it was the wrong thing to have said. She would have given anything to be able to take it back. But it was too late. The question hung over Josh like a dark cloud, and not even the brilliant sunset already fading into purple could burn it away.

"I'm sorry," she said quickly. God, she was an idiot. Because his reaction could only mean one thing.

He had done just that and it hadn't worked out.

"Don't be." His tone was casual, but she heard how forced it was. "It was just one of those things."

She wasn't buying that for a second. "Do you want to talk about it?"

"Not really. But I don't want to hide things from you." He set his plate on the coffee table and leaned back, his eyes fixed at some point way out over the lake. "Sydney. Her name was Sydney."

Was. That was possibly the worst word in the English language. *Was.*

"Graham Newport introduced us in my junior year. And, man, I was gone from the start."

She needed to say something here, something comforting and understanding that still kept things light. She was, after all, a professional at this sort of conversation. She had them weekly—daily, even. Bad news and loss were her constant companions.

But Josh wasn't her patient and Lucinda simply didn't know what to say.

He slid a sideways glance at her. "She was smart and fierce and she made me toe the line." He grinned, but it was a sad thing. It made Lucy's chest hurt. "She made me laugh. She's the reason I made it through law school. She didn't like it when I undersold myself, either. You would've loved her, Lucy."

"I would have," Lucy murmured. "You needed that."

"Yeah."

Silence fell between them as darkness fell outside.

Too late, Lucy realized that she didn't have any lights on in the apartment. One moment, she and Josh were sitting in a nearly light room. The next, they were in almost total darkness. "You asked why I left Chicago," Josh said in the darkness. "My life here was with her. And when she died…"

Lucy nodded, belatedly realizing that he probably couldn't see her. There was something comforting about the darkness, where she couldn't see his expression and he couldn't see hers. "So you went back to Cedar Point."

"I did."

They were quiet for some time longer. Lucy finished her wine and sat forward, leaving her glass on the coffee table next to the remains of her dinner.

When she sat back, her shoulder brushed against Josh's. It was another innocent touch, much like his kiss on her forehead earlier. But at the same time, it wasn't.

Josh shifted and his arm came around her shoulders. She wasn't sure if he pulled her against him or she was the one who moved first. The outcome was the same either way. She curled up against the side, her arm around his waist and her head against his shoulder as he held her.

There was an intimacy to the moment, but for once Lucy didn't overthink it. Josh had been right—they would always be friends. Right now, she wanted to let her friend know she was here for him and that she understood. More than anyone, she understood.

She didn't know how much time passed before Josh spoke again. "I didn't really mean for that to be quite such a downer." His voice was low and soft in her ear.

"It's okay." And, honestly, it was. "In case you've forgotten, I'm an oncologist. Death is a part of my life. You don't have to apologize for it."

He squeezed her tight. "Thank you," he said in a voice so quiet she had to look up to make sure she'd heard him correctly.

"For what?"

Somehow, she knew that he was looking down at her even though the room was almost pitch-black. Then he shifted and his fingertips brushed against her cheek and traced a path along her jaw. "For not telling me to get over it or move on or that it was God's will. Because that's what people always say and I hate it."

His fingers continued to move over her cheek in a slow, stroking motion. She wasn't surprised at what he'd said—she'd heard it all and more. "I would never dismiss your grief like that," she told him. Objectively, she knew all about the stages of grief and how people processed their loss.

But she wasn't thinking objectively right now. The arm that was around her side moved and his hand slid over her ribs and down her waist. She knew without even having to see that he was getting closer to her. She could feel the heat radiating off his chest, and the warmth of his breath against her forehead and then her nose. When he spoke again, she could feel the ghost of his lips moving against hers. "I missed you, Lucy."

This was wrong. So, *so* wrong. He was still in love with his wife and Lucy was married to her job, and it seemed as if there was something she was supposed to be doing right now—something that did not involve melting against him and trying to decide if she would wait for his kiss or just take one herself.

But she couldn't think of anything except Josh. Her hand skimmed up his chest and over his jaw and then there was no more space between them.

Once, she'd kissed him. She didn't remember very much of it because she'd been upset and desperate, and then there'd been the dawning horror that not only was he not kissing her back, but he was pushing her away and saying he couldn't do "this."

The memory was so painful that, for a moment, she was physically locked up with panic. She couldn't handle the humiliation, not again.

And then Josh sighed into her mouth, a sound of satisfaction and need like she'd never heard before, and Lucy stopped thinking about that first, terrible kiss. Instead, she lost herself in his lips and his arms. Here, in the dark, it was okay. Everything was okay and getting better by the second.

Then his tongue traced the seam of her lips and she opened for him and everything went from being okay to something else—something entirely different. Better. Hotter.

Because, all of a sudden, Lucy's skin started to tingle and her heart pounded and, unexpectedly, her nipples tightened to the point of pain—so much so that she arched her back to get closer to Josh in an effort to relieve the pressure. His sigh turned into a growl, a noise that she felt throughout her entire body. The space between her legs grew hot and heavy and the pressure was maddening.

It scared her a little, the intensity of the physiological responses that blossomed out of nowhere. Because suddenly, after years of convincing herself she did not need a physical relationship with a man—that she didn't need any physical relationship at all—she realized what a lie that had been.

She needed this. She needed *him*.

And she needed him now. She shifted, unsure of how to ask for what she wanted—unsure of what it was exactly that she wanted. But the pressure on her nipples and the weight between her legs were pushing her toward *something*.

As she tried to adjust her angle toward Josh, he surprised her by lifting her onto his lap. She straddled him, which made everything better and worse at the same time. "God, Lucy," he groaned before his hands slid down her back and his mouth captured hers again.

He gripped her bottom and settled her against him

more firmly. She whimpered as his erection made contact with her, hard and hot between her legs. All she could think was, *finally*. After all these years, she was *finally* going to find out what everyone else in the whole wide world already knew about.

Her head fell back as Josh ground against her, but he kept kissing her. His lips trailed down her neck and she arched into him again, her body begging for things she didn't have the words for. She was bracketed in his arms as his mouth moved lower. He grabbed the placket of her shirt in his teeth and pulled it to the side, exposing the top of her breast.

"I want this," she managed to say as she loosened her grip on him long enough to undo the stubborn buttons. This must be why people were always ripping shirts off in movies—buttons took too damn long.

Finally, she got three of the stupid things open. That was as far as she got before Josh was pushing her up and his mouth closed over her breast. Even though Lucy still had her bra on, the feeling of his mouth on her body was electric. Synapses and neurons all fired at once and the result had her shivering and shaking in his arms.

She wished she could see him. That was the only thing she'd change about this moment.

"Let me, babe," Josh said against her skin as she clung to him. His hands moved—one had stayed on her bottom and the other came around the front to cup her breast. He pulled her bra aside and then his lips wrapped around her nipple and his teeth were on her skin and—and—and—

"Josh!" His name was on her lips and his mouth was on her body, and she wanted this like she'd never wanted anything else. She'd always wanted this.

"That's it, Lucy. I just want to…" His voice trailed off

as he reached between her legs and began to stroke over the seam of her pants.

Lucy moaned. She understood the biology of the human female body. But she knew *nothing*. Nothing compared with what Josh was effortlessly doing to her. He sucked at her breast, gripped her bottom and rubbed her clit and there wasn't a single thing Lucinda could do about any of it. She was helpless in his arms and if she was making a fool of herself, then so be it.

She bore down on his hand and buried her fingers in his hair as she held him against her breast. Just when she didn't think she could take it for another second, Josh groaned, "Lucy," and she lost whatever control over herself she'd been clinging to.

She climaxed in his arms with such force that she almost pitched herself right off his lap. "Oh, God," she whispered in a shaky voice as Josh gathered her back in his arms and pulled her against his chest.

"You're beautiful," he got out before he was kissing her again with even more urgency.

She wasn't sure she could buy that—she wasn't beautiful and, besides, it was pitch-black in this room. But he grabbed her bottom again and was grinding up against her, and even though she didn't think she could handle another climax like that, she could already feel the pressure building again. "You," she tried to tell him in an authoritative voice. "Your turn."

His only response was to groan as she shifted against him. She didn't know what she was doing, but that didn't seem to matter. She kissed him and let her body move as it wanted to and—

Her phone buzzed and lit up, an unwelcome spotlight in their dark little world. Lucy jolted against him. "Ignore that," she told him. Whoever it was, they could just call back later. There was nothing in the world so important as what was happening right now between her and Josh.

Then he had to ruin it by asking, "What time is it?"

She froze. There was something that she was maybe supposed to be doing right now—she was supposed to be at the Winchester estate, seeing if they'd gotten a room set up for Sutton Winchester so he could continue his treatment at home.

"Oh, crap—the Winchesters." She pulled away from Josh and threw herself off the couch. She managed to get a light turned on without breaking anything and hurried to her phone. Yep, it was a series of texts from Nora Winchester, asking her where she was and if she was still planning on stopping by. "Oh, crap," she repeated again. It was nine o'clock.

She was late. God, how she hated being late. People depended on her. The least she could do was be dependable. Instead, she'd been throwing herself at Josh Calhoun—the very last person she should be screwing around with. She'd completely lost her mind, hadn't she? Because she was not the kind of person who put something as fleeting as physical desire ahead of her duties and responsibilities. There were lives on the line, damn it. She knew that.

But Josh had made her forget for a few glorious, humiliating moments. He'd made her forget everything, including herself. Especially herself. Shame burned at her cheeks and she couldn't meet his gaze when he said, "Lucy?"

One simple rule—she was not to embarrass herself in front of Josh. Not again. Never again.

And she'd done just that.

Damn it all.

Six

Josh sat on the couch in a state of shock. What the hell had just happened?

One minute, he was enjoying good Thai food with an old friend, watching the sunset over Lake Michigan and not actively hating Chicago.

The next, they were wrapped up in each other, hands and mouths everywhere. Although Josh was a little out of practice, he was pretty sure he'd made it good for her. He wasn't some green boy anymore. Lucy had moaned and writhed and shuddered against him, and damned if it hadn't been good. Amazing, even.

And then, just like all the light switches Lucy was actively flipping on, the whole thing was over and done.

He scrubbed his hand over his face and willed his erection to stand way the hell down as he tried to make sense of the situation. He wasn't having a lot of luck at that. He hadn't wanted—really and truly *wanted*—in such a damned long time that the whole thing had turned his brain into mush.

He shifted, trying to figure out what he needed to do next.

"I can't..." Lucy muttered. "I don't even know what to pack. And I'm late!"

That's what she was thinking about? He was trying to figure out how he could finish what they'd started together and she was worried about being *late*? "Lucy."

Not that she listened. She didn't. "I can't be late, Josh. I'm never late."

Well. At least she was acknowledging he was still in the room. "Why do you have to pack?"

"Because I'm supposed to stay at the house while Sutton's being treated," she replied, looking at him as if he were a special kind of stupid.

That made no sense. "But I thought he was still in the hospital?"

"He is," she snapped and then he thought she muttered something about...penguins?

He shook his head again, trying to get the blood to start flowing to his brain instead of other parts. He could still feel Lucy's weight as she straddled him, so close... "You're not going to discharge him tonight, are you?"

"Of course not!"

"Why are you packing right now, then?"

Lucy came to a dead stop. "What?" she asked in utter confusion.

Josh forced himself to stand, although this was not much more comfortable than sitting had been. "If Sutton isn't going home tonight, why do you need to stay there tonight?"

"I...don't?" She was completely, if adorably, flustered.

"I guess I thought I should—I don't know—already have my stuff over there? Before he got there?"

Josh couldn't help but grin at her. One of the smartest people he'd ever known—and she hadn't made that mental leap. "You know, there's such a thing as being too prepared."

She shot him one hell of a mean look—easily the meanest look she'd given him since he'd first seen her again. But if she was trying to scare him off, it wasn't working. In fact, it was having the opposite effect.

Because all he wanted to do was walk over there and kiss her until she stopped scowling at him.

He didn't, though. Being married for seven years had taught him a few things and he wasn't so slow as to forget what those things were. Kissing her right now would guarantee failure.

So, instead, he grabbed his keys and said, "Come on, let's go."

"What?"

"Let's go."

"You're not coming with me," she said in a tone of voice that made it clear this point was not up for discussion.

Except it was. "Yes, I am. Come on." He opened her door. And then he waited because he knew damn well she wasn't going to fall in line that easily. Not his Lucy.

Then he caught himself. When had she become his Lucy?

The moment he'd kissed her.

"No, you're *not*." It was at that point that Josh realized she might actually punch him. At the very least, she wanted to.

Unexpectedly, a wave of guilt hit him. "You've had some wine and you're upset." He hadn't thought it possible, but her glare got even meaner. This was going from bad to worse. "And we need to talk."

"No, we don't. Nothing to talk about." She grabbed her purse, slung it over her shoulder and began to wrangle her hair back into some semblance of order. "And you've had some wine, too."

He grinned at her again, not that she saw. He easily had sixty, maybe seventy pounds on her and he'd had half a glass of wine. "Lucy."

She stopped her frenetic movements, but she didn't meet his eyes. She didn't say anything, either. He had that odd sensation of guilt again—that he'd embarrassed her.

True, he'd kissed her—but she'd kissed him back. Enthusiastically. And he was pretty sure that she had said, "I want this," and he was even surer that she'd told him it was his turn.

So why the hell was she so embarrassed?

He tried a different approach. "I want to drive you. I want to spend more time with you."

She took a step back and he saw that she hadn't been ready for that line of attack. "You can't," she said definitively. "Patient privacy."

He had to go with his ace in the hole. She was not going to be happy about this. "Carson asked me to stop by the Winchester estate and make sure that everything was in order." Which was not something Josh was happy about. But he'd mentioned he was going to have dinner with Lucy before she went out to the Winchester estate and Carson had made his request. Josh had almost forgotten about it while he'd been in Lucy's arms and it about killed him to bring it up now.

The color drained out of Lucy's face.

"Oh. I see." And just like that, she shut down. It hurt

to watch. "Well. If you've been invited by family, then by all means."

She stalked past him, her head held high and her eyes focused anywhere but where he stood. He knew, without a doubt, that he was screwed.

As he followed her down the stairs, he tried to think—what would Sydney say? They'd had their share of disagreements and occasional fights in the ten years that they'd known each other. And Josh was known for being a peacemaker. He was the one who smoothed over fights, not the one who made them worse.

Which was clearly what he had done right now.

Lucy was not Sydney. While the two women probably would've gotten along and maybe even been friends, they were not the same woman. Appearances had been very important to Sydney. When a woman started her own high-end interior design business, appearances were everything. For her, Josh had willingly put away his hats and shoved his shit-kicker boots into the back of the closet. He'd worn corporate suits with the lawyerly ties because having a professional husband who made her look good had made Sydney happy.

Lucy, on the other hand… Today she wore basically the same outfit she'd been wearing at the hospital work site. A blouse, some dark slacks and her lab coat. She didn't have coordinating jewelry and her hair had a mind of its own. At best, her shoes could be described as serviceable—the round-toe things with thick heels that so many medical professionals wore.

She hadn't really changed that much. Exchange the slacks for jeans and the blouses for sweatshirts and she looked almost exactly the same as she had in high school.

Except for the curves. The soft, luscious curves that he had had in his hands for way too short a period of time.

The Lucy he remembered had been someone who hadn't blossomed yet. Maybe that was why she had always fit in with him and Gary so well—she'd been something of a tomboy and had certainly looked the part. No one in their right mind would have ever accused Sydney of being a tomboy.

No one in their right mind would have ever asked Sydney Laurence to go cow tipping on a Saturday night. But Lucy used to.

They made it out of the building and Josh pointed toward where he'd parked his truck. Lucy froze again. "Wait—you're still driving that truck?"

"Yeah. Is that a problem?"

"No…" He glanced down at her and saw that she was worrying her bottom lip—the very same lip he himself had been worrying not twenty minutes ago. "I would've figured you'd had a new car since then. That thing has to be twenty, twenty-five years old."

"Close. It's nineteen years old. I had the engine completely rebuilt about five years ago." When he'd come home from Chicago, actually. But he didn't tell her that part. "It looks like hell, but it runs great." He held the door for her.

She still had her car keys in her hand. "Do you even know where you're going? This isn't Cedar Point, you know. This is Chicago."

"Believe it or not, I know my way around this town. And after my last conversation with Carson, I programmed the Winchester estate address into my directions."

Lucy sighed and climbed up into the truck. As gallantly as he could, Josh closed the door—which took a bit of force, since he didn't use the passenger side door much and parts of it had rusted. Then he went around to the driver's side, climbed in and started the truck. The engine gurgled and then roared to life as he called up the directions on his phone.

They drove in silence for a few minutes. For once, traffic was not horrendous as they headed up the North Shore toward the Winchester estate.

Josh was at a loss as to what he was supposed to say now. If it were anyone else but Lucy sitting in the car next to him—anyone but a woman he had been kissing and hoping to do a whole lot more with—he would've known what to say. What was it about her that tied him in knots?

Wait, don't answer that, he told himself.

So he said nothing while the silence between them grew heavy. He didn't regret kissing her, though. He didn't regret touching her, either. He wanted to do it again. For the first time in five years, he wanted to hold a woman in his arms and lose himself in her touch and her sounds and her body.

Maybe that was part of the problem. He hadn't done this dance in such a long time—long before Sydney had died. He was thirty-five and the last time he'd started a new relationship had been fifteen years ago. He was rusty and it was showing.

But he wanted Lucy. It didn't make complete sense to him, but he *wanted* her. He wanted to go back to being tangled up with her on the couch in the dark and listening to her sigh his name. He wanted to know he could still do that for a woman.

He wanted to feel alive again, and for a few short minutes that was how Lucy had made him feel. No one else had given that to him.

And if he didn't get his head out of his ass, those few short minutes were all he was going to get.

At a stoplight, he glanced over at her. Her back was

ramrod straight and her eyes were focused straight ahead. She looked almost as if he were driving her to her doom. Was that because they were going to the Winchester estate or because she was in the car with him?

Discretion was the better part of valor. "I'm sorry."

She made an indelicate snorting noise. "Is that a general all-purpose apology? Because if you're hoping that will solve the world's ills, I'm here to tell you it won't."

Damn. Not that Sydney had ever bought that lame attempt, either. So he tried again—and this time, he was very specific. "I thought you were enjoying our time on the couch. I would never do anything to hurt you. Including putting you in an awkward position."

She snorted again, this time louder. Because, yeah, even he had to admit that the inside of this truck was awkward. "I don't want to talk about it."

Crap. He was in serious trouble here and he knew it. "It won't happen again."

He hit another stoplight and glanced at her again. He wouldn't have thought it was possible, but she was sitting up even straighter now. "No. Of course not." Her voice had gotten quiet and something in her tone pulled at him.

It was that guilt again, damn it. Not the same kind of guilt he'd felt when Sydney had died.

If it was possible for guilt to feel familiar, though, this did. It niggled at the back of his mind, like an old bug bite that he'd accidentally brushed so that it suddenly itched again. "Okay, I just apologized for the wrong thing. Are you going to explain why you're mad at me or should I just keep guessing?"

She didn't even snort this time. "The light is green." The moment she said it, horns began to blare behind them.

God, he hated Chicago. Josh accelerated through the

intersection and started to drive like he meant it. He hadn't expected to suddenly find himself weaving across traffic lanes like any native Chicagoan would do, but he was upset at Lucy and he was upset at himself. This whole situation stunk and he didn't know what else to do.

And he *always* knew what to do. That's what made him so good at his job. He ran the Calhoun Creamery because he had the vision to know what needed to be done to move the company into the future. He had the skills to negotiate with federal regulators and lobbyists and other dairy farmers. He had enough detachment that he could do things like walk into the middle of a fight between Eve Winchester and Carson Newport and identify the best course of action for everyone involved.

Everyone except for Lucy. He didn't have any detachment when it came to her.

It was going to be a problem. Hell, it was already a problem.

When she spoke, her voice was so soft that he almost missed it. "Do the Winchesters know you're coming? Or was your entire goal this evening to make it look like I invited you along?"

Oh. "You think I would use you like that?"

"Sutton Winchester is worth at least a billion dollars. Lots of people would do lots of things to get a piece of that. Including the Newports." She threw that out there as if that could explain everything.

Well, it didn't. "You realize I'm a multimillionaire in my own right, don't you? The Newport boys can't bribe me into doing things like that. I don't need the money and even if I did, I would *never* use you like that."

"What happened on the couch was merely…a fringe benefit, then?"

Josh was getting madder by the second. "You are acting like—"

"Oh, this I have to hear." She turned her full body toward him and stared. "How am I acting? Let me guess. Like a prim prude? Like an ice-cold bitch? Wait. I know. I'm not good enough for you. I have never been good enough for you." She paused, leaving a silence so sharp it could have cut glass. "Let me know when I'm getting close."

"No, goddamn it. Lucy, would you just listen? That's not it at all."

She crossed her arms just as Josh took a corner a little harder than he meant to. They were leaving the bright lights of Chicago proper behind. There was more open space as they moved into a more exclusive neighborhood. He was almost out of time and he was doing a piss-poor job of explaining himself. "I am not better than you. I never have been. If anything, I'm not good enough for you."

She threw her hands up. "Sure. I've heard that before, too."

"What the hell are you talking about?" Because it didn't sound like she was still talking about what happened on the couch. Enough of this crap. "You listen to me, Lucy Wilde. I like you. I have always liked you. I am *not* sorry for kissing you. I *am* sorry that we got interrupted because all I want to do is turn this truck around and take you back to your apartment and lay you out on that bed until you're screaming my name in pleasure. And the fact that I want that confuses me just as much as it confuses you because I didn't think I could still feel that anymore. So stop acting like I'm torturing you. We're not kids anymore and this is not a game I want to play. Now tell me why you're upset with me or get over it."

She didn't say anything. Again. And he honestly didn't know if he wanted to throttle her or pull her into a hug because he was pretty sure that she was over there doing her best not to cry.

But just then they found themselves at the gate of the Winchester estate. He got buzzed in and they drove toward the house.

A valet—an actual valet at a private home—opened Lucy's door and handed her out, took Josh's keys and stared at the stick shift in his truck in confusion before Josh told him to leave it there.

Then and only then, when he and Lucy had started up the grand staircase toward the front door, did he hear Lucy's reply. "There are some things," she said without looking at him, "that you just don't 'get over.' But I don't have to tell you that, do I?"

And then, without waiting for a response, she walked into the Winchester home and left him standing on the stoop.

Seven

This was why Lucy didn't have relationships. People in general and men in specific were distracting. As Lucy looked over the proper hospital-quality room that the Winchester girls had miraculously assembled in just over twenty-four hours, she was horrified to realize that she was having trouble concentrating on the pumps and computers.

Because she was thinking of Josh.

No, that wasn't it. Not entirely. Because she was thinking of how very badly she had embarrassed herself again. When would she learn? She could not trust herself around Josh Calhoun.

At least this time, she tried to tell herself, she had not done it all by herself. Not like the last time, anyway. She had not thrown herself at Josh Calhoun and begged for him to take her. He had not pushed her away and said no. It hadn't been like that at all.

It had been soft and sweet and natural and right. The most right thing in the world.

And then it stopped. All the good feelings, all the warmth and tenderness—gone.

And she still didn't know if it was real or not. Because if he had brought dinner over to her place, given her a glass of wine and kissed her senseless for the sole purpose of guaranteeing that she would take him with her to the Winchester home, then she would never forgive him. Never. It didn't matter how many times he claimed he would never use her like that.

"Well, what do you think?" Nora Winchester said, as they stood in the room the sisters had prepared for their father.

Tonight Lucy was dealing with the third Winchester sister, Nora—and Nora's little boy, Declan. He was snuggled in his mom's arms, his head resting on her shoulder. He had one thumb stuck in his mouth and was watching Lucy with the kind of naked curiosity that only small children could successfully pull off.

Lucy felt bad because she knew that she was keeping him up. If she had gotten here when she was supposed to, Nora would already be putting her son to bed, reading him stories and tucking him in with a kiss on his forehead.

"I'm impressed," Lucy told Nora. "I didn't think you'd be able to get everything I requested."

Nora shrugged, which jostled her son. "Sometimes, there are advantages to being a Winchester."

Before Lucy could respond to that, Declan began to fidget. He twisted out of his mother's grasp and made a break for the brand-new hospital bed. Oh. That's what had his attention—Lucy had tested the buttons to raise

and lower the bed, and that was too much a temptation
for any one kid.

"Whoa," Josh said, neatly stepping up and swinging
Declan into his arms. "Where you going, cowboy?"

Declan pointed shyly at the bed.

"I don't remember hearing you ask your mother if you
could jump on the bed—or Dr. Lucy. You've always got
to ask, you know that, buddy? Your grandpa is going to
be in this bed and you can't just jump on him, either."

Declan looked disappointed. Then Josh said, "Why
don't we ask now? Just this one time, though. When
Grandpa's in the bed, we can't play on it, okay?"

Nora smiled a tired smile. "No jumping on the bed,"
she said in a tone of voice that made Lucy think of an
old nursery rhyme. "We don't want to bump our heads.
But maybe Mr. Calhoun can help you work the buttons
for two minutes."

Lucy honestly didn't know who was happier about this
announcement—Josh or the child. Both of their faces lit
up in wide grins. "Let's go!" Josh said, carrying Declan
over to the bed. They sat down together and figured out
which button did what. "Whee!" they both called out.

And Lucy didn't know what to say. There was something about the way Josh played with the child that hurt
her at the same time that it made her happy. Because
it was a piece to a puzzle that she hadn't realized was
missing.

Josh had been married. Josh had been happy.

And Josh's wife had died.

She hadn't lied earlier when she told him she'd thought
he had settled down and had a couple of kids by now.
Josh was the kind of man who needed kids.

"He's really quite good," Nora said.

Lucy hadn't realized that the other woman had stepped in closer. "I'm sorry?"

"With Declan. Some men look at kids as if they were feral animals with contagious diseases. You can always tell which ones are the ones who will be good fathers and which ones won't."

"How can you tell?" Lucy asked as another "whee" came from the bed. It felt like a silly question, though, because it was obvious to anyone with two eyes that Josh was having just as much fun as Declan was.

Nora gave her a look that bordered on pitying. "I want to apologize on behalf of my sisters and Carson," she said without answering the question. "I don't think it's fair that you're being asked to relocate just so you can take care of our father."

Well, that was unexpected. Lucy wasn't sure how she was supposed to respond to that. Of all the Winchester daughters, Nora was the one with whom she'd had the least interaction. Thus far, her impression of Nora Winchester was that she would rather be anywhere but here. And that was a feeling Lucy could sympathize with.

"Cancer isn't fair," she said. And she meant it. "We're doing what we can to prolong his life, but you understand that this isn't about me? With your father's kind of cancer and how it progressed in his system before he sought treatment, we're risking all our gains by moving him out of the hospital."

Nora sighed heavily. "Oh, I understand. I also understand my sisters when they say they're concerned about his privacy." She gave Lucy a sympathetic smile. "There's just no good solution and sometimes we have to do the best with what we've got. Now," she went on in a more businesslike tone, "would you like to see the guest quarters? I was told you would be bringing your bags…"

"Again, my apologies for running late. I got held up at the hospital and didn't have time to pack." It wasn't a malicious lie. She just strategically left out the fact that it had been Josh who'd been holding her up. Physically. "I'm sorry if we screwed up bedtime." She angled her body so that Josh couldn't hear what she was about to say next. "I understand that Carson has asked Mr. Calhoun to check in on things, but you are under no obligation to open your home or your father's medical treatment to him."

That got her a funny look from Nora. "Dr. Wilde— after he got Carson and Eve to agree on something? I'm thinking of inviting him to Thanksgiving!" She laughed and Lucy tried to smile. She didn't think she made it, though, because Nora went on, "Carson told me Mr. Calhoun would be by, and that you and Mr. Calhoun were friends—old friends."

So Nora had been expecting Josh? Why hadn't anyone else thought it prudent to tell her what the damned plan was?

Still, Nora's response—and complete lack of concern about Josh—reassured Lucy somewhat. "We are. But he's not a member of the family and he's not a colleague of mine. And if you're truly concerned about your father's privacy…"

Another "whee" came from the bed. Nora looked to her son. "All right, sweetie—that's enough. Why don't we show Dr. Lucy where she's going to be staying, and then it's time for you to get a story and go to bed."

Declan said, "Aw."

But Josh said, "You heard her, buddy." He scooped Declan off the bed and jostled him in his arms.

Their little party, such as it was, followed Nora out into the hall and one door down. "We thought it best to keep you close to his room," Nora said in an apologetic tone as she opened the door. "I hope that's all right."

"That's fine," Lucy said as Nora flipped on the light. And then she gawked at the guest room.

Because the guest room was almost as large as her apartment. It had a massive queen-size four-poster bed in the middle of the room done in lush shades of blue and teal, with accents of orange in the pillows and drapes. There was a sitting area with the couch and two armchairs facing a fireplace with a flat-screen TV above the mantel. Off to one side was a small wet bar, complete with a minifridge.

"Nice place," Josh said.

Nora looked at Lucy and said, "Will this do?" She pointed to the small screen that was on the table next to the bed. "We had monitors installed so you'll have visual contact at all times. And here," she said, pointing to the computer on the coffee table, "is the monitor you requested. We'll have any meals you'd like delivered to the room—we don't expect you to join us in the dining room, unless you'd like to. If there's anything else you'd like to have, just let me know."

"This should be fine," Lucy said faintly.

It wasn't fine. This whole thing was insane. When she had become the head of the oncology department at Midwest, it had not come with a stipulation in the contract that she might occasionally have to go live with her patients. She didn't want to do this.

Then she thought of the expanded cancer pavilion that the Winchesters and the Newports were going to fund and how many people that was going to help and she sucked it up.

"Assuming his numbers are where I want them to be, I should be able to discharge him tomorrow afternoon—

the next day at the latest." She was trying her damnedest to sound professional at ten fifteen in the evening while watching Josh cuddle a two-year-old with such longing that it hurt. She wasn't sure she was making it. "I arranged for several of my most trusted nurses to pick up extra shifts when I cannot be on-site. As I've reminded your sisters, I will not compromise anyone else's care during this...experiment."

Nora nodded and reached out her arms for her son. Josh handed over the sleepy boy, and the look on his face...

"Can you find your way out?" Nora asked. She hugged her son and rubbed his back.

"Sure." Lucy felt almost dizzy with the surge of emotions that she couldn't name. On some level, she was still mad at Josh. And she still wanted him—which only made her madder. She didn't want to see the look of longing on Josh's face as they watched Nora carry her child to bed and she didn't want to think about what his marriage to his wife had been like. She didn't want to stay at the Winchester estate and, truthfully, she didn't want to be Sutton Winchester's oncologist anymore. But she also didn't want to turn down the chance to have that cancer pavilion bought and paid for.

As Nora had said, sometimes there were no good solutions. Lucy wished she wasn't the one who had to make the best of it. But giving a few weeks of her time to the Winchesters was for the greater good. She couldn't back out now.

Josh rested his hand on the small of her back and startled her. "Lucy?" She heard so many questions in that one word.

If only she had some answers. "I need to go home," she told him. Had he really brought her dinner and kissed her just to get out here to the estate? Or had it been a series of unfortunate coincidences? Everyone else seemed to know and accept that Josh would be here this evening.

Had he used her? Or did he really want her?

His hand was still on her lower back, warm and solid and somehow an answer to the question that she hadn't asked. "Would you like to go now?"

Her head was a mess and she didn't know what she was supposed to think anymore. "Yes," she said, turning into him. "I think I would."

Eight

The drive back to Lucy's apartment was quiet. She was probably still mad at him and he couldn't blame her for that. He'd handled the situation poorly—no doubt about that. He should have told her upfront that he'd planned on going to the Winchester estate. But he hadn't been using her, for God's sake.

Her accusations swirled around in his head with thoughts of that little kid.

He hadn't expected how seeing that boy would affect him. Technically, Declan was Carson's nephew—Josh was pretty sure, anyway. Sitting on a hospital bed and making it go up and down to keep the two-year-old from having a meltdown... It made him yearn for what he didn't have. And watching Nora Winchester take the boy from him and cuddle him against her chest?

That, too, was something he yearned for. He and Sydney had been waiting. Always waiting. She had wanted her business to be more established and Josh's career to be more settled and…

He didn't have anything.

That wasn't true. He had good friends like the Newport boys, and he had his family—his grandfather and his brothers and sisters. He ran a successful business and he didn't want for anything.

Anything but a family of his own.

There were times when he just didn't want to do this anymore. It always hurt when people told him to get over Sydney's death, but getting over it and moving on were what he desperately wanted to do. He wanted to close the door on that part of his life and bolt it shut. He didn't want to leave it cracked open so that at random times—like right now—that never-ending sense of loss could barge in and catch him unaware.

It was past eleven by the time he pulled up in front of Lucy's apartment building. Somehow, the thought of going back to Carson's place and reporting on what he'd found at Sutton's felt like a mountain he'd never finish climbing. Because he didn't want to do this anymore, either—be the go-between for Carson and his sisters and their father. He wanted to go back to the nice, busy life he'd made for himself in Cedar Point. There, at least, he didn't have Sydney's ghost waiting for him around every corner.

And after tonight he wasn't about to invite himself up to Lucy's place. He knew when to hold 'em and he knew when to fold 'em and, by God, he was going to fold tonight.

But she didn't get out of the truck. Lucy just sat there while the engine rumbled. Josh gave her twenty, thirty seconds and then figured that she didn't want to get out of the truck, so he turned the engine off and waited.

And they just sat there. She was looking straight ahead again, but she wasn't sitting ramrod straight anymore. She had her elbow on the truck door and her head leaned on her hand.

He knew that look. She was thinking—hard. So he let her think. Outside the truck, cars passed them and the occasional person walked down the sidewalk. She might tell him that she never wanted to see him again—but she might not.

He hoped not.

"We were so young," she said into the silence.

"When?" Because he was not going to make any assumptions whatsoever in the course of this conversation.

"When Gary died. I wasn't even eighteen."

Wait—was she still mad at him? It didn't sound like it. "It was a long time ago." Why was she bringing up Gary now? In all honesty, Josh hadn't thought that much about him after he'd gotten wrapped up with Sydney. Gary had become a bittersweet memory when Josh had chosen to think about him at all.

"Do you know," she said in a wistful voice, "that he was my first boyfriend?"

Josh sat up, instantly on alert. "That doesn't seem right."

"I didn't grow up in Cedar Point," she reminded him. "We moved so much—I know we never really talked about it, but my dad couldn't hold a job. I was surprised that I was able to stay in Cedar Point long enough to graduate. I was there for almost two whole years."

"But you were smart and cute." For the first time in a long time, she looked at him, even if it was only to roll her eyes. "I mean, in a tomboyish kind of way. You were fun."

"No, I wasn't. I've never had any sense of fashion or

style, and have never been cute. I was a know-it-all—
and an insufferable one, at that. We moved so much that
I rarely had friends. Until you. You and Gary."

She was making herself sound like some sort of loser,
which is not how he remembered her. "But we had fun
together."

That got him a smile that was sad around the corners. "We did, didn't we? An insufferable know-it-all,
the dying boy and you. The all-American boy next door."

He remembered something she'd said earlier, something that had hit him wrong. "I wasn't too good for you,
you know." Really, if it hadn't been for the fact that Gary
had been dying, who knew how it might have turned out?
"But you were with Gary."

She sat up again, looking stiffer. "And you were his
friend, first and foremost."

"I was. We'd been friends since kindergarten. There
are some things a man doesn't do to his friend." Like
steal his girl, for example.

Lucy was sort of bobbing her head, and Josh couldn't
tell if she was agreeing with him or thinking hard. Or
both.

Then she moved. She unbuckled her seat belt and
turned to face him with her entire body. "Like what?"

The hairs on the back of Josh's arm stood up. "What
do you mean?"

She scooted toward him on the old bench seat. "What
are some things that a man doesn't do to his friend?"

Josh didn't answer. He wasn't sure he could find his
voice, not with Lucy sliding toward him, an odd look in
her eyes.

"Like what?" she repeated more softly. There was a
note to her tone that hadn't been there earlier and Josh

couldn't help but think that she knew what he was trying not to say.

"Why do we have to talk about this?"

"Because," she said, reaching out and tracing the line of his jaw with her fingertips, "I think I understand now."

"Understand what?" But he was already leaning toward her, letting her pull him in closer. He had no idea what she was talking about, but he didn't care.

He simply did not care. He felt raw and exposed, as if someone had scraped off the top layer of his skin, and he didn't want to hurt anymore. He didn't want to think about his dead wife. He was tired of grief and sorrow, and he just wanted to get over it and he couldn't. He didn't know how.

Lucy was close enough to kiss now. Her breast brushed up against his arm and the warmth from her body calmed his raw nerves. "I understand." But she didn't kiss him and he wished like hell she would.

Because she was going to have to do it this time. There wasn't going to be any more confusion about this. If she wanted him, she had to come to him.

She tilted her head to one side and something in the air between them changed. "Will you come upstairs?"

"Lucy..." But already his body was responding to hers—her scent, her warmth. And what he really wanted was to go back to where they'd been earlier this evening. "If I come upstairs—"

"Stay," she whispered against his mouth. "Because I've missed you, too, Josh Calhoun."

It wasn't much of a kiss, the way her lips, light and sweet, brushed over his. It wasn't a kiss of passion or possession. But it was something else entirely—it was hopeful.

What the hell were they doing still sitting in the cab

of his truck? Because he wasn't a teenager anymore—
getting it on in the vehicle no longer held any appeal. "I
want to strip you out of those clothes and lay you out on
that bed and I don't care who hears us," he told her as he
wrenched off his seat belt.

"Yes," she hissed. "I want you on top of me, inside of
me—oh, God, Josh."

Somehow, they got out of the truck and into the building. Josh pulled her into his arms and fell back against
the wall next to the elevator. "You're really sure?" he
asked, trying to convince himself that whatever she said
would be okay.

"I've never wanted anything more in my life," she told
him. And then she grabbed his butt. The feeling of her
hands on his body did mighty interesting things to him.
It had been so long...

He didn't want to think about that. Not right now. Instead, he wanted to figure out a way to make this night
last for as long as possible.

He slid his hands over her body. She responded beau-
tifully, arching into his touch and rubbing her breasts
against his chest. But before he could do anything else,
the elevator doors opened and Lucy dragged him inside.

There was an itch in the back of his mind, a question
he didn't have the answer to. What did she understand?

But that question was buried under the sensation of
Lucy pulling him down into her, Lucy digging her hands
into his butt, Lucy moaning in his ear as he palmed her
breast. "I want you so badly," she whispered as she raked
her fingers through his hair and pulled his mouth to her.

Hell, that was all the permission he needed. He flattened her back against the wall of the elevator and hooked
one leg over his hand, lifting her up so he could thrust
against her.

"Oh, Josh," she moaned as her head fell back, exposing her neck. As he ground against her, he trailed his lips over her pale skin. "I want this shirt off you," he growled as he skimmed his teeth over the spot where her neck met her shoulders.

"Yes, yes," she panted as she clung to him.

Then the elevator dinged. Josh had to set her down and let her get her keys out, and the pause gave him back just enough self-control. He hadn't done this in a long time and he didn't want to screw it up. He wasn't under any illusions that this was going to be a regular thing, because she was in Chicago and after he left, he didn't know when he'd come back. He didn't know if he would come back for her.

So this had to count. It was so tempting to throw her on the bed and thrust into her until he came with mindless pleasure, but this was Lucy. She deserved more than that and he was going to give it to her.

"Sorry," she said, shooting him a guilty look over her shoulder as she fumbled with her keys.

He leaned down and put his lips against the back of her neck. "Nervous?" As he asked this, he settled his hands on her hips and began rubbing small circles with his thumbs.

She shrugged and got the door open. "Maybe a little."

He followed her inside, unwilling to break the physical connection. "We'll take it slow. I want to make this so good for you." He kicked the door shut behind him and leaned against it, pulling her back into him. His arms went around her waist and he just held her.

The feeling of her body against his—he had missed this. Five years of sleeping alone, of taking care of his own needs quickly—it hadn't been about pleasure. It hadn't been about want and need and another person.

He almost wanted to laugh. Because for the first time in years, he didn't feel the crushing loneliness. And that was thanks to Lucy.

"It's all right," she said in a soft voice as she reached up and slid a hand behind his neck.

Of course, it was all right—everything about this was just *fine*. Still, her words had an oddly reassuring effect on him and he hugged her even tighter. Then he began to move. Because a man couldn't get lucky if he stood by the door all night long. He splayed his hands over her ribs and began to stroke up, then down. "I want to take this off."

"Please do," she said, and underneath his lips, he could feel the pulse in her neck begin to beat faster.

He skimmed his hands up over her breasts to the buttons of her shirt. Slowly, he undid one and then the next until the entire shirt was open and he could slip his hands underneath. Her skin was warm to the touch—and touch it he did. He trailed his fingertips over her waist, over the smooth front of her bra. The whole time he stroked her, he kept his lips against her pulse and listened to her breath in his ear.

He wanted to make this all about her. Because this was Lucy. If all he cared about was getting laid, he could've accomplished that easily at any point in the last five years.

But he didn't just want to get off. He missed making love.

So that's what he was doing tonight. He was going to make love to Lucy with everything he had. They didn't have to worry about dating and that awkward getting-to-know-you period, and they didn't have to worry about long-term relationships. He already knew Lucy and he already liked her and he already loved making her gasp in that little way she was doing as he stroked her nipples with his fingertips.

"You like that, don't you?" he asked as he felt her nipples stiffen under his touch. He began lightly pinching them.

"Oh, Josh," she whimpered as he teased her flesh.

"Yeah, that's it, babe." One part of his brain wanted to remember that Sydney had always liked it when he played with her breasts, too, but he pushed that away. His wife was gone and he wanted to believe with all his heart that she would want him to do this. She would want him to grab a little bit of happiness, even if it was only for one night. Sydney would want him to find a piece of himself again with an old friend whom he could trust.

He relinquished Lucy's left breast and began to slide his hand lower, over the soft planes of her stomach and then down over the front of her pants. She sagged back against him and he was happy to carry her weight. Earlier, on the couch, he had just wanted to make her come. It had almost been as though he *needed* to make her come to prove that he hadn't forgotten how. But now he wanted this to be slow and sweet and so good that neither of them ever wanted it to end.

Her breathing got more labored as he rubbed slow circles against her sex. She clutched at his arms with her hands and shifted against him, the pressure of her bottom against his erection pushing any rational thought from his mind. This was what he wanted—not thinking, just doing. Just feeling.

Suddenly, she gasped and her fingernails dug into his arm. "Bed," she ordered. "Now."

"Yes, ma'am." He half turned her and leaned down so he could sweep her into his arms. She'd always been a small thing.

"Josh!" she squeaked as he settled her against his chest.

He grinned down at her. Her cheeks were flushed, her

pupils dilated wide—so wide, he almost couldn't see the blue in her eyes anymore. "I've got you," he reassured her as he carried her into the bedroom and over to the bed. He found the gap in the sheer curtain she'd hung around it and pushed it open. He sat her down on the bed and got rid of those doctor shoes she was wearing. Her socks quickly followed and then he took his time peeling her shirt off her arms.

"Look at you," he said, his voice wavering as he stared down at her. Her bra was what Sydney had always called serviceably beige—a plain beige. It wasn't all that sexy—but on Lucy? "I don't remember you having this body back in high school." He knelt on the bed so he could undo the bra.

"I didn't," she said, angling her body so he didn't have to stretch as far. "I was the definition of a late bloomer."

Josh was out of practice, so it took three tries before the bra hooks gave successfully. He tossed the bra to the side. "Wow, Lucy, your breasts were worth the wait."

Because they were fabulous—full and rounded and high on her chest. He fell to his knees before her and just took a moment to appreciate the beauty that was the female body.

She reached over and started working the buttons on his shirt. "Your turn," she said as she began to strip him.

She got his shirt off, but when she went for his jeans he pushed her hands out of the way. "Patience." He didn't know if he was admonishing her or himself.

"I'm tired of being patient," she told him. "You have no idea how long I've been waiting for this."

He thought she was going to say something else, so he cut her off the only way he knew how—he leaned down and wrapped his lips around her nipple. He sucked her into his mouth and was rewarded with a ragged gasp of pleasure. She threaded her fingers into his hair again and held him against her.

He was so hard in his jeans that it was becoming physically painful. He wasn't going to last. All of his good intentions about laying her out and making her scream were not going to amount to a hill of beans if he couldn't find a little more restraint.

But he couldn't help it. God, she felt so good in his mouth, under his hands. "Oh, Josh," she kept repeating as he sucked and licked and nibbled at first one breast, then the other. Somehow he managed to get the button and zipper of her pants undone. Reluctantly, he relinquished the hold he had on her nipples and laid her back on the bed so he could get her pants off.

As he stared down at her, he had a weird feeling of being out of time—that this was something that should've always happened, but the timing just hadn't been right.

"God, Lucy" was all he could say as he peeled her panties off her, and then she lay bare before him. Something clicked in his mind, and one word popped to the front of his consciousness.

Mine.

"I don't know how you think we're going to have sex if you stand there and stare at me all night," she said with what he hoped was an ironic smile. She lifted her foot and nudged his crotch. "And we're going to have sex—right?"

The next thing he knew, Josh was stripping out of his jeans and kicking off his boots—and coming to a dead halt. *Oh, no.*

"Josh?" Lucy pushed herself up and stared at him with new concern on her face.

"I don't have anything," he said in a shaky voice. "I didn't plan on this—I don't have any condoms." And he was no longer some stupid kid who could talk himself out of using one because "nothing would happen." He absolutely would not risk Lucy's health and safety with an accidental pregnancy just because he wanted to get laid for the first time in five years.

"Oh." Everything about her wilted. But then she perked up again. "Wait!" She threw herself off the bed and hurried to what Josh assumed was the closet. She hauled out a huge blue duffel bag and crouched down—which provided Josh with one hell of a view of her backside—as she rifled through it. "I think—oh, thank God." She stood up and turned around, holding three small foil squares in her hand. "I keep a fully stocked medical kit—for emergencies," she said, suddenly looking shy again. "You never know."

"I think this qualifies as an emergency," Josh told her. His erection heartily agreed.

She looked so innocent with that little grin on her face. "Will this be enough?"

That made Josh laugh out loud. "Babe, I'm not eighteen anymore." He took the condoms from her and pulled her into his arms again. As he kissed her, he realized that they fit together. God, it felt so good to hold her.

He lifted her up and laid her on the bed. Later, there would be time for niceties like oral sex and lots of foreplay. Right now, he couldn't wait—not a minute longer. He knelt between her knees and tore open one of the condom packets. She stared at him as he rolled it on. "Okay?" he asked.

"Okay," she said breathlessly. "I never…"

He leaned over her and reached down between her legs. She was wet to the touch, so ready for him. "I never thought this would happen, either. But I'm so glad it is. Lucy, you have no idea how glad."

She bucked at his touch and threw her arms around

his neck. "Me, too," she whispered as he positioned himself against her.

Slowly—as slowly as he could manage—he began to thrust into her.

Very slowly.

Too slowly.

"Don't stop," she said, clinging to him. Something wasn't right, but before Josh could ask her—maybe they did need to take the time for some oral sex—she kissed him, hard, while pulling him down into her. "Now," she demanded. "*Now*, Josh."

Her body gave a little against him and her fingernails dug into his back, pushing him forward. With a grunt, he sank into her. The feeling of her wet warmth surrounding him, taking him in—it short-circuited something in his brain. She moaned as her back arched and Josh couldn't hold himself back anymore.

He gave himself up to the sensations. Everything he had he gave to her. At one point, her nails bit into him so deeply that he had to grab her wrists and hold them over her head. "Oh, God, Josh," she whispered in a high, tight voice as she moved underneath him, rising up to meet him over and over again.

"You like that, don't you?" he asked as he stroked into her. He held both of her wrists with one hand and propped himself up so he could drive in deeper. "You like it hard like that, don't you?"

"Yes," she whimpered, her head thrashing from side to side as he buried himself in her body. "Make me come, Josh," she begged.

They were pretty, sweet words—and he hadn't known how much he needed to hear them until Lucy said them. He couldn't let go until she went first. Somehow he was able to shift so that he still had a hold of her wrists but he was sitting farther back on his knees so he could reach down between her legs and stroke his thumb over her clit. It didn't take much pressure—a few gentle strokes timed with a few hard thrusts—and her head came up off the pillow, her mouth open as she completely came apart.

Josh fought against the urge to let go. Instead, he forced himself to take in every memory of this moment. This was what he hadn't gotten on the couch earlier—the sight of Lucy letting go.

He'd done that. He'd given that to her. He still could.

It was nothing compared to what she was giving him.

It was only when her orgasm had passed and she'd fallen back on the pillow, panting, that Josh followed her over the edge. He leaned forward and kissed her hard as he pumped two, three more times. And then he came. The sweet release, her body surrounding him—God, he'd missed so much. *So* much.

He fell onto her and rolled off, not wanting to crush her. When he released her wrists, she threw her arms around him and held him tight. They didn't say anything.

What was there to say? He didn't know. He didn't have any words right now.

Finally, he pulled away and rolled out of bed. "I'll be right back," he said. It was then—and only then—that he glanced down and saw the blood.

Nine

"What the—*Lucy*?"

Something in Josh's tone made Lucy open her eyes. She didn't want to. She wanted to pull him back into her arms and curl around his chest—God, what a chest—and drift off into sleep. She wanted to wake up that way, too, and then she wanted him to hold her down again and make mad passionate love to her again and again and *again*.

She met his gaze and then he looked down at his penis. So she looked, too. She was allowed to look. They were lovers now and lovers got to openly stare at each other's naked bodies whenever they wanted, right?

That wasn't all she was looking at. It wasn't his manhood—it was the bloodstained condom.

And reality—that cruel, heartless bitch—came intruding into her happy dream.

"You were a virgin?" He asked in the same tone of voice he might use to ask if Bigfoot really existed.

Was there any good way to have this conversation? No. But there had to be a better way than this.

"Um," she started, and then stopped because that wasn't any sort of answer at all. "Yes?" She winced at the way it came out as a question. Because she knew it wasn't.

His eyes narrowed and he put his hands on his hips. "I'll be right back," he told her. "And then you and I are going to have a talk."

Without waiting for an answer, he turned and stalked away. Normally, she would've taken advantage of this opportunity to admire his butt. It was at that exact moment that she began to feel the effects of her first time. She was sore and stretched and her labia burned. Despite all that, she wanted him back in her bed again.

She sat up in bed, wincing as her delicate parts came into contact with the sheet. And then she winced again because there was probably more blood. She felt different—and that was an understatement. But at the same time, she didn't feel as different as she'd thought she would. She'd gained some firsthand knowledge—but she didn't think it had fundamentally altered who she was. She wasn't a virgin anymore, but she still felt like Lucy. She'd climaxed—two climaxes in one night wasn't bad for a first timer—but the heavens hadn't opened and the angels hadn't sung and she hadn't heard any fireworks go off.

She rubbed her temples. Being different and not different at the same time made her feel funny.

The bathroom door opened and Josh strode out. This was the stuff of fantasy, she had to admit. Because she had fantasized about this many times, except in her fantasies, Josh had always been leaner, more gangly. More awkward. He'd been the teenager she remembered.

He hadn't been this broad, muscled man with a sprinkling of dark chest hair. He also hadn't been this intimidating man with his jaw set and his eyes hard.

Before she could think of anything reasonable to say, he told her, "Your turn."

Lucy took the hint. She went to the bathroom and got cleaned up and then looked at herself in the mirror. She looked the way she felt—different and the same. Her hair was a disaster and her cheeks were flushed and her lips were red. She looked as though she had taken a lover. But she didn't look like a different woman. A more mature, more sophisticated version of herself was not staring back at her.

And now she had to go out and "have a talk" with Josh about this whole pesky virginity thing.

Was sex always this complicated?

She turned off the light before she opened the door, as if that would hide her. It didn't.

She saw that Josh had put his briefs back on, but nothing else. He was sitting on the edge of her bed, his forearms on his legs, and for the life of her, Lucy thought that he looked like he was praying. Oh, this was going to be bad, wasn't it? This was going to be complicated and messy and awkward and painful, and it was going to be all the worse because she didn't know how to have these conversations.

"Explain to me," Josh said in a low voice that bordered on dangerous, "how you were still a virgin." He didn't look up as she approached. He kept his head bowed and his gaze focused on the floor, on his toes or some imaginary speck of dust.

"I've been busy." That got his attention. His head popped up and he stared at her, and Lucy had a fleeting impression of...guilt? "Well, I have been. You don't get to be the youngest head of oncology in a hospital by having a social life."

She felt awkward standing before him, but she figured it would be even more awkward if she went and sat next to him. She looked around and saw her bathrobe on the floor near her closet. She must have launched it there when she was frantically trying to get packed earlier. She bent over and flipped it over her shoulders, belting it at the waist. Immediately, she felt less exposed.

"But that doesn't make any sense." He didn't remark on her bathrobe. At least it was a nice plain white bathrobe—not a fluffy penguin in sight.

"Yes, it does." Something in his eyes shifted. Instead of guilt, it looked more like he might feel sorry for her. And Lucy couldn't have that. "After high school, I wasn't exactly looking for another relationship. I threw myself into my studies. I got my BA in three years. Then there was med school and internships and residencies and… and my patients. I didn't make time for dating and I didn't have a lot of offers, so it worked out. I have my job and that's all I need."

Or it had been until Josh Calhoun had walked back into her life. Now? Now she wasn't so sure anymore.

And that, more than the loss of her virginity, was what had changed about her. Because Lucinda Wilde had been a doctor who hadn't needed a personal relationship, who had convinced herself that she didn't even want one.

But Lucy Wilde?

Josh stood and paced away from her. "No, that *doesn't* make any sense," he repeated with more authority. "What about you and Gary?"

This was always what it was going to come back to, wasn't it? No matter what curveballs life had thrown at them—and this sure as hell counted as a curveball—it would always begin back where it started.

"What about us?" She shifted from foot to foot, trying to find the posture that took a little more pressure off her newly sore parts.

"You guys were together—I mean, you dated for, like, two years!"

Lucinda Wilde, MD, would have stayed standing to make her best argument. But Lucy was tired. It was after midnight, and she had to get up tomorrow and keep dealing with Sutton Winchester and everyone else. So she sat on the bed and tried her best to keep from yawning. "And Gary was sick, Josh. I know that you guys were friends from childhood, but when I showed up at school, he was already sick. I never knew him when he was healthy."

He spun and stared at her. "What are you saying?"

She shrugged. "I wish I could tell you that we didn't go all the way because we were waiting for the right time or we thought he would get better and we'd get married or we knew we weren't mature enough to deal with it. But the truth was, he was sick."

She didn't want to tell Josh the rest. She wanted to let that part of Gary stay buried. But she knew, just from looking at Josh's face, that she wasn't going to be able to do that. She sent up a silent prayer for forgiveness to Gary's spirit, wherever he was.

"But he loved you," Josh said. He sounded so young and idealistic—as if he really did believe love could cure the world of all its ills. Lucy couldn't help but smile. "And you loved him—didn't you?"

"I did. He was a good kisser—not that I had anything to compare him to—and we fooled around. Just because I was a virgin didn't mean I've never done anything. The spirit was willing but his flesh was…weak." No matter how hard she'd tried, Gary Everly had died a virgin in the strictest sense of the word.

She wanted that to be the end of it. "Will you stay with me? I'm tired, Josh."

He took two steps toward her and then stopped. Lucy braced herself because she knew it was coming and she knew she couldn't stop it. "You—after Gary's funeral when you kissed me—what was *that* about, then?" He looked horrified.

She tried to smile, as if they were reminiscing about lighthearted tales of frivolity instead of life-and-death issues. "Why did you kiss me tonight? Earlier, after you told me about your wife?" His mouth opened and then he shut it again. "Why did you come upstairs with me tonight—after you played with that little boy?"

The color drained out of his face and he looked as if she'd slapped him. Hard.

She stood up and walked over to him, laying her palm against his cheek. "I understand," she told him gently.

For a moment, she thought he was going to give. His arms twitched as if he wanted to pull her tight against his chest. And that was what she wanted.

But that was not what happened. "Did you—did you just have *pity sex* with me? Is that what that was? You give up your virginity after all these years to make me feel better about my dead wife?" His voice had risen until he had shouted that last part.

She stumbled back. "No! That's not what this was, Josh!"

"Then what was it?"

"I *like* you," she told him, trying to keep the panic out of her voice. This was not how it was supposed to go. Even a novice like herself knew that. "I've always liked you. And I thought—after you explicitly told me—that you liked me, too!"

"Jesus, Lucy." He pushed past her and started gathering up his clothes.

Now she was panicking in earnest. "What are you doing?"

"Leaving," he told her shortly as he shoved his legs into his pants and then his feet into his boots. "This was a mistake. God, what was I thinking?"

That did it. Some of her panic flipped over into anger. "Boy, you sure know how to make a girl feel special, don't you? Just what every virgin wants to hear, that she was nothing but a mistake. Would you just listen to me? This wasn't pity sex!"

He jammed his arms into his shirt and didn't even bother to button it up. "Wasn't it?" He made a break for the door. She grabbed his arm and tried to hold him still. "A thirty-five-year-old virgin and a widower and you're going to tell me that's not pitiful?"

She gasped in shock, humiliation blossoming in her chest. "I am not pitiful," she said, her voice shaking with anger. "And neither are you."

He cut her a mean look and opened his mouth. She tensed, but he didn't say anything. Instead, he spun on his heel and walked right out of her apartment.

All she could do was watch him go.

And that?

That was pitiful.

Ten

Somehow, Josh found himself outside Carson's place. He didn't get out of the truck immediately; instead, he sat there, fighting the urge to bash his forehead against the steering wheel in frustration.

What had just happened? He found himself repeating that question over and over again—not that repeating it got him any closer to an answer.

He had slept with Lucy. She had been a virgin. Those facts were just that—facts.

It was also a fact that he had—and this was an understatement—flipped out. And the hell of it was, he had no idea why. Not one single idea. But he was pretty damn sure that in the process of flipping out he had grievously insulted Lucy. Which just made everything that much worse.

He had screwed up. That was bad enough. Technically, he'd screwed up twice. Basically, his evening with Lucy had had three stages—plumbing the depths of his grief, seducing her and insulting her.

Only one of those had been any fun. And he'd screwed that up, too.

It was well past one when Josh finally dragged himself into the house. He was surprised to find all three Newport brothers sitting in a parlor. For a moment, he had a flashback to high school, of trying to sneak in past his curfew only to find his grandfather sitting up and waiting for him.

But he wasn't in high school anymore and nobody was going to ground him. The first person to try was going to get a fat lip for his troubles.

Here they all sat, each one of them looking at him expectantly. Because he had been assigned a task—go to the Winchester estate and make sure that Sutton Winchester would be well cared for in a private setting.

And, idiot that he was, he had used Lucy for that purpose.

"We were beginning to wonder where you'd gotten off to," Graham said in a diplomatic tone. Before Josh could tell him exactly where he could go, Graham added, "Whiskey?" as he held up his own tumbler. It was mostly empty.

Yeah, he could use a drink. But he was in no mood to drink in present company. "Lucy has given her approval of the setup. She's waiting on one set of test results and then she'll discharge him."

Brooks rolled his eyes, Graham threw back the rest of his drink and Carson sat forward, looking interested.

"Anything else?" Carson asked.

Josh had always been a peacemaker. Ever since he'd buried his parents, he'd had to be. His grandfather had leaned on him in his time of sorrow. His brothers and sisters had needed him to step up, especially after his elder brother, Lincoln, had joined the military and bailed on them. His employees had disputes that needed settling. Even his friends—the Newports especially—had been well served by Josh's calm, steady presence.

And he was tired of it.

"The estate is lovely. Your sister Nora is a sweet soul. Your nephew Declan is adorable."

"Problem?" Graham asked, reaching over for a crystal decanter to refill his glass. "Are you sure you don't want some whiskey?"

"No, damn it, I don't want any whiskey."

Brooks snorted. "What crawled up your butt and died?" he asked, and Josh thought he seemed to be enjoying himself a little too much.

Josh glared at him—at them all. "You're just waiting for him to die. Can't you let a man die in peace?"

Brooks shrugged. "He doesn't even deserve that much, you know. I'd have tossed him on the street if I could." Brooks glanced at Carson and muttered a halfhearted, "Sorry."

"No, you're not," Josh snapped. "You're hell-bent on this vendetta." He turned to Graham. "I haven't figured out what your angle is yet, but I know you too well to know you're *not* working on an angle."

Carson ignored this outburst. "You agreed that moving him was a good idea. In fact, you're the one who convinced me it might get him to talk."

"Of course I did. I was keeping the damn peace. I always keep the peace." Except tonight. Except with Lucy. God, what a mess. He felt like his skin was turning inside out. It was too much. He never should have come back to Chicago. "The next time you want to find out what's happening at your father's house, go there yourself. In the meantime, stop expecting me to do your dirty work. Because now Lucy has to rearrange her entire life so that she can coddle a man no one else wants to coddle."

The three brothers exchanged knowing—and irritating—looks. "Who is Lucy, again?" Brooks asked.

Carson stared at Josh. "Dr. Lucinda Wilde. Sutton's oncologist—and apparently a former old friend of Josh's." There was a pause while Brooks and Graham digested this information, and then Carson added, "Or perhaps, she's not that former a friend."

"Go to hell," Josh retorted. "I am *your* friend. You want advice? Fine. You want to talk about it? Fine. But I'm not your errand boy and I'm not your employee—not anymore. I didn't come back to Chicago for the first time in five long, dark years just so you could use me and Lucy to fight some proxy battle. If you can't get that—any of you—then I'll be gone by morning. I have a business to run."

He turned and started to stalk out of the room, but Carson called after him, "Josh?"

He stopped at the doorway, but he didn't turn back around. "What?"

"We know it wasn't easy for you to come back. But we're glad you did."

"Whatever." And then Josh did something that was normally uncharacteristic of him—but something he'd done twice tonight, nevertheless.

He walked away without looking back.

"What's wrong with you?"

Lucy startled and glanced up from her tablet. Sutton Winchester was a man who looked sick. Ever since they'd started chemo and radiation, his skin had taken on a sickly gray pall. He'd lost a lot of weight and all of his hair in a very short period of time, which gave him a nearly skeletal appearance.

But Lucy saw reasons for hope. He was able to keep some food down and the last scan of his lungs has shown that the tumor appeared to be shrinking.

"Sorry?"

Sutton sighed and repeated himself. "What's wrong with you? Somebody die? Wasn't me, was it?" That last bit he wheezed out.

"No, actually. Nothing's wrong. Your numbers are looking good and I think we're starting to see your tumor shrink."

Sutton's head was propped up on the pillows, and he seemed so weak that he could barely keep his eyes open at half-mast. But appearances, she knew, could be deceiving, and she got the feeling that Sutton was watching her far more closely than he should be. "You look like somebody dumped you," he went on. "I've got three daughters. I know these things."

Great. Just what she needed. "Mr. Winchester, not that it's relevant to your treatment, but I'm not seeing anyone. Ergo, no one can dump me."

Sutton's eyes drifted shut and she hoped that maybe he was going to fall asleep. But today was not her lucky day. "Someone sent you flowers—the nurses were talking about it. You're too good for him."

This wasn't exactly an unknown phenomenon. Sometimes, when people were facing death, they became more philosophical about the trials and tribulations of life. Those regrets were then projected onto those around them. If they'd been neglectful parents, they would cajole and beg the nurses and doctors to take better care of their own families. If they'd been unfaithful, they would talk of love and honor and respect, of vows they hadn't kept and now wished they had.

Just her luck that Sutton Winchester would fall into more than one of those categories. "Mr. Winchester," she began in a stern tone. "My personal life has no bearing on your treatment—and that's the thing that you and I should both be concerned with at this time. Your family has gone to great lengths to have you transferred out of this hospital and returned to your home."

Sutton cracked open one eye and Lucy thought maybe he looked a little alarmed. "What? Why?"

"They want me to continue your treatment at home, where you will have greater control over your privacy."

His other eye opened and he stared at her. "You're not sending me home to die, are you?"

"No. I'm not giving up on you and you should not give up, either. In fact," she went on, staring at her tablet and nothing in particular, "I'm going to be living at the estate in the room next to yours for the time being so that I can ensure that you're receiving the best care possible twenty-four hours a day."

Sutton didn't respond immediately. She couldn't tell if this announcement surprised or pleased him—or made him furious. Finally, he said, "You don't come cheap, I assume?"

No, but the fact that she was selling her services to the highest bidder had a way of making her feel pretty damned cheap. "The Newports and the Winchesters have generously agreed to provide the bulk of the funding for the new cancer pavilion expansion here at Midwest."

Sutton exhaled and seemed to sink back into his pillows. The conversation had clearly worn him out. "Should've held out for more," he said in a tone of voice that would've been scolding if he'd had any energy. "You need to be a tougher negotiator."

"Yes, well, you and I are going to have a lot of time together over the next several weeks. I look forward to hearing how you would recommend I go about doing just that."

She watched him for a moment longer, but he'd settled in to sleep.

As she walked out of Sutton's room, she almost ran into John Jackson, the vice president of the hospital. "Dr. Wilde! Just the person I was hoping to see!" he gushed.

Lucy didn't necessarily believe in a sixth sense, but if she had one, hers was telling her to run. Quickly. "Mr. Jackson, how can I help you today?"

"I wanted to be the one to tell you," he went on, grinning like a loon. "It's simply wonderful!"

She began to back away from him. "I already know about the cancer pavilion," she reminded him.

"No, no! I mean, well—yes. This is about the cancer pavilion. Sort of."

"Mr. Jackson," Lucy said, pinching the bridge of her nose under her glasses. "I'm making my rounds—if you could be so kind as to get to the point?"

"Yes, yes—of course. The Newports are hosting a gala benefit for the children's hospital they're building."

She stared at him because that wasn't exactly news. Nor was it relevant to her. "So?"

"So!" He clapped his hands. "They want you to be the guest of honor!"

Oh, God. "Why?"

"Why?" Jackson blinked at her. "It's because of everything you're doing for them. This is wonderful! The publicity—the visibility!"

Lucy could feel all eyes from the nurses station on

her. Her life was no longer her own and everyone knew it. She did her best to put on a brave face, though. "How delightful. And when are the festivities scheduled?"

"Three weeks!" Jackson was physically bouncing on the balls of his feet, which made him look like a four-year-old who was so excited about a birthday present he couldn't stand still. "I'm sure we can make time for you to attend—what with you being the guest of honor and all."

Translation? This was not an optional event. Attendance was mandatory.

She remembered what Sutton had said to her just a few minutes ago. "And what are we going to get out of it?" There. That was her being a better negotiator.

Jackson's smile cracked, but Lucy was done with the social niceties. They never got her anywhere, anyway. "It will be a fund-raising event. With the Winchesters and the Newports hosting, the cream of Chicago's high society will be in attendance."

If she was going to give up yet another part of her life—and her self-determination—she needed to make sure it was for a greater cause. She wanted to tell Jackson that the children's hospital should have the best damned children's oncology department in the country—but she knew that Jackson was only concerned with Midwest. "That cardiac cath lab you wanted—I won't go unless we get a commitment of funds for that," she told Jackson.

"Yes, well, yes," Jackson blustered, as if the idea of an oncologist caring about cardiology was so foreign as to be hilarious. "I'll see what I can do."

As much as Lucy wanted to hide in her office, she was doing rounds. So she forced herself to nod at the nurses who were busy *not* eavesdropping before she went in to see her next patient, Mr. Gadhavi.

There was nothing good about this. She was so well-known for her lack of a social life that the appearance of flowers had the entire department gossiping. She was so unpracticed at being dumped—if you could call two almost-dates with Josh "dating"—that even an old cad like Sutton Winchester could tell that she was upset. And now she was going to have to get dressed up and go to the benefit and smile for all the people who were making her miserable.

Well, not all of them. With any luck, Josh Calhoun would not be at the benefit.

She wanted so badly to blame this on Josh, but it wasn't his fault—not entirely. Lucy had made herself a promise that she would not humiliate herself in front of Josh again, and yet she'd managed that not once but twice in the course of a few hours.

Worse than the embarrassment—worse than having her virginity thrown back in her face—was that she hadn't seen his parting insult coming. Long ago, she'd stopped thinking of her sexual status as something to be pitied, condemned or fixed. It was a nonissue to her. Sure, she wished she dated. She wanted someone to come home to, someone to do things with. She wanted someone in her bed in the morning and at night. She wanted to love someone and she wanted to know that she was lovable.

But, ultimately, that was not how Josh had made her feel. When it came down to it, all of her choices, her hopes, her dreams—they had all been reduced to one simple label.

Thirty-five-year-old virgin.

And now she wasn't even that anymore.

She never wanted to see Josh Calhoun again.

The following days passed in a blur. Lucy packed up and relocated to the Winchester state. Sutton Winchester was discharged and transported home. When he had some energy, he complained loudly about the color of the walls, the remote for the TV that his daughters had picked out, the noises of the machines. When he was tired, he yelled or snipped or tried to browbeat Lucy and her nurses.

Lucy was pulling eight-to ten-hour days at Midwest. Then she would spend a couple of hours taking care of her personal business before she went to the Winchester estate and spent hours with Sutton Winchester or his daughters. Then she would sleep poorly, get up and do it all over again the next day.

She did not hear from Josh. Which was fine. She didn't want to.

Carson Newport came by to see his father on a regular basis—although the older man did not seem any more inclined now to answer Carson's questions than he had been when in the hospital.

Sutton's daughters stopped by to see him often, too. And they made sure that Lucy had anything she could possibly need. Staying at the Winchester estate was almost like being at a spa retreat—a working spa retreat, but still. Sutton's chef was excellent, Lucy's minifridge was well-stocked with soda and wine—not that she drank a lot while she was on call, which was all the time, but still—and a maid made up her room every day. In all honesty, it was as close to a vacation as she had gotten in years. Except for the man fighting for his life next door, that was.

Except for the fact that she didn't hear from Josh.

She'd been at the Winchester estate for six nights when she came home to find Carson sitting by Sutton's bed. They weren't talking, but Lucy got the feeling that Sutton was only pretending to be asleep. "How are we tonight?"

she asked, wanting nothing more than a good soak in the enormous two-person whirlpool tub that was in her bathroom and knowing she couldn't. Not yet.

Carson stood and, with a glance back at his father, went to meet her in the doorway. "Is he always this quiet, or is he just avoiding talking to me?"

She thought she saw Sutton turn his head slightly at the sound of Carson's voice.

"Well…" she hedged. Her first priority was, as always, her patient. "The alternative seems to be yelling. Lots of yelling." The light in the room was dim, but she was almost positive she saw the corner of Sutton's mouth curve up. That old man wasn't fooling anyone right now.

Anyone except for Carson. "Dr. Wilde," he said in an even quieter voice, which made her lean in. "I wanted to apologize to you."

Lucy took a step back. "Why? Have you done something else that's going to…" She let her voice trail off because there was no way she could complete that sentence while maintaining a polite, professional exterior.

"I wanted to tell you that I appreciate everything you've done on behalf of our family. You've gone above and beyond the call of duty—you and Josh."

Lucy stiffened at the mention of Josh's name. "Oh? What else have you had him doing?"

A muscle in Carson's jaw clenched. "Nothing, actually. He's been back in Iowa for a week. I get the feeling that he's not talking to us. Me and my brothers," he quickly corrected. "I asked him to come with you last week to make sure the room was acceptable. As I understand it, that was not the best way to handle the situation and I put both of you in an uncomfortable position."

Lucy could feel all of the blood draining out of her face, but she did her level best not to have any other reaction. "Yes, well." That seemed to be the only thing she was capable of saying.

It should not matter that Josh had returned to Cedar Point without telling her. Why would it? He'd shown up in Chicago without letting her know, after all. He was under no obligation to keep her apprised of his movements. But, somehow, the fact that he'd not only walked out of her apartment without a look back but walked away from Chicago just stung all the more.

She really did mean that little to him. And that wasn't just an observation about the sex and the aftermath. Their years of friendship and their bond over Gary—it actually hadn't meant that much at all.

She must not have gotten any better recently at hiding her emotions, because Carson gave her a worried look and then gestured for her to step out into the hallway. He closed the door behind them. "I really am sorry," he said again.

Lucy tried to wave this away. "He mentioned that you guys were old friends. I understand how those things go."

Carson gave her an odd look. "Did something happen? If he was a jerk, I can go beat him up for you."

She lifted an eyebrow at him. "That won't be necessary." But her curiosity got the better of her. "You knew his wife, didn't you?"

"Sydney? Yes. We all loved her. It was funny how it shook out. I think Graham was actually interested in her when he introduced her to Josh. It was the sort of thing that could have ended a friendship. But Josh was the peacemaker."

"Yeah, he's always been that way." Except when it came to her, apparently. No, that wasn't fair. When they were around other people, it was fine. It was only when it was the two of them alone. That was when it all went to hell.

Carson seemed to consider this. "Have you ever seen him mad?"

"Of course," she said, trying not to think about the way things had ended. "Why?"

Carson ran a hand through his hair. "Because after he came back from here the other week, he was mad at us and told us to stop jerking you around. Not in so many words, but the message was the same."

Lucy tried to synthesize this information without actually reacting to it. "Yet the very next day, I was informed I would be a guest of honor at a gala banquet—instead of being asked."

Carson winced. "It wasn't my fault. That was entirely the doing of my sisters."

Lucy sighed. "It's fine."

She didn't mean it and she was pretty sure that Carson knew it. "If there's anything I can do to make it up to you..." he said.

"That won't be necessary." God only knew how he might try. "Now if you'll excuse me, I have a patient to attend."

Carson stepped aside and she moved past him. But against her better judgment, she paused with her hand on the doorknob. "If you do talk to Josh," she said, "could you make sure he's doing all right?"

Which was an admission of failure and she knew it. If she were really Josh's friend, she should be able to ask him that herself.

But she couldn't.

Carson nodded. "Yeah, I can do that."

Lucy managed to muster a wan smile and then went in to see her patient, closing the door behind her.

Sutton wasn't pretending to be asleep anymore. "You're back again," he said in the tone of voice that suggested he had a little more energy today. Which meant he was going to be cranky and Lucy was going to take the brunt of it. "Who is this Josh?"

"So you're feeling better," Lucy said, determined not to give him anything more to work with.

"I don't want you here anymore," Sutton snapped at her. "I want all these tubes out. I'm not that sick."

Lucy gave him a stern look, but the old man didn't even blink. "Did you chase Jenelle off?" she asked, looking around for the nurse who was supposed to be on duty.

"Carson told her to go get something to eat," Sutton grumbled. He lay back against the pillow and closed his eyes. "He looks so much like his mother."

Lucy did not want to be drawn into the Newport/Winchester family drama any more than she had to be—but right now she'd rather deal with their drama than her own. "Have you told him that?"

Sutton didn't answer. Apparently, he was going to pretend to be asleep to any question he didn't feel like answering.

"Did you know your children are hosting a gala benefit for the new children's hospital the Newports are building? And I'm the guest of honor?"

That got his attention. "Why are they doing that?"

"Because I haven't killed you yet," she told him briskly. "And I took your advice—I negotiated for the cardiac cath lab funding at Midwest in exchange for being dressed up and paraded around like a trophy. Indirectly, you're helping a great many people who can't afford this level of care on their own—you know that, right?" She shot a snarky smile at him. "You might even get Humanitarian of the Year at the rate you're going."

When he didn't answer, she peeked at him again, expecting to find him asleep. But he was watching her closely. "This Josh was a fool to let you go."

She cringed. "Mr. Winchester, does this constitute flirting for you?"

That got the old man to grin. He still looked terrible—two steps above death warmed over—but grinning was an improvement. Laughter was the best medicine, after all. "If I were a stronger man, I'd have you on my arm at this benefit. And in my bed afterward." The smile still on his face, his eyes started to drift shut, and this time Lucy was sure that he wasn't faking sleep. His chest rose and fell in even breaths and a little color was coming back into his cheeks. It wouldn't last—this next round of chemo was due to hit tomorrow morning and he was going to look only one step above death warmed over then. But he hadn't given up.

Jenelle came back in, and she and Lucy conferred over Sutton's status.

When this was all over and Lucy went back to her normal life, she was sure she would feel like herself again. But that wasn't going to happen anytime soon.

She had a gala benefit she needed to get ready for, a patient to save and a hospital administrator to keep in line—not to mention all of her other patients.

She did not have a single moment to waste thinking about Josh Calhoun.

Finally, she went to her room.

There was a bouquet of daisies and sunflowers on her coffee table.

The card read, "L—you deserve a better class of friends. J."

Now what the hell was *that* supposed to mean?

Eleven

Josh's phone rang as he was trying to make sense of the latest sales for Calhoun Creamery's new Greek yogurt line. The numbers were sagging. They might've entered this market a little too late, he was forced to conclude as he answered the phone. "This is Josh," he said, putting the call on speakerphone.

"If I ask you to come back to Chicago," Carson Newport said, "will you hate me forever? Or just for a couple of days?"

"I won't hate you," Josh told him, setting his report aside. "But I'm not coming back to Chicago." *Ever*, he mentally added.

"My sisters," Carson went on as if Josh hadn't spoken, "have decided the best way to honor the extraordinary efforts of one Dr. Lucinda Wilde is to make her the guest of honor at the gala benefit we're hosting on behalf of the new children's hospital we're building."

Josh might have groaned. He wasn't sure.

"Dr. Wilde has requested that some funds raised at this benefit go to a new cardiac cath lab, seeing as we've already paid for the cancer pavilion expansion," Carson added.

This was a trap. Josh could feel it. The question was, what kind of trap was it? He hadn't figured Lucy to go cry on anyone's shoulder. She hadn't even cried on his shoulder. Of course, she hadn't punched him, either— and he certainly deserved a good walloping.

This was a huge mess and, apparently, it wasn't a mess that was going to go away if he ignored it.

"So you're building a new children's hospital, funding a cancer pavilion and now a new cardiology lab? Business must be better than I thought." Of course, Lucy would ask for something so selfless. She'd said her dad died of a heart attack, right? A less scrupulous person would have pocketed that cash or demanded a finder's fee or something.

But not his Lucy. Every single bit went right back into her hospital and her patients.

And he had called her pitiful. To her face.

"Philanthropy is good business," Carson said. "You should know that by now."

"You've neglected to mention why you're telling me this," Josh said.

"You're invited. To the benefit, that is."

Josh waited, but Carson didn't have anything else to say. "That's it? You're not going to ask me to snoop around or convince your sisters to do something for you? Has Brooks gone off the deep end? Does he need to be hauled back into reality again?"

"No," Carson said simply. "We overstepped and this is our way of making it up to you."

"If that isn't the damnedest thing I've ever heard. How do you figure that asking me to come back to Chicago is making anything up to me?"

There was a moment of silence, during which Josh's grandfather stuck his head into the office. "Everything okay?" he asked. If his grandfather had heard him, it probably meant that Josh was shouting.

Dammit. He tried to keep calm. "Carson's asking me to go to some benefit in Chicago." He hadn't exactly filled his grandfather in on the details of his disastrous trip to Chicago. And he didn't want to.

Still, his grandfather knew him too well. "Does this have something to do with our Lucy?"

"Dr. Lucinda Wilde is the guest of honor," Carson chimed in. "I think she'd want to have her friends around her. She doesn't strike me as the kind of woman who is used to a lot of media scrutiny."

Josh's grandfather gave him a warm smile. "Maybe you should go."

If Josh didn't know any better, he would have said that the two men had planned this entire ambush. "I'm still trying to get caught up from the last time I was in Chicago," he told both of them at the same time.

"Reports will keep," his grandfather said.

"There are going to be a lot of movers and shakers at this event," Carson reminded him. "It's going to be a hell of a networking opportunity."

Josh scowled at his grandfather.

Carson, however, did not see the scowl. "Look, I was talking with Dr. Wilde the other day and she asked me to make sure you are doing okay."

"She did?" Josh said. "I mean, she asked about me?"

His grandfather cocked an eyebrow at this as Carson

said, "She did. I think she was worried about you. I can't really blame her—you took off like a bat out of hell."

No one could blame her. Josh knew exactly where the blame lay—with him.

Was this his penance, then? He'd made an ass of himself with Lucy, so was he going to have to suck it up and go back to Chicago to make it up to her?

He needed to apologize to her. There was no guarantee that she would forgive him, but the guilt of how he'd treated her was eating away at him.

His grandfather said, "She was a good friend of yours," as if that was supposed to reassure Josh instead of making him feel worse.

"Well?" Carson said. "Shall I put your name down on the guest list?" Josh's grandfather nodded encouragingly.

Josh needed to make it up to her. And he couldn't do that from Iowa. "Fine, I'll go. Send me the information I need."

"One grumpy ice-cream maker, check," Carson teased. "Anything else you need?"

Josh dropped his head into his hands and thought. He knew Lucy—or he thought he did, anyway. No, that was a cop-out. He *did* know her. And he knew that if she was going to be the guest of honor at a big gala with the movers and shakers of Chicago's high society, she'd drive herself crazy trying to decide what to wear. Because he had a feeling this was not the sort of event that she could a wear lab coat to—or even that dress she'd worn to the pizzeria.

"Yeah," he told Carson. "Can you give me your sister Nora's phone number?"

Lucy paused only long enough to drop her bag off in her room before she headed next door to see Sutton.

She was, for all intents and purposes, dead on her feet. It was only Tuesday but she had worked through two weekends in a row trying to stay caught up at the hospital while keeping tabs on an increasingly grumpy Sutton Winchester. Just yesterday, she'd had to threaten to strap him down to his hospital bed to keep him from pulling out his chemo port. If love was a battlefield, this was an all-out war.

She hadn't even had time to go back to her apartment and stare helplessly at her closet. The gala was on Friday night and she was the guest of honor and she had absolutely nothing to wear. She had no idea what she was even *supposed* to wear. She had a feeling that if she showed up in the blue dress and the white cardigan she'd worn to the pizzeria with Josh—again, her thoughts went back to Josh—that John Jackson might have a stroke right then and there.

She had no time to get a dress and, frankly, at this point, she was too tired to care.

"And how are we doing…today?" she asked as she walked into Sutton's room and saw that all three Winchester daughters—Nora, Eve and Grace—were talking with Elena. That was unusual enough—she hadn't yet seen all three women in here at the same time. But the way all four women suddenly stood up straighter, wearing nearly identical fake smiles, set her nerves on edge. "Is everything okay?"

"None of these girls will bring me a rum and Coke," Sutton grumbled. "And I want a cigar."

It was official. She was in no mood to deal with his crap. "And I'd like a pony, Mr. Winchester. Sadly, neither of us is going to get what we want today." She glanced at the four women, who were staring at her like dogs eyeing a bone. "What?"

The Winchesters looked at Elena. "Dr. Wilde," Elena said in a gentle voice, and Lucy decided that maybe Elena was no longer her best work friend. "The Winchesters would like to talk to you about something. You and I can go over Sutton's vitals in a little bit."

Lucy's gaze traveled over the three Winchester sisters' faces. She knew instinctively that this was going to be yet another thing she didn't want to do and she knew she was too tired to care. "Okay, what?"

Grace Winchester was the one to step forward first. "Can we talk to you in your room?"

What would they want from her now? She shuddered to think. She wasn't going to marry anyone. She wasn't going to carry anyone's surrogate baby. She wouldn't be donating a kidney to Sutton Winchester should his suddenly decide to fail. She would not be moving into this house permanently.

Nora Winchester stepped up and slipped her arm through Lucy's. "It won't be bad," she promised as she turned Lucy around and they headed toward the open door.

"Hold out for more!" Sutton yelled behind them. For some reason, that made Nora giggle.

"Daddy!" Eve said in an exasperated tone.

Lucy was marched out of the sickroom and into her guest quarters in short order. Nora sat her down in one of the armchairs and the sisters stood around her like the three Furies. Resistance was futile. Lucy knew she was about to be assimilated. "Do I want to know?"

"We were thinking," Grace said, clapping her hands together with excitement, "that you might appreciate a little assistance in getting ready for the gala."

Lucy slumped back in the chair and stared dully at

the three sisters. "Is it that obvious that I'm going to be hopeless at it?"

Eve leaned over and looked at the fading bouquet of sunflowers and daisies on the coffee table. Too late, Lucy realized she hadn't hidden the card. When Eve straightened, she had a smile on her face. It was not comforting. "Look," she said in a brisk tone, "it's our way of making it up to you. We didn't ask if you wanted to be a guest of honor at the benefit and we've been made aware of the fact that you might not have the appropriate wardrobe."

They'd "been made aware" of that? What did that mean?

But before she could formulate her thoughts into an actual question, Grace went on, "So, we're here to help!" She came over to the chair and pulled Lucy to her feet. "I love a good makeover," she said with way too much enthusiasm for Lucy's current energy levels. "A dress, obviously, plus shoes, a bag, new hair, makeup—how committed are you to those glasses?"

"There's nothing wrong with my glasses," Lucy said defensively, putting her hands up and shielding the frames on her face. At that point, she couldn't be sure that someone wouldn't whisk off her glasses, never to be seen by her again. Because she needed her glasses to find her glasses.

All three sisters exchanged looks that could only be described as pitying. And Lucy was not having any of that. "I'm keeping my glasses and that's final," she said in her sternest voice. "And, okay—I might not have the things to wear on Friday. But I also do not have time to go clothes shopping and get my hair done and whatever it is that people do before they go to balls or galas or whatever you call them. May I remind you—again—that I am pulling down a full-time job plus caring for your father?"

"Not a problem," Grace said warmly. "Elena has already agreed to extend her shift for an extra hour or two the next couple of nights so that we can spend a little time polishing you up. We'll do it here," she said, gesturing at the room they were in.

"She seems to think it will be good for you," Nora added in a sympathetic tone. At least Lucy hoped it was sympathetic and not just pitying.

The traitor, Lucy thought. "I suppose she's getting something out of this, too?"

"She's invited, of course," Nora said. "Jenelle will be taking the shift."

Lucy sighed heavily. At least no one had asked her to donate a kidney—yet. The day wasn't over yet, though. "Do I have much of a choice?"

The three women exchanged worried looks. "If you have something you'd rather wear…" Grace started.

Lucy shook her head. "No, actually—I don't." She looked down at her boring blouse and her boring work pants and her boring shoes and the boring lab coat. Boring—that was her in a nutshell.

"And as for the cost, it's all being taken care of," Nora said. "See? I told you it wouldn't be that bad."

Lucy had the distinctive feeling that there was something she was missing about this conversation. "Fine. But I swear to all that is holy, this is the last thing I will be railroaded into on your behalf. The moment your father is stabilized, I'm going to be returning to my regularly scheduled life. Is that understood?" It wasn't much of a negotiation, but it was all she wanted at this point. Before Sutton Winchester and his various and sundry children—and Josh Calhoun—had steamrolled her life, she hadn't minded being boring. In fact, right now she missed it.

The three sisters nodded and assured her that, once

they basically got done playing dress up with a real-life doll, things would be "much calmer."

Lucy let herself believe the lie simply because she was too tired to argue. Besides, getting professionally made up was almost a Cinderella dream come true.

But she was keeping her damned glasses. That was final.

Twelve

God, he hated Chicago.

Which did nothing to explain why Josh was back here for the second time in less than three weeks after having successfully managed to avoid the godforsaken city for over five years. Nor did it explain why he was climbing the steps of the Chicago Cultural Center in a tuxedo. He supposed that, at the rate he was going, he should be thankful that this wasn't where he and Sydney had gotten married. He was trying to be a better human at this point, but when faced with that sort of memory, he wasn't sure he could pull it off.

Hell, he still wasn't sure of anything as he fought the urge to yank at the bow tie around his neck and headed straight for the bar. He didn't know if it was lucky or not, but he saw that Brooks Newport was already there.

Brooks was talking to a large man in a tux that barely seemed to contain his shoulders and—if Josh didn't know any better—the man had a piece under his jacket. That was interesting. Private security or private investigator? An investigator, Josh decided. Brooks could handle his own security. Either way, the other man moved on as Josh got closer.

"Brooks."

Brooks started and turned to look at him. "I'll be damned," he said with a wide grin. "You actually showed up. I owe Graham fifty bucks." He shook Josh's hand and slapped him on the back.

"You're in a good mood," Josh said as he ordered a beer. There was no way he was getting through tonight without a shot of liquid courage. "Make any progress on your end of things?"

"Some." He took a long pull of his drink. "Get this—before he got sick, Sutton was trying to block our birth father from finding our mom, the bastard."

"And that's got you smiling?" Josh asked. He had not come back to get involved in the family drama again. He'd come back for one reason and one reason only. Still, Brooks was his friend and Josh was worried about him.

Brooks shrugged. "Because I'm going to bury Sutton Winchester if it's the last damn thing I do. His daughters thought I was doing a full-court press before?" He snorted. "They have no idea what's coming. None."

"Brooks…" Josh put a hand on his shoulder and dug deep for the thing to say that would pull his friend back from the brink of what sounded like madness. It was insane, it really was.

But Brooks looked past Josh and said, "Who is *that*? Damn. She's gorgeous."

The moment was lost. Josh followed his gaze and felt his breath catch. A stunning woman had just entered the room. She wore a dark blue gown—but it was a vibrant blue, not a conservative navy. The top of the dress was a loose-fitting satin that was wide open at the neck, revealing sloping, graceful shoulders. Her light blond hair had been arranged in delicate curls and she held a silver bag in her hand. Even at this distance, Josh could see the jewels that glittered in her ears.

The only thing he recognized was her glasses.

Otherwise, he never in a million years would have figured it was Lucy. When he'd called Nora Winchester and told her that Lucy was going to need some help getting ready for the gala, he had no idea that *this* would be the result. He'd just wanted to get her into an appropriate outfit so that she wouldn't feel overwhelmed. It'd been a selfless act. After all, Lucy was the girl who'd worn a mother-of-the-bride's dress—complete with tacky jacket—that she'd bought at a thrift store to senior prom.

He hadn't anticipated that the Winchester girls would turn her into a goddess, though. And he especially hadn't anticipated how seeing her would affect him. His lungs quit working and his chest seized up, and regret—regret like he'd never felt before—beat him over the head with a two-by-four.

He was only vaguely aware that Brooks had shoved him forward. All he knew was that he was getting closer to Lucy as she peered around the room, her eyes large behind her glasses. She was thinking about fleeing, he realized. And then her gaze settled on him.

She took a step back. "What are you doing here?" she said, and he heard the terror in her voice.

"Apologizing," he told her. He reached over to pick up her hand and kiss the back of it. He needed to keep her from bolting. "Also, telling you how beautiful you look."

She stood stiffly as his lips brushed over her skin.

"Apology accepted," she said, each syllable sounding like she was chewing on glass.

From where he was bent over her hand, he lifted his eyes until he met her gaze. "No, I don't think it is. You're still furious with me. Frankly, I'm surprised you haven't punched me yet."

"I should, you know."

"You absolutely should." He stood and smoothly tucked her hand into the crook of his arm. "You look gorgeous tonight." He began to lead her toward the bar, but he saw that Brooks had bailed. Damn that man's hide.

"Josh, please spare me. I'm already nervous. Don't make it worse than it already is."

He had opened his mouth to reassure her, when a voice called out, "Dr. Wilde!"

"It just got worse," she said in a low whisper as they turned toward the sound of the voice. Josh didn't recognize the man who was working his way through the crowd toward them, but Lucy did.

"Old boyfriend?" he whispered back.

"Later? I'm going to kill you," she muttered. Then, in a fake cheerful voice, she said, "Mr. Jackson! This appears to be quite a success thus far. The place is packed. John Jackson, this is an…old friend of mine, Josh Calhoun. Josh, this is John Jackson, the vice president of Midwest. He's been working closely with the Winchesters and the Newports to manage my time and their many generous donations."

Josh shook the man's hand. Why had he said that? Why had he risked further antagonizing Lucy, asking if this guy was a boyfriend? Later, when she killed him, he was going to deserve it. "This is quite a party," he said, which was one of those meaningless things people said at parties because somebody had to say something.

"Isn't it? I'm beginning to think that anything the Winchesters and the Newports touch turns to gold." He stepped back and gave Lucy the once-over, which make the hair on the back of Josh's neck stand up. "Including our dear Dr. Wilde. If it weren't for the glasses, I'm not sure I would've recognized you."

Josh's free hand clenched into a fist, but he should've known that Lucy didn't need him to defend her. "Don't get used to it," she said in a short voice. "This is a one-time-only event. Sutton Winchester is improving and the moment he is no longer my patient, I'm no longer going to be your dog at this dog-and-pony show. So you'd better get all the donations for that cardiac cath lab out of this that you can now. The clock is ticking."

John Jackson wilted for just a second before he rallied. "Right. Well, we can't say that you haven't done your best. Now if you'll excuse me... Keep up the good work," he said over his shoulder as he merged back into the crowd.

Josh rolled his eyes and turned to Lucy. "Vice president, huh?"

She exhaled heavily. "Just count yourself lucky I didn't tell him about the Calhoun Creamery—he'd have been all over you. Lord," she added, and Josh could hear her roll her eyes. "I can see this evening is going to be a smashing success. I need a drink."

Josh grinned at her. She hadn't pulled her hand away from his arm yet, which, given how big an ass he'd made of himself, was a hell of a good sign. "Look. We are conveniently located next to a bar. Champagne?" She scowled at him. "We are at a gala benefit, may I remind you. Champagne is the drink of choice."

"Fine."

Josh got two flutes of champagne and handed her one.

She sipped at it nervously as her eyes scanned the room. Josh did the same. He could just make out Graham Newport, tucked behind one of the alcoves in the bar, leaning in close to talk to…

Was that Eve Winchester?

But before he could get a better view, Nora Winchester made her way over to him on the arm of a tall, striking man. "Dr. Wilde," she said in her gentle voice. "You do look beautiful tonight. May I introduce my fiancé, Reid Chamberlain? Reid, this is Dr. Lucinda Wilde—she's been caring for my father. And this is Josh Calhoun, of the Calhoun Creamery. He's a friend of the Newports."

"Dr. Wilde," Chamberlain said in a deep voice. "The Winchesters have been singing your praises."

Josh didn't even have to look at Lucy to know that she was blushing. He could feel the heat pouring off her. For her sake, he hoped that she wasn't turning bright red.

"Thank you," she said in a tight voice.

Josh had been wrong earlier. Lucy might not need to be rescued from the likes of hospital administrators, but in the face of sincere compliments from handsome men, she was not as well equipped. So Josh jumped into the fray. "Where's Declan?" He turned to Chamberlain. "We tested out the hospital bed that his grandfather's using the night Dr. Wilde approved of the setup. He's a great kid."

Chamberlain didn't smile, but his eyes crinkled a little bit and he looked pleased. "He's at home with the nanny. I couldn't pass up an opportunity to take my future wife out for a night on the town like this."

Nora looked at Reid and smiled warmly, but next to Josh, Lucy giggled. It was a sound right out of the past—high-pitched to the point of squeaking, and it meant one thing only. She was panicking.

He put his hand on the small of her back, hoping that

would reassure her. At the very least, it would piss her off, which would redirect all of her nervous energy toward him.

Nora looked at Lucy with concern. "I hope after your speech, you'll be able to enjoy yourself."

Lucy giggled again. "Oh, I'm sure I will be able to. This is all…wonderful."

Nora and Reid glanced at each other. No, Lucy wasn't fooling anyone at the moment. "If you'll excuse us," Nora said. "I'm looking for Eve."

"I thought I saw her over there," Josh said, pointing toward the alcove where he'd seen Graham earlier. But the space was empty now. "Or maybe not. Sorry."

Nora just smiled sweetly. "No worries. I'm sure she's somewhere. Mr. Calhoun, Dr. Wilde." With that, she and Reid Chamberlin disappeared back into the crowd.

"How are you doing?" Josh asked. It wasn't his fault that he had to step in a little closer to make himself heard over the noise.

"I didn't expect it to be this crowded," Lucy said in a small voice. And Josh could tell that she was worried about all these people staring at her.

"Just pretend that this is high school graduation and you're giving your valedictorian address again," he told her.

She shot him a mean look. "I was nervous before that, too."

"But it didn't stop you from giving a damn fine speech," he reminded her.

She took a longer drink of her champagne. "Flattery will get you exactly nowhere, Joshua Calhoun. I'm not listening to any of your apologies."

"Not even the ones I really mean?"

Her shoulders stiffened. "Perhaps we could save time

if you just point out now which ones you didn't really mean?"

He set his champagne flute on the bar and stepped in closer so he could whisper in her ear. "I could apologize for asking the Winchester sisters to work their magic on you, but I wouldn't really mean it."

She inhaled sharply. "You did *what*?"

"I asked them to make sure that you would be ready for this—on my dime. But it was worth it because you are a goddess tonight. And any good goddess has her moments of wrath. So, to save time, I'll keep this simple." He inhaled deeply, giving her a chance to pull away. She didn't. "What I said was cruel and heartless and uncalled-for. It had nothing to do with you and it had everything to do with me. That's not an excuse—but it is the truth. I screwed up and I'm sorry." Her nostrils flared, but she didn't tell him off. "Now it's up to you whether you destroy me or show benevolent mercy. My fate is in your hands."

She drank the rest of her champagne, set her glass down on the bar behind him with a *thunk* and turned to him. Forgiveness was not in her eyes. "No, it's not. Now if you'll excuse me, I have a speech to give."

Lucy didn't remember giving her little speech. On a basic level, she turned on autopilot, read from her prepared notes and smiled a big fake smile for the photos. There were a *lot* of photos. Lucy was positioned between the Newports and the Winchesters. The hospital administrators also had to get their pictures taken with everyone in seemingly every permutation. Then Lucy had to stand and smile while millionaires and billionaires posed and grinned for the society pages. She was vaguely aware that these people were all writing checks to the new children's hospital and Midwest, and at one point John Jackson leaned over and whispered there was now a bidding war to see who would get to name the new cardiac cath lab. He seemed excited about this.

It *was* exciting, she supposed. So why wasn't she more excited?

Because no matter where she looked, Josh Calhoun—the bane of her existence—was there. That was bad enough, but the fact that he looked absolutely stunning in a custom-fit tuxedo? The fact that, even when he appeared to be in conversation with another beautiful woman, his eyes were always on her—as though she was the only woman in the room? As though she was a goddess, for crying out loud? It was all unbearable.

She was not a goddess. Not now, not ever.

She wanted to be so mad at him for hijacking yet another part of her life. Sure, it hadn't been that bad trying on gorgeous, expensive dresses with one or more of the Winchester sisters pointing out how good she looked in this one, how flattering the cut of that one was on her. And, no, it hadn't been the worst thing in the world to have a hairstylist and a makeup artist appear in her guest quarters to transform her into—well, into someone who still wasn't a goddess, but someone who at least fit in at this red-carpet event. And the relief of knowing that people wouldn't look at her and see a hopeless case counted for a lot, actually.

But was this an apology? Between the dress, the shoes, the jewels—yes, even the underwear—she was wearing about six thousand dollars' worth of stuff. All stuff Josh had paid for. For her. Maybe that was how millionaire business owners apologized?

But she didn't feel like herself. Not Dr. Lucinda Wilde, not Lucy Wilde. She felt like was…window dressing.

After all the speeches—and there were a lot of them—were done and the photos had all been taken, the band started up. Because what was a gala benefit ball without the dancing?

She knew what was coming and before she'd even made it four steps toward the bar, Josh Calhoun was at her side again. "You're doing great," he whispered in her ear and damn it all, it made her feel better. Because she had no way to tell if she was being gracious or professional or respectable. The whole evening was a blur of flashbulbs and microphones.

But she didn't want his reassurances. She didn't want him to make her feel better. Not when she knew that he could make her feel worse with a cutting look and a few well-placed barbs.

"Dance with me?" he asked.

Oh, lovely. A request. Not an order.

"Or do you need a drink first? I can get us some more champagne."

Us. There was no *us.*

Which did not explain why she heard herself say, "Champagne would be great."

"Don't move. I'll be right back." Then he was gone, cutting a swath through the crowd at an impressive rate of speed.

She did move, though. She took several steps back into the shadows, away from the dance floor and the people and the noise. Could she go home? And not back to the Winchester estate, either. Back to her apartment with its comfortable couch and floor-to-ceiling windows. Back to fuzzy pajamas with fluffy penguins on them and a pint of Calhoun Creamery ice cream to eat while she watched a silly movie.

"There you are," Josh said, handing her a flute of champagne. "Can you make it just a little bit longer?"

She stared at him. She didn't like how easily he could read her right now. It felt…dangerous. "I haven't forgiven you for anything. You can stop being so nice."

Amazingly, his mouth curved up in a small smile. "Good. You're still feeling feisty. I was getting worried about you. And I think you have it backward. I fail to see how me being continually rude at this point would encourage you to forgive me. This, more than anything, is a situation that calls for niceness."

Lucy took a long, cool sip of her champagne. "Why are you here, really?"

"I came back for you."

Unexpectedly, Lucy's throat closed up and she felt dangerously close to tears. Tears, for God's sake! She was overly tired, that's all it was.

Josh took her champagne flute out of her hand and set it on a tray. "Come here," he said, leading her out onto the dance floor. "If you keep your forehead against my shoulder—yes, like that—then no one can see."

She wanted to ask, *see what*? But she knew. Her eyes were watering and her mouth was pulling down into a frown, and she wanted him to stop being so damned nice to her. She didn't want to feel as if he was trying to protect her. She didn't want to need protecting.

But the simple fact was that she was out of her league here and he—of all people—wasn't.

Even weirder was the fact that Josh Calhoun could dance. Dance! "This is new," she whispered, trying to talk around the stupid lump in her throat. "As I recall, didn't you squash the hell out of my toes at prom once?"

"I did. I also squashed the hell out of Sydney's toes before we got married. Therefore, I was subjected to several long months of dance lessons so that I would not make a fool of myself at my wedding reception. Funny," he said as he spun Lucy in a small circle. She had no idea what dance they were doing. She just let him lead her around the dance floor. "I had forgotten I knew how to dance."

She leaned against him and let him guide her. "I don't know what to do about you, Josh."

He took a deep breath and let it out slowly before he answered. "What do you mean?"

"I mean, I keep promising myself that I'm going to stop embarrassing myself with you. And I do okay with that when we're around other people. But I can't seem to be alone with you without something happening."

"Something good—or something bad?"

"Both."

They took another turn around the dance floor before he said anything else. "Help me out here. When, exactly, have you embarrassed yourself in front of me?"

"Are you serious?"

"Completely. Hang on." The next thing she knew, Lucy had been dipped down low—which meant she wasn't hiding her face against his shoulder anymore. With a look on his face that she couldn't read, Josh held her there for two heartbeats before he pulled her back into his arms and began to move around the floor again. "Because I'm pretty sure I'm the one who has been busy making a fool of himself."

"Okay, fine. If this is how you want to play it, *fine*. I didn't think I could be any more humiliated than I was when you turned me away after Gary died. And I felt like an idiot after we made out on the couch and you made it seem like that was part of your plan to get into the Winchester estate. And I am not now, nor have I ever been, a pitiful virgin." She knew she was turning bright red.

"Not to mention that saying all of those things out loud to you is embarrassing all over again. And the fact that we are having this conversation in the middle of a crowded dance floor in front of the highest of Chicago's high society is not helping."

"I would have this conversation with you anywhere," he told her, and, damn him, he sounded like he meant it. "Because that's not how I remember it, Lucy. I remember making an ass of myself and hurting your feelings over and over and over again. I remember lashing out at you when what you needed was a friend. I remember being so lost in my own grief that I couldn't think about yours." He swallowed, his Adam's apple bobbing dangerously near her nose. God, he even smelled good.

"I remember failing you," he went on in a low voice. "And I'm trying so hard not to fail you again. You are the kindest, most compassionate, most intelligent person I know, and I've never understood why you put up with me." She buried her face against his shoulder, swallowing reflexively, but it didn't move the lump in her throat. He held her close and began stroking her back. "God, Lucy, don't cry. I'd rather you punched me, instead."

"I don't want to punch you," she told him, her voice cracking over the words. "I don't know what I want anymore. And what's more, I don't know what to do with you."

"Hang on again," he said, and spun Lucy out and then pulled her back into his arms. Compared to the prom where he had nearly broken every single one of her toes, this was like moving on a cloud. He must've had one hell of a dance teacher. "What do you want to do with me?" he asked when he had her back firmly in his arms.

This, she thought. Wasn't this what normal people did? Okay, so maybe not the whole gala benefit ball thing, but like Nora and Reid Chamberlain—this was a date night for them. They got dressed up, went out on the town, had some champagne…

They fell in love.

Was it wrong to want that? Was it wrong to stop thinking about her patients and cancer and malignant growth and hospitals and death, just for a little while?

Was it wrong to want to be swept off her feet? To know that, when she looked up in the middle of a crowded room, that Josh would be standing right there waiting for her? Telling her she was a goddess, that she was doing a great job?

"It's been five years since I was with another woman," Josh whispered, low and close to her ear. "I didn't want to be with anyone. I didn't want to risk the pain again. That's what I told myself. But the truth is, there hasn't been anyone else who's been worth the risk. But you are, Lucy. I made a mess of it. I had trouble reconciling the girl I used to like with the woman I'm attracted to now and I reacted poorly."

"That's one way to put it." She tried to say it ironically, but her heart was pounding too hard.

"I know I don't deserve a second chance—or even a third one," he added, leaning her back so that he could look down into her eyes. "But I didn't come here this time to keep the peace between the Newports and the Winchesters. I came to Chicago to make it up to you. So let me do that."

They'd come to a stop somewhere on the dance floor. Vaguely, she was aware that music was still playing and people were still laughing and drinking, but it didn't register. She was in the arms of a handsome man who knew her better than anyone else.

She shouldn't want this—*him*. She shouldn't crave his

touch or his body. She shouldn't need him. She shouldn't feel so alone without him. She had her work and her patients and…and her work.

And it wasn't enough.

"Can we get a do-over?"

He cupped her cheek in his palm and stroked his thumb over her skin. "What do you mean?"

"A girl's first time should be special and magical. When she decides to take a lover, he should put her feelings and her pleasure first." She had no idea where these words were coming from, but they sounded good, so she kept going. She poked him in the chest. "He should whisper sweet nothings in her ear and hold her afterward. If she wants to fall asleep in her lover's arms and wake up there in the morning, then that's what she should get."

One corner of his mouth worked up into a smile. "That sounds right to me."

"I didn't get that because you 'reacted poorly.' So you owe me a night, Joshua Calhoun. I want a do-over." She poked him in the chest again. *"Now."*

His hands settled on her waist, and all she wanted to do was close her eyes and lean into him. "Can we at least go back to your place?" he asked with a sly grin.

She'd have to text Jenelle, but surely it would be okay if she didn't go back to the Winchester estate tonight. Right now, she didn't have anything else that she could give to the Newports or the Winchesters. She just needed a little time. For once, she wanted to do something for herself. "You'd better make it up to me."

Something wicked glinted in his eyes and a shiver went through her body. "I will."

Thirteen

Josh kissed her in the back of the cab, his hands cupping her face and his breath fluttering over her skin. He slung an arm around her waist and held her tight as he walked her toward the elevator in her apartment building. Once the doors closed and shut out the rest of the world, he pulled her into his arms and whispered, "I *had* to come back for you. I couldn't stay away." Then he trailed his lips over her jaw, her mouth, the hollow in her throat.

"Yes," she moaned, angling her head back to give him better access. The first time—in fact, all the other attempts—had been a mask for sadness. They had both needed the physical release so they wouldn't have to think about everything they'd lost.

But that's not what this was tonight. This wasn't about mindlessly giving herself over to pleasure. This was about actively choosing pleasure.

This was about choosing Josh and this was about Josh

choosing her. Not as a substitute, not as a replacement—not to fill a void left behind by someone else.

He'd come back for her. She was worth the risk.

She had things she wanted to say, but she was too busy kissing Josh back to say them. His hands slid up the silk of her dress, caressing her body at a maddeningly slow pace. Her skin began to tingle and then burn under his touch, as if her dress had suddenly become too hot and she needed to take it off *right now*.

Somehow, they got into her apartment. It barely registered that she'd scarcely been here in weeks. All she could think about was Josh's hands on her. All she wanted to think about was this night—a night of romance. A night to feel special and wanted and—yes—irresistible.

"Tell me what you want," Josh breathed in her ear as he found her zipper and pulled it down notch by notch. "Do you want it slow and seductive or do you want it hard? You liked it hard last time, babe." She quivered at the memory. Josh exhaled against her neck and she felt his arms shake as they slid over the silk covering her breasts. "Yes, you liked it when I held you down and thrust into you and made you come, didn't you?"

"Josh," she breathed as he stroked her nipples through her dress.

"Look at you," he said in a reverential tone. "Don't hold anything back, babe. Give me all of it."

She reached back behind her to stroke the length of him through his tuxedo pants. He was hard and hot and maybe it was shameless, but she wanted him inside of her. She needed him. God, she needed him like she'd never needed anyone before in her life.

Years of sexual denial all melted away as he put his hand on the back of her neck and tilted her head forward. "I'm going to give you exactly what you want, but this time, I'm going to make sure you're ready for it." With that, he slid the dress off her shoulders and shoved it down over her hips. The expensive silk pooled at her feet and she was left in nothing but a tasteful pair of pale pink panties and a matching bra, because the Winchester sisters had had enough foresight to insist that she wear beautiful underthings with a beautiful dress. She needed to remember to send a thank-you note for that little bit of advice because listening to Josh inhale sharply as his hands stroked over her breasts and down her bottom was worth it.

"God, Lucy," he groaned, and the next thing she knew, he fell to his knees behind her and bit her bottom. Not hard, but with the feel of his teeth on her in such a hidden, intimate place, she couldn't fight the shudder that went through her.

"What are you doing?"

"Loving you," he said simply. He pulled her panties down and kissed the spot he'd bitten. Then he kissed the other side. As he did so, his hands came up between her legs and he began to stroke her.

She wasn't used to her heels and the things he was doing to her—his mouth on her, his fingers on her, his fingers *inside* of her. "I can't stand." She wasn't sure how much of it she could take. "Josh, please."

"What? 'Josh, please' what?" His fingers found her clitoris as his thumb slipped inside of her and he began to move his hand in a way that turned her brain to complete mush. "Josh, please make me come? Is that what you want to say?"

"Yes," she hissed, trying to find a way to stand that would keep her from falling over.

He bit her again, a little harder this time. Everything about Lucy's body tightened up as the climax shook her. She moaned as her knees gave, but Josh caught her. "There's my girl," he said. She couldn't help but think that he sounded a little relieved. "God, you're so beautiful when you come."

"Bed," she said weakly.

"Hmm. You can still talk. I think I need to try harder." He scooped her into his arms and stood effortlessly, as if it were the easiest thing in the world. Then he carried her to the bedroom and set her on the edge of the bed.

He got her bra undone as she worked at his pants. "Lucy—" he said through clenched teeth as she freed him from his boxer briefs and wrapped her lips around him. "What are you doing?"

"Something I've never done before," she told him as she ran her tongue up his length.

"Lucy…" he groaned. "I'm supposed to be making this up to you, not the other way around." But even as he said it, he fisted his hand in her hair—there were advantages to not always having her hair pulled back in a bun.

Maybe she wasn't doing this right—maybe she should let him be in charge. But he didn't pull her away. "You should stop." He sounded as if he was hanging on to his self-control by the very thinnest of margins.

Granted, she didn't know a lot about oral sex. Okay, so she didn't know about sex in general. So she had no idea if it was supposed to be such a turn-on to have pushed Josh to the edge like this. But it was. The space between her legs throbbed with need as she swirled her tongue around his tip and he groaned again. She knew that in a few moments he'd take back control and throw her down on this bed and do bad, bad things to her. But, right now, she was in control. And he wasn't.

His skin was smooth in her mouth—that wasn't so unexpected. But the way he tasted—that was something she hadn't anticipated. He was salty and musky and he tasted like Josh should taste. She tried to suck him into her mouth, but it didn't go quite the way she wanted it to, so she went back to licking.

"Lucy," he said, the warning in his voice clear. This time, he did pull her away from him. He bent over and kissed her hard, tangling his tongue with hers. She could feel danger in his touch. It was exciting, that danger. His teeth skimmed her lips and his hand slid between her legs, stroking her again. "You're so wet for me," he whispered into her mouth as his fingers raced across her skin.

She was buzzing with desire as Josh pulled away, pushing her down on her back and pulling her to the edge of the bed. He braced her legs under his arms. Pausing only long enough to roll on the condom, he grabbed her wrist and held it down by her side. "You let me know if this is too rough."

She couldn't stop her hips from shimmying from side to side. "I need you now," she told him, her voice shaking. "Now, Josh."

He pressed against her, his length sliding against her sex. "Impatient," he teased as she squirmed against him.

"I've been waiting decades for this," she snapped, squeezing him with her thighs and pulling him toward her. "I'm not waiting for you any longer."

Unexpectedly, he paused. "You have, haven't you?" Then he shifted his hips as he pressed against her opening. "Then I won't make you wait another second."

Lucy tensed, even though it hadn't exactly hurt last time—maybe that was the advantage of being an older virgin.

"I've got you," he said reassuringly. Then he thrust into her. There was no pain this time—just friction. Just the need to move against him, with him, as he filled her.

He was not terribly gentle. He hadn't been last time, either. She hadn't realized that it would work for her—but it did. He kept her knees trapped under his arms and held her wrists against her side and drove into her over and over again and all she had to do was lie there and let wave after wave of pleasure wash over her. She didn't have to make any life-or-death decisions. She didn't have to supervise nurses or tiptoe around administrators. Josh took care of everything.

But her orgasm danced just out of her reach until Josh let go of one of her wrists and cupped her breast. He tweaked her nipple in time with his thrusts and the shock of the sensation pushed her over the edge. She arched into his touch and moaned as her release shook her.

Josh gripped her hips and pounded into her. When he came, he made a sound that was almost animalistic. Then he withdrew, sliding down to his knees so he could rest his head against her stomach. "God, Lucy. I didn't know I could still feel this way."

She lay on her back, staring up at the ceiling, her heart pounding and her body still shaking as she tangled her fingers in his hair. Anything to touch him. "I didn't know I could feel this way at all," she admitted.

He looked up at her and grinned. "It's a good thing, I hope?"

She brushed hair out of his eyes. "It is."

"I'll be back." He had turned to go, but then paused and turned back. "And this time I'm not going to screw it up."

Lucy laughed and watched him go. He did have a damned fine butt.

She flopped back on the bed. He was getting cleaned up and then she would get cleaned up and then… And then she would go to sleep in his arms. And she would wake up there, too. And maybe in the morning, they could make love again before…

Before she had to go back to the Winchester estate. Back to being Sutton Winchester's oncologist and the head of the oncology department at Midwest.

A sense of loss invaded her happiness. She hadn't known she could feel this way—and now she did. She was discovering she liked sex and that she liked her partner to be in control. But more than that, she liked Josh. When he wasn't driving her nuts, at least. But when she went back to being Dr. Lucinda Wilde, he was going to go back to being Josh Calhoun, head of the Calhoun Creamery—based in Cedar Point, Iowa.

She shouldn't miss him. After all, they'd gone almost seventeen years without seeing each other, right? And maybe…

And maybe what? He hated Chicago and she hadn't been back to Cedar Point since after Gary's funeral. Those weren't exactly the makings of a long-distance relationship—if he even wanted one. If she even wanted one—and she didn't know if she did. It would take a lot of time away from her job and her patients.

If she wanted something more with Josh—would she be putting lives in danger?

Boy, she was overthinking this by a lot. If ever there was a situation that called for a one-day-at-a-time approach, this was it. She shouldn't be thinking about anything past breakfast tomorrow morning. Everything else could wait.

Josh came out of the bathroom and she took her turn. And then, finally, she climbed in between the sheets and curled up in Josh's arms. By some unspoken agreement, they didn't talk. That's when it all had gone wrong last time—the talking.

Instead, Josh rubbed lazy circles into her shoulder as she drifted off to sleep thinking that she was definitely going to miss *this*.

For the first time in years, Josh woke up in a woman's arms. There'd been a part of him that had been afraid of this—of being with another woman. Would he be able to fully let himself go? Or would he constantly be thinking about Sydney? The reason he hadn't started dating again was not that he was afraid he would call another woman by his wife's name, but it was still a little fear that bothered at the back of his mind.

But he knew from the moment he began to float out of sleep that it was Lucy, not Sydney, in his arms. And, honestly, he didn't know if that was a relief or something that scared him even more, because he didn't want to forget about Sydney. But he also didn't want her ghost to be between him and Lucy.

He had no idea how to honor his wife and move on with his life at the same time. But for the first time in five years, he thought he might want to try. Because he had missed this. Not just the sex—although the sex was surprisingly good. She got an *A* for effort. Enthusiasm made up for lack of experience.

Even just thinking about the way she had licked him was making him hard. Yes, enthusiasm made up for a lot.

"Humph," Lucy groaned from somewhere near his chest. She rolled onto her back and flung an arm over her forehead. She had pulled the sheets down around her waist and her breasts… God, her breasts.

Josh rolled into her and began licking her nipple. "Good morning."

"What time is it?" she mumbled. And then she moaned

again. "Oh. Good morning, indeed." Her hand snaked down under the sheets and found his throbbing erection.

"A man could get used to this," he told her, shifting over her so that he covered her body with his. He was not going to insult her honor or her virtue or her work ethic. He had promised that he was going to make it up to her and he would be damned if he screwed that up.

Because this was what he wanted. Lucy was who he wanted. As he joined his body to hers, he knew that this was the only way forward for him. Lucy understood him in a way that no one else did.

Their lovemaking was quieter in the morning hours, and he was able to take his time and learn her better. He didn't have to rush anything. Somehow, they would make this work.

And when she came apart in his arms again, he let himself go and followed her over the edge. "Mine," he whispered into her hair when he fell onto her. "My beautiful Lucy."

She wrapped her arms around his chest and held him tight. "That's not too bad for a sweet nothing," she said in a shaky voice.

Something about the way she said that struck a note of fear in the back of his mind. It hadn't been what he'd expected her to say, but more than that, it was the way she said it. Aside from the shakiness, she had not sounded like a woman who had just come in his arms.

She sounded…distant, almost.

Josh levered himself up and looked down at her. Her brow was wrinkled and she had that faraway look in her eyes that meant she was thinking too hard again. "Lucy? I want to keep doing this."

A tight smile danced across her lips and then was gone. "I wish we could, but I have to work."

She put her hands on his chest and pushed him aside before she rolled out of bed.

He felt that note of fear again.

And it didn't go away when she came out of the bathroom and went to stand in front of her closet instead of coming back to bed or even smiling at him. "How much longer are you here for?"

He sat on the edge of the bed and stared at her. Where had he screwed up? There'd been no discussions of his late wife, no mention of Lucy's high school sweetheart—and he certainly hadn't accused her of being a virgin again. So why was she acting like this? "You tell me," he said in a cautious tone. "I came back for you, you know."

She tossed a nervous smile over her shoulder and then pulled out one of her basic button-up blouses. "I won't ask you to stay. I am, for the foreseeable future, still living at the Winchester estate and I know how much you hate Chicago."

That sounded final and he didn't like it. "I'm not planning on moving back here, but I thought that maybe we could…"

Lucy took a deep breath and turned to face him. Her blouse barely came to her hips and her hair was mussed, and damn it all, she was still beautiful. "I don't think we can," she told him in a carefully controlled voice, and he found himself wondering if this was what she sounded like when she talked to patients with terminal diagnoses. "This was wonderful—don't get me wrong—but I've thought about it, and I just don't think there's any way that this could be an ongoing thing."

"You what?" He couldn't believe his ears. "Lucy, don't you realize what we have?"

"It doesn't matter," she told him.

Maybe he was still asleep. Maybe this was a nightmare. He could wake up now. That would be okay. "Of course, it matters. You matter to me, Lucy."

She exhaled heavily, her shoulders slumping. "Josh, you say that now—but what happens the next time I ask a question about your wife? What happens the next time you play with a little kid and I get to watch the shadows creep into your eyes and you have to do something—anything—not to think about it until you can't avoid the truth anymore?"

"That's not what this was. Okay, maybe our first time was a little bit of that—but not this time. Damn it, Lucy. You are not just a distraction for me." The moment the words left his mouth the fear in the back of his mind blossomed into something larger. Something he could name. "And I'm not just a distraction for you—am I?"

She didn't answer right away, which was all the answer he needed. "Damn it, Lucy—I never meant to hurt you. I want to love you."

She came over to him, sorrow in her eyes. But she didn't cry. She touched his cheek and then leaned up and kissed the spot where her fingertips had warmed his skin. "I love you, too—but it doesn't change things. What happened between us…"

"It matters," he told her fiercely. "Don't you dare tell me it doesn't matter."

"It does." For the first time, he heard weakness in her voice. "But don't you understand? I was a thirty-five-year-old virgin for a reason, Josh. I am, for all intents and purposes, married to my job. I save lives. And yes—" she cut him off as he opened his mouth to argue "—part of it is that I've never had anyone I cared enough about to have a relationship with. But I do the most good fighting cancer, one patient at a time. It would be wrong to turn my back on that just because I'm in love with you.

People will die if I don't do my job to the very best of my abilities."

He realized he was shaking with anger. "People die," he told her through clenched teeth. "People die all the time and there's nothing that you or I or anyone can do about it. My wife died in one of the best hospitals in Chicago because she had an aneurysm. I spent years blaming myself—*years*, Lucy. But there's nothing I could have done. There's nothing the doctors could have done. People die. Gary died. My parents died. Every day, I live in terror that my older brother Lincoln will die in whatever war-torn country he's in right now. My grandfather could die tomorrow in his sleep and be contented with his long and happy life. And there's not a goddamn thing you can do about any of it."

"You don't understand," she said, dropping her gaze and turning away from him. He caught her arm and forced her to turn back. "There *is* something I can do about it. I've spent my entire adult life doing something about it. I know I can't save Gary, but this whole thing with the Winchesters and the Newports? The children's hospital they're building? That cancer pavilion they're going to fund? Do you realize how many people that will help because I was there to take care of their father?"

"But that doesn't have to be your entire life, Lucy. You don't have to be this selfless angel. You get to have your own life, too. Just because my wife died doesn't mean I died. I'm still here. I'm still fighting. I haven't given up—and I'm sure as hell not going to give up on you. I didn't understand all those years ago why you came on to me. I didn't want to betray Gary's memory by taking his girlfriend. But turning you down and walking away from you has been one of the biggest regrets of my life and now I've got a second chance to show you how much you mean to me. I'm not going to screw that up again."

"It won't work," she said stiffly. "My job and my life are here. Your job and your life are back in Cedar Point." Her mouth twisted into a frown and he thought she might be about to cry.

Good, he thought. That stoic crap sucked.

But she didn't. Instead, she squared her shoulders and said, "Thank you for the wonderful evening—the dress and everything. Thank you for looking out for me. It's something that I hadn't realized I was missing. I accept your apology. You can go back to Iowa with a clear conscience."

He couldn't hurt any more than if she had actually punched him. "You're just going to walk away from this? From us? You don't understand how special this is. I didn't come back here because I needed a clear conscience. I came back here because I love you, damn it."

Then she cracked, just a little. "You're making this harder than it has to be," she said in a small voice.

Wasn't that rich? "That's because I'm willing to fight for what I want. And I want you."

The look she shot him was so forlorn that it cut right through him. But then she said, "It wasn't meant to be seventeen years ago and it's not meant to be now. Please, if you'll excuse me, I have to get to work. Goodbye, Josh." With that, she turned around and walked into the bathroom.

And once again Josh was all alone.

God, he hated this city.

Fourteen

Normally, on Saturdays and Sundays Lucy went down to the lakefront or did her shopping. But for the third Saturday in a row, Lucy was sitting by Sutton Winchester's bed. It wasn't as if she had to watch him every moment of the day. The treatments were working, which meant he slept a lot. Still, Lucy felt a responsibility to be here, just in case. Her nurses needed a break, anyway, and all of this time gave her the chance to review her other patient files.

Whether he realized it or not, Sutton Winchester was a test case. Inoperable cancer that had already metastasized to the lymph system was not an easy thing to treat and the fact that he was responding at all was encouraging. What worked for him might work for others, too.

Which was what was important here. Not the way her heart felt—as if it had been cut out of her chest and put in a cooler full of ice to be donated to someone else who needed it more. Not the way Josh's face had crumpled when she'd said goodbye.

Not the way she'd had one magical, romantic, *perfect* night. Her only one.

She caught herself staring at the old man. She'd seen pictures of him in his prime, of course. Sutton Winchester was hard to miss and the press had loved him. The man who was sleeping in the bed next to her workstation bore almost no resemblance to that captain of industry. She knew about his reputation—the mistresses and his willingness to get dirty when it came to business. By all accounts, Sutton Winchester was possibly the most selfish man she'd ever had the privilege to treat.

And, somehow, he was also turning out to be one of the most generous. The money that his children had donated to Midwest—in addition to the money that the Newports were already sinking into the new children's hospital—would save countless lives. As much as she did not want to personally like Sutton Winchester—and he made it very hard to like him sometimes—she couldn't help but be thankful for him.

Because of one of the most selfish, egotistical men in the world, people like Gary might have a better chance. If he'd been able to get the kind of treatment that Sutton was getting now, surely his leukemia wouldn't have killed him before he turned eighteen.

She shook her head and tried to focus on her files. She was feeling maudlin, that was all. She was tired, her feet hurt after an evening in unfamiliar high heels—and she couldn't stop thinking about Josh.

A small but insistent part of her brain was convinced she was making a mistake. A huge mistake. Because she was pretty damned sure she loved Josh.

Oh, who was she kidding? She'd loved him for years.

Years. Even while she'd been dating Gary, she'd loved Josh. It hadn't been this passionate, intense kind of love—but even then he was a good man who protected those he cared for. He'd made a dying boy and a socially awkward girl happy simply by being himself.

And now…now he'd made her love him even more. He'd sent her flowers and brought her dinner and made love to her. Okay, yes, he'd also revealed himself to be painfully human and capable of mistakes. But everyone made mistakes. He'd made it up to her. Oh, how he had made it up to her.

But what was she supposed to do? He'd blown back into her life like a tornado—and she certainly felt destroyed. Her life was in Chicago. His was in Iowa. He couldn't stand being in Chicago because everything about it reminded him of his dead wife—and that still left open the question of children. There was no *us*, not for her and Josh. There couldn't be.

A maid delivered Lucy's lunch. There were copies of both the *Sun-Times* and the *Chicago Tribune* on the tray. Sutton roused himself and demanded to see the newspapers. Lucy handed them over without a second thought. Today's lunch was a quiche Lorraine with two slices of fresh-baked bread and delicate asparagus spears wrapped in bacon. This was not hospital food and as much as she wanted to get back to her regularly scheduled life, she was going to miss having a personal chef.

"Who is this?" Sutton said, his tone of voice demanding.

Lucy sighed and finished chewing her bite of quiche. "Who is who?"

"This is you, right? Who is this fellow you're dancing with?" Instead of holding the paper out for Lucy to see, Sutton held it up to his eyes. "My girls did a good job

with you. If I were a stronger man, you'd have been dancing with me—and doing a whole lot more than dancing."

"It's good to see you're feeling better," Lucy said patiently as she set her tray aside and moved to stand next
to his bed. She didn't encourage patients to hit on her—
no woman in her right mind would—but it was a good
sign that Sutton still had a lot of fight left in him. "Let
me see." Even as she said that, she realized who had to
be in the picture with her.

She'd only danced with one man. Josh Calhoun.

Sutton tilted the paper so that she could see the picture
of her and Josh. Oh, God—it was a really big picture—
almost half a page. The rest of the page was a write-up of
the event. The entire next page of the *Sun-Times* was nothing but photos of the Newports and the Winchesters and
all of the other rich and famous people who'd been there.

"Is that the fellow who keeps sending you flowers?"
Sutton asked.

Lucy didn't like the way his voice had dropped and
taken on a slightly suspicious tone. She paused as if she
was trying to remember his name. "That's…Josh Calhoun. I think he runs the Calhoun Creamery."

That wasn't much a lie, was it? No, not really. She had
conveniently failed to answer the question of whether or
not Josh had been sending her flowers. It also didn't answer the question of whether or not Josh would send her
any more flowers.

She didn't want him to. Was it wrong to just want a
clean break?

Sutton looked as though he was thinking, so Lucy
headed him off at the pass. "It was quite an event. Your
daughters—and your son—did an amazing job of planning it. The hospital administrators were so happy and I
think people had a really good time."

She backed away from the bed to sit down with the remains of her lunch. But she didn't have much of an appetite. She shoved the tray aside and returned her attention to her computer. Lives were on the line, after all. Her patients and their families relied upon her to be the cool, levelheaded voice of reason in a scary and dark time. She couldn't afford to be distracted by something like love.

And, really, she should be better at this. She had years of practice of holding herself apart, of keeping up a wall between her personal emotions and those of her patients. She had to—it was the only way to stay sane.

So why couldn't she keep up a wall with Josh right now?

The back of her neck prickled and she glanced over to see Sutton staring at her intently. And it was only twelve forty-five in the afternoon. How was she going to make it through the next day and a half until her nurses came back on duty without letting this grumpy old billionaire barge into her personal life?

"Yes?" Might as well get this over with. She didn't do well with dread.

"You remind me of her," Sutton said in a voice that was so quiet she almost didn't hear the words.

"Excuse me?"

His eyes drifted closed. "The look on your face… The greater good. That's what she used to say. The greater good for her sons. The greater good of my reputation. She had all these reasons why we couldn't be together…"

Lucy sat very still. What questions was she supposed to ask? Because there were questions that needed answers—she knew that. Carson Newport had been coming to visit this old man for days in the hopes that he would say something—anything—about his mother. And Sutton hadn't opened his mouth. Except to her.

Why her?

"I wish I'd fought harder," he said, his voice starting to drift. "Don't talk yourself out of what you need. She was so beautiful. You remind me of her…"

And then he was breathing deeply, his chest rising and falling.

Lucy sat there, every hair on her body standing at attention—she felt as though someone had applied the defibrillation paddles to her chest and forgotten to yell *Clear*.

The greater good? Of course, she had to be concerned with the greater good. She was a doctor. She saved lives. Everything she did was for the greater good—moving into this house, attending that gala ball. Her entire life was about the greater good. What did having her heart broken once—okay, twice—mean when held up against all of the people she had saved? It didn't mean a damned thing. What mattered was advancing cancer treatments. What mattered was comforting people during hard times in their lives. What mattered was…

What mattered was that kids like Gary died because they didn't have access to good doctors and proper treatment.

What didn't matter—what had never mattered—was that she had been a thirty-five-year-old virgin. That she had been frumpy and ugly and unable to connect with the people who surrounded her.

It didn't matter that she had been alone and that she had been lonely.

So, yes—she had her reasons. Really good reasons.

And she was already fighting as hard as she could.

Somehow, Josh found himself at the cemetery where Sydney was buried. He was pleased to see that the grass was neatly mowed and there were flowers at the headstones. He'd had very little contact with his in-laws in the preceding years—they had tried to get together that next Christmas after Sydney had died, but it was too painful for all of them and they'd drifted away until it was just cards on holidays and birthdays.

"Syd, I screwed up," he told her as he knelt and pulled a stray weed away from her headstone. "I should've come to see you sooner. I'm sorry. But it just hurt too much." He sat there for a moment, waiting for the overwhelming grief he'd always felt whenever he thought about coming to visit her grave.

It didn't come. He was filled with a sense of sorrow, of regret for a life they hadn't been able to spend together— but it wasn't the crippling pain that he'd come to associate with the memory of his wife. Maybe he was finally getting over it. "I found someone," he said in a low voice. "You remember me telling you about her? Lucy. Lucy Wilde. We ran into each other again and… And there was something there. Something good. I didn't expect it and now…" He shook his head. "Now I don't know what to do. I'm the one who always knows what to do, but not this time." He scrubbed his eyes with the heels of his palms. "She says it can't work. She's married to her job and her job is here, and I can't be here because this is where you and I were. When I'm at home in Iowa, I'm okay."

Even as he said it, though, he knew that that wasn't the truth. He knew that he hadn't been okay until he came back to Chicago for Lucy. He did his job and he ran his company and he worked with his siblings—but that wasn't okay. That was just barely keeping it together.

He was so tired of keeping it together. He didn't even want to settle for being okay anymore. He wanted to feel good again.

He wanted to eat Thai food and drink wine and watch

the sunset with Lucy. He wanted to take her out on the town and dance her around. He wanted to go to sleep with her in his arms and he wanted to wake up that way, too.

He swiped his eyes again. "I want to make this work with her, but I don't know how."

He didn't know how long he sat there—long enough for the back of his neck to get hot from the sun. He desperately wanted to feel Sydney's presence, to hear her voice telling him that it was going to be okay. Just as she had before the doctors had wheeled her into surgery.

But he didn't. Sydney was gone.

Josh was alone, the way he'd been for the past five years.

And if he didn't find a way to change Lucy's mind, that's how he was going to stay.

Fifteen

A week had passed since the morning Josh had realized that Lucy was not going to come out of the bathroom anytime soon and he'd gathered his clothes and walked away from her. In the seven days since, the urge to go back and force her to see reason hadn't gotten any less strong.

It was noble, really, how selfless she was. How she put her patients ahead of herself.

Josh was not that selfless. By comparison, he was a selfish, selfish person.

But more than that, he was a selfish person with a plan.

"So," his grandfather said, once Paige, Trevor and Josh's youngest sister, Rose, had all settled in the conference room at the Calhoun Creamery. "What's this all about?"

"Philanthropy," Josh told him. "I was recently reminded that philanthropy is good for business."

Paige, Trevor and Rose exchanged concerned glances,

but their grandfather just smiled. "What did you have in mind?" he asked.

"I've been thinking that it's time for us to invest in the Cedar Point community more heavily. I'd like to start with the Cedar Point Regional Hospital." He took a deep breath. Sometimes, the line between selfish and selfless was so thin as to be nearly invisible. "A long time ago, my best friend died of leukemia."

Paige leaned over and placed her hand on top of his, giving him a reassuring squeeze. "Gary—I remember him."

"If he'd had a better doctor and top-notch care, the outcome might have been different." Everything might have been different. But if there was one thing he'd learned in his life, it was that there was no going back. He had to keep moving forward. "My friends, the Newports, recently donated a significant amount of money to sponsor a cancer pavilion expansion at Midwest Regional Medical Center in Chicago. Thanks to their generosity, they're going to make it one of the most advanced cancer-fighting hospitals in the country. I know we can't replicate that level of success here—but surely we can help Cedar Point Regional build a better cancer unit."

Paige and Rose exchanged another worried glance as Trevor said, "Are you feeling all right? I mean, this is a great idea and I think we're all happy to get behind it— but you've spent the last five years hoarding the profits from the business."

Josh winced. That was true—but he hadn't thought of it like that. He had just thrown himself into the business. It hadn't been about the money. It had been about pretending to be okay. And he was done pretending.

But his grandfather was grinning widely. "I think this is a brilliant idea. But, you know, the hospital is going to need to bring in someone to run this new oncology unit. Jim Cook is a fine doctor, but I don't think he's up-to-date on the latest in cancer treatments."

Josh resisted the urge to snort with amusement. He had completely befuddled his siblings, but he wasn't fooling his grandfather. Not even a little bit. "I think I know someone who might be interested in the job." He hoped, anyway. Cedar Point Regional would never be comparable to a world-class institution like Midwest.

But people lived here. They were born here, they got married here and they died here. The best that Dr. Cook could do for most people suffering from rare forms of cancer was refer them to Des Moines to see a specialist.

Lucy was a specialist. She was one of the best. Bringing her out here was selfless because she would want to help people who didn't have any other options.

And it was 100 percent selfish because if Lucy was in Cedar Point, saving lives and curing cancer one patient at a time, then maybe…

"It sounds like a fine idea," his grandfather declared. "You just tell us what you need us to do."

So Josh laid out his plans. He was committed. No matter what happened, the Calhoun Creamery was going to start making a difference. Paige began to formulate ideas to turn this philanthropic bent into a marketing campaign for the company. Trevor was friends with a doctor at the hospital and volunteered to make the first contact, and Rose suggested doing some limited-time flavors of ice cream with the proceeds going to the hospital fund or the American Cancer Society. Through it all, their grandfather sat there, beaming at Josh. At one point, while his siblings were busy arguing over flavors, their grandfather leaned over and said in a voice just for Josh, "I'm proud of you, son."

"I may have to make another trip to Chicago," he told his grandfather.

He clapped Josh on the back. "I think we can hold down the fort for just a little bit longer." He stood. "There always was something between you two, you know that?"

"Yeah." Now he just had to convince Lucy that that was the truth.

It was the kind of day that shook Lucy's faith. Mr. Gadhavi had died. He'd gone peacefully and his family had accepted his death—at least for the time being.

But she hated it when she lost a patient. She hated it more now because everything felt more personal than it had before...

Before Josh Calhoun had come back into her life.

She was tired. Losing a patient always took a lot out of her. It felt like a failure all over again. But on top of that, she was still living at the Winchester estate. Sutton Winchester was showing signs of, if not improving, at least holding steady. But she hadn't had a day off since the gala ball and even that hadn't been a day off. She had been professional and gracious for most of the evening. She didn't think that one dance with Josh and then coming home to make love with him and sleep in her own bed truly constituted a day off.

Part of her knew that she couldn't keep doing this. She was burning all of her candles at all ends, but she couldn't stop. People depended on her. What did being tired matter when lives were on the line?

She trudged into the Winchester mansion and stopped at her room to drop off her things before she dragged herself over to see Sutton and deal with whatever abuse he felt like dishing out today.

As she did so, Josh's words came back to her. She

wanted a life back. She missed him and that was something she hadn't expected, either. She shouldn't have
missed him, because she was used to not having him
around. But what she wouldn't give to have dinner with
him and drink a bottle of wine and make out on the
couch. Or the bed.

She hadn't heard anything from him in ten days, but
she'd asked for that. What had she thought would happen when she'd told him it wasn't going to work and
she wasn't going to make it work? Still, the radio silence hurt.

Maybe she should take some time off. She hadn't been
back to Iowa since she'd first moved into the dorms for
her freshman year of college. It might be nice to go back
to the one place that she considered a hometown.

And she could find Josh and...

And what? Tell him that she was tired? Tell him that
she missed him? Maybe they could try to do something
long-distance? It wasn't as though Iowa was on the opposite side of the planet. It probably wasn't more than a
seven-or eight-hour drive. That was doable on the weekends, right?

She didn't know. She had not been kind to Josh the last
time they'd seen each other. He would be well within his
rights to tell her that he couldn't do long-distance and he
couldn't do weekends.

She washed her face in her private bathroom and
stared in the mirror. First things first. She had to get to
a point where her presence here wasn't required at either
the hospital or the Winchester estate every hour of the
day. Then she had to get to the point where she wasn't
working weekends. Once she did that...

Well, it was a start.

She headed over to see Sutton. "And how are we...

today?" She came to a dead halt as she realized it was not Elena or Jenelle next to Sutton's bedside.

It was a man. And not Carson Newport, either.

Josh Calhoun was sitting next to Sutton Winchester. Even stranger, Josh had one of Sutton's thin hands in his. He appeared to be comforting the sick man.

As Lucy stood there and gaped, both men turned to look at her. And then it just got weirder because Josh smiled at her and Sutton smiled at her, as well. "There you are," Josh said. "We were waiting on you."

"We?" She realized her mouth was hanging wide open, but she was powerless to get it closed. "What are you doing here? You hate Chicago!"

"Hold out for more," Sutton said. He sounded weaker today, but then again he was smiling.

"Mr. Winchester and I were just reminiscing," Josh explained patiently. He patted the top of Sutton's hand and then stood.

"About what?" As far as Lucy knew, they'd never even met before.

"Women," Sutton croaked. "Fight harder."

For once, Lucy wished she didn't know what he was talking about. "He's right," Josh explained. "We were discussing women we've loved and lost and let go. We were discussing things we wish we'd done differently."

"Oh. That's good. Carson will be..." Josh stepped forward as Lucy's words trailed off. An unfamiliar emotion had her looking around. "Where's Elena?"

"Told her to take a break. She's been working too hard. You all have."

Sutton leaned back against his pillow and closed his eyes. "I'm tired. You guys are bothering me. Send a pretty nurse back in."

Josh raised his eyebrows at her. "I think the man needs his rest. Can I talk to you outside?"

"Hold out for more," Sutton shouted at her as Josh ushered her from the room.

"Should I even ask what he's talking about?" Josh asked as he put his hand on the small of her back. Even that small touch was enough to make her skin warm.

"Probably not. What are you doing here? And don't tell me you just came back to make nice with Sutton because Carson asked you to." She didn't know why she'd said that. It was just that she was so glad to see Josh that she couldn't think of anything else. She wanted him to be here for her. She had no right to want that, but she did.

Without even realizing it, he was directing her toward her room. They went in and he closed the door behind them. "I didn't come back because Carson asked me to," he said, and then he was cupping her face in his hands and kissing her.

And she was letting him. She was kissing him back because he was here again and she'd spent the last ten days thinking about him and trying to convince herself that she didn't want or need him. What she needed was what she'd always needed—to save lives and make people better.

She still needed that. But she needed something more. She needed Josh.

"I missed you," she told him. "Josh, I'm so sorry. I said horrible things and I think I might've been wrong."

He leaned back against the door and grinned down at her. "You missed me?"

She could feel the heat in her cheeks. "Of course, I did. And I've been trying to figure out how I can make this work."

He lifted his eyebrows. "Come up with any solutions?

I've got to tell you, I have a vested interest in the outcome." He stroked his thumbs over her cheeks and pulled
her in closer.

God, it felt so good. "Cedar Point isn't that far away.
We could try to do a long-distance thing. On the weekends. You wouldn't have to stay in Chicago very long,
and I…"

"And you wouldn't have to give up your job," he said,
tucking her head under his chin and holding her tight.

"It could work, right?" He didn't answer right away
and she heard herself keep going. "I want to fight harder
for you. For us. I didn't think I needed to. But I've realized that I do."

He sighed heavily and Lucy's heart almost stopped.
"Long-distance could work, I suppose. But it wouldn't
work for long. It wouldn't work forever. Sooner or later,
we'd get tired of the drive. And I know that I would get
tired of only having you in my bed once a week."

It sounded like a *no*. But he was right. A long-distance
relationship like that was not a long-term solution. "Oh.
Okay then."

And then he was chuckling. Actually chuckling, as if
she had told a mildly amusing joke instead of admitting
defeat. "I'll have you know," he told her, leaning down so
he could whisper right into her ear, "that I've been trying
to figure out how to make this work, too."

She looked up at him. "How? You hate Chicago and
my job is here and if it's not a long-distance thing, then
I don't know what it could be."

"Oh, Lucy," he said, and that definitely was not a *no*.
"I would never ask you to give up your job. I know how
much it means to you."

She stared at him because that also did not sound like

a *yes.* "It's who I am." But even that didn't feel entirely honest, not anymore. It's who she had been. But now?

She felt as though she might be something more than just Dr. Lucinda Wilde. But she had no idea what that actually meant.

"I have a proposition for you," he said, tightening his grip on her waist.

"A proposition?" That was possibly the least romantic sounding word in the English language.

"I would never ask you to give up your job," he repeated. "But here's the funny thing—it turns out there's more than one hospital in the United States. And equally funny is the fact that many of these other hospitals also treat cancer."

She blinked at him. "So, you mean, like, get a job in Des Moines?" What the hell was he talking about? Sure, Cedar Point was a lot closer to Des Moines than it was to Chicago, but why would she relocate and essentially start her career over in a new hospital if she wasn't going to move to Cedar Point…

"Calhoun Creamery has recently decided to make an investment in the community of Cedar Point," he went on, suddenly sounding more like a CEO than a farm boy. "We're going to be endowing a fund for a brand-new cancer pavilion at Cedar Point Regional Hospital. We're still working out the details, but the hospital administrators and I agree that it would be best to bring in someone new to handle the transition. The current oncologist on staff, Dr. Jim Cook, is well into his seventies." Her eyes bugged out of her head. "It's good publicity for the creamery," he added. "I learned that from the Newports."

"Josh, what are you saying?" Because it sounded like he was saying—

"Marry me," he said. "Marry me and come home to

Cedar Point and take over the oncology department at the hospital. I don't want you to give up your job. I don't want you to stop saving people and I don't want you to stop trying to beat cancer. But I do want you by my side. I want you by me today and tomorrow and for the rest of our lives. There are no guarantees in this life, Lucy, but you are worth the risk to me."

She gaped at him. Was this really happening? Because she might have collapsed in her bed and fallen asleep and had the most wonderful dream ever. *Ever.*

Josh must have taken her silence the wrong way. Instead of pulling her closer, he pushed her away, just a little bit. "I just hope that I'm worth the risk to you, too. But if I'm not, I understand."

Oh, God, she was not screwing this up. "No! I mean, yes! I mean…" She hauled him down to her and kissed him.

He stiffened in her arms, but only for a second. Then he was pulling her tight and kissing her hard.

"You're worth the risk," she told him. Giving up her job at a prestigious urban hospital and relocating to a small town in Iowa certainly was a risk.

But then, not doing either of those things was a risk, too. She'd be risking her heart and her sanity. She'd be risking a lonely life and she needed to hold out for more.

God bless Sutton Winchester, but that was exactly what she was going to do.

"Just so we're clear," Josh said with a smile. "Was that a yes or no to the marriage proposal? Because I'm not going to give up on you, Lucy."

She hiccupped, and even she didn't know if she was laughing or crying. It didn't matter because suddenly she felt right again. "Yes. Yes, I'll marry you, because I'm never going to give up on you, either."

"I love you, Dr. Lucinda Wilde."

"And I love you, Joshua Calhoun. I always have." She knew that now.

He kissed her again, harder, and in between kisses, he said, "And if I have anything to say about it, you always will."

* * * * *

Available now from Mills & Boon Desire!

***

MILLS & BOON®

Desire™

PASSIONATE AND DRAMATIC LOVE STORIES

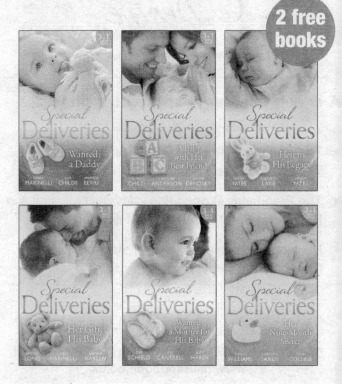